Song of Albion
Book Three

THE ENDLESS KNOT

For Jan Dennis

Song of Albion
Book Three

THE ENDLESS KNOT

Stephen Lawhead

A LION BOOK

Oxford · Batavia · Sydney

Published by
Lion Publishing
1705 Hubbard Avenue, Batavia, Illinois 60510, USA
ISBN 0 7459 2231 7
Lion Publishing plc
Sandy Lane West, Oxford, England
ISBN 0 7459 2231 7
Albatross Books Pty Ltd
PO Box 320, Sutherland, NSW 2232, Australia
ISBN 0 7324 0670 6

First edition 1993

Library of Congress Cataloging-in-Publication Data
Lawhead, Steve
       The endless knot / Stephen Lawhead
       (Song of Albion : bk 3)
       ISBN 0-7459-2231-7
       I. Title. II. Series: Lawhead, Steve. Song of Albion : bk. 3
    PS3562.A865E5   1993
    813'.54–dc20   92-44645   CIP

A catalogue record for this book is available
from the British Library

Printed and bound in Great Britain
by HarperCollins Manufacturing, Glasgow

Contents

*"Since all the world is but a story,
it were well for thee to buy the
more enduring story, rather than
the story that is less enduring."*

The Judgment of St. Colum Cille
(St. Columba of Scotland)

Hear, O Son of Albion, the prophetic word:

Sorrow and be sad, deep grief is granted Albion in triple measure. The Golden King in his kingdom will strike his foot against the Rock of Contention. The Worm of fiery breath will claim the throne of Prydain; Llogres will be without a lord. But happy shall be Caledon; the Flight of Ravens will flock to her many-shadowed glens, and ravensong shall be her song.

When the Light of the Derwyddi is cut off, and the blood of bards demands justice, then let the Ravens spread their wings over the sacred wood and holy mound. Under Ravens' wings, a throne is established. Upon this throne, a king with a silver hand.

In the Day of Strife, root and branch shall change places, and the newness of the thing shall pass for a wonder. Let the sun be dull as amber, let the moon hide her face: abomination stalks the land. Let the four winds contend with one another in dreadful blast; let the sound be heard among the stars. The Dust of the Ancients will rise on the clouds; the essence of Albion is scattered and torn among contending winds.

The seas will rise up with mighty voices. Nowhere is there safe harbor. Arianrhod sleeps in her sea-girt headland. Though many seek her, she will not be found. Though many cry out to her, she cannot hear their voices. Only the chaste kiss will restore her to her rightful place.

Then shall rage the Giant of Wickedness, and terrify all with the keen edge of his sword. His eyes will flash forth fire; his lips shall drip poison. With his great host he will despoil the island. All who oppose him will be swept away in the flood of wrongdoing that flows from his hand. The Island of the Mighty will become a tomb.

All this by the Brazen Man is come to pass, who likewise mounted on his steed of brass works woe both great and dire. Rise up, Men of Gwir! Fill your hands with weapons and oppose the false men in your midst! The sound of the battleclash will be heard among the stars of heaven and the Great Year will proceed to its final consummation.

Hear, O Son of Albion: Blood is born of blood. Flesh is born of flesh. But the spirit is born of Spirit, and with Spirit evermore remains. Before Albion is One, the Hero Feat must be performed and Silver Hand must reign.

Banfáith of Ynys Sci

1

Dark Flames

A fire rages in Albion. A strange, hidden fire, dark-flamed, invisible to the eye. Seething and churning, it burns, gathering flames of darkness into its hot black heart. Unseen and unknown, it burns.

These flames of darkness are insatiable; they grow, greedy in their spreading, consuming all, destroying all. Though the flames cannot be seen, the heat scorches and singes, searing flesh and bone alike; it saps the strength, and withers the will. It blisters virtue, corrodes courage; it turns love and honor to hard, dark embers.

The dark fire is an evil and ancient enemy, older than the Earth. It has no face, no body, limbs, or members to be engaged and fought, much less quenched and conquered. Only flames, insidious tongues, and hidden dark sparks that blow and scatter, blow and scatter on every fretful wind.

And nothing can endure the dark fire. Nothing can stand against the relentless, scathing corruption of the unseen flames. It will not be extinguished until all that exists in this worlds-realm is dead cold ash.

The oxhide at the door rippled as Tegid Tathal stepped into the hut. His quick eyes searched the darkness; he could see again. His blindness had been healed, or at least transmuted somehow into vision by the renewing waters of the lake. For he saw me sitting in the straw on the floor, and he asked, "What are you doing?"

"Thinking," I replied, flexing the fingers of my silver hand one by one. That hand! Beauty made tangible in fine, flawless silver. A treasure of value beyond imagining. A gift to me—a warrior's compensation, perhaps—from a deity with a most peculiar sense of humor. Most peculiar.

Tegid assures me that it is the gift of *Dagda Samildanac*, the Swift Sure Hand himself. He says it is the fulfillment of a promise made by the lord of the grove. The Swift Sure Hand, by his messenger, granted Tegid his inner sight, and gave me my silver hand.

Tegid observed me curiously while my thoughts drifted. "And what are you thinking about?" he said at last.

"About this," I raised my metal hand. "And fire," I told him. "Dark fire."

He accepted this without question. "They are waiting for you outside. Your people want to see their king."

"I had to get away for a while. I had to think."

The sound of merrymaking was loud outside; the victory celebration would continue for days. The Great Hound Meldron was defeated and his followers brought to justice, the drought was broken, and the land restored. The happiness of the survivors knew no bounds.

I did not share their happiness, however. For the very thing that secured their safety and gave wings to their joy meant that my sojourn in Albion had come to an end. My task was finished and I must leave—though every nerve and sinew in me cried against leaving.

Tegid moved nearer and, so that he would not be speaking down to me, knelt. "What is wrong?"

Before I could answer, the oxhide lifted once again and Professor Nettleton entered. He acknowledged Tegid gravely, and turned to me. "It is time to go," he said simply.

When I made no reply, he continued, "Llew, we have discussed this. We agreed. It must be done—and the sooner the better. Waiting will only make it worse."

Tegid, regarding the small man closely, said, "He is our king. As *Aird Righ* of Albion it is his right—"

"Please, Tegid." Nettleton shook his head slowly, his mouth pressed into a firm line. He stepped nearer and stared down at me. "It is permitted no man to stay in the Otherworld. You know that. You came to find Simon and take him back, and you have done that. Your work is finished here. It is time to go home."

He was right; I knew it. Still, the thought of leaving cut me to the heart. I could not go. Back there I was nothing; I had no life. A mediocre foreign student, a graduate scholar woefully deficient in almost every human essential, lacking the companionship of men and the love of a woman; a perpetual academic with no purpose in life save to scrounge the next grant and hold off the day of reckoning, to elude life beyond the cocooning walls of Oxford's cloisters.

The only real life I had ever known was here in Albion. To leave would be to die, and I could not face that.

"But I have something more to do here," I countered, almost desperately. "I must have—otherwise, why give me this?" I lifted my silver hand; the cold metal appendage gleamed dully in the darkness of the hut, the intricate tracery of its finely wrought surface glowing gold against the soft white of silver.

"Come," the professor said, reaching down to pull me up. "Do not make it more difficult than it already is. Let us go now, and quietly."

I rose to my feet and followed him out of the hut. Tegid followed, saying nothing. Before us the celebration fire blazed, the flames leaping high in the gathering dusk. All around the fire people rejoiced; snatches of song reached us amid the happy tumult. We had not taken two steps when we were met by Goewyn carrying a jar in one hand and a cup in the other. Behind her a maid carried a plate with bread and meat.

"I thought you might be hungry and thirsty," she explained quickly, and began pouring the ale into the cup. She handed the cup to me, saying, "I am sorry, but this is all I was able to save for you. It is the last."

"Thank you," I said. As I took the cup, I allowed my fingers to linger upon her hand. Goewyn smiled and I knew I could not leave without telling her what was in my heart.

"Goewyn, I must tell you—" I began. But before I could finish, a pack of jubilant warriors swarmed in, clamoring for me to come and join them in the celebration. Goewyn and the maid were pushed aside.

"Llew! Llew!" the warriors cried. "Hail, Silver Hand!" One of them held a haunch of meat which he offered to me and would not desist until I had taken a healthy bite from it. Another saw my cup in my hand and poured ale from his own cup into mine. "*Sláinte*, Silver Hand!" they cried, and we drank.

The warriors seemed intent on carrying me away with them, but Tegid intervened, explaining that I wished to walk among the people to enjoy the festivity. He asked them to guard the king's peace by removing any who would disturb me, beginning with themselves.

As the warriors went their noisy way, Cynan appeared. "Llew!" he cried, clapping a big hand upon my shoulder. "At last! I have been looking for you, brother. Here! Drink with me!" He raised his bowl high. "We drink to your kingship. May your reign be long and glorious!"

With that he poured ale from his bowl into my already full cup.

"And may our cups always overflow!" I added, as mine was spilling over my hand at that moment. Cynan laughed. We drank, and before he could replenish my cup, I passed it quickly to Tegid.

"I thought we had long since run out of ale," I said. "I had no idea we had so much left."

"This is the last," Cynan remarked, peering into his bowl. "And when it is gone, we will have long to wait for fields to be tilled and grain to grow. But this day," he laughed again, "this day, we have everything we need!" Cynan, with his fiery red hair and blue eyes agleam with delight and the contents of his cup, was so full of life—and so happy to be that way after the terrible events of the last days—that I laughed out loud with him. I laughed, even though my heart felt like a stone in my chest.

"Better than that, brother," I told him, "we are free men and alive!"

"So we are!" Cynan cried. He threw his arm around my neck and pulled me to him in a sweaty embrace. We clung to one another, and I breathed a silent, sad farewell to my swordbrother.

Bran and several Ravens came upon us then, saluted me and hailed me king, pledging their undying loyalty. And while they were about it, the two kings, Calbha and Cynfarch, approached. "I give you good greeting," said Calbha. "May your reign ever continue as it has begun."

"May you prosper through all things," Cynfarch added, "and may victory crown your every battle."

I thanked them and, as I excused myself from their presence, I glimpsed Goewyn moving off. Calbha saw my eyes straying after her, and said, "Go to her, Llew. She is waiting for you. Go."

I stepped quickly away. "Tegid, you and Nettles ready a boat. I will join you in a moment."

Professor Nettleton glanced at the darkening sky and said, "Go if you must, but hurry, Llew! The time-between-times will not wait."

I caught Goewyn as she passed between two houses. "Come with me," I said quickly. "I must talk to you."

She made no reply, but put down the jar and extended her hand. I took it and led her between the cluster of huts to the perimeter of the *crannog*. We slipped through the shadows along the timber wall of the fortress, and out through the untended gates.

Goewyn remained silent while I fumbled after the words I wanted to say. Now that I had her attention, I did not know where to begin. She watched me, her eyes large and dark in the fading light, her flaxen hair glimmering like spun silver, her skin pale as ivory. The slender torc shone like a circle of light at her throat. Truly, she was the most beautiful woman I had ever known.

"What is the matter?" she asked after a moment. "If there is anything that makes you unhappy, then change it. You are the king now. It is for you to say what will be."

"It seems to me," I told her sadly, "that there are some things

15

even a king cannot change."

"What is the matter, Llew?" she asked again.

I hesitated. She leaned nearer, waiting for my answer. I looked at her, lovely in the fading light.

"I love you, Goewyn," I said.

She smiled, her eyes sparkling with laughter. "And it is this that makes you so unhappy?" she said lightly, and leaned closer, raising her arms and lacing her fingers behind my head. "I love you, too. There. Now we can be miserable together."

I felt her warm breath on my face. I wanted to take her in my arms and kiss her. I burned with the urge. Instead, I turned my face aside.

"Goewyn, I would ask you to be my queen."

"And if you asked," she said, speaking softly and low, "I would agree—as I have agreed in my heart a thousand times already."

Her voice . . . I could *live* within that voice. I could exist on it alone, lose myself completely, content to know nothing but the beauty of that voice.

My mouth went dry and I fought to swallow the clot of sand that suddenly clogged my throat. "Goewyn . . . I—"

"Llew?" She had caught the despair in my tone.

"Goewyn, I cannot . . . I cannot be king. I cannot ask you to be my queen."

She straightened and pulled away. "What do you mean?"

"I mean that I cannot stay in Albion. I must leave. I must go back to my own world."

"I do not understand."

"I do not belong here," I began—badly, it is true, but once begun, I was afraid to stop. "This is not my world, Goewyn. I am an intruder; I have no right to be here. It is true. I only came here because of Simon. He—"

"Simon?" she asked, the name strange on her tongue.

"Siawn Hy," I explained. "His name in our world is Simon. He came here and I came after him. I came to take him back—and now that is done and I have to leave. Now, tonight. I will not see you any more after—"

Goewyn did not speak; but I could see that she did not understand a word I was saying. I drew a deep breath and blundered on. "All the trouble, everything that has happened here in Albion—all the death and destruction, the slaughter of the bards, the wars, Prydain's desolation... all the terrible things that have happened here—it is all Simon's fault."

"All these things are Siawn Hy's doing?" she wondered, incredulously.

"I am not explaining very well," I admitted. "But it is true. Ask Tegid; he will tell you the same. Siawn Hy brought ideas with him— ideas of such cunning and wickedness that he poisoned all Albion with them. Meldron believed in Siawn's ideas, and look what happened."

"I do not know about that. But I know that Albion was not destroyed. And it was not destroyed," Goewyn pointed out, "because you were here to stop it. But for you, Siawn Hy and Meldron would have reigned over Albion's destruction."

"Then you see why I cannot let it happen again."

"I see," she stated firmly, "that you must stay to prevent it from happening again."

She saw me hesitate and pressed her argument further. "Yes, stay. As king it is your right and duty." She paused and smiled. "Stay here and reign over Albion's healing."

She knew the words I wanted to hear most in all the world, and she said them. Yes, I could stay in Albion, I thought. I *could* be king and reign with Goewyn as my queen. Professor Nettleton was wrong, surely; and Goewyn was right: as king it was my duty to make certain that the healing of Albion continued as it had begun. I could stay!

Goewyn tilted her head to one side. "What say you, my love?"

"Goewyn, I will stay. If there is a way, I will stay for ever. Be my queen. Reign with me."

She came into my arms then in a rush, and her lips were on mine, warm and soft. The fragrance of her hair filled my lungs and made me light-headed. I held her tight and kissed her; I kissed her ivory throat, her silken eyelids, her warm moist lips that tasted of honey and wild flowers. And she kissed me.

I had dreamed of this moment countless times, yearned for it, longed for it. Truly, I wanted nothing more than to make love to Goewyn. I held the yielding warmth of her flesh against me and knew that I would stay—as if there had ever been any doubt.

"Wait for me," I said, breaking off the embrace and stepping quickly away.

"Where are you going?" she called after me.

"Nettles is leaving. He is waiting for me," I answered. "I must bid him farewell."

2

Three Demands

Darting along the timber wall, I hurried to join Tegid and Professor Nettleton in the boat. I gave the boat a push and jumped in; Tegid manned the oars and rowed out across the lake. The water was smooth as glass in the gathering twilight, reflecting the last light of the deep blue sky above.

We made our landing below Druim Vran, and quickly put our feet to the path leading to Tegid's sacred grove. With every step, I invented a new argument or excuse to justify my decision to stay. In truth, I had never wanted to leave anyway; it felt wrong to me. Goewyn's urging was only the last in a long list of reasons I had to dismiss Professor Nettleton's better judgment. He would just have to accept my decision.

The grove was silent, the light dim, as we stepped within the leafy sanctuary. Tegid wasted not a moment, but began marking out a circle on the ground with the end of his staff. He walked backwards in a sunwise circle, chanting in a voice solemn and low. I did not hear what he said—it was in the Dark Tongue of the *Derwyddi*, the *Taran Tafod*.

Standing next to Nettles, my mind teemed with accusation, guilt, and self-righteous indignation—I was the king! I had built this place! Who had the right to stay here if not me?—I could not make myself say the words. I stood in seething silence and watched Tegid prepare our departure.

Upon completing the simple ceremony, the bard stepped from the circle he had inscribed and turned to us. "All is ready." He looked at me as he spoke. I saw sorrow in his gaze, but he spoke no word of farewell. The parting was too painful for him.

The professor took a step towards the circle, but I remained rooted to my place. When he sensed me lagging behind, Nettleton looked back over his shoulder. Seeing that I had made not the slightest move to join him, he said, "Come, Lewis."

"I am not going with you," I said dully. It was not what I had planned to say, but the words were out of my mouth before I could stop them.

"Lewis!" he challenged, turning on me. "Think what you are doing."

"I cannot leave like this, Nettles. It is too soon."

He took my arm, gripping it tightly. "Lewis, listen to me. Listen very carefully. If you love Albion, then you *must* leave. If you stay, you can only bring about the destruction of all you have saved. You must see that. I have told you: it is permitted no man—"

I cut him off. "I will take that risk, Nettles."

"The risk is not yours to take!" he charged, his voice explosive in the silence of the grove. Exasperated, he blinked his eyes behind his round glasses. "Think what you are doing, Lewis. You have achieved the impossible. Your work here is finished. Do not negate all the good you have done. I beg you, Lewis, to reconsider."

"It is the time-between-times," Tegid said softly.

"I am staying," I muttered bluntly. "If you are going, you had better leave now."

Seeing that he could not move me, he turned away in frustration and stepped quickly into the circle. At once, his body seemed to fade and grow smaller, as if he were entering a long tunnel. "Say your farewells, Lewis," he urged desperately, "and come as soon as you can. I will wait for you."

"Farewell, my friend!" called Tegid.

"Please, for the sake of all you hold dear, do not put it off too long!" Nettleton called, his voice already dwindling away. His image rippled as if he were standing behind a sheet of water. The rims of his glasses glinted as he turned away, and then he vanished, his words hanging in the still air as a quickly-fading warning.

Tegid came to stand beside me. "Well, brother," I said, "it would seem you must endure my presence a little longer."

The bard gazed into the now-empty circle. He seemed to be peering into the emptiness of the nether realm, his features dark and his eyes remote. I thought he would not speak, but then he lifted his staff. "Before Albion is One," he said, his voice hard with certainty, "the Hero Feat must be performed and Silver Hand must reign."

The words were from the *Banfáith*'s prophecy, and, as he reminded me from time to time, they had yet to prove false. Having delivered himself of this pronouncement, he turned to me. "The choice is made."

"What if I made the wrong choice?"

"I can always send you back," he replied, and I could sense his relief. Tegid had not wanted to see me leave any more than I had wanted to go.

"True," I said, my heart lightening a little. Of course, I could return any time I chose to, and I would go—when the work I had begun was completed. I *would* go one day. But not now; not yet.

I forced that prospect from my mind, soothing my squirming conscience with sweet self-justification: after all I had endured, I well deserved my small portion of happiness. Who could deny it? Besides, there was still a great deal to be done. I would stay to see Albion restored.

Yes, and I would marry Goewyn.

Word of our betrothal spread through Dinas Dwr swifter than a shout. Tegid and I arrived at the hall, and walked into the ongoing celebration which, with the coming of darkness, had taken on a fresh, almost giddy, euphoria. The great room seemed filled with light and sound: the hearthfire roared and the timber walls were lined with torches; men and women lined the benches and thronged in noisy clusters around the pillar-posts.

Only the head of the hall, the west end, remained quiet and empty, for here the Chief Bard had established the Singing Stones in their wooden chest supported by a massive iron stand—safe under perpetual guard: three warriors to watch over Albion's chief treasure at all times. The guards were replaced at intervals by other warriors, so that the duty was shared out among the entire warband. But at no time, day or night, were the miraculous stones unprotected.

The din increased as we entered the hall, and I quickly discovered the reason.

"The king! The king is here!" shouted Bran, rallying the Ravens with his call. He held a cup high and cried, "I drink to the king's wedding!"

"To the king's wedding!" Cynan shouted, and the next thing I knew I was surrounded, seized, and lifted bodily from the ground. I was swept back across the threshold and hoisted onto the shoulders of warriors to be borne along the paths of Dinas Dwr, the crowd increasing as we went. They marched along a circuitous route so that the whole *caer* would see what was happening and join us.

In a blaze of torchlight and clamor of laughter, we arrived finally at the hut which Goewyn and her mother had made their home. There the company halted, and Cynan, taking the matter in hand, called out that the king had come to claim his bride.

Scatha emerged to address the crowd. "My daughter is here," she said, indicating Goewyn who stepped from the hut behind her. "Where is the man who claims her?" Scatha made a pretence of scanning the crowd, as if searching for the fool who dared to claim her daughter.

"He is here!" everyone shouted at once. And it suddenly occurred to me, in my place high above the pressing crowds, that this was the preamble to a form of Celtic wedding I had never witnessed before. This in itself was not surprising; the people of Albion know no fewer than nine different types of marriage and I had seen but few.

"Let the man who would take my daughter to wife declare

himself," she said, folding her arms over her breast.

"I am here, Scatha," I answered. At this the warriors lowered me to the ground and the crowd opened a way before me. I saw Goewyn waiting, as if at the end of a guarded path. "It is Llew Silver Hand who stands before you. I have come to claim your daughter for my wife."

Goewyn smiled, but made no move to join me; and as I drew near, Scatha stepped forward and planted herself between us. She presented a fierce, forbidding aspect and examined me head to heel—as if inspecting a length of moth-eaten cloth. The palm of my flesh hand grew damp as I stood under her scrutiny. The surrounding crowd joined in, calling Scatha's attention to various desirable qualities—real or imagined—which I might possess.

In the end, she declared herself satisfied with the suitor, and raised her hand. "I find no fault in you, Llew Silver Hand. But you can hardly expect me to give up such a daughter as Goewyn without a bride price worthy of her."

I knew the correct response. "You must think me a low person indeed to deprive you of so fine a daughter without the offer of suitable compensation. Ask what you will, I will give whatever you deem acceptable."

"And you must think me slow of wit to imagine that I can assess such value on the instant. This is a matter which will require long and careful deliberation," Scatha replied haughtily. And even though I accepted her reply as part of the ritual game we were playing, I found myself growing irritated with her for standing in my way.

"Far be it from me to deny you the thought you require. Take what time you will," I offered. "I will return tomorrow at dawn to hear your demands."

This was considered a proper reply and all acclaimed my answer. Scatha inclined her head and, as if allowing herself to be swayed by the response of the people, nodded slowly. "So be it. Come to this place at dawn and we will determine what kind of man you are."

"Let it be so," I replied.

At this, the people cheered and I was swept away once more on a tideflood of acclaim. We returned to the hall where, amidst much laughter and ribald advice, Tegid instructed me on what to expect in the morning. "Scatha will make her demands, and you must fulfill them with all skill and cunning. Do not think it will be easy," Tegid warned. "Rare treasure is worth great difficulty in the getting."

"But you will be there to help me," I suggested.

He shook his head. "No, Llew; as Chief Bard I cannot take one part over against the other. This is between you and Scatha alone. But, as she has Goewyn to assist her, you may choose one from among your men to aid you."

I looked around me. Bran stood grinning nearby—no doubt he would be a good choice to see me through this ordeal. "Bran?" I asked. "Would you serve me in this?"

But the Raven Chief shook his head. "Lord, if it is a strong hand on the hilt of a sword that you require, I am your man. But this is a matter beyond me. I think Alun Tringad would serve you better than I."

"Drustwn!" cried Alun when he heard this. "He is the man for you, lord." He pointed across the ring of faces gathered around me, and I saw Drustwn ducking out of sight. "Ah, now where has Drustwn gone?"

"Choose Lord Calbha!" someone shouted.

Before I could ask him, someone else replied, "It is a wife for Silver Hand, not a horse!"

Calbha answered, "It is true! I know nothing of brides; but if it is a horse you require, Llew, call on me."

I turned next to Cynan, who stood beside his father, Lord Cynfarch. "Cynan! Will you stand with me, brother?"

Cynan, assuming a grave and important air, inclined his head in assent. "Though all men desert you, Silver Hand, I will yet stand with you. Through all things—fire and sword and the wiles of bards and women—I am your man."

Everyone laughed at this, and even Cynan smiled as he said it. But his blue eyes were earnest, and his voice was firm. He was giving me a pledge greater than I had asked, and every word was from the heart.

I spent a restless, sleepless night in my hut, and rose well before dawn, before anyone else was stirring. I took myself to the lakeside for a swim and a bath; I shaved and washed my moustache, even. It was growing light in the east by the time I returned to the hut, where I spent a long time laying out my clothing. I wanted to look my best for Goewyn.

In the end, I chose a bright red siarc and a pair of yellow-and-green checked breecs. Also, I wore Meldryn Mawr's magnificent belt of gold discs and his gold torc, and carried his gold knife—all of which had been retrieved for me from among Meldron's belongings. "As the rightful successor, they are yours," Tegid had told me. "Meldron had no right to them. Wear them with pride, Llew. For by wearing them you will reclaim their honor."

So I wore them, and tried to forget that the Great Hound Meldron had so recently strutted and preened in them.

Cynan came to me as I was pulling on my buskins. He had also bathed and changed, and his red curls were combed and oiled. "You look a king attired for his wedding day," he said in approval.

"And you make a fine second," I replied. "Goewyn might well choose you instead."

"Are you hungry?" he asked.

"Yes," I replied. "But I do not think I could eat a bite. How do I look?"

He grinned. "I have already told you. And it is not seemly for a king to strain after praise. Come," he put his large hand on my shoulder, "it is dawn."

"Tegid should be close by," I said, "let us go and find him." We left my hut and moved towards the hall. The sun was rising and the sky was clear—not a cloud to be seen. My wedding day would be bright and sunny, as all good wedding days should be. My wedding day! The words seemed so strange: wedding . . . marriage . . . wife.

Tegid was awake and waiting. "I was coming to rouse you," he said. "Did you sleep well?"

"No," I replied. "I could not seem to keep my eyes closed."

He nodded. "No doubt you will sleep better tonight."

"What happens now?"

"Eat something if you like," the bard replied. "For although it is a feast day, I doubt you will have much time for eating."

Passing between the pillar-posts we found a place at an empty table and sat down. Bran and the Ravens roused themselves and joined us at the board. Although it was still too early for anything fresh from the ovens, there was some barley bread left over from last night's meal, so the others tucked in. The Ravens broke their loaves hungrily, stuffing their mouths and, between bites, urging me to eat to keep up my strength. "It is a long day that stretches before you," Bran remarked.

"And an even longer night!" quipped Alun.

"It grows no shorter for lingering here," I said, rising at once.

"Are you ready?" asked Tegid.

"Ready? I feel I have waited for this day all my life. Lead on, Wise Bard!"

With a wild, exuberant whoop warriors tumbled from the hall in a rowdy crush. There was no way to keep any sort of order or decorum, nor any quiet. The high spirits of the troop alerted the whole crannog and signalled the beginning of the festivities. We reached Scatha's hut with the entire population of Dinas Dwr crowding in our wake.

"Summon her," Tegid directed, as we came near the door.

"Scatha, Pen-y-Cat of Ynys Sci," I called, "it is Llew Silver Hand. I have come to hear and answer your demands."

A moment later, Scatha emerged from her hut, beautiful to behold in a scarlet mantle with a cream robe over it. Behind her stepped Goewyn, and my heart missed a beat: she was radiant in white and gold. Her long hair had been brushed until it gleamed, then plaited with threads of gold and bound in a long, thick braid. Gold armbands glimmered on her slender arms. Her mantle was white; she wore a white cloak of thin material, gathered loosely at her bare shoulders and held by two large gold brooches. Two wide bands of golden threadwork—elegant swans with long necks and wings fantastically intertwined—graced the borders of her cloak and the hem of her robe. Her girdle was narrow and white with gold laces tied and braided in a shimmering fall from her slim waist. She wore earrings of gold, and rings of red gold on her slender, tapering fingers.

The sight of her stole my breath away. It was like gazing into the brightness of the sun—though my eyes were burned and blinded, I could not look away. I had never seen her so beautiful, never seen any woman so beautiful. Indeed, I had forgotten such beauty could exist.

Scatha greeted me with frank disapproval, however, and said, "Are you ready to hear my demands?"

"I am ready," I said, sobered by her brusqueness.

"Three things I require," she declared curtly. "When I have received all that I ask, you shall have my daughter for your wife."

"Ask what you will, and you shall receive it."

She nodded slowly—was that a smile lurking behind her studied severity? "The first demand is this: give me the sea in full foam with a strand of silver."

The people were silent, waiting for my answer. I put a brave face on it and replied, "That is easily accomplished, though you may think otherwise."

I turned to Cynan. "Well, brother? We are days from the sea, and—"

Cynan shook his head. "No. She does not want the sea. It is something else. This is the impossible task. It is meant to demonstrate your ability to overcome the most formidable obstacle."

"Oh, you mean we have to think symbolically. I see."

"The sea in full foam—" Cynan said, and paused. "What could it be?"

"Scatha laid particular stress on the foam. That may be important. 'The sea in full foam—'" I paused, my brain spinning. "'A strand of silver'... Wait! I have it!"

"Yes?" Cynan leaned over eagerly.

"It is beer in a silver bowl!" I replied. "Beer foams like the sea and the bowl encircles it like a strand."

"Hah!" Cynan struck his fist into his palm. "That will answer!"

I turned to the crowd behind me. "Bran!" I called aloud. The

Raven Chief stepped forward quickly. "Bran, fetch me some fresh beer in a silver bowl. And hurry!"

He darted away at once, and I turned to face Scatha and wait for Bran to return with the bowl of beer. "What if we guessed wrong?" I whispered to Cynan.

He shook his head gravely. "What if he can find no beer? I fear we have drunk it all."

I had not thought of that. But Bran was resourceful; he would not let me down.

We waited. The crowd buzzed happily, talking among themselves. Goewyn stood cool and quiet as a statue; she would not look at me, so I could get no idea of what she was thinking.

Bran returned on the run, and the beer sloshing over the silver rim did look like sea waves foaming on the shore. He delivered the bowl into my hands, saying, "The last of the beer. All I could find— and it is mostly water."

"It will have to do," I said and, with a last hopeful look at Tegid—whose expression gave nothing away—I offered the gift to Scatha.

"You have asked for a boon and I give it: the sea in full foam surrounded by a strand of silver." So saying, I placed the bowl in her outstretched hands.

Scatha took the bowl and raised it for all to see. Then she said, "I accept your gift. But though you have succeeded in the first task, do not think you will easily obtain my second demand. Better men than you have tried and failed."

Knowing this to be part of the rote response, I still began vaguely to resent these other, *better* men. I swallowed my pride and answered, "Nevertheless, I will hear your demand. It may be that I will succeed where others have failed."

Scatha nodded regally. "My second demand is this: give me the one thing which will replace that which you seek to take from me."

I turned at once to Cynan. "This one is going to be tough," I said. "Goewyn means the world to her mother—how do we symbolize that?"

He rubbed his chin and frowned, but I could tell he was relishing his role. "This is most difficult—to replace that which you take from her."

"Maybe," I suggested, "we have only to identify one feature which Scatha will accept as representing her daughter. Like honey for sweetness—something like that."

Cynan cupped an elbow in his hand and rested his chin in his palm. "Sweet as honey... sweet as mead..." he murmured, thinking.

"Sweet and savory..." I suggested, "sweetness and light... sweet as a nut—"

"What did you say?"

"Sweet as a nut. But I do not think—"

"No, before the nut. What did you say before that?"

"Um... sweetness and light, I think."

"Light—yes!" Cynan nodded enthusiastically. "You see it? Goewyn is the light of her life. You are taking the light from her and you must replace it."

"How?" I wondered. "With a lamp?"

"Or a candle," Cynan prompted.

"A candle—a fragrant beeswax candle!"

Cynan grinned happily. "Sweetness and light! That would answer."

"Alun!" I called, turning to the Ravens once more. "Find me a beeswax candle, and bring it at once."

Alun Tringad disappeared, pushing through the close-packed crowd. He must have raided the nearest house, for he returned only a moment later, holding out a new candle, which I took from him and offered to Scatha, saying, "You have asked for a boon, and I give it: this candle will replace the light that I remove when I take your daughter from you. It will banish the shadows and fill the darkness with fragrance and warmth."

Scatha took the candle. "I accept your gift," she said, raising the candle so that all might see it. "But though you have succeeded in the second task, do not think you will easily obtain my third demand.

Better men than you have tried and failed."

I smiled confidently and repeated the expected response. "Nevertheless, I will hear your demand. It may be that I will succeed where others have failed."

"Hear then, if you will, my last demand: give me the thing this house lacks, the gift beyond price."

I turned to Cynan. "What is it this time? The impossible task again?" I wondered. "It sounds impossible to me."

"It could be," he allowed, "but I think not. We have done that one. It is something else."

"But what does her house lack? It could be anything."

"Not anything," Cynan replied slowly. "The one thing: the gift beyond price."

"She seemed to stress that," I agreed lamely. "The gift beyond price... what *is* the gift beyond price? Love? Happiness?"

"A child," suggested Cynan thoughtfully.

"Scatha wants me to give her a child? That cannot be right."

Cynan frowned. "Maybe it is you she wants."

I pounced on the idea at once. "That is it! That is the answer!"

"What?"

"Me!" I cried. "Think about it. The thing this house lacks is a man, a son-in-law. The gift beyond price is life."

Cynan's grin was wide and his blue eyes danced. "Yes, and by joining your life to Goewyn's you create a wealth of life," he winked and added, "especially if you make a few babies into the bargain. It *is* you she is asking for, Llew."

"Let us hope we are right," I said. I took a deep breath and turned to Scatha, who stood watching me, enjoying the way she was making me squirm.

"You have asked for a gift beyond price and a thing which you lack," I said. "It seems to me that your house lacks a man, and no one can place a value on life." So saying, I dropped down on one knee before her. "Therefore, Pen-y-Cat, I give you the gift of myself."

Scatha beamed her good pleasure, placing her hands on my

shoulders, bent and kissed my cheek. Raising me to my feet, she said, "I accept your gift, Llew Silver Hand." She lifted her voice for the benefit of those looking on. "Let it be known that there is no better man than you for my daughter, for you indeed have succeeded where other men have failed."

She turned, summoned Goewyn to her and, taking her daughter's left hand, put it in mine, and then clasped both of ours in her own. "I am satisfied," she declared to Tegid. "Let the marriage take place."

The bard stepped forward at once. He thumped the earth three times with his ashwood staff. "The Chief Bard of Albion speaks," he called loudly. "Hear me! From times past remembering the Derwyddi have joined life to life for the continuance of our race." Regarding us, he said, "Is it your desire to join your lives in marriage?"

"That is our desire," we answered together.

At this, Scatha produced the bowl which I had given her and passed it to Tegid. He raised it and said, "I hold between my hands the sea encircled by a silver strand. The sea is life; the silver is the all-encircling boundary of this worlds-realm. If you would be wed, then you must seize this worlds-realm and share its life between you."

So saying, he placed the silver bowl in our hands. Holding it between us, I offered the bowl to Goewyn and she drank, then offered the bowl to me. I also took a few swallows of very watery beer and raised my head.

"Drink!" Tegid urged. "It is life you are holding between you, my friends. Life! Drink deep and drain it to the last."

It was a very large bowl Bran had brought. I took a deep breath and raised the bowl once more. When I could not hold another drop, I passed the silver bowl to Goewyn, who took it, raised it, and drank— so long and deep and greedily I thought she would never come up for air. When she lowered the vessel once more, her eyes were shining bright. She licked her lips and, handing the bowl to Tegid, cast a sidelong glance at me.

Putting the bowl aside, Tegid said, "Goewyn, do you bring a gift?"

Goewyn said, "Neither gold nor silver do I bring, nor anything which can be bought or sold, lost or stolen. But I bring this day my love and my life, and these I do give you freely."

"Will you accept the gifts that have been offered?" Tegid asked.

"With all my heart, I do accept them. And I will cherish them always as my highest treasure, and I will protect this treasure to the last breath in my body."

Tegid inclined his head. "What token do you offer for your acceptance?"

Token? No one had told me about that; I had no token to offer. Cynan's voice sounded in my ear. "Give her your belt," he suggested helpfully.

I had no better idea, so I removed the belt and draped the heavy gold band across Tegid's outspread hands. "I offer this belt of fine gold," I said and, on a sudden inspiration, added, "Let its excellence and value be but a small token of the high esteem in which I hold my beloved, and let it encircle her fair form in shining splendor like my love which does encompass her for ever—true, without end, and incorruptible."

Tegid nodded sagely and, turning, offered the belt to Goewyn, who lowered her head as it was placed in her hands. She gathered the belt and clutched it to her breast. Were those tears in her eyes?

To Goewyn, Tegid said, "By this token your gift has been accepted. If you will receive the gift you have been given will you also offer a token of acceptance?"

Without a word, Goewyn slipped her arm around my neck and pressed her lips to mine. She kissed me full and free and with such fervor that it brought cheers from the onlookers gathered close about. She released me, breathless, almost gasping. The ardor in her clear brown eyes made me blush.

Tegid, smiling broadly, thumped the earth once more with his staff, three times, sharply. Then he raised the staff and held it horizontally over our heads. "The gifts of love and life have been exchanged and accepted. By this let all men know that Llew Silver Hand and Goewyn are wed."

And that was that. The people acclaimed the wedding loudly and with great enthusiasm. We were instantly caught up in a whirlwind of well-wishing. The wedding was over, let the celebration commence!

3

The Wedding Feast

Swept away on a floodtide of high exuberance, Goewyn and I were propelled through the crannog. I lost sight of Tegid, Scatha and Cynan; I could not see Bran or Calbha. At the landing we were bundled into a boat and rowed across to the lakeside where Scatha's field was quickly prepared for games.

Feast days and festivals are often accompanied by contests of skill and chance. Wrestling and horse racing are by far the favorites, with mock combat and games of hurley. An earthen mound was raised facing the field, with two chairs placed upon it. One of the chairs was made from stag antler, and adorned with a white oxhide—this was to be mine. And from this vantagepoint, Goewyn and I were to watch the proceedings and dispense prizes.

The sport would come first, the food and drink later—giving the cooks time to see everything properly prepared, and the competitors and spectators opportunity to build an ample appetite. Better to wrestle on an empty stomach, after all, than with a bellyful of roast pork. And after a few bowls of strong wedding mead, who would be able to sit a horse, let alone race one?

When the hastily erected mound was finished, Goewyn and I ascended to our chairs and waited for the company to assemble. Already, many had made their way across the lake from the crannog, and more were arriving. I was happy to wait. I was a happy man—perhaps for the first time in my life, truly happy.

All I had ever known of joy and life, and now love, had been found here, in the Otherworld, in Albion. The thought touched a guilty nerve in my conscience, and I squirmed. But surely, Professor Nettleton was wrong. He *was* wrong, and I would not destroy the thing I loved; he was wrong, and I could stay. I would sooner give up my life than leave Albion now.

I looked at Goewyn, and smothered my guilt with the sight of her gleaming hair. She sensed me watching her, and turned to me. "I love you, my soul," she whispered, smiling. And I felt like a man who, living his entire life in a cave, that instant steps out into the dazzling light of day.

Tegid arrived shortly, attended by his *Mabinogi*, led by the harpbearer, Gwion Bach. Another carried his staff. "I have given Calbha charge of the prizes," Tegid told us. "He is gathering them now."

"Prizes? Ah, yes, for the games."

"I knew you would not think of it," he explained cheerfully.

Calbha carried out his charge in style. He came leading a host of bearers, each carrying an armload of valuable objects—and some in twos lugging heavy wicker baskets between them. They piled their offerings around our chairs. Soon the mound was knee-deep in glittering, gleaming booty: new-made spears with decorated heads and shafts, fine swords inset with gems, shields with rims of silver and bronze, bone-handled knives... Wherever I looked there were cups and bowls—bowls of copper, bronze, silver, and gold; wooden bowls cunningly carved; cups of horn with silver rims, small cups and large cups; cups of stone even. There were fine new cloaks and piles of fluffy white fleeces. Armbands of bronze and silver and gold gleamed like links in a precious chain, and scattered among them were brooches, bracelets and rings. As if this were not enough, there were three good horses which Calbha could not resist adding.

I gaped at the glittering array. "Where did you get all this?"

"It is yours, lord," he replied happily. "But do not worry, I have chosen only the finest for such a celebration as this."

"I thank you, Calbha," I replied, eyeing the treasure trove. "You have served me well. Indeed, I did not know I was so wealthy."

There was so much, and all so lavish, that I wondered aloud to Tegid, "Can I afford this?"

The bard only laughed and indicated the shimmering mound with a sweep of his hand. "The greater the generosity, the greater the king."

"If that is the way of it, then give it all away—and more! Let men say that never in Albion was such a wedding celebration as this. And let all who hear of it in later days sicken with envy that they were not here!"

Cynan, arriving with some of his men just then, looked upon the treasure and declared himself well ready to win his share. Bran and the Ravens came behind him, calling loudly for the games to begin. Alun challenged Cynan then and there to chose whatever game of skill or chance he preferred—and he should be bested at it.

"You are a wonder, Alun Tringad," Cynan crowed. "Can it be you have forgotten the defeat I gave you when last you tried your skill against me?"

"Defeat?" Alun cried. "Am I to believe what I am hearing? The victory was mine, as you well know."

"Man, Alun—I am surprised your teeth keep company with your tongue, such lies you tell. Still, for the sake of this festive day," Cynan declared, "I will not hold your impudence against you."

"It was your voice, Cynan Machae, cried mercy as I recall," Alun replied amiably. "Yet, like you, I am willing to forget what is past for the sake of the day."

They fell to arguing then about the size of the wager—pledging prizes not yet won—and quickly drew a crowd of onlookers eager to back one or the other of the champions and so reap a share of the rewards.

They were still settling the terms when Goewyn leaned close. "If you do not begin the games soon, husband, we will be forced to listen to their boasting all day."

"Very well," I agreed, and rose from my chair to address the crowd. Tegid called for silence and, when the people saw that I would speak, they quieted themselves to listen. "Let us enjoy the day given to us!" I said. "Let us strive with skill and accept with good grace all that chances our way, that when the games are done we may retire to the feasting-hall better friends than when the day began."

"Well said, lord," Tegid declared. "So be it!"

Wrestling was first, followed by various races, including a spectacular horse race which had everyone exhausted by the time the winner—a young man from Calbha's clan—crossed the finish line. I awarded him a horse and, much to the crowd's amusement, he promptly retired from the games lest he lose his prize in a foolish wager.

I tried at first to match each award to its winner, but I soon gave up and I lost track and took whatever came to hand. Indeed, as the games proceeded I called on Goewyn to help, so that sometimes I awarded the prizes and sometimes the winners received their trophies from Goewyn—which I suspected most preferred. I noticed that many who came to the mound to marvel at the prizes, stayed to feast their eyes on Goewyn. Time and again I found myself stealing glances at her—like a beggar who has found a jewel of immense value, and must continually reassure himself that it is not a dream, that it does exist and, yes, that it belongs to him.

One young boy came to the mound and found a copper cup which, once he had picked up the thing, he could not bring himself to put down. "You like that cup," I said, and he blushed, for he did not know he was observed. "Tell me, how would you win it?"

He thought for a moment. "I would wrestle Bran Bresal himself," he answered boldly.

"Bran might be reluctant to risk his great renown by engaging one so young," I answered. "Perhaps you would be persuaded to pit your strength against someone more your own size?"

The boy accepted my suggestion and a match was agreed. It ended well and I was pleased to award him his prize. Thus began a succession of children's games and races, no less hotly contested than the trials of their elders.

The contests progressed and, little by little, the treasure mound was reduced. Tegid disappeared at some point in the proceedings and I was so caught up my role as gift-giver that some long time passed before I missed him. Turning to Goewyn, I said, "I wonder where Tegid has gone. Do you see him anywhere?"

Before she could reply, there came a rush at the mound behind us. I heard the swift approach and saw a confused motion out of the corner of my eye. Even as my head swivelled towards the sound and movement, I saw hands reaching for Goewyn. In the same instant that I leapt to my feet, she was pulled from her chair. "Llew!" she cried, and was borne roughly away.

I hurled myself after her, but there were too many people, too much confusion. I could hardly move. Head down, I drove forward into the mass of bodies. Hands seized me. I was pressed back into my chair. Goewyn cried out again, but her voice was farther away and the cry was cut off.

I kicked free of the chair and made to leap from the mound. Even as I gained my feet, I was hauled down from behind, thrown to the ground, and pinned there. Voices strange and loud gabbled in my ears. I fought against those holding me down. "Let me go!" I shouted. "Release me!" But the hands held firm, and the chaos of voices resolved itself into laughter. They were laughing at me!

Angry now, I struggled all the more. "Tegid!" I bellowed. "Tegid!"

"I am here, Llew," Tegid's voice replied calmly.

I looked around furiously, and saw Tegid's face appear above me. "Release him," the bard instructed.

The weight of hands fell away; the circle of faces drew back. I jumped to my feet. "They've taken Goewyn," I told him. "We were sitting here, and they—"

There were smiles and a spattering of laughter. I halted. Tegid, his fingers laced around his staff, appeared unconcerned. "What is happening?" I demanded. "Did you hear me?"

"I heard you, Llew," the bard replied simply.

His lack of concern appalled me. I opened my mouth to protest, and again heard the laughter. Gazing at those gathered around us, I saw their faces alight with mischief and mirth. It was only then I realized that I was the object of a prank. "Well, Tegid, what is it? What have you done?"

"It is not for me to say, lord," he answered.

It came to me then that this was another of those peculiar Celtic marriage customs. The trick required me to work the thing out for myself. Well, prank or custom, I was not amused. Turning away, I called, "Bran! Cynan! Follow me!"

I strode down from the mound, a path opening before me as I hastened away. "Bran! Cynan!" I called again, and when they did not join me, I turned to see them standing motionless. "Follow me!" I shouted. "I need you."

Cynan, grinning, moved a step forward, then stopped, shaking his head slightly.

"I go alone," I remarked.

"That is the way of it," Bran said.

"So be it!" Exasperation turning to anger, I whirled away across the field in the direction I had last seen Goewyn. It was a stupid jest, and I resented it.

The trail led to the lakeside where I lost it on the stony shore. They might have gone in either direction—one way led along the lake towards Dinas Dwr, the other rose to the heights and the ridge of Druim Vran above. Looking towards the crannog, I saw no sign of flight, so I pivoted the opposite way and strode towards the heights and Tegid's grove.

I reached the path and began the climb. The crowd followed behind, streaming along the lake in a happy hubbub. The trees gradually closed around me, muffling the sound of the following throng. It was cool among the silent trees, and the sun-dappled shadows seemed undisturbed. But I heard the creak of a bough ahead and knew my instincts were true. I quickened my pace, pushing recklessly ahead: ducking low-hanging branches, dodging trunks and shrubs.

Tegid's sacred grove lay directly ahead, and I made straight for it. Putting on a final burst of speed, I ascended the final leg of the trail and gained the grove. I entered with a rush to find a bower of birch branches had been erected in the center of the grove. And before the bower stood seven warriors, armed and ready.

"Put down your weapons," I commanded, but they did not move. I knew these men; they had followed me into battle and stood with me against Meldron. Now they stood against me. Though I knew it to be part of the ritual, the ache of betrayal that knifed momentarily through me was real enough. There was no help for me. I stood alone against them.

Steeling myself, I moved closer. The warriors advanced menacingly towards me. I stopped and they stopped, staring grimly at me. The smiles and laughter were gone. What, I wondered as I stood staring at them, was I supposed to do now?

The first of the onlookers reached the grove. I turned to see Bran, Cynan and Tegid entering behind me and, rank upon rank, my people surrounding the sacred circle. No one spoke, but the eagerness in their eyes urged me on.

If this was a mock abduction, it seemed I would have to undertake a mock battle to win my queen. I had no weapon, but, turning to the task before me, I stepped boldly forth and met the first warrior as he swung the head of the spear level. Moving quickly under the swinging shaft, I caught it with my silver hand and pulled hard.

To my surprise, the warrior released the spear and fell at my feet as if dead. Taking the shaft, I turned to meet the next warrior, who raised his spear to throw. I struck the man's shield with the tip of the spearblade: he dropped his weapon and fell. The third warrior crumpled at the touch of my spear against his shoulder—the fourth and fifth, likewise. The two remaining warriors attacked me together.

The first one struck at me, drawing a wide, lazy arc with his sword. I crouched as the blade passed over my head, and then drove into them, holding my spear sideways. At the lightest contact, the two warriors toppled, fell, and lay still.

Suddenly, the grove shook to a tremendous shout of triumph as I stepped to the bower's entrance. "Come out, Goewyn," I called. "All is well."

There was a movement from within the bower, and Goewyn stepped forward. She was as I had seen her only a few moments before, and yet she was not. She had changed. For, as she stepped from the deep green shadow of the birch-leaf bower, the sunlight struck her hair and gown and she became a creature of light, a bright spirit formed of air and fire: her hair golden flame, her gown shimmering sea-foam white.

The crowd, so noisily jubilant before, gasped and fell silent.

Dazzling, radiant, glowing with beauty, she appeared before me and I could but stand and stare. I heard a movement beside me. "Truly, she is a goddess," Cynan whispered. "Go to her, man! Claim your bride—or I will."

I stepped forward and extended my silver hand to her. As she took my hand, the sunlight caught the metal and flared. And it seemed that a blaze sprang up between us at the union of our hands. Though it was only a game, it was with genuine relief that I clasped her to my heart. "Never leave me, Goewyn," I breathed.

"I never will," she promised.

The sun had begun its westward plunge by the time we returned to the crannog. Tables had been set up outside the hall to accommodate the increased numbers the king would entertain this night. I would have preferred to remain outside—after the brilliant day, the night would be warm and bright—but the interior of the hall had been festooned with rushlights and birch branches to resemble the leafy bower in the grove. With all this preparation specially for us, it would have been unkind not to acknowledge the honor and enjoy it.

Famished with hunger and aflame with thirst, the warriors called loudly for food and drink as soon as they crossed the threshold. The tables inside the hall had been arranged to form a large hollow square so that we could all see one another. As the first were finding their places at the board, the platters appeared—borne on the shoulders of the servers—huge trenchers piled high with choice cuts of roast beef, pork, and mutton; these were followed by enormous platters of cooked cabbages, turnips, leeks and fennel. A fair-sized vat had been set up at the end of each table so that no one would have to go far to refill cup or bowl. Alas, there was no ale left, so tonight the vats had been filled with water flavored with honey and bullace. Along the center of each table were piled small loaves of honey-glazed *banys bara*, or wedding bread—fresh-baked and warm from the ovens.

As the platters were passed, each diner, man or woman, was offered the most succulent portions. Within moments the clamor sank to a muffled din as hungry mouths were filled with good food. The privilege of eating first carried with it the obligation of serving; those who served now would be guests later. Thus, order and right were admirably maintained. The guards watching over the Singing Stones were the only exceptions. They neither served nor ate, but stood aloof from the celebration, as watchful and wary as if they were alone in a hostile land.

Looking out across the crowded hall, my heart swelled with joy to see my people so happy and content. It came to me why it was that the mark of a king was linked to his benevolence: his people lived on it, looking to the king for their sustenance and support; through him they lived, or died. I filled my bowl with the savory morsels served me, and began to eat with a ready appetite.

When everyone had been served, a loud thumping drum resounded through the hall, and into the hollow square advanced eight maidens at a slow and solemn pace. Each maiden gathered her loose-hanging hair and wound it into a knot at the nape of her neck. They then drew up the hems of their mantles so that their legs were bare, and loosened the strings of their bodices. Each maiden then approached a warrior at table and begged the use of his sword.

The warriors—eager accomplices—gave up their swords willingly, and the maidens returned to the center of the square where they formed a circle, each placing her sword on the ground at her feet so that the swordpoints touched. Tegid, harp at his shoulder, appeared and began to play. The harpstrings sang, each note plucked with definite accent; and the maidens began to dance, each step deliberate and slow.

Around the sunburst of swords they danced, treading their way slowly over the hilts and blades, eyes level, fixed on a point in the distance. Around and around, they went, adding an extra step with each pass. By the sixth pass the harpsong began to quicken and the footwork grew more complicated. By the twelfth pass, the harp was humming and the dance had become fantastic. Yet, the maidens danced with the same solemn attitude, eyes fixed, expressions grave.

The music reached a crescendo and the maidens, spinning swiftly, performed an intricate maneuver with their arms. Then, quick as a blink, they stopped, spun around, stooped, and each seized her sword by the hilt and lofted its point to the rooftrees above, shedding the tops of their mantles in the same motion.

The music began again, slowly. Lowering the swords, the maidens began the dance once more, their steps measured and precise. The swords flashed and gleamed, creating dazzling arcs around the twirling lissome shapes. The tempo increased, and those looking on began beating time with their hands on the tables, shouting encouragement to the dancers. The young women's skill at handling the swords was dazzling; handwork and footwork elaborate, cunning, and deft: hands weaving enigmatic patterns, feet tracing complex figures as the keen-edged swords shimmered and shone.

Torchlight and rushlight glimmered on the sweat-glistening flesh of slender arms, rounded shoulders and breasts. The harpsong swelled; the sword-dance whirled to its climax. With a shriek and a shout, the maidens leaped, striking their blades together in simulated battleclash. Once, twice, three times, the weapons sang. They froze for an instant, and then fell back, each maiden clutching the naked blade to her breast. They knelt and lay back until their heads touched the ground and the swords lay flat along their taut chests and stomachs.

Slowly raising the swords by the hilts, they rose to their knees once more, brandishing the blades high. Suddenly, the harp struck a resounding chord. The swords plunged. The maidens collapsed with a cry.

There was a moment's silence as we all sat gazing raptly at the swaying blades standing in the packed earth floor. And then cheers filled the hall, loudly lauding the dancers' feat. The maidens gathered their clothes and retreated from the square.

I looked at Goewyn, and then at the bowl in my hands. All thought of food vanished from my mind—instantly replaced by a hunger of an entirely different, though no less urgent, variety. She sensed me looking at her and smiled. "Is something wrong with the food?" she asked, indicating my half-filled bowl.

I shook my head. "It is just that I think I have discovered something more to my liking."

Goewyn leaned close, put her hand to my face and kissed me. "If you find *that* to your liking," she whispered, "then join me when you have finished." Rising from her chair, she let her fingers drift along my jaw. Her touch sent a delicious shiver along my ribs.

I watched her go. She paused at the door and cast a backward glance at me before disappearing. It seemed to me that the close-crowded hall, so festive only moments before, grew suddenly loud and the crush of people oppressive.

Cynan noticed that I was not eating. "Eat!" he urged. "This night above all others you will need what little strength you possess."

Bran, sitting next to him, said, "Brother, can you not see it is food and drink of a different kind that he craves?"

Others offered their own opinions on how best to maintain strength and vigor in such circumstances. I forced down a few bites and swallowed some ale, but my friends thought my efforts lacked conviction, and redoubled their exhortations. Calbha filled my cup from his own and insisted I drain it in a single draught. I sipped politely and laughed at their jests, though my heart was not in it.

The feasting and dancing would continue through the night, but I could not tolerate another moment. Rising from the table, I tried to make an unobtrusive exit, which proved impossible. I was forced to endure much good-natured, bibulous advice on how to conduct myself on my wedding night.

As I moved past Tegid, he slipped a skin of mead into my hands so that my wedding night should lack neither sweetness or warmth. "In mead is found the flavor of the marriage bed. Twice blessed are lovers who share it on this night."

The more garrulous seemed anxious to accompany me to the hut where Goewyn waited. But Tegid came to my rescue, urging them to sit down and celebrate the new-wedded couple's happiness in song. He took up his harp and made a great show of tuning it. "Away with you," he murmured under his breath, "I will keep order here."

Cradling the mead in the crook of my arm, I hurried across the yard to the nearby hut which had been prepared for us. The house, like the hall, had been transformed into a forest bower with fragrant pine and birch branches adorning walls and ceiling, and rushlights glowing like ruddy stars, creating a dimly pleasant rose-hued light.

Goewyn was waiting, greeted me with a kiss, and drew me inside, taking the meadskin. "I have waited long for this night, my soul," she whispered as she wrapped her arms tightly around me.

Our first embrace ended in a long, passionate kiss. And as the sleeping-place was prepared—fleeces piled deep and spread with cloaks—we tumbled into it. I closed my eyes, filling my lungs with the warm scent of her skin as our caresses grew more urgent, taking fire.

Thus occupied, I do not know whether it was the shout or the smoke that first called me from the bed. I sat up abruptly. Goewyn reached for me, tugging me gently back down. "Llew..."

"Wait—"

"What is it?" she whispered.

The shout came again, quick and urgent. And with it the sharp scent of smoke.

"Fire!" I said, leaping to my feet. "The crannog is on fire!"

4

A Fine Night's Work

"The fire is on the western side," Goewyn said, watching the rusty stain seeping into the night sky. "The wind will send it towards us."

"Not if we hurry," I said. "Go to the hall. Alert Tegid and Bran. I will return as soon I can."

Even as I spoke, I heard another cry of alarm: "Hurry, Llew!" I kissed her cheek and darted away.

The smoke thickened as I raced towards the fire, filling my nostrils with the parched and musty sharpness of scorched grain: the grain stores! Unless the fire was extinguished quickly, it would be a lean, hungry winter.

As I raced through the crannog along the central byway joining the various islets of our floating city, I saw the yellow-tipped flames, like clustered leaves, darting above the rooftops. I heard the fire's angry roar, and I heard voices: men shouting, women calling, children shrieking and crying. And behind me, from the direction of the hall, came the battleblast of the carynx, sounding the alarm.

The flames leapt high and ever higher, red-orange and angry against the black sky. Dinas Dwr, our beautiful city on the lake, was garishly silhouetted in the hideous glow. I felt sick with dread.

Closer, I saw people running here and there, darting through the rolling smoke, faces set, grimly earnest. Some carried leather buckets, others had wooden or metal bowls and cauldrons, but most wielded only their cloaks which they had stripped off, soaked in water, and now used as flails upon the sprouting flames.

I whipped off my own cloak and sped to join them. My heart sank like a stone. The houses, so close together, their dry roof-thatches nearly touching, kindled like tinder at the first lick of flame. I beat out the flames in one place only to have them reappear elsewhere. If help did not come at once, we would lose all.

I heard a shout behind me.

"Tegid! Here!" I cried, turning as the bard reached me. King Calbha, with fifty or more warriors and women came with him, and they all began beating at the flames with their cloaks. "Where are Bran and Cynan?"

"I have sent Cynan and Cynfarch to the south side," Tegid explained. "The Ravens are on the north. I told them I would send you to them."

"Go, Llew," instructed Calbha, wading into battle. "We will see to matters here."

I left them to the fight, and ran to aid the Ravens, passing between huts whose roofs were already smoldering from the sparks raining down upon them. The smoke thickened, acrid and black with soot. I came to a knot of men working furiously. "Bran!" I shouted.

"Here, lord!" came the answer, and a torso materialized out of the smoke. Bran carried a hayfork in one hand and his cloak in the other. Naked to the waist, his skin was black from the smoke; his eyes and teeth showed white, like chips of moonstone. Sweat poured off him, washing pale rivulets through the grime.

"Tegid thought you might need help," I explained. "How is it here?"

"We are trying to keep the fire from spreading further eastward. Fortunately, the wind is with us," he said, then added, "but Cynan and Cynfarch will have the worst of it."

"Then I will go to them," I told him, and hurried away again. I rounded a turn and crossed a bridge, meeting three women, each carrying two or three babes and shepherding a bedraggled flock of young children, all of them frightened and wailing. One of the women stumbled in her haste and trod on a child; she fell to her knees, almost dropping the infants she clutched so tightly. The child sprawled headlong onto the bridge timbers and lay screaming.

I scooped up the child—so quickly that the youngster stopped yowling, fright swallowed by surprise. Goewyn appeared beside me in an instant, bending to raise the woman to her feet and shouldering an infant all in one swift motion. "I will see them safe!" she called to me, already leading them away. "You go ahead."

I raced on. Cynfarch stood as if in the midst of a riot, commanding the effort. I ran to him, shedding my cloak. "I am here, Cynfarch," I said. "What is to be done?"

"We will not save these houses, but—" he broke off to shout orders to a group of men pulling at burning thatch with wooden rakes and long iron hooks. A portion of the roof collapsed inward with a shower of sparks, and the men scurried to the next hut. "These houses are ruined," he continued, "but if the wind holds steady we may keep it from spreading."

"Where is Cynan?"

"He was there," the king glanced over his shoulder. "I do not see him now."

I ran to the place Cynfarch indicated, passing between burning buildings into a valley of fire. Flames leapt all around me. The heat gushed and blasted on the breeze. Everything—the houses to the right and left, the wall ahead, the black sky above—shimmered in the heat-flash.

I heard a horse's wild scream, and directly in front of me a man burst through a bank of smoke holding tight to the reins of a rearing horse. The man had thrown his cloak over the terrified animal's head, and was leading it away from the fire. Immediately behind him came four more men with bucking, neighing, panicky horses, each with their heads bound in the men's cloaks. Only a few horses and kine were kept on the crannog; all the rest ranged the meadow below the ridgewall. But those we stabled in Dinas Dwr we could least afford to lose.

I helped the men lead the horses through the narrow, fire-shattered path between the burning wrecks of houses and sheds. Once on the wider path, I retraced my steps and hurried on. Smoke billowed all around, obscuring sight. Covering my nose and mouth with the lower part of my siarc, I plunged ahead and came all at once into a clear place swarming with people. Fire danced in a hazy shimmer all around. I felt as if I had been thrust into an oven.

Cynan, with a score of warriors and men with axes, chopped furiously at the timber wall. They were trying to cut away a section as a fire-break to keep the flames from destroying the entire palisade. Threescore men with sopping cloaks beat at the wooden surfaces and the ground, keeping the surrounding flames at bay, while more men with buckets doused the smoldering embers of the ruins they had reclaimed. Black curls of soot and grey flakes of ash fell from the sky like filthy snow.

"Cynan!" I called, running to him.

At the sound of my voice he turned, though the axe completed its stroke. "Llew! A fine wedding night for you," he said, shaking his head as he chopped again.

I scanned the ragged, fire-ravaged wall. "Will your fire-break hold?"

"Oh, aye," he said, stepping back from the wall to look at his labor. "It will hold." He raised his voice to shout the order. "Pull it down! Pull it down, men!"

Ropes stretched taut. The wall section wobbled and swayed, but would not fall.

"Pull!" shouted Cynan, leaping to the nearest rope.

I joined him, lending my weight to the effort. We heaved on the ropes and the timbers groaned. "Pull!" Cynan cried. "Everyone! All together! Pull!"

The timbers sighed and then gave way with a shuddering crash. We stood gazing through a clear gap at the lake beyond. "Those houses next!" Cynan ordered, stooping for his axe.

Two heartbeats later, a score of axes shivered the roof-trees of three houses as yet untouched by the relentlessly encroaching flames.

Seizing one of the rakes, I began attacking the smoldering thatch of a nearby roof, throwing the rake as high up the slope as I could reach and pulling, pulling, pulling down with all my might, scattering the bundled thatch, and then beating out the glowing reeds as they lay at my feet.

When I finished one roof, I rushed to another, and then another. My arms ached and my eyes watered. I choked on smoke. Live embers caught in the cloth of my siarc, so I stripped it off and braved the burns of falling thatch. The heat singed my hair; it felt as if my skin was blistering. But I worked on, sometimes with help, more often alone. Everyone was doing whatever could be done.

"Llew!" I heard someone shout my name. I turned just in time to see a pair of long horns swing out of the smoke haze. I dodged to one side as the curved horn cut a swathe through the air where I stood. An ox had broken free from its tether and, frightened out of its dim wits, was intent on returning to its pen. The stupid beast was running among burning huts looking for its shed. Snatching up my siarc, I waved and shouted, turning the animal away. It rumbled off the way it had come, but no one gave chase. We had enough to do trying to stay ahead of the flames.

Everywhere I turned, there was a new emergency. We flew to each fresh crisis swiftly, but with a little less energy than the one before. Strength began to flag—and then to fail. My arms grew heavy and numb. My hand was raw from the rake handle, and from burns. I could not catch my breath; my lungs heaved and the air wheezed in my throat. Still, I doggedly planted one foot in front of the other and labored on.

And when I began to think that we must abandon our work to the flames, Bran and the Ravens appeared with several score men and warriors. With a shout they swooped to the task. Within moments of their arrival, or so it seemed to me, we were working harder than ever before. Raking thatch, beating flames, smothering sparks—raking, beating, smothering, over and over and over again and again.

Time passed as in a dream. Heat licked my skin; smoke stung my nose and my eyes ran. But I toiled on. Gradually, the fire's glare dimmed. I felt cooler air on my scorched skin and I stopped.

A hundred men or more stood around me, clutching tools, vessels, and cloaks in unfeeling hands. We stood, heads bowed, our arms limp at our sides, or kneeling, leaning on our rakes for support. And all around us the quiet hiss of hot embers slowly dying...

"A fine night's work," growled Cynan in a voice ragged as the remains of his burnt tatters of clothing.

I raised my head and turned raw eyes to a sky showing grey in the east. In the pale, spectral light Dinas Dwr appeared as a vast heap of charred timber and smoking ash.

"I want to see what is left," I told Cynan. "We should look for the injured."

"I will look after the men here," Bran said. He swayed on his feet with fatigue, but I knew he would not rest until all the others were settled. So I charged him to do what he deemed best, and left him to it.

In the grim grey dawn, Cynan and I stumbled slowly through the devastation of the caer. The damage was severe and thorough. The western side of the stronghold had been decimated; precious little remained standing, and that little had been ravaged by flame and smoke.

Calbha met us as we pursued our inspection; he had been arranging temporary storage for salvaged food stocks and supplies, and holding-pens for horses and cattle until they could be conveyed to pasturage on the meadows.

"Was anyone hurt here?" I asked him.

Calbha gave a quick shake of his head. "A few with burns and such," he answered, "but no one seriously hurt. We were fortunate."

We left him to his work and continued on, picking our way through smoking rubble. In the center of a small yard formed by the charred remains of three houses, we found Tegid and several women working with the injured. The bard, nearly black with smoke and soot, knelt over a thrashing body, applying unguent from a clay pot. Lying on the ground around him were a dozen more bodies: some gasping and moaning, or struggling to rise; others unnaturally still, and wrapped head to foot in cloaks. Several of these cloak-covered corpses were no bigger than a bundle of kindling.

The full weight of sadness descended upon me then, and I staggered beneath it. Cynan caught my arm and bore me up.

Scatha moved among the living, bearing the marks of one who had walked through flames—as indeed she had. For when the alarm sounded, she had organized a search of each house on the western side. Nearly everyone was at the wedding feast, but a few—especially mothers of small children—had retired to sleep. Scatha had roused them and conducted them through smoke and flames to safety, returning again and again, until the fire grew too hot and she could do no more.

"How many?" She glanced up quickly at the sound of my voice, and then proceeded with her work of bandaging a young man's burned upper arm.

"If there had been time," she replied, "these might have been saved. But the fire spread so swiftly . . . and these young ones were asleep." She lifted a hand to the tiny bundles. "They never woke, and now they never will."

"Tell me, Scatha," I said, my voice husky with fatigue and remorse. "How many?"

"Three fives and three," she replied, then added softly, "Two or three more will join that number before nightfall."

Tegid finished and joined us. "It is a wicked loss," he muttered. "Smoke took them while they slept. It was a merciful death, at least."

"But for the feast," Cynan put in, "it would have been much worse. Almost everyone was in the hall when it started."

"And if almost everyone had not been in the hall, it would never have started in the first place," Scatha suggested.

I was in no mood for riddles. "Are you saying that this was not an accident?" I demanded bluntly.

"It was no accident kindled the flame." Cynan was adamant.

Tegid agreed. "Flames arising in three places at once—the wall, the houses, the ox pens—is not negligence or mishap. That is willful and malicious."

Lord Calbha, coming upon us just then, heard Tegid's

pronouncement. "Someone set the fires on purpose—is that what you are saying?" charged Calbha, unwilling to believe such a thing could happen in Dinas Dwr. "What man among us would do such a thing?"

"Man or men," Cynan replied, his voice raw from smoke and shouting. "There was maybe more than one." He regarded the smoldering ruins narrowly. "Whoever it was knew their work, and did it well. If the wind had changed we would have lost the caer— and many more lives besides."

The sweat on my back turned cold. I turned to those around me, silently scanning their faces. If there was a killer among us, I could not imagine who it might be. A call from one of the women took Tegid away. "Speak of this to no one," I charged the others, "until we have had time to learn more."

Scatha returned to her work, and Cynan, Calbha and I went back to where Bran and the Ravens were sifting the rubble of a storehouse. Closer, I saw that they were slowly, carefully lifting a collapsed roofbeam from a body which was trapped beneath it.

Cynan and I hastened to add our strength to the task. Grasping the blackened timber, we heaved it up, shifting it just enough for the broken body beneath to be withdrawn. The man was pulled free of the debris and carried from the ruin where they laid him gently down and rolled him onto his back.

Bran's head came up slowly, his expression grave. He glanced from me to Cynan. "I am sorry, Cynan..."

"Cynfarch!" exclaimed Cynan. Falling to his knees, he raised his father's body in his arms. The movement brought a faint whimper of a moan. The Galanae king coughed and a thin trickle of blood leaked from the corner of his mouth.

Calbha stifled an oath; I put my hand on the man nearest me. "Fetch Tegid," I ordered. "Hurry, man!"

Tegid came on the run, took one look at the body on the ground, and ordered everyone back. Bending over Cynfarch's side, the bard began to examine the stricken king. He gently probed the body for wounds, and turned the head to the side. Beneath the filthy coating of ash, Cynfarch's flesh was pale and waxy.

Cynan, his broad shoulders hunched, clasped his father's hand in his and stared hard at the slack features, as if willing vigor to reappear. "Will he live?" he asked as Tegid finished his scrutiny.

"He is hurt inside," the bard replied. "I cannot say."

These words were scarcely fallen from his lips when another call claimed our attention. "*Penderwydd*! Llew! Help! Come quickly!"

We turned to see a warrior running towards us. "What is it, Pebin?" I called to him. "What has happened?"

"Lord," Pebin replied, "I went to the hall to take up my watch..." he paused, glancing around quickly. "You had better come at once."

5

Good Counsel

"I will look after my father," Cynan said. "Leave me."

"Take Cynfarch to my hut," the bard ordered. "Sioned will tend him there."

Then Tegid, Pebin and I threaded our way back towards the center of the crannog, passing knots of people hurrying to the site of the fire. The embers were still smoking and ash still hot, but the clean-up was commencing. Those who had taken refuge on the shore were returning to begin the restoration.

Crossing the bridge on the main pathway we came to the cluster of low round houses that sheltered in the shadow of the great hall. Except for the smell of smoke, which permeated everything in the fortress, the houses and hall were untouched by the fire. All appeared safe and secure.

We moved quickly among the huts and across the yard separating them from the hall. "Stay here, Pebin," I instructed the warrior. "Do not let anyone in." Passing between the massive doorposts, I followed Tegid inside. Even in the dim light I could see that the iron stand had been overturned. The wooden chest bearing the Singing Stones was gone. Closer, I saw two figures huddled against the far west wall, and a third sprawled face down on the bare earth floor. They did not stir as we entered.

Approaching the nearest man, I stooped and shook him by the shoulder. When my jostling awoke no response, I rolled the man towards me. His head flopped loosely on his chest, and I knew he was dead.

"One of the warband," I said. I had seen the man before, but did not know his name.

"It is Cradawc," Tegid informed me, leaning near to see the man's face.

I lowered the body gently to the floor, cradling his neck in my hand so that his head would not strike the ground. My hand came away sticky and wet. A sick feeling spread through my gut as I looked at the dark substance on my hand. "The back of his head has been crushed," I murmured.

Tegid moved to the second man, and pressed his fingertips against the man's throat.

"Dead?" I asked.

He answered me with a nod, and turned at once to the third warrior.

"This one as well?"

"No," Tegid answered. "This one still lives."

"Who is it?"

Just then the man groaned and coughed.

"It is Gorew. Help me get him outside."

Carefully, Tegid and I carried the body from the hall and laid it gently on the ground outside. Stretching his long fingers over the fallen warrior, Tegid turned Gorew's head to the side. It was then I saw the hideous blue-black bruise bulging like an egg on the side of his temple above the right eye.

The movement brought another moan. "Gorew," Tegid said loudly, firmly.

At the sound of his name, the warrior's eyes fluttered open. "Ahhh..." The groan was a whisper.

"Rest and be easy," Tegid told him. "We are here to help you."

"They are... gone," Gorew said, his voice a faint rattle in his throat.

"Who is gone?" Tegid asked, holding Gorew with his voice.

"The stones..." the warrior answered. "Gone... stolen..."

"We know, Gorew," I replied. The injured warrior's eyes fluttered. "Who did this to you?" I asked. "Who attacked you?"

"I, ahh... saw someone... I thought..." Gorew sighed, and closed his eyes.

"The name, Gorew. Give us the name. Who did this?" But it was no use; Gorew had lost consciousness once more.

"We will learn nothing more for the moment," Tegid said. "Let us carry him to my hut."

Pebin, staring down at Gorew, made no move, so I took his arm and directed him to help lift the wounded warrior. We carried Gorew to Tegid's hut where Cynan and Bran were now waiting. Inside, Sioned, a woman much skilled in healing, was watching over the more badly injured. Sioned spread a cloak for him over a mat of straw, and we laid Gorew down beside Cynfarch. "I will tend him now," she said.

"Who would do this?" Pebin asked as we stepped from the hut.

Who indeed, I wondered? Twenty dead so far—with more likely to follow—half the caer ruined, and the Singing Stones stolen. The damage was severe as it was brutal. I determined to lay hands to the thieves before the sun set on this day.

Summoning Bran and Cynan to me, I informed them of the theft. "The thieves set fire to the caer and used the resulting confusion to steal the Singing Stones. Gorew and the other guards were attacked and overpowered."

"The Treasure of Albion stolen?" Bran wondered. "And the guards?"

"Two were killed outright; Gorew still lives. He may yet tell us something."

Cynan's blue eyes narrowed dangerously. "He is a dead man who did this."

"Until we raise the trail, we do not know how many are involved."

"One man or a hundred," Cynan muttered, "it is all the same to me."

"Bran," I said, moving towards the hall, "raise the warband. We will begin the search at once."

The Chief Raven sped away, and Cynan and I began walking back towards the hall. As we came into the yard, the booming battlehorn sounded, and a few moments later the Ravens began flocking to the call: Garanaw, Drustwn, Niall, Emyr, Alun. Scatha arrived too, and a few moments later Bran entered with a score of warriors. All gathered around the cold hearth.

"We have been attacked by enemies," I explained, and told them about the assault during the fire. "So far, twenty are dead, and others are badly injured—Cynfarch and Gorew among them. The Singing Stones are stolen." This revelation brought an instant outcry. "We will catch the men who did this," I pledged, and my vow was echoed by a dozen more. "The search will begin at once."

I turned to Bran Bresal, my battlechief, leader of the Raven Flight. "Make ready to leave. We will ride as soon as horses are saddled."

He hesitated, glancing quickly at Scatha; a look I could not read passed between them.

"Well?" I demanded.

"It will be done as you say, lord," Bran replied, touching the back of his hand to his forehead. Calling the warband to follow him, they hurried from the hall to attend to their various tasks, leaving Cynan and Scatha alone with me.

"I am sorry, Cynan," Scatha said, touching the brawny warrior on the arm.

"The blood debt will be paid, Pen-y-Cat," he replied quietly. "Never doubt it." The pain bled raw in his voice.

Turning to me, Scatha said, "I would serve you in this, lord. Allow me to lead the warband and capture the thieves."

"I thank you, Pen-y-Cat," I declined, "but it is my place. You will serve better here. Tegid will need your help."

"Your place is here as well, Llew," she persisted. "It is time for you to think beyond yourself to those who depend on you. You need rest," Scatha suggested, pressing her point. "Stay here and rule your people."

Her words meant nothing to me. Rage flowed hot and potent through my veins, and I was in no mood for unravelling riddles. I saw but one thing clearly: the men who had practised this outrage on me would be caught and judged. "A bath is all I need," I grumbled. "The cold water will revive me."

Aching in every joint, I dragged myself back to my hut intent on bathing and changing clothes before departing. I reeked of stale sweat and smoke; my hair was singed in a dozen places, and my breecs and buskins looked as if they had been attacked by flaming moths. Inside the hut, I paused only long enough to retrieve a change of clothes, a chunk of the heavy tallow soap, and the strip of linen I used for a washcloth. I had started across the yard when Tegid emerged from his hut. I went to him.

"Gorew may recover," the bard said. "I will know more when he awakes."

"And Cynfarch?" I asked.

"Death is strong, but Cynfarch may yet prove stronger," the bard replied. "The battle will be decided before this day is done."

"Either way, I mean to have the thieves caught and the stones returned before this time tomorrow," I said.

"And are you thinking of going after them yourself?" he asked pointedly.

"Of course! I am the king. It is my duty."

The bard bristled at this, and opened his mouth to object. I did not want to hear it, so I cut him off. "Save your breath, Tegid. I am leading the warband, and that is that."

Turning on my heel, I stalked away across the yard, through the gate, and out to the boat landing. At one end of the landing, the rock base of the crannog formed a shallow area many used as a bathing-place. But there was no one else about.

I stripped off my clothes and slipped into the water; the icy sting on my scorched hide felt like a balm. Sinking gratefully into the water, I floated submerged except for forehead and nose.

The sun rose higher, burning through the thin grey mist while I busied myself with the soap. I washed my hair and scrubbed my skin raw with the cloth. When I lowered myself into the water to rinse, I felt like a snake sloughing off its old dead skin.

I was shaking water from my hair when Goewyn arrived.

"Scatha has told me what has happened," she said. She stood on the landing above me with her arms crossed. Her face was smudged with soot, and her hair was tangled and powdered with ash. Her once-white mantle was leopard-spotted with black and brown burnmarks.

I almost salmon-leaped from the water for, until the moment I saw her again, I had completely forgotten that I was a married man now and had a wife waiting for me.

"Goewyn, I am so sorry, I forgot that—"

"She says you are planning to ride out," she continued coldly. "If you care anything for your people, or what has happened here this night, you will not go."

"But I must go," I insisted. "I am the king; it is my duty."

"If you are a king," she said, flinging each word separately for emphasis, "stay here and act like a king. Rule your people. Rebuild your stronghold."

"What of the Singing Stones? What of the thieves?"

"Send your battlechief and warriors to bring them back. That is what a true king would do."

"It is my place," I replied, moving towards her.

"You are wrong. Your place is here with your people. You should not be seen chasing these—these *cynrhon!*" She used a word seldom used of another in Albion; I had never seen her so angry. "Are you above them?"

"Of course, Goewyn, but I—"

"Then show it!" she snapped. "Are these thieves kings that it takes a king to capture them?"

"No, but—" I began, and was quickly cut off.

"Hear me, Llew Silver Hand: if you allow your enemy to prevent you from ruling, he is more powerful than you—and the whole of Albion will know it."

"Goewyn, please. You do not understand."

"Do I not?" she demanded, and did not wait for my answer. "Will not Bran serve you with the last breath of his body? Will not Cynan move mountains at your word? Will not the Ravens seize the sun and stars to please you?"

"Listen—if I am a king at all, it is because the Singing Stones have made me so."

"You are not just another king. You are the Aird Righ! You *are* Albion. That is why you cannot go."

"Goewyn, please. Be reasonable." I must have presented a forlorn spectacle standing up to my navel in cold water, shivering and dripping, for she softened somewhat.

"Do not behave as a man without rank and power," she said, and I began to see the shape of her logic. "If you are a king, my love, then *be* a king. Demonstrate your authority and might. Demonstrate your wisdom: send Bran and the Raven Flight. Yes. Send Cynan. Send Calbha and Scatha and a hundred warriors. Send everyone! But do not go yourself. Do not become the thing you seek to destroy."

"You sound just like Tegid," I replied, attempting—clumsily—to lighten the mood. It seemed absurd for both of us to be angry.

"Then you should listen to your wise bard," she replied imperiously. "He is giving you good counsel."

Goewyn stood with her arms crossed over her breast, regarding me with implacable eyes, waiting for my reply. I was beaten and I knew it. She was right: a true king would never risk the honor of his sovereignty by chasing criminals across the kingdom.

"Lady, I stand rebuked," I said, spreading my hands. "Also I stand shivering and cold. I will do as you say, only let me come out of the water before I freeze."

"Far be it from me to prevent you," she said, her lips curving ever so slightly at the corners.

"So be it." I took another step towards her, climbing from the water. She stooped and shook out the cloak, holding it out for me to step into.

I turned my back to her and she draped the cloak over my shoulders. Her hands travelled slowly down my back, and then her arms encircled my waist. I turned in her embrace, put my arms around her and held her close. "You will get wet," I told her.

"I need a bath," she replied, then, realizing the truth of what she had said, at once pushed me away and held me at arm's length.

"I have washed," I protested.

"But I have not." She withdrew a quick step.

"Wait—"

"Come home, husband," she called, "but not until you have told Tegid that you are staying in Dinas Dwr, and not until you have sent the Raven Flight to work your will."

"Goewyn, wait, I will go with you—"

"I will be waiting, husband," she called, disappearing through the gate.

I pulled on my breecs, stuffed my arms into the sleeves of the siarc, snatched up my buskins, and hurried back to Tegid's hut to inform him of my change of plan.

6

Cynan Two-Torcs

I called Tegid from his hut. He emerged looking hunched and old; his dark hair was grey with ash, and his face seemed just as colorless. His eyes were bloodshot from smoke and exhaustion. He must have been dead on his feet. I instantly felt guilty for taking a bath, leaving everyone else to do the work.

"Wise Bard," I said, "I have changed my mind. I am staying in Dinas Dwr. I will send Bran and the Raven Flight to capture the thieves and bring back the Singing Stones."

"A prudent decision, lord," Tegid said, nodding with narrow satisfaction.

"Yes, so I am told."

Emyr Lydaw hailed me just then and came running to say that the warband was ready. "Assemble at the landing," I commanded. "Tegid and I will join you there."

"Come," I told Tegid, taking him by the arm and leading him towards the hall, "we will eat something before we join them. The king and his bard must not be seen to swoon with hunger."

Tegid declared himself well satisfied with this sentiment—it showed I was beginning to think like a king. We stopped long enough for a loaf and a drink of the sweetened water left over from the wedding feast. Thus refreshed, we made our way to the landing.

The Ravens, singed and bedraggled from the night's ordeal, were loading the last of their provisions into the boats. Cynan stood a few paces apart, a spear in each hand, staring at the water. Alun and Drustwn greeted me as we approached. Bran turned from the task to say, "All is ready, lord. We await your command."

"I am needed here—I will not accompany you. And you do not require my help to capture these low criminals," I explained. "I charge you to do this work swiftly and return with all haste."

Bran, somewhat relieved by my change of plan, replied, "I hear and will obey, lord."

Cynan, his jaw hard and his brow set in a lethal scowl, said nothing, but stared away across the lake to the strand where Niall and Garanaw waited with the horses. "Good hunting, brother," I told him.

He nodded curtly and climbed into one of the boats. The others joined him, and the boats pushed away from the landing. We bade them farewell then, and the boats withdrew. The oarsmen had not pulled three strokes, however, when the woman Sioned appeared at the gate.

"Penderwydd!" she called, and came running when she saw him.

"What is it, Sioned?" Tegid turned to meet her, grey eyes quick with concern.

"He is dead," she said hastily. "King Cynfarch has died, Penderwydd. Eleri is with him. He just stopped breathing and—that was all."

Tegid made to hurry away; he took two quick steps, then paused, glancing back over his shoulder towards the departing boats. He opened his mouth to speak, but I spoke first. "Go," I told him. "I will tell Cynan."

While the Chief Bard hastened towards the gate, I called the boats back. "Cynan," I said when he was close enough to hear, "it is your father."

He saw the figures of Tegid and the woman hurrying away, and he guessed the worst. "Is my father dead?"

"Yes, brother. I am sorry."

At my words, Cynan stood upright in the boat, rising so suddenly that he almost tipped it over. As soon as the oarsman brought the vessel near the landing, Cynan leaped from the boat and started towards the gate.

I caught him as he passed. "Cynan, I am sending the Raven Flight without you."

His face darkened and he started to protest, but I held firm. "I know how you feel, brother, but you will be needed here. Your people are without a king now. Your place is with them."

He glanced away, the conflict hot within. "Let them go, Cynan," I urged. "It is for Bran to serve me in this. It is for us to stay."

Cynan's eyes flicked from mine to the boat and back again. Without a word he turned and hurried away.

From the boat Bran called, "Would you have us wait for him, lord?"

"No, Bran," I replied, sending the Raven Chief away. "Cynan will not accompany you now."

I watched as the boats landed on the opposite shore and the pack animals were quickly loaded. The Ravens mounted; Bran lofted a spear and the warriors moved off along the lakeshore. I raised my silver hand in salute to them, and held the salute until they were well away. Then I turned and began walking back to the hall. In truth, I was secretly glad not to be riding with them. Weary to the bone, I longed for nothing more than sleep.

Instead, I returned to Tegid's hut where Cynan had taken up vigil beside his father's body. "There is nothing to be done here," Tegid told me. "You need rest, Llew. Go now while you may; I will summon you if you are needed."

Unwilling to leave, I hesitated, but the bard placed his hand firmly on my shoulder, turned me, and sent me away. I started across the small yard to my hut, and then remembered I had a different home now. I turned aside and went instead to the hut prepared for Goewyn and me. It seemed an age since our wedding night.

Goewyn was waiting for me inside. She had bathed and put on a new white robe. Her hair was hanging down, still wet from washing. She was sitting on the bed, combing out the tangles with a wide-toothed wooden comb. She smiled as I came in, rose, and welcomed me with a kiss. Then, taking my silver hand in both of hers, she led me to the bed, removed my cloak and pushed me gently down onto the deep-piled fleece. She stretched herself beside me. I put my arms around her, and promptly fell asleep.

I came awake with a start. The hut was dark, and the caer was quiet. Pale moonlight showed beneath the oxhide at the door. My movement woke Goewyn, and she put her warm hand on the back of my neck.

"It is night," she whispered. "Lie down and go back to sleep."

"But I am not tired any more," I told her, lowering myself onto my elbow.

"Neither am I," she said. "Are you hungry?"

"Ravenous."

"There is a little wedding bread. And we have mead."

"Wonderful."

She rose and went to the small hearth in the center of the room. I watched her, graceful as a ghost in the pale moonlight, kneeling to her work. In a few moments, a yellow petal of flame licked out and a fire blossomed on the hearth. Instantly, the interior of our bower was bathed in shimmering golden light. Goewyn retrieved the meadskin and cup, and two small loaves of *banys bara*.

She settled herself beside me on the bed once more, broke the bread and fed me the first bite. Whereupon, I broke off a piece and fed her. We finished the first loaf, and the second, then pulled the stopper from the meadskin and lay back to savor its sweetness and warmth, sharing the golden nectar between us in a string of kisses, each more ardent than the last.

I could wait no longer. Laying aside the meadskin, I reached up and gathered her to me. She came into my arms, all softness and warmth, and we abandoned ourselves to the heady delight of our bodies.

Conscious that my metal hand would be cold, I did my best to keep it from touching her—no easy task, for I desired nothing more than to stroke her hair and caress her skin. But Goewyn put me at my ease.

Kneeling beside me, she opened her robe and took my silver hand in both of hers. "It is part of you now," she said, her voice soft and low, "so it shall be no less part of me." Raising my metal hand she pressed it between her exquisite breasts.

The tenderness of this act filled me with awe. I lost myself then in passion. Goewyn was all my universe and she was enough.

Later, we poured mead into a golden cup and drank it in bed. Our wedding night, although untimely interrupted, was all we could have hoped it would be.

"It seems as if I have never lived until now," I told her.

Lips curling deliciously, Goewyn raised the cup to her lips. "Do not think this night is finished yet," she said.

And so we made love again, with passion, to be sure, but without the haste of our previous coupling; we could afford to take our pleasure more slowly this time. Some time towards dawn we fell asleep in one another's arms. But I do not recall the closing of my eyes. I remember only Goewyn, her breath sweet on my skin, and the warmth of her body next to mine.

That night was but a moment's respite from the cares and concerns of the days that followed. Yet, I rose next morning invincible, more than a match for whatever the future held in store. There was work to be done, and I was eager to begin.

I found Tegid and a somber Cynan in the hall, sitting at bread, discussing Cynfarch's funeral. It had been decided that Cynan would return with his people to Dun Cruach for the burial. They must leave at once.

"I would it were otherwise," Cynan told me. His eyes were red and his voice a rasp. "I had wished to stay and help rebuild the caer."

"I know, brother; I know," I answered. "But we have hands enough to serve. I wish I could go with you."

Our talk turned to provisioning his people for the journey. Because of the fire and the long drought before it, our supplies were not what they might have been. Still, I wanted to send him back with enough not only for the journey but for a fair time beyond it.

Lord Calbha, who would be returning to his own lands one day soon, oversaw the loading of the Galanae wagons. After a while, Calbha entered the hall to announce that all was ready; we rose reluctantly, and followed him out. "I will send word when we have caught the thieves," I promised as we stepped out into the yard.

"Until that day," Cynan replied gravely, "I will drink neither ale nor mead, and no fire shall burn in the hearth in the king's hall. Dun Cruach will remain in darkness."

Some of the Galanae warriors standing near heard Cynan's vow and approached. "We would have a king to lead us home," they said. "It is not right that we should enter our realm without a king to go before us."

Tegid, hearing their request, placed a fold of his cloak over his head and said, "Your request is honorable. Have you a man of nobility worthy to be king?"

The Galanae answered, "We have, Penderwydd."

"Name this man, and bring him before me."

"He is standing beside you now, Penderwydd," they said. "It is Cynan Machae and no other."

Tegid turned and placed his hand on Cynan's shoulder. "Is there anything to prevent you from assuming your father's throne?" Tegid asked him.

Cynan ran his hand through his wiry red hair, and thought for a moment. "Nothing that I know," he replied at last.

"Your people have chosen you," Tegid said, "and I do not think a better choice could be made. As Chief Bard of Albion, I will confer the kingship at once if you will accept it."

"I will accept it gladly," he replied.

"It would be well to establish your reign with the proper ceremony," Tegid explained. "But the journey will not wait, therefore we will hold the kingmaking now."

Cynan's kingmaking was accomplished with the least possible ceremony. Scatha and Goewyn stood with me, Calbha watching, and the Galanae gathered close about as Tegid said the words. It was simply done and quickly over—the only interruption in the swift affair came when Tegid made to remove Cynan's torc and replace it with the one Cynfarch had worn.

"The gold torc is the symbol of your sovereignty," Tegid told him. "By it all men will know that you are king and deserving of respect and honor."

Cynan agreed, but would not surrender his silver torc. "Give me the gold torc if you will, but I am not giving up the torc my father gave me."

"Wear it always—and this as well." So saying, the bard slipped the gold torc around Cynan's neck and, raising his hands over him, shouted, "King of the Galanae in Caledon, I do proclaim you. Hail, Cynan Two-Torcs!"

Everyone laughed at this—including Cynan, who from that moment wore his new name as proudly as he wore his two torcs.

I embraced him—Scatha and Goewyn likewise—and in the next breath we were bidding him farewell. Cynan was anxious to return to the south to bury his father and begin his reign. We crossed to the plain and accompanied him on horseback as far as Druim Vran, where we waited on the ridgetop as the Galanae passed. When the last wagon had crested the ridge and begun its long, slow way down the other side, Cynan turned to me and said, "Here I am, sorry to be gone and I have not yet left. The burden of a king is weighty indeed." He sighed heavily.

"Yet, I think you will survive."

"It is well for you," he replied, "but I have no beautiful woman to marry me and I must shoulder the weight alone."

"I would marry you, Cynan," Goewyn offered amiably, "but I have already wed Llew. Still, I think you will not long suffer the lack of a bride. Certainly a king with two torcs will be a most desirable husband."

Cynan rolled his eyes. "Och! I am not king so much as a single day and already wily females are scheming to separate me from my treasure."

"Brother," I said, "think yourself fortunate if you find a woman willing to marry you at any price. Ten torcs would be not one torc too many to give for a wife."

"No doubt you are right," Cynan admitted. "But until I find a woman as worthy as the one you have found I will keep my treasure."

Goewyn leaned across and kissed him on the cheek. We then waved him on his way, watching until he reached the valley below and took his place at the head of his people. Goewyn was quiet beside me as we rode back to the lake.

I turned to her and said, "Marry me, Goewyn."

She laughed. "But I have already married you, best beloved."

"I wanted to hear you say it again."

"Then hear me, Llew Silver Hand," she said. She straightened in the saddle, holding her head erect and proud. "I marry you this day, and tomorrow, and each tomorrow until tomorrows cease."

7

The Ravens' Return

Work on the restoration of Dinas Dwr proceeded at once with brisk efficiency. The people seemed especially eager to eliminate all traces of the fire. The people, my people—my patchwork cloak of a clan, made up of various tribes and kin, warriors, farmers, artisans, families, widows, orphans, refugees each and every one—labored tirelessly to repair the damage to the crannog and put everything right once more. As I toiled beside them, I came to understand that Dinas Dwr was more to them than a refuge; it had become home. Former bonds and attachments were either broken or breaking down, and a new kinship was being forged: in the sweat of our striving together, we were becoming a singular people, a clan as distinct as any tribe in Albion.

Life in the crannog, so cruelly assaulted by fire and the Great Hound's desolations, soon began to assume its former rhythm. Tegid summoned his Mabinogi and reinstated their daily lessons in bardic lore. Scatha likewise mustered her pupils and the practice yard rang to the shouts of the young warriors and the clatter of wooden swords on leather shields once more. The farmers returned to their sun-ravaged crops, hopeful of saving some part of the harvest now that the drought had broken. The cowherds and shepherds devoted themselves to replenishing their stocks as the meadows began greening once more.

As I surveyed the work of restoration, it seemed to me that everyone had determined to put the recent horror behind them as quickly as possible and sought release from the hateful memories by striving to make of Dinas Dwr a paradise in the north. But the wounds went deep and, despite the ardent industry of the people, it would be a very long time before Albion was healed. This, I told myself, was why I must stay: to see the land revived and the people redeemed. Yes, the healing had begun; for the first time in years men and women could face the future with something other than deepest dread and despair.

Thus, when the Raven Flight reappeared with their prisoner a scant few days after riding out, we all deemed it a favourable sign. "You see!" men said to one another. "No one can stand against Silver Hand! All his enemies are conquered at last."

We greeted the Ravens' return warmly, and acclaimed the obvious success of their undertaking: riding with them was a sullen, doleful, solitary prisoner—made to sit backwards in the saddle, with hands bound behind his back and his cloak wound over his head and shoulders.

"Hail, Raven Flight, and greetings!" I called as the boat touched shore. A number of us had rowed from the crannog to meet them; we scrambled ashore as the Ravens dismounted. "I see you enjoyed a successful hunt."

"Swift the hunt, great the prize," Bran agreed tersely. "But not without sacrifice, as Niall will soon tell you."

"How so?" I asked and, turning, saw the blood-soaked bandage beneath Niall's cloak.

The injured Raven dismissed my alarm with a wave of his hand—though even that slight movement made him wince. "Zeal made me careless, lord," he replied, speaking through clenched teeth. "It will not happen again, I assure you. Yet, I was fortunate; the swordstroke caught me as I fell. It might have been worse."

"His head might have parted company with his neck," Alun Tringad informed me. "Though whether that be for the worse, or for the better, we cannot decide."

This brought a laugh from the small crowd that had gathered to hail the Ravens' success and learn the identity of the malefactor they had captured.

"A most disagreeable prisoner, this one," Bran affirmed. "He chose death and was determined to have us accompany him."

"We came upon him by surprise," Drustwn offered, "or he would surely have taken two or more of us down with him."

It was then I saw that both Drustwn and Emyr were also wounded: Drustwn held his arm close to his body, and Emyr's leg was wrapped in a thick bandage just above the knee. When I inquired about their injuries, Drustwn assured me that they would heal far faster than the pride of their prisoner, which he reckoned had suffered harm beyond recovery.

"The worse for us, if he had not slipped on the wet grass and fallen on his head," Garanaw added; he made a motion with his hand, indicating how it happened, and everyone laughed again. It was a far from happy sound, however; they laughed out of relief mostly, and also to humiliate the captive further. Not for a moment had anyone forgotten the outrage done to us.

"I am glad none of you were more seriously hurt," I told them. "Your sacrifice will not be overlooked. All of you," I said, raising my silver hand to them, "have earned a fine reward and the increased esteem of your king."

Bran declared himself satisfied with the latter, but Alun avowed that for his part the former would not be unwelcome. The prisoner, who had maintained a seething silence up to then, came to life once more. Twisting in the saddle, the man strained around to yell defiantly: "Loose me, sons of bitches! Then we will see how well you fare in an even fight!"

At these words, a chill touched my heart—not for what he said, but for the voice itself. I knew this man.

"Get him down," I instructed. "And take away the cloak. I want to see his face."

The Ravens hauled the captive roughly from the saddle and

forced him to his knees before me. Bran seized a corner of the cloak, untied it, and pulled the cloak away to reveal a face I recognized and did not care to see again.

Paladyr had not changed much since last I saw him: the night he had put a knife through Meldryn Mawr's heart. True, I had glimpsed him momentarily on the clifftop at Ynys Sci when he had hurled Gwenllian to her death, but I had not had a good look at him then. Seeing him now, I was amazed again at his immense size—every limb enormous, thick-muscled shoulders above a torso that might have been hewn from the trunk of an oak tree. Even men like Bran, Drustwn and Alun Tringad seemed slight next to Prydain's one-time champion.

He had not given up without a fight, however, and the Ravens had not been over-gentle with him. An ugly purple bruise bulged at one temple, his nose was swollen, and his lower lip was split. But his arrogance was as staggering as ever, and his fiery defiance undimmed.

"Bring Tegid," I said to the man nearest me, unwilling to turn my back on Paladyr. "Tell him to come at once."

"The Chief Bard is here, lord," the man replied. "He is coming now."

I turned to see Tegid and Calbha hastening to join us. The sight of Paladyr kneeling before us halted both men in their steps.

Tegid regarded the defiant captive with grim satisfaction. Upon seeing the Chief Bard of Albion, Paladyr clamped his mouth shut, malice burning from his baleful eyes. After a moment, Tegid turned to Bran, "Had he the Singing Stones with him?"

"That he had, Penderwydd," replied Bran. He gestured to Drustwn, who produced a leather bag from behind his saddle, and brought it to us.

"We caught him with them," Garanaw explained. "And we are pleased to restore them to their rightful place in Dinas Dwr." He opened the chest briefly to show that the pale stones were indeed still within; then he passed the chest to Tegid's keeping.

"Was he alone? Did you find anyone with him?" Lord Calbha

asked. I watched Paladyr's expression carefully, but he remained stony-faced, without the slightest flicker of a sign that what I said concerned him.

"No, lord," the Raven Chief answered. "We searched the region, and watched well the trail behind us. We saw no sign of anyone with him."

Turning to some of the men who had gathered with us, I said, "Make ready a storehouse here on the shore to receive our prisoner, for I will not allow him to set foot on the crannog again."

To Lord Calbha, I said, "Send your swiftest rider to Dun Cruach. Tell Cynan we have captured the man responsible for his father's death, and we await his return so that justice can be satisfied."

"It will be done, Silver Hand," the king of the Cruin replied. "He is not so many days away—we may overtake him before reaching Dun Cruach." Calbha then summoned one of his clansmen and the two moved at once.

"What will you do with the Stones of Song?" asked Tegid, holding the bag.

"I have in mind a place for them," I answered, tapping the bag with a finger. "They will not be so easily stolen again."

Leaving our prisoner in the care of a score of warriors, Tegid, Calbha and the Ravens returned with me to the hall where I pointed to the firepit in the center of the great room. "Raise the hearthstone," I said, "and bury the Singing Stones beneath it. No one will be able to take them without alerting the whole crannog."

"Well said, lord," Bran agreed. Tools were brought and, after a great deal of effort, the massive hearthstone in the center of the hall was raised and held in place while a small hole was dug beneath it. The oak chest was put in the hole and the hearthstone lowered into place once more.

"All men bear witness!" declared Tegid, raising his hands in declamation. "Now is Dinas Dwr established on an unshakable foundation."

I dismissed the Ravens to their well-earned rest, and then summoned Scatha and Goewyn to the hall where I informed them that the thief responsible for killing Cynfarch, stealing the stones, and setting fire to the caer had been captured. "It is Paladyr," I said.

Goewyn allowed a small gasp to escape her lips; Scatha's face hardened and her manner grew brittle. "Where is he?"

"He had the Singing Stones with him. There is no doubt he is guilty."

"Where is he?" she asked again, each word a shard of frozen hate.

"We have locked him in a storehouse on the shore," I answered. "He will be guarded day and night until we have decided what is to be done with him."

She turned at once. "Scatha, wait!" I called after her, but she would not be deterred.

When I caught up with her again, Scatha was standing outside the storehouse, railing at the guards to open the door and let her go in. They were relieved to see me approach.

"Come away, Pen-y-Cat," I said. "You can do nothing here."

She turned on me. "He killed my daughters! The blood debt must be paid!" She meant to collect that debt then and there.

"He will not escape again," I soothed. "Let it be this way for now, Pen-y-Cat. I have sent word to Cynan, and we will hold court as soon as he returns."

"I want to see the animal who killed my daughters," she insisted. "I want to see his face."

"You shall see him," I promised. "Soon—wait but a little. Please, Scatha, listen to me. We can do nothing until Cynan returns."

"I will *see* him." The pleading in her voice was more forceful than my own misgivings.

"Very well." I gestured to the guards to open the door. "Bring him out."

Paladyr shambled into the light. His hands were bound and chains had been placed on his feet. He appeared slightly less insolent than before, and gazed at us warily.

Quick as the flick of a cat's tail, Scatha's knife was out and at Paladyr's throat. "Nothing would give me greater pleasure than to gut you like a pig," she said, drawing the knife across the skin of his throat. A tiny red line appeared behind the moving knifepoint.

Paladyr stiffened, but uttered no sound.

"Scatha! No!" I said, pulling her away. "You have seen him, now let it be."

Paladyr's mouth twitched into a faintly mocking smile. Scatha saw the smirk on his face, drew herself up and spat full in his face. Anger flared instantly, and I thought he would strike her, but the one-time champion caught himself. Trembling with rage, he swallowed hard and glared murderously at her.

"Take him away," I ordered the guards and, turning back to Scatha, I watched her walk away, head high, eyes brimming with unshed tears.

Upon Cynan's return a few days later, I convened the first *llys* of my reign; to judge the murderer. Meting out judgment was the main work of a king's llys, and if anyone stood in need of judgment it was Paladyr. The verdict was a forgone conclusion: death.

My chair was established at the head, or west end, of the hall. Wearing Meldryn Mawr's torc and the Great King's oak-leaf crown, I stepped to the chair and sat down: Goewyn and Tegid took their places—my queen standing beside me, her hand resting on my left shoulder, and my Chief Bard at my right hand.

When everyone had assembled, the carynx sounded and the Penderwydd of Albion stepped forward. Placing a fold of his cloak over his head, he raised his staff and held it lengthwise above him. "People of Dinas Dwr," he said boldly, "heed the voice of wisdom! This day your king sits in judgment. His word is law, and his law is justice. Hear me now: there is no other justice but the word of the king."

With three resounding cracks of his staff on the stone at my feet, Tegid returned to his place beside me. "Bring the prisoner!" he called.

The crowd parted and six warriors led Paladyr forward. But if his captivity had cowed him even in the slightest, he did not show it. Prydain's one-time champion appeared as haughty as ever, smiling smugly to himself, his head high and his eye unflinching. Clearly, he had lost none of his insolence in captivity. He stalked to the foot of my throne and stood there with his feet apart, and a smirk on his face.

When Bran saw how brazenly his prisoner regarded me, the Raven Chief forced Paladyr to kneel, dealing him several sharp blows behind the knees with the butt of his spear. Not that this altered the prisoner's demeanor appreciably; he still regarded me with a strange disdainful expression—the condemned man's way of displaying courage, I thought.

The hall was deathly silent. Every man and woman present knew what Paladyr had done, and more than a few burned to see the blood-debt settled. Tegid regarded the prisoner coolly, gripping his staff as a warrior would a spear. "This is the court of Llew Silver Hand, Aird Righ of Albion," he said, his voice a lash of authority. "This day you will receive the justice you have long eluded."

At Tegid's mention of the High Kingship, Paladyr's eyes flicked from Tegid to me. He seemed somewhat taken aback by that, and it produced the first hint of anything approaching fear I had ever seen in Prydain's former champion. Or was it something else?

The Chief Bard, acting as my voice, continued, grave and stern. "Who brings grievance against this man?"

Several women—the mothers of suffocated infants—cried out at once, and others—the wives of the dead warriors—added their voices to the chorus. "Murderer!" they screamed. "I accuse him! He killed my child!" some said, and others, "He killed my husband!"

Tegid allowed the outcry to continue for a time, and then called for silence. "We have heard your accusation," he said. "Who else brings grievance against this man?"

Scatha, cold and sharp as the blade at her side, stepped forward. "For the murder of my daughter, Gwenllian, Banfáith of Ynys Sci, I do accuse him. And for his part in the murder of my daughter, Govan, Gwyddon of Ynys Sci, I do accuse him." These words were spoken with icy clarity and great dignity; I realized she had rehearsed them countless times in anticipation of this day.

Bran Bresal spoke next, taking his place beside Scatha. "For stealing the Treasure of Albion, and killing the men who guarded that treasure, I do accuse him."

Stepping forward, Cynan shouted, "For starting the fire that took my father's life and the lives of innocent men, women, and children, I do accuse him."

His voice cut like a swordstroke through an atmosphere grown dense with pent-up rage, and his words brought another outburst, which Tegid patiently allowed to play itself out. Then he asked for silence again. "We have heard your accusations. For the third and last time, who brings grievance against this man?"

When no one else made bold to answer, I stood. I did not know if it was proper for me to speak in this way, nor did I care. I had a grievance that went back further than any of the others and I wanted it heard. "I also bring grievance against this man," I said, pointing my finger in Paladyr's face. "It is my belief that you, with the help of others now dead, sought out and murdered the Phantarch, thereby bringing about the destruction of Prydain."

This revelation sent a dark murmur coursing through the tight-pressed crowd. "However," I continued, "as I possess no proof of your part in this unthinkable crime, I cannot bring accusation against you." Raising my silver hand, I pointed my finger directly at him. "But with my own eyes I saw you murder Meldryn Mawr, who held the kingship before me. While pretending repentance you took the Great King's life. For this act of treachery and murder, I do accuse you."

I sat down. Tegid raised and lowered his staff three times slowly. "We have heard grievous accusations against you, Paladyr. We have heard how by your hand you murdered your king, Meldryn Mawr. We have heard how by your hand you murdered Gwenllian, Banfáith of Ynys Sci, and violated the ancient *geas* of protection which was the right of all who sheltered in that realm.

"You contrived to steal the Treasure of Albion, using flames to conceal your crime—flames which took the lives of a score of men, women, and infant children. In order to obtain the treasure, you did strike down the warriors pledged to guard it, and by stealth did you remove the treasure from Dinas Dwr."

The Chief Bard continued, slashing like a whip, his voice ringing in the rooftrees. "Ever and again you have betrayed your people and repaid loyalty with treachery; you have practised treason against the one you were sworn to protect with your life. You sought gain through deception in the service of a false king; you sold your honor for promises of wealth and rank, and squandered your strength in evil. By reason of these acts your name has become a curse in the mouths of men."

No one moved; not a sound was heard when he had finished. The people stood as if stunned into silence by the enormity of Paladyr's crimes. For his part, however, the prisoner seemed vaguely contrite but not overly concerned by his predicament. He merely stared with downcast eyes—as if contemplating the patch of floor between him and my throne. I imagine he had long ago come to terms with the risks of his wrongdoing.

"For these crimes, no less than for the crimes you pursued in the service of the Great Hound Meldron, you are condemned," Tegid declared. "Do you have anything to say before you hear the judgment of your king?"

Paladyr remained unmoved, and I thought he would not speak. But he slowly raised his head and looked Tegid square in the eye. Arrogant to the end, he said, "I have heard your words, bard. You condemn me and that is your right. I do not deny it."

His eyes flicked to me then, and I felt my stomach tighten in apprehension. Looking directly at me, Paladyr said, "But now you tell me that I am in the presence of the High King of Albion. If that is so, let us prove the kingship he boasts. Hear me now: I make the claim of *naud*."

The words hung in the silence of the hall for a moment. Tegid's face went white. Everyone else stared at the kneeling Paladyr in mute and somewhat dazed astonishment. Unwilling to believe what we had all heard quite plainly, Tegid said, "You claim naud?"

Emboldened by the effect of his claim, Paladyr rose to his feet. "I stand condemned before the king. Therefore, I do make the claim of naud for my crimes. Grant it if you will."

"No!" someone shouted. I looked and saw Scatha, swaying on her feet as one wounded by the thrust of a spear. She shouted again, and Bran, beside her, put his arms around her—whether to comfort or to keep her from attacking Paladyr, I could not say. "No! It will not be!" she screamed, her face contorted with rage.

"No..." moaned Goewyn softly. Lips trembling, eyes blinking back tears, she turned her face away.

Cynan, fists clenched, fought forward, straining like a bull; Drustwn, Niall and Garanaw threw their arms around him and kept him from the prisoner's neck. Behind them, the crowd surged forward dangerously, calling for Paladyr's death.

Stern and forbidding, Tegid shouted them down. "Silence!" he cried. "There will be silence before the throne!" The Ravens took it in hand to hold back the crowd, and in a moment the crisis passed. Having restored a semblance of order, the Chief Bard turned to me, visibly upset. He bent low in consultation.

"I will refuse him." I said.

"You cannot," he said; though stunned and heartsick, he was thinking more clearly than I.

"I do not care. I will not allow him to walk away from this."

"You must," he said simply. "You have no choice."

"But why?" I blurted in frustration. "I do not understand, Tegid. There must be something we can do."

He shook his head gravely. "There is nothing to be done. Paladyr has made the claim of naud, and you must grant it," he explained, "or the Sovereignty of Albion will belong to a treasonous murderer."

What Tegid said was true, practically speaking. The claim of naud was partly an appeal for clemency—like throwing oneself on the mercy of the court. But there was more to it than that, for it went beyond justice, it transcended right and wrong and went straight to the heart of sovereignty itself.

In making the claim, the guilty man not only invoked the king's mercy, he effectively shifted responsibility for the crime to the king himself. The king had a choice, of course—he could grant it, or he could refuse. If he granted the claim, the crime was expunged: the punishment that justice demanded, justice itself would fulfill. Naturally, only the king could reconcile himself to himself.

If the king refused the claim, however, the guilty man would have to face the punishment justice decreed. A simple enough choice, one would think, but in refusing to grant naud, the king effectively declared himself inferior to the criminal. No king worthy of the name would lower himself in that way, nor allow his kingship to be so disgraced.

Viewed from the proper angle, this backwards logic becomes curiously lucid. In Albion, justice is not an abstract concept dealing with the punishment of crime. To the people of Albion, justice wears a human face. If the king's word is law to all who shelter beneath his protection, then the king himself becomes justice for his people. The king is justice incarnate.

This personal feature of justice means that the guilty man can make a claim on the king which he has no right to make: naud. And once having made the claim it is up to the king, in his role as justice, to demonstrate his integrity. Justice, then, is limited only by the king's character—that is, justice is limited only by the king's personal conception of himself as king.

Thus, the claim of naud swings on this question: how great is the king?

Paladyr had rightly divined the question, and had determined to put it to the test. If I refused his claim, it would be tantamount to admitting that my sovereignty was restricted in its breadth and power. What is more, all men would know the precise limits of my authority.

If, on the other hand, I granted Paladyr his claim of naud, I would show myself greater than his crimes. For if my sovereignty could extend beyond even Paladyr's offences, then I must be a very great king indeed. As Aird Righ, my kingly power and authority would be deemed well-nigh infinite.

Oh, but it was a very hard thing. In essence, I had been asked to absorb the crime into myself. If I did that, a guilty man would walk free.

Tegid was frowning, glaring into my face as if I were the cause of his irritation. "Well, Silver Hand? What is your answer?"

I looked at Paladyr. His crimes screamed for punishment. Certainly, no man ever deserved death more.

"I will grant him naud," I said, feeling as if I had been kicked in the gut. "But," I added quickly, "am I allowed to set conditions?"

"You may establish provisions for the protection of your people," my bard cautioned. "Nothing more."

"Very well, let us send him to some place where he cannot harm anyone again. Is there such a place?"

Tegid's grey eyes narrowed in sly approval. "Tir Aflan," he said.

"The Foul Land? Where is that?" In all my time in Albion, I had rarely heard mention of the place.

"In the east, across the sea," he explained. "To one born in Albion it is a joyless, desolate place." Tegid allowed himself a grim smile. "It may be that Paladyr will wish himself dead."

"So be it. That is my judgment: banish him to Tir Aflan, and may he rot there in misery."

Tegid straightened and turned to address Paladyr. He raised his staff and brought it down with a crack. "Hear the judgment of the king," he intoned. "You have made the claim of naud and your claim is granted."

This declaration caused an instant sensation. Shouts filled the hall; some cried aloud at the decision, others wept silently. Tegid raised his staff and demanded for silence before continuing. "It is the king's judgment that, for the protection of Albion's people, you are banished from all lands under his authority."

Paladyr's expression hardened. Likely, he had not foreseen this development. I could see him working through the implications in his mind. He drew himself up and demanded, "If all lands lie under your authority, Great King," the words were mockery in his mouth, "where am I to go?"

A good question, which showed Paladyr was paying attention. If I was the High King, all of Albion was under my authority. Clearly, there was no place on the Island of the Mighty, or any of its sister isles, where he could go. But Tegid was ready with the answer.

"To Tir Aflan you will go," he replied bluntly. "And wherever you find men to receive you, there you will abide. Know you this:

from the day you set foot in Tir Aflan it is death to you to return to Albion."

Paladyr accepted his fate with icy dignity. He said nothing more, and was escorted from the hall by Bran and the Ravens. Tegid declared the llys concluded. And the people began filing grimly from the hall, shattered, their hearts broken.

8

The Cylchedd

At dawn the next morning, the Ravens and some of the warband left Dinas Dwr to escort Paladyr to the eastern coast where he would be shipped across Mór Glas and set free on the blasted shore of Tir Aflan. Cynan, bitter and angry, left a short while later to return to Dun Cruach. In all, it was a miserable parting.

Over the next days, work on the fire-damaged caer progressed. New timber was cut and hauled from the ridge forest to the lakeshore where it was trimmed and shaped to use for rooftrees and walls. Reeds for thatch were cut in quantity and spread on the rocks to dry. The burnt timber was removed and the ground prepared for new dwellings and storehouses; quantities of ash were transported across the lake and spread on the fields. I would have been happy to see this work to its completion—the sight of the fire-blackened rubble ached in me like a wound, and the sooner Dinas Dwr was restored, the sooner the pain would cease. But Tegid had other ideas.

At supper one night after the Ravens had returned from disposing of Paladyr, Tegid rose and stood before the hearth. Those looking on assumed he meant to sing, and so began calling out the names of songs they would hear. *"The Children of Llyr!"* clamored some. *"Rhydderch's Red Stallion!"* shouted someone else, to general acclaim. *"Gruagach's Revenge!"* another suggested, but was shouted down.

Tegid simply shook his head and announced that he could not sing tonight or any other night.

"Why?" everyone wanted to know. "How is it that you cannot sing?"

The wily bard answered, "How can I think of singing when the Three Fair Realms of Albion stand apart one from another with no king to establish harmony between their separate tribes?"

Leaning close to Goewyn, I said, "I smell a ruse."

Turning to me, Tegid declared that as Aird Righ it must certainly be foremost among my thoughts to ride the circuit of my lands and establish my rule in the kingdom.

"To be sure," I replied lightly, "my thoughts would have arrived there sooner or later." To Goewyn, I whispered, "Here it comes."

"And since you are High King," he announced, brandishing his staff with a flourish, "you will extend the glory of your reign to all who shelter beneath your Silver Hand. Therefore, the *Cylchedd* you contemplate will include all lands in the Three Fair Realms so that Caledon, Prydain and Llogres will be brought under your sovereign authority. For all must own you king, and you must receive the honor and tribute of the Island of the Mighty."

This speech was delivered to a largely unsuspecting throng and so took them by surprise. It took me somewhat unawares as well, but as he spoke I began to see the logic behind Tegid's highflown formality. Such an important undertaking demanded a certain ceremony. And the people of Dinas Dwr promptly understood the significance of Tegid's address.

It was not the first time the Chief Bard had used the title Aird Righ, of course. However, it was one thing to speak the words here in Dinas Dwr among my own people, but quite another actively to proclaim this assertion in the world beyond the protecting ridge of Druim Vran.

Whispers hissed through the crowd: "Aird Righ! Llew Silver Hand is the High King!" they said. "Did you hear? The Chief Bard has proclaimed him Aird Righ!"

There was a solid reason behind Tegid's proclamation: he was anxious to establish the Sovereignty of Albion beyond all doubt. A worthy venture, it seemed to me. All the same, I wished he had warned me. Strictly speaking, I did not share Tegid's enthusiasm for the High Kingship—which is, no doubt, why he chose to announce the Cylchedd the way he did.

Whatever my misgivings, Bran and the Raven Flight, and the rest of the warband, supported Tegid and fairly thundered their endorsement. They banged their cups and slapped the board with their hands; they raised such an uproar that it was some time before Tegid could continue.

The Penderwydd stood there smiling a supremely self-satisfied smile, watching the commotion he had caused. I felt the touch of a cool hand on my neck and glanced up. Goewyn had come to stand beside me. "It is no less than your right," she said, her breath warm in my ear.

When the furore had subsided somewhat, Tegid continued, explaining that the circuit would begin in Dinas Dwr as I held court among my own people. And then, when all the proper preparations had been made, I would ride forth on a lengthy tour of Albion.

Tegid had a lot more to say, and said it well. I listened with half an ear, wondering if, as he claimed, the circuit would actually take a year and a day—an estimate I took to be more a poetic approximation than an actual calculation. Be that as it may, I knew it would not be accomplished quickly or easily, and I found myself working out the details even as Tegid spoke.

"Listen, bard," I said as soon as we were alone together, "I am all for riding the Cylchedd, but you might have told me you were going to announce it."

Tegid drew himself up. "Are you displeased?"

"Oh, sit down, Tegid. I am not angry. I just want to know. Why did you do it?"

He relaxed and sat down. We were together in my hut; since the wedding Goewyn and I preferred the privacy of the one-room hut to the busy bedlam of the hall.

"Your kingship must be declared before the people," he said

simply. "When a new king takes the throne it is customary to make a Cylchedd of his lands. Also, as Aird Righ, it is necessary to obtain the fealty of other kings and their people in addition to that of your own chieftains and clansmen."

"I understand. How soon will we leave Dinas Dwr?"

"As soon as adequate preparation can be made."

"How long will that take? A couple of days? Three or four?"

"Not longer." He paused, regarding me eagerly. "It will be a wonderful thing, brother. We will establish the honor of your name and increase your renown throughout all Albion."

"Has it occurred to you that some of Meldron's mongrel horde may yet ride free? They might disagree with you."

"All the more reason for the Cylchedd to be made at once. Any who still lack proper understanding must be convinced. We shall travel with a warband."

"And will it really take all year? I am newly married, Tegid, and I had hoped to stay close to home for a while."

"But Goewyn will accompany you," he said quickly, "and anyone else you choose. Indeed, the larger the procession, the greater your esteem in the eyes of the people."

I could see that Tegid considered the circuit a great show of pomp and power. "This is going to be a huge undertaking," I mused.

"Indeed!" he declared proudly. "It will be like nothing seen in Albion since the time of Deorthach Varvawc." I saw that this meant more to him than he let on. Well, I thought, let him have his way. After all he had been through with Meldron, he had earned it. Maybe we both had.

"Deorthach Varvawc," I remarked, "now who could forget a name like that?"

The preparations went forward with all haste. Four days later I was looking at a veritable train of wagons, chariots and horses. It appeared that the entire population of Dinas Dwr planned to make the journey with us. Enough would stay behind, I hoped, to look after the fields and proceed with the restoration of the crannog. All well and good to go wandering all over Albion, but there were crops to be gathered and herds to be maintained, and someone had to do it.

In the end, it was agreed that Calbha would remain in Dinas Dwr while we were gone. Meldron had destroyed the Cruin king's stronghold at Blár Cadlys, so gathering enough supplies, tools and provisions to begin rebuilding would occupy Calbha a good while yet. Thus, he became the logical choice to stay behind. Much as he would have liked to accompany us, he agreed that time was best spent looking after the affairs of his people.

And, as there were young warriors to train, Scatha elected to stay behind with her school. Three Ravens would stay with her to aid the training of the young, and enough warriors to protect Dinas Dwr.

The day before we were due to set off, Tegid summoned the people to the hall. When all had gathered, I took the throne and, looking out upon the faces of all those gazing expectantly at me, I felt—not for the first time—the immense weight of duty settling upon me. This would have been daunting if I had not sensed an equally great strength of tradition helping to shoulder the burden. I could bear the weight, because others had borne it before me and their legacy lived on in the spirit of sovereignty itself.

It came to me as I sat there on my antlered throne that I could be a king, even a High King, not because I knew anything about being a king—much less because I was somehow more worthy than anyone else—but because the people *believed* in my kingship. That is to say, the people believed in sovereignty and were willing, for the sake of that belief, to extend their conviction to me.

It might be that the Chief Bard held the power to confer or withhold kingship, but that power derived from the people. "A king is a king," Tegid was fond of saying, "but a bard is the heart and soul of the people; he is their life in song, and the lamp which guides their steps along the paths of destiny. A bard is the essential spirit of the clan; he is the linking ring, the golden cord which unites the manifold ages of the clan, binding all that is past with all that is yet to come."

At last, I began to grasp the fundamental fact of Albion. I understood, too, Simon's deadly design: in attacking sovereignty, he had struck at the very heart of Albion. Had he succeeded in killing kingship at the root, Albion would have ceased to exist.

"Tomorrow," the Chief Bard announced, "Llew Silver Hand will leave Dinas Dwr to make Cylchedd of his lands and receive the homage of his brother kings and the tribes of the Three Fair Realms. Before he gains the esteem of others, however, it is fitting for his own people to pledge faith with him and honor him."

Tegid raised his staff and thumped it on the floor three times. He called for all chieftains—be they kings, noblemen, or warriors—to pay homage to me, and to swear oaths of fealty which he spoke to them. I had only to receive their pledges and grant them protection of my reign. As each chieftain finished reciting the oath, he knelt before me and placed his head against my chest in a gesture of submission and love.

One by one, beginning with Bran Bresal, they came before me: Alun, Garanaw, Emyr, Drustwn, Niall, Calbha, Scatha, Cynan. These were followed by several of those who had come to Dinas Dwr during Meldron's depredations, and lastly by those who had surrendered at Meldron's defeat. To receive the honor of such men touched me deeply. Their oaths bound them to me and, no less securely, bound me to them.

When the ceremony was finished, I was more than ever a king— and more than eager to see Albion once more.

We crossed Druim Vran just as the sun was rising behind the encircling hills. As we started down the ridge trail, I paused to look back along the line to see that the last of the wagons had yet to leave the lakeside.

If, as Tegid suggested, the size of an entourage could increase a king's esteem, then mine was multiplied a hundredfold at least. Altogether there were sixteen wagons with supplies and provisions, including livestock—a larder on the hoof—and extra horses for the hundred or so men and women attending us as cooks, camp hands, warriors, messengers, hunters and stockmen. Leading the cavalcade were my Chief Raven, Bran Bresal, Emyr Lydaw bearing the great battle carynx, and Alun Tringad, astride high-stepping horses. Next came the Penderwydd of Albion attended by his Mabinogi and, behind them, Goewyn, on a pale yellow horse, and myself on a roan. Following us were the warband, and behind them the wagons in a long, long rolling file.

The valley below flooded with light, glowing like an emerald, and my heart soared at the prospect of travelling through this extraordinary land—the more so with Goewyn by my side and the fellowship of amiable companions. I had forgotten how fair Albion could be. Ablaze with color and light: the rich greens of the tree-filled glens and the delicate mottled verdure of the high moors, the dazzling blue of the sunwashed sky, the subtle greys of stone and the deep browns of the earth, the sparkling silver of water, the shimmering gold of sunlight.

I had ranged far through the land on my various forays, and still it held the power to astonish. A glimpse of white birches stark against a background of glossy green holly, or the sight of blue cloudshadow gliding down distant hillsides could leave me gasping with wonder. Marvellous it was—all the more so since Albion had endured the ravages of fire and drought and unending winter. The land had suffered through the desolation of Lord Nudd and his demon horde, and the depredations of the Great Hound Meldron. Yet it appeared reborn.

There must have been some unseen agent toiling away to bring about a continual renewing of the land, for there was no trace of desolation anywhere, no lingering scars, no visible reminders of the tortures so recently endured. Perhaps its splendors were constantly restored, or perhaps Albion was somehow created anew with each dawn. For it seemed that every tree, hill, stream, and stone had just burst into existence from sheer creative exuberance.

After two days of this I was a man enraptured with existence— not only my own, but the entire universe as well. My enchantment extended to the moon and stars and the dark void beyond. Had I been a bard, I would have sung myself dizzy.

As we travelled further, I grew, slowly but surely, more sensitive to the beauty of the land around me. I began to sense a momentous glory radiating from every form that met my eye—every limb and leaf, every blade of grass ablaze with unutterable grandeur and majesty. And it seemed to me that the world I saw before me was merely the outward manifestation of a vastly powerful, deeply fundamental reality that existed just out of sight. I might not discern this veiled reality directly, but I could perceive its effects. Everything it touched it set vibrating like a string on Tegid's harp. I thought that if I listened very hard I might hear the hum of this celestial vibration. Sometimes I imagined that I did hear it—like the echo of a song which lingered just beyond the threshold of hearing. I could not hear the melody, only the echo.

The reason for this delight was, partly, Goewyn. I was so enraptured by her that even Nudd's hostage pit would have seemed like paradise if she were there. As we travelled through the revived splendor of Albion I began to realize that I now viewed the world through different eyes. No longer a sojourner, a trespassing transient merely visiting a world that was not my home, I belonged; Albion *was* my home now. Indeed, I had taken an Otherworld woman for my wife. So far from being a stranger, I was now a king. I was the Aird Righ. Who belonged in Albion if not the High King?

The king and the land were connected in an intimate and mysterious way. Not in some abstract philosophical way, but actually, physically. The relationship of the king to the land was that of man to wife—the people of Albion even spoke of it as a marriage. And now that I was married myself, I was beginning to understand—no, to *feel* it: the concept was still well beyond my comprehension, but I could discern wisdom taking shape in my flesh and bones. I could sense an ancient, primal truth I could not yet put into words.

Thus, the Cylchedd began to take on the quality of a pilgrimage, a journey of immense spiritual significance. I might not apprehend the full meaning of the pilgrimage, less still its more delicate implications; but I could feel, like gravity, its irresistible, inexorable, inescapable power. I did not find this in any way burdensome; all the same, like a soul clothed in flesh, I knew that I would never move without it again.

By day we journeyed through a landscape made sublime by the light of a fulgent sun, imparting an almost luminous splendor to all it touched, creating shimmering horizons and shining vistas on every side. By night we camped under an enormous skybowl bursting with stars, and went to our rest with the blessed sound of harpsong in our ears.

In this way we reached our first destination: Gwynder Gwydd, clan seat of the Ffotlae in Llogres. As it happened, there were Ffotlae with us, and they were eager to discover whether their kinsmen still survived.

We established camp on a meadow near a standing stone called *Carwden*, the Crooked Man, which the Ffotlae used as a meeting place. There was a lively brook running through the meadow which was surrounded by woodlands of young trees. As soon as the tents were erected, Tegid sent the Raven Flight out as messengers into the region and we settled back to wait.

Meanwhile, we had brought my stag-antler chair with us, and Tegid directed that a small mound be raised before the Carwden stone and the chair placed on the mound. The next morning, following Tegid's counsel, Goewyn and I dressed in our best clothing—for Goewyn a white shift with Meldryn Mawr's golden fishscale belt I had given her, and a skyblue cloak; for me, a cloak of red edged with gold over a green siarc, and blue breecs. I wore a belt of huge gold discs, an enormous gold brooch, and my gold torc. Goewyn had to help me with the brooch—I had grown accustomed to managing without a right hand, but I was still unused to my silver hand.

Goewyn fastened the brooch for me, then stepped quickly away again to appraise me with a critical eye. She did not like the way I had folded the cloak, so she deftly adjusted it. "Everything in place?" I asked.

"If I had known you were going to make such a handsome king, I would have married you long ago," she replied, slipping her arms around my neck and kissing me. I felt the warmth of her body and was suddenly hungry for her. I pulled her more tightly to me . . . and the carynx sounded.

"Tegid's timing is impeccable," I murmured.

"The day is yet young, my love," she whispered, then straightened. "But now your people are arriving. You must prepare to greet them."

We stepped from the tent to see a fair-sized throng advancing across the meadow to the Carwden stone. The people of Gwynder Gwydd and surrounding settlements had gathered—sixty men and women, the remnant of four or five tribes. The Ffotlae among us were overjoyed to see their kinsmen again, and welcomed them with such cheering and crying that it was some time before the llys could begin. Then Tegid commanded Emyr to sound the carynx once more. The bellow of the battlehorn signalled the beginning of the court; Goewyn and I walked to the mound and took our places: myself on the throne, and she beside it where she would be most conspicuous. Tegid wanted them to recognize and honor their queen.

The people of Gwynder Gwydd, eager to cast their eyes on this wonder of a new king—and his ravishing queen—crowded close to the mound for a good view. This gave me a chance to observe them as well. Plainly, they had suffered. Some were maimed, many were scarred from beatings or torture, and despite the renewing of the land all were still gaunt from misery and lack of food. They had come dressed in their best clothes, and these were but well-laundered tatters, for the most part. Meldron had exacted a heavy price for his kingship, and they had been made to pay it.

The Chief Bard opened the proceedings in the usual way, proclaiming to one and all the remarkable thing which had come to pass. A new High King had arisen in Albion, and now was making a Cylchedd of the realm to establish his rule . . . and so on.

The Ffotlae wore the hopeful, if not entirely convinced, expressions of people who had grown used to being cheated and lied to at every turn. They were respectful, and appeared willing to believe, but the mere sight of me did not altogether reassure. Very well, I would have to win their trust.

So, when Tegid finished, I stood. "My people," I said, "I welcome you." I raised my hands; the sun caught the silver and flashed like white fire. This caused a great sensation and everyone gaped wide-eyed at my silver hand. I held it before them and flexed the fingers; to my surprise, they all fell on their faces and hugged the ground.

"What is this?" I whispered to Tegid, who had joined me on the mound.

"They fear your hand, I think," he replied.

"Well, do something, Tegid. Tell them I bring them peace and goodwill—you know what to say. Make them understand."

"I will tell them," Tegid replied sagely. "But only you can make them understand."

The Chief Bard raised his staff and told the frightened gathering what a fine thing it was rightly to revere the king and pay him heartfelt respect. He told them how pleased I was to receive their gift of homage, and how, now that Meldron had been defeated, they had nothing to fear, for the new king was no rampaging tyrant.

"Give them a cow," I whispered, when he concluded. "Two cows. And a bull."

Tegid raised his eyebrows. "It is for you to receive *their* gifts."

"Their gifts? Look at them, they have nothing."

"It is their place to—"

"Two cows and a bull, Tegid. I mean it."

The bard motioned Alun to him and spoke some words into his ear. Alun nodded and hurried away, and Tegid turned to the people, telling them to rise. The king knew of their hardship in the Day of Strife, he said, and had brought them a gift as a token of his friendship and a symbol of the prosperity they would henceforth enjoy.

Alun approached then with the cattle. "These kine are given from the Aird Righ's own herd for the upbuilding of your stock." Then he asked for their chief to take possession of the cattle on behalf of the tribe.

This provoked some consternation among the Ffotlae; for, as one of the clansmen with us quickly explained, "Our lord was killed, and our chieftain went to serve Meldron."

"I see." I turned back to Tegid. "It seems we must give them a chief as well."

"That is easily done," the bard replied. Raising his staff, he stood before the people and said that it was the High King's good pleasure to give them a new lord to be their chief and to look after them. "Who among you is worthy to become the lord of the Ffotlae?" he asked. There followed a brief deliberation in which various opinions were expressed, but one name eventually won out, apparently to everyone's satisfaction. "Urddas!" they clamored. "Let Urddas be our chief."

Tegid looked to me to approve the choice. "Very well," I said, "have Urddas step forward. Let us have a look at him."

"Urddas," Tegid called. "Come and stand before your king."

At this the crowd parted and a thin, dark-haired woman approached the mound. She regarded us with deep, sardonic eyes, a look of defiance on her lean, expressive face. "Tegid," I said under my breath, "I think Urddas is a woman."

"Possibly," he replied in a whisper.

"I am Urddas," she said, removing any doubt. I glanced at Goewyn, who was obviously enjoying our momentary confusion.

"Hail, Urddas, and welcome," Tegid offered nicely. "Your people have named you chieftain over them. Will you receive the respect of your clan?"

"That I will," the woman replied—three words, but spoken with such authority that I knew the Ffotlae had chosen well. "Nor will it be to me an unaccustomed honor," she added, "for I have been leading my clan since their lord, my husband, was killed by Mór Cù. If I am acknowledged in this way, it is no less than my right."

Her speech had an edge—and why not? the clan had been through hell, after all—but it was not rancor or pride that made her speak so. I think she simply wanted us to know how things were with them. No doubt she found blunt precision more suited to her purpose than affable ambiguity. It could not have been easy ruling a clan under Meldron's cruel regime.

"Here, then, is your king," Tegid told her, and asked, "Will you acknowledge his sovereignty, pledge him fealty, and pay him the tribute due him?"

Urddas did not answer at once—I believe I would have been disappointed if she had. But she cast her cool, ironic eyes over me as if she were being asked to estimate my worth. Then, still undecided, she glanced across at the cattle I had bestowed upon the clan.

"I will own him king," the woman replied, turning back. But I noticed she was looking at Goewyn as she answered—as if whatever lack she saw in me was more than made up by my queen. Presumably, if I could woo and win a woman of Goewyn's distinction, then perhaps there was more to me than first met her dubious eye.

Tegid administered the oath of fealty then, and when it was completed, the woman came to me, knelt before me and held her head against my breast. When she rose once more, it was to the acclaim of the Ffotlae. She ordered some of the younger men to take the cows and bull—lest I change my mind.

"Urddas," I said as she made to return to her place. "I would hear from you how you have fared through this ill-favored time. Stay after the llys is completed and we will share a bowl between us—unless something else would please you more."

"A bowl with the Aird Righ would please me well," she replied forthrightly. Only then did I see her smile. The color came back to her face, and her head lifted a little higher.

"That was well done," Goewyn said softly, stroking me lightly on the back of the neck.

"Small comfort for the loss of a husband," I said, "but it is something at least."

There were several lengthy matters to arbitrate—mostly arising from the troubles that had multiplied under Meldron. These were prudently dealt with, whereupon Tegid concluded the llys and, after leading the combined tribes in a simple oath of fealty, declared clan Ffotlae under the protection of the Aird Righ. To inaugurate this new accord, we hosted them at a feast and the next day sent them back to Gwynder Gwydd loudly praising the new king.

This was to become the pattern for the rest of the circuit through Llogres. Sadly, some previously well-populated districts or *cantrefs* were now uninhabited, either abandoned or destroyed. Our messengers rode far and wide, to the caers and strongholds and to the hidden places in the land. And at each place where we found survivors—at Traeth Eur, Cilgwri, Aber Archan, Clyfar Cnûl, Ardudwy, Bryn Aryen, and others, our messengers proclaimed the news: The High King is here! Gather your people, tell everyone, and come to the meeting place where he welcomes all who will own him king.

The years of Meldron's cruelty had wrought a ghastly change in the people. The fair folk of Albion had become pale, thin, haggard wraiths. It tore at my heart to see this noble race degraded so. But I found solace in the fact that we were able to deliver so many from the fear and distress that had held them for so long. Take heart, we told them, a new king reigns in Albion; he has come to establish justice in the land.

As the Cylchedd progressed, we all—each man and woman among us—became zealous bearers of the glad tidings. The news was everywhere greeted with such happiness and gratitude that the entire entourage strove with one another to be allowed to ride with the message—just to share in the joy the tidings brought.

Indeed, it became my chief delight to see the transformation in the listeners' faces when they at last understood that Meldron was dead and his war host defeated. I could almost see happiness descend upon the people like a shining cloud as the truth took hold within them. I saw bent backs straighten, and dead eyes spark to life. I saw hope and courage rekindled from dead, cold ashes.

The Year's Wheel revolved and the seasons changed. The days were already growing shorter when we finished in Llogres and turned towards Caledon. We had arranged to winter at Dun

Cruach, before resuming the Cylchedd. I was for going home, but Tegid said that once begun, I could not return to Dinas Dwr until the round was completed. "The course must not be broken," he insisted. So, Cynan would have the pleasure of our company through Sollen, Season of Snows.

9

Alban Ardduan

We arrived at Dun Cruach in Caledon just as the weather broke. Rain pelted down and wind whined as we passed through the gates. It had been a good journey, but it was a relief to abandon our tents for the warmth and light of a friendly hall. Cynan and the Galanae threw open the doors and gathered us in.

"Llew! Goewyn!" Cynan cried, throwing his arms around us. "*Mo anam*! But we expected you days ago. Did you get lost?"

"Lost! Goewyn, did you hear that? I will have you know, Cynan Two-Torcs, that I have personally inspected every track, trail, and footpath in Llogres and most of Caledon. Truly, the deer in the glens will lose their way before Llew Silver Hand."

"Ah, Goewyn," Cynan sighed, and I noticed he had not taken his arm from around her. "Why did you ever marry such an ill-tempered man? You should have married me instead. Now look what you must suffer." He shook his head sadly and clucked his tongue.

Goewyn kissed him lightly on the cheek. "Alas, Cynan," she sighed, "if only I had known."

"All this talk of marriage," I remarked. "Are you trying to tell us something?"

The big warrior became suddenly bashful. "Now that you say it, brother, I believe I have found a woman much to my liking."

"That is half the battle, to be sure," I replied. "But, more to the point, will she have you?"

"Well," Cynan allowed with uncommon reticence, "we have talked and she has agreed. It so happens, we will be married while you are here."

"At the solstice perhaps," suggested Tegid; he had overheard everything. "It will be a highly favorable time—the *Alban Ardduan*."

"Welcome, Penderwydd," Cynan said warmly, grasping his arms and embracing Tegid like a wayward brother.

"What is this Alban Ardduan?" I wondered aloud. "I have never heard of it."

"It is," the bard explained slowly, "the one solstice in a thousand coinciding with a full moon."

"And," Goewyn continued, taking up where Tegid had left off, "both setting sun and rising moon stand in the sky at once to regard one another. Thus, on the darkest day, darkness itself is broken."

I remembered with a pang that Goewyn, like her sisters, had once been a Banfáith in a king's house. Govan and Gwenllian were dead, and of the three fair sisters of Ynys Sci, Goewyn alone survived.

"That is why," Tegid resumed, "it is a most auspicious time—a good day to begin any endeavor."

"Yes, do it then," I urged. "If ever a man stood in need of such aid, it is you, brother." My eyes swept the busy hall. "But where is she, Cynan? I would meet the lady who has won your heart."

"And I thought you would never ask!" he cried happily. He turned and motioned to someone standing a little behind him. "Ah! Here she comes with the welcome cup!"

We all turned to see a willowy young woman with milk-white skin and pale, pale blue eyes, advancing towards us with a great steaming bowl of mulled ale between her long, smooth hands. It was easy to see how she had captured Cynan's notice, for her hair was as fiery red as his. She wore it long and it hung about her shoulders in such a mass of curls as a man could get lost in. She stepped briskly, regarding us steadily; there was an air of boldness about her. In all, she looked more than a match for Cynan.

"My friends," said Cynan expansively, "this is Tángwen, the fortunate woman who has agreed to become my wife."

Smiling, she offered the bowl to me, saying, "Greetings, Silver Hand." Her voice was low and smoky. At my expression of surprise she smiled knowingly and said, "No, we have never met. You would remember if we had, I think. But Cynan has told me so much about you that I feel I know you like a brother. And who else wears a hand of silver on his arm?" She gave me the bowl, and as I took it from her, she let her fingertips stroke my silver hand.

I drank the warming liquid and returned the bowl to Tángwen. She passed it to Tegid. "I give you good greeting, Penderwydd," she said. "You, I would know even without the rowan. There is only one Tegid Tathal."

Tegid raised the bowl, drank, and returned it, watching the red-haired charmer all the while. Tángwen, cool under his gaze, turned next to my queen. "Goewyn," she said softly, "I welcome you most eagerly. Since coming to Dun Cruach, I have heard nothing but praise for Llew's queen. We will be good friends, you and I."

"I would like that," Goewyn replied, accepting the bowl. Though she smiled, I noticed that Goewyn's eyes narrowed as if searching for some sign of recognition in the other woman.

Then Tángwen raised the bowl to her own lips, saying, "Greetings and welcome, friends. May you find all you wish to find in your stay among us, and may that stay be long."

All this was accomplished under Cynan's proud gaze. Obviously, he had schooled her well. She knew us all and spoke frankly and directly. Her forthright manner took me aback somewhat, but I could see how it would appeal to Cynan; he was not a man to endure much simpering.

Having served us, Tángwen moved on to welcome Bran and the Ravens who had just entered. We watched her lithe form glide away. Cynan said, "Ah, she is a beauty, is she not? The fairest flower of the glen."

"She is a wonder, Cynan," I agreed. "But who is she, and where did you find her?"

"She is no stranger to a king's hall," Goewyn observed. "I am thinking Tángwen has served the welcome bowl before."

"You cut straight to the heart of it," Cynan replied proudly. "She is the daughter of King Ercoll, who was killed in a battle with Meldron. Her people have been wandering Caledon in search of a steading and came to us here. I saw at once that she was of noble bearing. She will make a fine queen."

Gradually, the hall had filled with people. Food had been prepared in anticipation of our arrival and, when it appeared, Cynan led us to our places at his table. We ate and talked long into the night, enjoying the first of many pleasant meals around the winter hearth.

Thus we passed the winter at Dun Cruach amiably. When the sun shone we rode over the misty hills or walked the soggy moors, slipping over wet rocks and scaring up grouse and partridges. When the sleet rattled on the thatch or snow swirled down in the north wind's frigid wake, we stayed in the hall and played games— *brandub* and *gwyddbwyll* and others—as we had done when wintering on Ynys Sci.

Each night Tegid filled the hall with the enchanting music of his harp. It was joy itself to sit in that company, listening to the stories Albion's kings had heard from time out of mind. I counted every moment blessed.

As the day of Cynan and Tángwen's wedding drew near, Tegid let it be known that he was preparing a special song for the occasion. Though many asked what the tale would be, he would say no more than that it was an ancient and powerful story, and one which would bring great blessing to all who heard it.

Meanwhile, Goewyn and Tángwen attended to the preparations for the celebration. They were often together and appeared to enjoy one another's company. I thought them a strikingly beautiful pair, and thought Cynan and myself the two most fortunate men in all Albion to boast such women as wives.

Cynan was well pleased with his choice, and remarked often on the happy circumstance that brought her to his door. "She might have wandered anywhere," he said, "but she happened to come here, to me."

I saw little more than simple chance in it, but what did that matter? If Cynan wanted to believe that some extraordinary destiny had brought them together, who was I to disagree?

In any event, Tángwen had firmly established herself at the center of Cynan's household. Neither timidity nor humility found much of a patron in her; she was intelligent and capable and saw no reason to affect a meekness or modesty she did not naturally possess. Still, there was something about her—something driven, yet strangely constrained. She often stood apart when Tegid sang, watching from the shadows, her expression almost derisive, scornful—as if she disdained joining us, or spurned the pleasure of the gathering. Other times, she seemed to forget herself and joined in with a will. I felt somehow she was following the dictates of a scheme, rather than the promptings of her heart. And I was not the only one to notice.

"There is a hidden place in her soul," Goewyn said one night when we had retired to our sleeping quarters. "She is confused and unhappy."

"Unhappy? Do you think so? Maybe it is just that she is afraid of being hurt again," I suggested.

Goewyn shook her head slightly. "No, she wants to befriend me, I think; but there is something cold and hard in her that will not let her. Sometimes I wish I could just reach into her heart and pluck it out, and then all would be well with her."

"Perhaps that is her way of covering the pain."

Goewyn looked at me oddly. "Why do you say she has been hurt?"

"Well," I said slowly, thinking aloud, "Cynan said that her father had been killed in a battle against Meldron. I suppose I simply assumed Tángwen, like so many we have met along the way, still carried that grief."

"Perhaps," Goewyn allowed, frowning in thought.

"But you think otherwise?"

"No," she said after a moment. "That must be it. I am certain you are right."

The days dwindled, shrinking down toward Alban Ardduan and

Cynan's wedding. The Galanae warband and the Raven Flight had stocked the cookhouse with wild game of all kinds, and the cooks kept the ovens glowing hot, preparing food for the feast. The brewer and his helpers, foreseeing strong demand for the fruit of their labor, worked tirelessly to fill the vats with mead and ale. On the day before the wedding, the fattened pigs were slaughtered, and next morning we awoke in the dark to the aroma of roast pork.

After breaking fast with a little bread and water, we all dressed ourselves in feast-day clothes and assembled in the hall, eager for the festivities to begin. Torches fluttered from scores of holders, banishing shadows from every dark corner. On this day the torches would burn brightly from dawn to dawn in observance of Alban Ardduan.

Cynan appeared first, resplendent in red-and-orange checked breecs and yellow siarc. He wore a blue-and-white striped cloak and his father's great gold brooch. He had brushed his long red beard and fanned it out across his broad chest, and he had allowed his wiry red hair to be gathered and tied at the back of his head. His gold and burnished silver torcs gleamed like mirrors. He fretted and preened, patting his belt and adjusting his cloak.

"A more regal groom has never been seen in Caledon," I told him. "Stand still, now. Do you want her to think she is marrying a twitch?"

"What can be keeping them?" he asked, glancing nervously around the hall for the third time in as many moments.

"Be at ease," I told him. "You have endured your solitary ways a long time, you can endure yet a little longer."

"What if she has changed her mind?"

"Goewyn is with her," I reassured him. "She will not change her mind."

"What can be keeping them?" He craned his neck around, inspecting the hall yet once more. "Here they come!" he said, darting forward.

"Relax—it is Tegid."

"Oh, it is only Tegid." He began patting himself again, as if he were searching for something he had lost somewhere about his person. "How do I look?"

"Handsome enough for any two men. Now stand still, you are wearing a hole in the floor."

"Only Tegid?" wondered the bard.

"Ignore him," I told Tegid. "Cynan is not himself today."

"My throat is on fire," Cynan complained. "I need a drink."

"Later—after the wedding."

"Just one cup."

"Not a drop. We do not want the king of the Galanae falling down during his own wedding ceremony."

"I tell you I am dying!"

"Then do it quietly."

Tegid broke in, saying, "Here they are." At that instant, a ripple of voices sounded from the far end of the hall. Cynan and I turned to see Goewyn and Tángwen approaching.

Cynan's bride was a vision—a blaze of fiery beauty: two long braids bound in bands of gold swept back from her temples and lost themselves in the luxurious fall of flaming curls that spilled over her shoulders. She wore a crimson cloak and a robe of apricot yellow over a salmon-colored shift. Her feet were bare, and on each ankle was a bracelet of thick gold so that each step glittered. On her breast was a splendid silver brooch set with glowing red gems around the ring; the pin was joined to the ring by a tiny silver chain, and the head shone with a blazing blue jewel. No doubt the eye-catching object was her father's chief treasure.

Cynan could restrain himself no longer. He strode to meet her, gathered her in his arms, and all but carried her to where we stood by the wide, central hearth. "To be surrounded by battle-tried friends in a shining hall," he crowed, "with his arms around a beautiful woman— this is the greatest joy a man can know!" He turned to Tángwen, kissed her, and declared, "This is the happiest day of my life!"

At this, Tángwen put a hand to his ruddy face and turned his lips to hers, kissing him ardently and long. "Come, Tegid," Cynan said, "the bride is here; the hall is filled, and the feast is waiting. Perform the rite and let us begin the celebration!"

With raised staff and a loud voice, Tegid called the assembly to witness the marriage of Cynan and Tángwen. Everyone crowded close and the ceremony began. Cynan's wedding was very like my own. Gifts and tokens were exchanged and, as the bowl was shared, I felt Goewyn's hand slip into mine. She put her lips to my ear and whispered her love to me, nipping my earlobe as she withdrew.

Three sharp raps of the Chief Bard's staff and the wedding was over. Cynan whooped loudly and lifted his bride from her feet. He carried her to the table and set her upon it. "Kinsmen and friends!" he called. "Here is my wife, Tángwen. Hail her everyone, Queen of the Galanae!"

The room resounded with the chorused cries as the Galanae welcomed their queen. Tángwen, her face flushed with happiness, smiling, radiant, stood on the board, receiving the adulation of the people. The expression on her face, at first charmed, took on an aspect of triumph—as if she had won a close-fought campaign.

Cynan reached up to her and Tángwen tumbled into his arms. They embraced to the loud acclaim of everyone. And then Cynan ordered ale to be brought so that we could all drink the health of the happy couple. The brewer and his men brought forth the first vat and placed it beside the hearth. Cups and bowls were plunged deep and brought out frothing. We raised our bowls and our voices. "*Sláinte! Sláinte môr!*" We drank to life and health and happiness. We drank to the prosperity of Cynan's reign.

Outside it began snowing. Cold wind streamed over the hills, lashing the snow which fell from a blanched sky. Inside the hall, the feast began: steaming joints of venison and pork were carried in on their spits; platters of sweet breads of various sorts; huge rounds of pale yellow cheese, and mounds of crisp apples. We ate, and drank, and talked, and ate and drank some more, passing the dark day in the light-filled hall surrounded by fellowship and plenty. And when at last we sat back, stuffed and satisfied, a call went up for a story. Taking up his harp, Tegid came before us, standing at the hearth in the center of the hall, the fire bright around him.

He strummed the harp, waiting for everyone to find a place and for quiet to claim the crowd. Gradually, the hall fell hushed. Lifting his voice, the bard declared, "It is right to celebrate the union of man and woman with weddings and feasts and songs—more so than the victories of warriors and the conquests of kings. It is right to pay heed to the stories of our people, for that is how we learn who we are and what is required of us in this life and the life beyond.

"On this day above all others, when the light of Alban Ardduan burns in the high places, it is right to give ourselves to revelry, it is right to draw near the hearthfire to hear the songs of our race. Gather then and listen, all who would hear a true tale—listen with your ears, Children of Albion, and listen with your hearts."

So saying, he bowed his head and fell silent. Then, fingers stirring on the strings of the harp, he conjured a melody from the air, drew breath, and began to sing.

10

The Great King's Son

The sweet-sounding notes of the harp spilled like glittering coins from Tegid's fingers; or like bright sparks sprung from the lusty fire, swirling up on rising draughts to the dark-shadowed rooftrees. The Chief Bard's voice rose to join the melody of the harp, and the two twined about one another in matchless harmony as he began to sing the tale he had prepared for Alban Ardduan. And this is what he sang:

"In the first days of men, when the dew of creation still glimmered upon the earth, there arose a great king who ruled many realms and held authority over divers clans. The great king's name was Cadwallon, and he ruled long and wisely, ever increasing the fortunes of those who sheltered beneath his shield. It was his custom in the evening to climb the council-mound beside his stronghold and gaze out upon his lands, to see for himself how matters stood with his people. And this is the way of it . . .

"One twilight, as Cadwallon sat on his high mound, gazing out upon his lands, it came to him that his holdings had grown vast beyond reckoning. 'I can no longer see from one end of my dominion to the other, nor can I count the number of my people—just to tell out the names of their tribes would take my bard three whole days.

" 'What shame,' thought he, 'if trouble were to threaten and I did not hear of it in time to prevent harm befalling my people. This could easily happen, for the kingdom has grown too great for one king to rule. Therefore, I must find someone to help me rule my realm and keep my people safe.'

"As it happened, there was no lack of would-be kings eager to help him rule. Sadly, not all of them cared as much for the welfare of the clans as Cadwallon, and it distressed the great king to think that a self-serving man should gain power at his command. So, he took himself to his *gorsedd* mound to think the thing through, saying, 'I will not come down until I have discovered a way out of this predicament.'

"Through three sunrises and three sunsets, Cadwallon did not stir; and through three more, and yet three more, until at dusk on the ninth day he hit upon a way to determine which of his noblemen was most worthy to aid him. He rose and walked down to his stronghold in confidence.

"The next day messengers rode to the four quarters of the kingdom bearing the message, and it was this: Noblemen all, the great king invites you to attend him for a season and take your ease in his hall where there will be feasting and gaming, and where the circling of mead cups will not cease.

"When the chieftains received this summons, they hastened to their lord. And when they saw the wealth of food and drink which had been prepared for them, they were well pleased and exclaimed that of all lords, Cadwallon must certainly be the most generous and benevolent ever known.

"When they had taken their places at table according to their rank, the feast began. They ate as much as they cared to eat and drank as much as they cared to drink, and after the sharp edge of hunger and thirst had been dulled somewhat, they began to talk, as men will, about the various adventures that had befallen them. One after another spoke, and each told his best tale to delight the others.

"The great king listened to the talk around him and stared unhappily into his cup. When they asked him why he frowned so, the great king replied, 'We have heard some strange tales told among us, but none more strange than the one I shall tell. For of all adventures, mine is the strangest. On my life, I wish someone would tell me what it means.'

" 'Fortunate are you, O king, if that is all that troubles you,' the noblemen replied. 'We are ready to do your bidding. You have but to tell us your story, and we will soon put your heart at ease.'

" 'Listen then,' the king said, 'but do not imagine you will discover the meaning as easily as you think. For I am persuaded that this tale will cause you all no little dismay before the end.'

" 'Know you, Great King, that we fear nothing. Indeed, your words provoke our interest as nothing we have heard before. Speak how you will, you cannot dismay us.'

" 'No doubt you know what is best,' mused the king. So saying, Cadwallon began to relate his adventure.

" 'I was not always the king you see before you,' he told the chieftains. 'In my youth I was very high-spirited and arrogant, supposing that no one could surpass me in any feat of weapons. Thinking I had mastered every feat known in this worlds-realm, I equipped myself and rode to the wild places far from the fields we know. To win glory and renown with my skill was my intent, to hear my name lauded in song was my desire.'

" 'What happened?' they asked. 'What did you find?'

" 'I found the loveliest valley any man has ever seen. Trees of every kind grew in the woods, and a wide river flowed through the valley. I crossed the river and struck a path and rode until I came to a measureless plain blooming with every kind of flower. The path went before me, so I followed. Three days and three nights I rode, and at last came to a shining fortress beside a restless sea of blue.

" 'I approached that fortress and two boys met me—each with hair so dark it made me think of crows' wings—and both dressed in princely garb with fine green cloaks and silver torcs on their necks. Each lad carried a bow of horn with strings of deer sinew, and shafts of walrus ivory with points of gold and eagle feathers. Their belts were silver and their knives were gold. And they were shooting their arrows at a shield covered with white oxhide.

111

" 'A little distance away stood a man with hair so light it made me think of swans' wings. His hair and beard were neatly trimmed, and he wore a torc of gold on his neck. His cloak was blue and his belt and buskins were of fine brown leather.

" 'I rode to meet this man with a ready greeting on my lips, but he was so courteous as to greet me before I could speak. He bade me enter the fortress with him, which I was eager to do for it was a marvel to behold. I saw others inside the fortress, and observed at once that they were a prosperous people, for the least one among them displayed the same wealth as the first man, nor did the greatest one among them display less than three times as much as the least.

" 'Five grooms took my horse and stabled it better than the best grooms I ever saw. And then the man led me to the hall, which had pillars of gold and a roof made of the feathers of speckled birds. Inside were handsome men and beautiful women—and all of them pleasantly conversing, singing, playing games and taking their ease. Twenty maidens were sewing by the window, and the least lovely maiden among them was more beautiful than any maiden in the Island of the Mighty. And as we entered the hall, these maidens rose to greet me and welcomed me most enjoyably.

" 'Five of them drew off my buskins and took my weapons, and five of them took from me my travel-worn clothes and dressed me in clean clothes—siarc and breecs and cloak of finest craft. Five maidens laid the board with good cloth and five maidens brought food on five huge platters. And the five who had taken my buskins and weapons now brought new fleeces for me to sit upon, and the five who had dressed me led me to the table.

" 'I sat beside the man who had brought me, and others of that exalted company sat around us. There was not a single cup or bowl or platter on that table that was not gold or silver or horn. And the food—such food! I have never tasted anything so pleasing to the tongue and satisfying to the stomach as I tasted in that hall surrounded by that bright company.

" 'We ate, but never a word was spoken to me from the first bite to the last. After a time, the man beside me, perceiving that I had finished my meal, turned to me and said, "I see that you would sooner talk than eat."

" ' "Lord," I said, "it is high time I had someone to talk with. Even the best food is poor fare when it is shared in silence."

" ' "Well," answered the man, "we did not like to disturb your meal. But if I had known how you felt about it, we would certainly have spoken sooner. But let us talk now if nothing prevents you." And he asked me what sort of man I was and what was the errand that had brought me to them.

" ' "Lord," said I, "you see before you a man of no small skill in weapon-play. I am roaming the wild places of the world, hoping to find someone who might overcome me. For I tell you the truth, it is no sport to me to overcome men of lesser skill than mine, and it is long since any warrior in my own country could offer me the sport I crave."

" 'The great lord smiled and said, "My friend, I would gladly guide you to your goal if I did not believe some harm would follow."

" 'At his words my face fell in sad disappointment. Seeing this, the lord said, "However, since you desire evil rather than good, I will tell you. Prepare yourself."

" 'To this I replied, "Lord, I am always prepared."

" ' "Then hear me, for I will say this but once. Spend the night here and rise tomorrow at dawn and take the path that brought you to this fortress until you reach a forest. A short distance into that forest, the path will split in two; take the left turning and follow on until you come to a clearing with a mound in the center. On that mound you will see a huge man. Ask this man where to go and, though he is often uncivil, it is my belief he will show you how to find that which you seek."

" 'That night was endless. All the ages of the world end to end would not last longer than that night lasted. As often as I looked at the sky, morning was no closer than when I last looked. At last, however, I saw the sky greying in the east and knew that night was ending. I rose and put on my clothes and went out and mounted my horse and set off on my way. I found the forest, and found the divided path, followed the left turning, and found the clearing with the mound in the center, the very same which the great lord had described to me.

" 'There was a man sitting on the mound. My host had told me that the man was huge, but he was far bigger than I had imagined—and and far uglier. He had but one eye in the middle of his forehead, and one foot; thick black hair covered his head and grew on his shoulders and arms. He carried an iron spear which would have been a burden for any four warriors, yet this man carried it easily in his hand. And around this man, both upon the mound and all around it, there grazed deer and pigs and sheep and forest animals of every kind—thousands of them!

" 'I greeted this Keeper of the Forest, and received a harsh reply. But it was no less than I expected, so I asked him what power he possessed over the animals gathered so closely about him. Again he made a rude reply. "Little man," he scoffed, "you must be the dullest of your kind not to know this. Nevertheless, I will show you what power I possess."

" 'The huge, hairy man took up his spear and aimed a blow at a nearby stag. He struck the animal with the butt of the spear, causing the stag to bell. And the belling of the stag shook the trees and trembled the very ground beneath my feet. Wild animals of every kind came running to the sound, gathering from the four quarters of the world. By the thousands and tens of thousands the animals came until there was hardly any room for my horse to stand among the wolves and bears and deer and otters and foxes and badgers and squirrels and mice and serpents and ants and all the rest.

" 'The animals gazed upon the huge Keeper as obedient men honor their lord, and he called to them and commanded them to graze, and at once they began to graze. "Well, little man," he said to me, "now you see the power I hold over these animals. But I am thinking you did not come here seeking assurance of my power, undoubtedly great though it is. What do you want?"

" 'I told him then who I was and what I sought, and he replied uncouthly to me. In short, he told me to go away. But I persisted, and he said, "Well, if you are stupid enough to seek such a thing, it is not for me to prevent you." Raising his iron spear, he pointed with it and said, "Follow the path you find at the end of the clearing. After a time you will discover a mountain; climb the slope of the mountain until you reach the summit and from there you will see a great glen the like of which you have never seen before. And in the middle of that glen you will see a yew tree that is both older and taller than any other yew tree in the world. Beneath the branches of that yew tree is a pool, and beside the pool is a stone, and on the stone is a silver bowl with a chain so that the bowl and stone cannot be separated. Take up the bowl, if you dare, and fill it with water and throw the water on the stone. Do not ask me what happens next, for I will not tell you—not even in a thousand years of asking."

" ' "Great Lord," I said, "I am not the sort of man to shrink from anything. I must know what happens next even if I stand here for a thousand and one years."

" ' "Was there ever a more ignorant and foolish man than you?" the Forest Keeper asked. "Nevertheless, I will tell what happens next: the rock will thunder with such force that you will think the heavens and earth must crack with the noise, and then will come a shower of water so fierce and cold that you will probably fail to survive. Hailstones big as loaves will fall! Do not ask me what happens next, for I will not tell you."

" ' "Great Lord," I said, "I believe you have told me enough. The rest I can find out for myself. I thank you for your help."

" ' And it is "Ha!" he says, "what is your thanks to me, little man? As for the help you have had, it will likely be your doom. Though I hope I never meet another as foolish as you, I will bid you farewell."

" 'I followed the path he had shown me, and rode to the mountain summit and spied the great glen and the tall yew tree. The tree was far taller and far older than the Forest Keeper had told me. I rode to the tree and discovered the pool and the stone and the silver bowl and chain—all as I had been told.

" 'Eager to try my skill, I wasted not a moment, but took up the bowl, filled it with water from the pool and dashed the water onto the stone. At once there arose a thunder far louder than the great lord had described, and then a squall of rain with hailstones huge as loaves. My friends, I tell you the truth—if I had not squeezed myself beneath the stone, I would not be here to tell the tale. Even so, my life was on the point of leaving me when the shower and hail stopped. There was not one green spear left on the yew tree, but the weather had cleared and now a flock of birds alighted on the bare branches and began to sing.

"'I am certain that no man before or since has heard music sweeter and more poignant than I heard then. But when the music was most pleasant to me, I heard a most mournful groaning which grew until it filled the great glen. And the groans became words: "Warrior, what do you want of me? What evil did I ever inflict on you that you should do to me and my realm what you have done?"

"'"Who are you, lord?" I demanded. "And what evil have I done to you?"

"'The mournful voice answered, "Do you not know that owing to the shower which you have thoughtlessly provoked neither man nor beast remains alive in my realm? You have destroyed everything."

"'With those words there appeared a warrior on a black horse, dressed all in black; his spear was black and his shield was black, and black the sword on his thigh from hilt to tip. The black horse pawed the ground with a black hoof and without another word the dread warrior charged.

"'Although the appearance was abrupt, I was prepared. Thinking that at last I would achieve everlasting renown, I quickly raised my spear and made my attack. I exulted in the power of the horse beneath me and in the swift advance of the great warrior. But though my charge was far more skillful than the best attack I have ever made, I was quickly swept from my horse and thrown ingloriously down upon the ground. Without so much as a look or word, my dark opponent passed the spearshaft through the bridle rein of my horse and took the animal away, leaving me there alone. He did not think it worth his while to take me hostage or even so much as retrieve my weapons.

" 'Thus I was forced to return by the path I had taken before, and when I reached the clearing the Keeper of the Forest met me, and it is a wonder that I did not melt into a puddle for the shame that sharp-tongued lord heaped upon me. I let him have his say, and he said it with eloquence most rare, and then I sighed and began making my long, slow way back to the shining fortress by the sea.

" 'There I was greeted more joyfully than before, and was made even more welcome and served even better food—if that is possible—than I received the first time. I was able to talk to the men and women in that fair place as much as I liked, and they talked fondly to me. However, no one made mention of my journey to the Black Lord's realm, nor did I speak of it myself. As vast as my former arrogance, so great was now my disgrace.

" 'I spent the night there and, when I rose, I found a splendid bay horse with a mane the color of red lichen. I gathered my weapons and bade the lord of that place farewell, and then returned to my own realm. The horse remains with me to this day, and I am not lying when I say that I would sooner part with my right hand than give up that horse.'

"The king then raised his eyes and looked around his table. 'But it is the truth I tell you when I say that I will give half my kingdom to the man who can explain to me the meaning of my adventure.'

"At this, Cadwallon concluded his peculiar tale. His lords sat stunned by the humility of their king in telling such a story against himself—as much as by the strangeness of the tale itself. Then up spoke a bold warrior-lord named Hy Gwyd.

" 'Noblemen all,' he said, 'our lord has told us a tale worth hearing. And, unless I am much mistaken, our most canny king has also set a challenge before us, and it is this: to discover for ourselves the meaning of this strange adventure. Therefore, let us behave as bold men ought; let us go forth to meet the king's challenge and discover the meaning of the tale.'

"And the noblemen began to discuss the matter among themselves. They talked long and earnestly, for not everyone agreed with Hy Gwyd. In the end the noblemen decided that nothing good could come of interfering in such mysteries, thus the matter was better left where it stood. They turned again to their feasting and eating. But Hy Gwyd, ambitious as he was clever, was unwilling to let the matter rest; he continued pressing his argument and in the end won his way with his friend, a warrior named Teleri.

"So, while the others ate and drank at table, the two warriors crept from the hall. They saddled their horses, took up their arms, and rode out from Caer Cadwallon in the grip of the mystery their king had posed for them. They rode far and wide in search of the foreign fields that had been described to them. In good time, the two friends reached the forest and the path, and knew it to be the same forest and the same path Cadwallon had described.

"They followed the path and came to the wonderful valley and crossed the wide, shining river where they found the track leading to the endless plain blooming with every kind of flower. The fragrance of the flowers filled their lungs and the pleasure of that land filled their eyes as they rode along. Through three days and three nights they rode and at last came to the gleaming fortress beside the ever-changing sea of deepest blue.

"Two boys with silver torcs and bows of horn were shooting ivory arrows at a white shield—just as Cadwallon had described. A golden-haired man stood watching the boys, and all three greeted the riders warmly, and welcomed them to come into the fortress to sup with them. The people they saw inside the stronghold were even more fair, and the maidens more lovely than they had imagined. These beautiful women rose up to serve the warriors just as they had served Cadwallon, and the meal they ate in that wondrous hall far surpassed anything they had ever tasted before. When the meal was finished, the lord who had greeted them addressed them and asked them what errand they were on.

"Hy Gwyd answered him and said, 'We are seeking the Black Lord who guards the pool.'

"'I wish you had said anything but that,' the lord replied, 'but if you are determined to seek the truth of this matter for yourselves, I will not prevent you.' And he told them everything, even as he had told Cadwallon.

"At dawn the two rode through that fair realm until they reached the forest clearing where stood the Forest Keeper on his mound. The Keeper of Animals was even more ugly and impressive than they had been led to believe. Following the disagreeable lord's grudging directions, they reached the vale beyond the mountain and the vale where the yew tree grew. There they found the fountain and the silver bowl upon the stone. Teleri was for returning the way they had come, but Hy Gwyd laughed at him and taunted him. 'We have not come this far to turn back now,' he said. 'I feel certain that we will win the renown our king failed to gain. Certainly, we have it in our power to become greater than Cadwallon ever was.' So saying, he took up the bowl, filled it with water from the pool, and dashed the water over the stone.

"There followed both thunder and a hail storm much more severe than Cadwallon had said. They thought they must surely die, and were on the point of doing so when the sky cleared and the birds appeared in the leafless yew. The song of the birds was finer and more pleasing than they could have imagined, but when the singing had filled their hearts with pleasure, the groans began. Indeed, such was the groaning that it seemed as if the whole world was in misery and dying. The two warriors looked and saw a lone rider approaching them: the Black Lord they had been told to expect.

"The Black Lord gazed mournfully upon them and said, 'Brothers, what do you want of me? What evil did I ever inflict on you that you should do to me and my realm what you have done?'

"'Who are you, lord?' asked the two warriors. 'And what evil have we done to you?'

"The mournful voice answered, 'Do you not know that owing to the shower which you have thoughtlessly provoked neither man nor beast remains alive in my realm? You have destroyed everything.'

"The two warriors turned to one another and bethought themselves what they might do. 'Brother, we are in need of a plan,' Teleri observed. 'For it is as our king has said and we are no nearer the truth of this mystery than when we first began. I say we go back now before something happens we will all regret.'

" 'Am I to believe what I hear?' Hy Gwyd hooted in derision. 'We are this close to winning glory and power beyond reckoning. Lash a spear to your spine if you must, but follow me. There is no turning back.'

"With that Hy Gwyd raised his shield and lofted his spear. When the Black Lord saw that they meant to face him, he attacked, unhorsing both warriors with as little effort as if they had been inept children. The dread one made to take their horses; but the two warriors, warned by the example of their king, leapt up at once, grasped the black spear and pulled their foe from his mount. The Black Lord rose to his knees, and his hand found the hilt of his sword. But Hy Gwyd was quicker.

"Up with his sword and down: the Black Lord's head rolled free of his shoulders and his body toppled to the ground like a felled oak. Hy Gwyd leaned on his sword, breathing hard, but well pleased with himself nonetheless. 'We have done it, brother,' he said. 'We have succeeded where our king has failed. Now his renown is ours and we are his betters.'

'Teleri was still searching for his tongue to make reply when there arose a moaning far greater than the groans they had heard previously. The moan grew to a keening wail. Piteous in its misery and mournful in its grief, the sound of this wailing would wring tears from stones. Indeed, if all the misery in the world were suddenly given voice it could not sound more lamentable. The two warriors thought they would not long survive the onslaught of such sorrow.

"They gazed about them to discover the source of this cry, and saw a woman drawing near them, and oh! she was hideous to behold. If all the womanly beauty in the world were turned rancid at a single stroke and bestowed upon the bony back of the most repulsive crone, it still would never match for ugliness the sight which the two warrior friends beheld. Her face was a mass of wrinkles; her teeth black and twisted in her crack-lipped maw. Her sagging flesh was a mass of maggoty sores; lice and worms worked ceaselessly in her hair. The finest of clothes had once been hers, but now the remnants hung on her disgusting body in filthy rags.

"The wails of grief were coming from the throat of this loathsome woman, more mournful with every approaching step. When she arrived at the pool, she looked upon the corpse of the Black Lord and keened even louder than before. Birds dropped dead from the trees at the sorrowful sound.

" 'Woe be upon you!' she cried, tears of sadness streaming down her ruined cheeks. 'Look at me! As ugly as I am now, I was once so beautiful. What will happen to me?'

" 'Lady, who are you?' asked Teleri. 'Why do you beseech us so?'

" 'You have killed my husband!' the loathly lady screeched. 'You have taken my man from me and left me desolate!' She stooped to the corpse before her and lifted the severed head by the hair, and kissed it on the mouth. 'Woe! Woe! My lord is gone. Who is there to care for me now? Who will be my comfort and support?'

" 'Calm yourself, if you can,' Teleri said. 'What is it you want from us?'

" 'You have slain the Guardian of the Pool,' the appalling woman said. 'He was my husband. Now one of you must take his place. One of you must take me to wife.'

"At this, the hideous crone approached the two warriors. A smell came from her that made their legs go weak and their bowels tremble. Red-eyed from crying, her nose running and spittle flowing from her lips, the crone spread her arms to them; her rags parted, revealing a body so wasted and repugnant that both men shut their eyes lest they retch at the sight.

" 'No!' they shouted. 'Do not come any closer or we shall faint.'

" 'Well?' the Black Hag asked. 'Which is it to be?' She turned first to Hy Gwyd. 'Will you embrace me?'

"Hy Gwyd turned his face away. 'Get you from me, hag!' he shouted. 'I will never embrace you!'

"She turned to Teleri. 'I see that you are a man of more heart. Will you embrace me?'

"Teleri's stomach squirmed. He felt sweat on the palms of his hands and the soles of his feet. He gulped air to keep from fainting.

'Lady, it is the last thing I will do,' Teleri replied.

"At this the woman began wailing again and so powerful was her keening that the sky darkened and the wind began to blow and the rain began to fall and thunder rolled across the sky. The very ground beneath their feet trembled and the whole world quaked at the sound of trees being uprooted and mountains sliding into the sea.

"The sudden onset of such a storm frightened the two warriors. 'Let us leave this place at once,' shouted Hy Gwyd. 'We have achieved all we came here to do.'

"But, though his heart quailed within him, Teleri was unwilling to leave the woman if he could help put the matter right. 'Lady,' he said, 'although it makes my flesh crawl, I will embrace you.'

"'You are a fool, Teleri!' shouted Hy Gwyd. 'You deserve her.' With that, he leapt onto his horse and rode swiftly away, though the storm crashed all around him.

"Teleri plucked up his courage and stepped toward the hag. His eyes watered—but whether from the sight of her, or the stench of her, he knew not. His arms shook and his strength flowed away like water. He thought his poor heart would burst for the shame and loathing coiling within him.

"Yet he raised his shaking arms and put them around the woman. He felt her hands on him, cold as ice, gripping him, bony fingers digging into his flesh. 'Woman,' he said, 'I have embraced you, and a cheerless embrace it is. Cold death could not be more desolate, nor the grave more grim.'

"'Now you must lie with me,' the hag told him, her breath foul in his face. Close up she was even uglier—if that were possible—and more ghastly and more repulsive than before.

"'Lie with you?' Teleri almost lost his reason. He thought to flee, but the Black Hag had him in her clutches and as there was no escape he resolved to see the thing through. 'I fear it will be a most abhorrent coupling. Yet, if that will satisfy you, I will do it—for your sake alone, the Good God knows I will receive no pleasure from it.'

"So Teleri took the Black Hag in his arms and lay down with her. He put his lips to her stinking mouth and kissed her. They made love, firm flesh to brittle bone, but Teleri could not endure the feat and he fainted.

"When he awoke, he was lying in the arms of the most beautiful maiden he had ever seen. Her long hair was yellow as pollen, and her limbs firm and supple; her breasts were shapely and her legs slender and long. Up he jumped with a startled cry. 'Where am I?' he said, holding his head. 'What happened to the other woman who was here?'

"The maiden sat up and smiled, and it was as if the sun had never shone upon Teleri until that moment. 'How many women must you have to satisfy you?' she asked, and oh! her voice was the melting of sweet honey in the mouth.

"'Lady,' Teleri said, 'you are all the woman I require. Only promise me you will remain with me!'

"'I will remain with you through all things, Teleri,' the maiden replied. 'For, if I am not mistaken, I am your wife and you are my husband.'

"'What is your name?' Teleri asked, feeling foolish that he had a wife but did not know her name.

"But the maiden answered soothingly. 'Beloved, my name is that word which is most pleasing to your ear. You have but to speak it and that is what I shall be called.'

"'Then I will call you Arianrhod,' he said, 'for that is the name most pleasing to me.'

"Teleri gathered his lovely Arianrhod in his arms and embraced her; her skin was soft and smooth and the touch of her filled him with delight. He kissed her and his soul rose into the heights of ecstasy. His love knew no bounds.

"They dressed themselves then, drawing on the kind of garments with which kings and queens array themselves. Teleri found his horse grazing nearby and mounted. He settled his new wife before him and rode from the pool, returning to his former realm the same way he had come.

"By and by, Teleri and Arianrhod returned to Caer Cadwallon where they were greeted and made welcome. His former friends exclaimed much over Teleri's good fortune at finding a woman so beautiful and wise to be his wife.

"'Welcome home, Teleri,' said King Cadwallon. 'You have returned at last. And here I was thinking that I would have to rule my realm alone, for I could find no one worthy to help me.'

"'What are you saying, lord?' asked Teleri. 'Hy Gwyd left before I did. He it was who killed the Black Lord.'

"'Ah, but it is not Hy Gwyd I see before me,' Cadwallon answered, 'nor is it Hy Gwyd who has entered my presence arrayed in splendor with so fair and queenly a wife.' The great king shook his head slowly. 'The man you speak of has not returned, and I think he never will. Therefore, let no man speak of him more. For I have found the one who is worthy above all others to share my throne, and whom, for this reason, I desire to elevate above all other men in my realm. From this day you are my own son, and as my son you will enjoy the benefit of my power and prosperity.'

"So saying, the Great King removed the torc from his own throat and placed it around Teleri's throat, thereby conferring a kingship no less sovereign than his own, nor yet less honorable. Teleri could not believe his good fortune.

"Cadwallon proclaimed a season of feasting throughout the realm and caused great rejoicing among all who held him sovereign. Then he placed half his kingdom under Teleri's authority, and removed himself to the other side of his realm where he watched with the greatest delight and joy all that Teleri did. For in everything Teleri showed himself an astute and able king, and as Teleri's eminence grew, so did Cadwallon's; and as Teleri's honor increased among the people, so did the great king's prestige increase through that of his adopted son.

"For his part, Teleri was well pleased with his lot and ever looked to increase the great king's honor among men. But of Hy Gwyd he heard nothing more, nor did any man ever lay eyes on him again. It was as if that man had never been born.

"Teleri and Arianrhod ruled long and wisely, ever exulting in their delight. And the love with which they loved one another increased until it filled the whole of the great king's realm with a potent and powerful goodness.

"Here ends the tale of the Great King's Son. Let him hear it who will."

11

The Boar Hunt

On a high-skied, sunbright day in early spring we left Dun Cruach. Snow still veiled the high ground, but I was eager to return to Dinas Dwr. The necessity of completing the circuit of Albion required a lengthy sojourn in Prydain and Caledon. There were still many clans and settlements to visit in the south, and it would likely be some time yet before we could at last turn our steps once more to Dinas Dwr in the north.

My entourage had swelled in number since setting out. It seemed that we added new members at each place visited. Dun Cruach was no exception—Cynan insisted on escorting us on our journey through southern Caledon, claiming it had been too long since a Galanae king had made the circuit. Now that he was king it was his right; besides, it would increase his renown to be seen in the company of the Aird Righ.

The real reason, I suspect, was that he just wanted to show off his new bride. But I did not mind. It gave us an opportunity to ride together once more, which I enjoyed.

As before, messengers rode before us, summoning the people to the king's llys. We made camp in the holy places—at crossroads, at standing stones and gorsedd mounds. There I received the fealty of the Caledonian tribes, and—as in Prydain and Llogres—placed the people under my authority and protection.

Ever and again, my thoughts turned toward Dinas Dwr, my splendid Water City. I wondered how the people fared, how the herds and crops were growing. I missed the place, missed my motley tribe, and wondered if they missed me. I longed for my hearth and hall. The minimal pleasures of a nomadic life were beginning to pall—the amusement of sleeping in a tent had long since worn off.

"There are only four or five tribes left to visit in the south," Tegid offered by way of consolation. "And as there are still very few people in Prydain at present, it will not be long before we begin making our way north again."

"How long?" I asked.

"Twenty—" the bard replied.

"Twenty days!" I shouted. My impatience got the better of me.

"—or thirty," Tegid added quickly. "Perhaps more. I cannot be certain until we have visited all the gathering places in the south."

"It will be Samhain before we get home again—if ever."

"Not at all. We should be within sight of Druim Vran before Lugnasadh—well before harvest time." He paused, almost beaming with pleasure. "We have done well. The tribes honor your kingship. Your brother kings welcome you. It is all we had hoped."

Truly, the circuit had been a triumph. As Tegid pointed out, people did accept me as Aird Righ, and I could already see a direct benefit. After such a time as we had just been through with Siawn Hy and Meldron, the High Kingship offered a substantial degree of stability—not to mention tranquility. If observing the ancient rite of the Cylchedd had helped bring this about, I would do it all over again. I would do anything to make Albion again what it had been when I came. Absolutely anything.

"Why not go hunting with Bran?" Tegid suggested, stirring me from my thoughts. "We will reach our destination just past midday. Bran and some of the others are planning to explore some of the game runs Cynan has told us about. You could go with them."

"Trying to get rid of me, brother bard?"

"Yes. Go. Please."

Bran was more than happy to include me in his hunting party. It had been a long time since I had ridden the hunt with him, or with anyone else. "It will not do for the High King's spearpoints to rust from neglect," he remarked. I took it as a kindly way of saying he did not want me growing soft now that I sat a throne more often than a charging horse. Fair enough.

Upon reaching our camping place for the night, we gathered our spears and rode to the forest. It was just past midday, as Tegid had said it would be, and the day was warm. We struck the first game run shortly after entering the wood, but decided we would be unlikely to find anything so near to the outer fringes of the forest, and so pressed deeper into the heart of the wood.

There were six of us in our party altogether and, upon reaching a second run, we divided ourselves into three groups and proceeded along the track two abreast. Bran and I rode in the center, three to four spear-lengths between us; and though I could not see the others through the tangled wood, I knew they were within easy hailing distance.

We rode in silence for some time, and at last came upon the spoor of wild pigs. Bran dismounted for a closer look. "How many?" I asked.

Bran, kneeling on the trail, raised his head and said, "A small herd. Four at least—maybe more." He stood and glanced ahead into the shadow-dappled trail. "Let us ride a little further and see what we find."

We proceeded with caution. This is always a tense situation, for until the pigs are sighted there is the very present danger of riding into them or overtaking them unawares. That is when accidents happen. Many is the hunter who has had his horse cut from under him—or worse—by a charging pig he did not see. Wild pigs are fearless fighters and will not hesitate to attack when pressed too close—though, like most animals, given the chance they prefer to flee.

Bran and I proceeded a short distance further down the run, and paused to listen. The air was still in the depths of the forest; only the quick tak-tak, tak-tak of a woodpecker broke the dull silence. Then, a little way ahead, we heard a low, grunting huff—which was followed by the snap of twigs and the shifting of dry leaves. Lowering his spear, Bran pointed into the dense thicket ahead and to the left of us. We waited, motionless, and in a moment a good-sized sow stepped onto the run before us, just beyond a sure throw. Pigs do not see well, though their hearing is acute and their sense of smell is keen. There was no wind, however, and if we kept quiet there was the chance she might wander nearer.

We waited.

Two piglets, small—they had been born only days before—joined their mother on the trail. They were joined by three more, all of them making small mewing sounds and scampering under the sow's belly and between her legs as she moved, snout down, along the run.

Bran shook his head slowly; we would not take the sow and leave the young without a mother. Accordingly, we made to turn off the track to give them a wide berth—a new mother feeling protective of her young would be extremely touchy and we had no wish to upset her. But, just as we turned aside, the thicket gave a shake and out burst a huge old boar.

He seemed more startled than angry, for he halted in the center of the run, turning this way and that—trying to locate the source of his agitation, I suppose—before gathering himself for a foray in our direction. This gave us time to ready ourselves and we were moving forward, spears low, when he charged. He closed the distance between us with surprising speed. We were ready, however, and had decided how to take him; Bran would strike the beast high in the shoulder, and I would go for his ribs.

The boar was a doughty old warrior, wise in his strength. He made his first charge a bluff, breaking off at the last instant so that we were forced to reign up and wheel our mounts to keep him between us. High-backed, his crest bristling over his sharp shoulders, he paused for a moment in the shadows, head down, tusks gleaming, slobbering as he pawed the turf. The sow and her brood had scattered, meanwhile, squealing as they fled down the run.

Bran and I readied ourselves for another charge. My pulse beat in my temples. I felt my blood warming to the challenge of this old boar.

Not waiting for the pig to decide the matter, we urged our horses forward to take him on the run. The beast did not move, but stood his ground and waited. Our spears were almost upon him when he broke sharply to the left, toward me—presenting his massive side as an easy target for my spear. I drew back to throw.

The boar must have sensed the movement, for he swerved and came headlong at me. His legs were a blur, and his tusks a glimmer of white in the gloom as he drove at me, grunting as he came. I braced myself for the impact, having already decide to let him come as near as possible before releasing my spear. Bran raced to join me, hoping to get in a second strike if mine missed.

All at once, there arose a great squeal and two more pigs darted into the run. I saw them only as two dark smudges speeding at an angle towards me. Bran shouted, his cry loud with surprise. I jerked the reins back hard, and my mount's legs all but folded under it as the creature struggled to halt and turn itself in one swift motion.

The first pig darted under the horse's rearing forehooves. The other I managed to ward off with a quick spearthrust as it made to rip into my mount's flank. I got a good look at the beast as it swerved aside to avoid the spear. It was a young tusker, not yet come into its full growth: thin in the hindquarters, and light in the chest. Yet, what it lacked in bulk, the beast more than made up for in speed and determination. For, no sooner had it passed one way than it charged again from another.

I shouted at Bran to warn him, and saw him, out of the corner of my eye, slashing at the second pig with a short, chopping motion of the spear. The pig fell, rolled on its back, legs kicking in the air, and then scrambled away, screaming as it fled.

This gave Bran a brief respite. He raised himself in the saddle and called for help, his voice ringing in the wood. I thought to give voice as well, but was soon too preoccupied to shout. The old boar had passed Bran and was now behind me. I heard a snuffling grunt as he lunged forward. I wheeled my horse and brought the spear down hard and fast. The blade caught the beast on the ridge of tight-muscled flesh atop his hump.

The spear bent and then came a loud, splintering crack as the shaft snapped in two. The next thing I knew I was falling sideways onto the forest floor.

I threw my leg over the saddle as I fell, and landed hard on my side. But at least my leg was not trapped beneath the horse. I scrambled to my feet and dived for another spear—bundled behind the saddle of my floundering mount.

Bran, seeing my predicament, threw his own spear to me. It struck the earth two paces beside me. I dived for it, snatched it up, and then whirled to my horse, seizing the reins and urging it upright. Blood flowed from its hock and I hoped the wound was not serious.

"Llew!" Bran shouted. A spear streaked past my shoulder as I turned. The missile hit the charging boar a glancing blow—only enough to turn it aside. I spun and thrust with my spear as it went past, but missed completely as the wily animal dodged aside, streaming fluid from its nostrils and foam from its tusks.

Just then I heard behind me a crashing sound, and turned to meet Emyr and Alun as they rode to our aid. At the appearance of the newcomers, the pigs turned and began racing away down the trail.

"They're running!" cried Alun, urging his horse to the chase.

Emyr and Bran were next away. I hooked an arm over the neck of my mount and swung myself up into the saddle. An instant later I was bolting after them. The pigs kept to the side of the hunting run, low among the branches, where they were hardest to reach. Our only hope of roast pig was to keep pace with them, and strike when they broke cover and dashed into the open.

We readied our spears and ranged ourselves accordingly. Then, as we drew even with our fleet-footed quarry, the hunting run turned suddenly and we found ourselves in a sunlit, bramble-hedged glade. In the center of the glade stood a dolmen: three upright stones capped by a single huge slab which formed a roof. The dolmen was surrounded by a shallow, grass-grown ditch and ring.

The old boar put his head down and ran straight across the clearing, skirting the dolmen and driving into the thicket on the far side of the glade. His young companion, however, was not so canny. The pig scurried across the ditch and disappeared behind the dolmen with Emyr right behind. Alun and I peeled away, racing for the opposite side to cut off his escape. Bran halted at the entrance to keep the brash porker from retreating back down the run.

The pig cleared the dolmen, saw us, and continued on around for the second time. Emyr picked him up as he passed and gave chase. Then it was Alun's and my chance once more. But the speedy pig darted among the stones and eluded us. Emyr shouted as the pig appeared on his side once more, and then I saw the brown blur as it rounded the ring and sped on for a third circuit.

Alun lofted a spear as the pig appeared once more. The spear struck the soft ground just in front of the young boar's jaw. The pig gave a frightened grunt and lunged for the cover of the dolmen stones.

I saw it scramble into the deep shadow under the capstone—I saw its silhouette sharp against the bright green beyond. And then it disappeared.

The pig simply melted from sight. I saw it go. Rather, I saw it, and then I did not see it any more. The creature had evaporated—tusks, tail, bristles and all—leaving not so much as a squeal behind.

I saw it go and my stomach tightened. My heart sank and I suddenly felt weak. My spear fell from my slack fingers; I made a clumsy grab for it and missed. The spear dropped on the ground.

"Where is it?" shouted Emyr. He looked to Alun, who leaned poised in the saddle with his spear raised, ready to throw. Neither had seen the pig vanish.

"The beast is hiding!" replied Alun, indicating the crevice between stones.

Cautiously, Emyr approached the dolmen and jabbed his spear beneath the capstone, thinking to drive the pig out. With trembling fingers, I gathered the reins and turned my mount, leaving the glade. Bran hailed me as I passed. "Have they made the kill?" he called. "Llew!"

I made no answer. Overcome by the enormity of the crisis, I could not speak. I simply spurred my horse away.

"Llew! What has happened?" Bran called sharply.

I knew what had happened: the web between the worlds had now grown so thin and tenuous that a frightened pig could cross the threshold in broad daylight. The balance between the worlds was skewed; the Endless Knot was unravelling. The Otherworld and the manifest world I had left behind were collapsing inward each upon the other. Chaos loomed.

I could hear the shriek of the void loud in my ears as I passed from the glade. The chill touched my heart—and my hand: my silver hand had grown cold on the end of my arm. The cold spread to my bones. Blackness swarmed the borders of my vision.

"Are you injured, lord?" called the Raven Chief behind me.

Ignoring Bran, I rode on . . .

I had almost reached the edge of the forest when the others caught me. They were puzzled by my actions, and disappointed at having to abandon the hunt. No one spoke, but I could feel their tacit bewilderment at my behavior. We rode back to camp without explanation and, upon dismounting, I turned to Bran. "Bring Tegid," I said, and ducked into my tent.

Goewyn was not there. No doubt she was away somewhere with Tángwen. I sat down on the red oxhide in the center of the tent, crossed my legs, folded my arms across my chest and bent my head until it almost touched my knees. I waited, feeling a cold tide of desperation rising within me. If I did not think about what I had seen, and what it meant, I could keep the tide from overwhelming me.

"Hurry, Tegid," I murmured, rocking slowly back and forth.

In this way I held the tide at bay and kept it from swallowing me and carrying me away. I do not know how much time passed, but I heard the brushing tread of a step at the doorway and then felt a presence beside me. I opened my eyes and raised my head.

Tegid was bending over me, concern creasing his brow. "I am

here, brother," he said softly. "The hunt went well?"

I shut my eyes again and shook my head. When I did not reply, he said, "What has happened?" He paused. "Llew, tell me. What has happened?"

I raised my silver hand to him. "It is cold, Tegid. Like ice."

He bent down and touched the metal hand thoughtfully. "It feels the same to me," he offered, straightening once more. "Tell me about the hunt."

"Three pigs," I began, haltingly. "They gave us a good hunt. We chased them—deep into the forest. One escaped. We followed two into a clearing. There was a dolmen and ring. We chased one of the pigs around the dolmen and ... and then it disappeared."

"The dolmen?"

I cast a quick, disgusted glance at the bard to see if he was baiting me. "The pig. The pig disappeared. I saw it go, and I know where it went."

"Did the others see it?" he asked.

"That is hardly the point—is it?" I spat.

Tegid watched me closely.

"I have seen the pig before," I told him. "Before I came to Albion, I saw that pig. It is just like the aurochs, you see?"

Tegid did not see. How could he? So I explained to him about the aurochs—the aurochs we had hunted on our flight to Findargad, and which had disappeared into a mound the same way the pig had vanished.

"But we killed it," Tegid protested. "We ate its meat and it fed us."

"There were *two*!" I said. "One disappeared and the other we killed. That aurochs is what brought Simon and me to Albion; the one we chased was the one that brought us. And the pig I chased today was the one I saw before I came."

Tegid shook his head slowly. "I hear you, brother, but I still do not understand why this upsets you," he said. "It is unfortunate, but—"

"Unfortunate!"

Tegid stood looking at me for a moment, then sat down facing me. He settled himself, and said, "If you want me to understand, you must tell me what it means." He spoke slowly, but crisply. He was restraining himself, but with obvious effort.

"It means," I said, closing my eyes again, "that Nettles was *wrong*. The balance is not restored. The Knot—the Endless Knot is still unravelling."

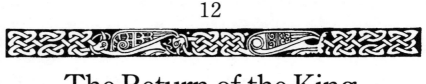

12

The Return of the King

Though Tegid and I talked at length, I was unable to make him grasp the significance of the vanishing pig. Probably I could not explain properly, or at least in a way he could understand. He seemed willing enough, but my explanation lacked some element crucial to persuasion. I could not make him see the danger.

"Tegid," I said at last, "it is late and I am tired. Let us get something to eat."

Tegid agreed that might be best; he rose stiffly, and left the tent. Gloom and doom had so permeated my thoughts that I was amazed to find a stunning sunset in progress—pink, carnelian, copper, wine and fuchsia flung in gorgeous splashes against a radiant hyacinth sky. I blinked my eyes and stood staring at it for a moment. The air was warm still, with just a hint of evening's chill. Soon the stars would come out, and we would be treated to yet another spectacle of almost staggering grandeur.

Through all its travails, Albion still endured. How was that possible? What preserved it? What sustained it in the very teeth of cataclysm and disaster?

"What do you see?" asked Goewyn softly.

"I see a miracle," I replied. "I see it and I wonder how such things can endure."

Upon seeing Tegid emerge from the tent, Goewyn had quickened her step to meet me. She had kept herself away from the tent while Tegid and I talked, but now she was eager to discover the subject of our discussion. "Are you hungry?" she asked, taking my flesh hand in hers. She did not say that she had been waiting long; the curiosity in her dark brown eyes was evident enough.

"I am sorry," I told her. "I did not mean to exclude you. Tegid and I were talking. You should have joined us."

"When a king and his bard hold council, no one must intrude," she replied. There was no irritation in her tone, and I realized that despite her curiosity, which was only natural, she would have fought anyone who tried to disturb us.

"Next time I will send for you, Goewyn," I said. "I am sorry. Forgive me."

"You are troubled, Llew." She reached a cool hand to my forehead and smoothed my hair back. "Walk. Take your ease. I will have food brought to the tent and await you there."

"No, walk with me. I do not want to be alone just now."

So we walked together a while. We did not talk. Goewyn's undemanding presence was a balm to my agitated spirit, and I began to relax somewhat. As the stars began to waken in the sky, we returned to the tent. "Rest now. I will see that food is brought." She moved away, and I watched her go. My heart soared to see her in motion. I loved every curving line.

My melancholy lifted at once. Here was love and life, full and free before me. Here was a soul shining like a beacon flame, shining for me. I wanted to gather her in my arms and hold her for ever.

Never leave me, Goewyn.

Entering the tent once more, I found Tegid and Bran waiting. Tegid had also rousted Cynan from his tent and brought him along. Rushlights had been lit and placed on stands around the perimeter of the tent, casting a rosy glow over the interior. They ceased talking when I appeared.

"This was not necessary, Tegid," I told him.

"You are troubled, brother," the bard replied. "I have failed to console you, so I brought your chieftains to attend you."

I thanked them all for coming, and insisted that it was not necessary to attend me. "I have Goewyn to console me," I explained.

"It is unfortunate that the pig got away," Bran sympathized. "But we can find another one tomorrow."

"The hunting runs are full of them," offered Cynan helpfully.

Shaking my head gently, I tried once more to explain. "It is not the pig. I do not care about the pig. It is what the pig's disappearance represents that worries me. Do you see that?"

I could tell by the way they looked at me they did not see that at all. I tried again.

"There is trouble," I said. "There is a balance between this world and my world, and that balance has been disturbed. I thought defeating Siawn Hy and Meldron would restore the balance—Nettles thought so, too. But he was wrong, and now . . ."

The blank stares brought my lecture to an abrupt halt. I had lost them again.

"If there is trouble, we will soon know it," Bran suggested. "And we will conquer it."

Spoken like a fighting man. "It is not that kind of trouble," I answered.

"We are more than a match for any enemy," Cynan boasted. "Let it come. There is no enemy we cannot defeat."

"It is not that simple, Cynan." I sighed, shaking my head again. "Believe me, I wish it were."

Tegid, desperate to help, observed, "The Banfáith's prophecy has proven true through all things. All that has happened, and all that is yet to happen, is contained in the prophecy."

"There, you see?" agreed Cynan with satisfaction. "There is nothing to worry about. We have the prophecy to guide us if trouble should come. There is nothing to worry about."

"You do not understand," I said wearily. It was as if a gulf stood between us—a gulf as wide and deep as that which separates the worlds, perhaps. Maybe there was no way for them to cross that gap. If Professor Nettleton were here, he would know what to say to make them understand. Nettles would know what it meant... or would he? He had been wrong about my remaining in Albion; obviously there was still some work for me to finish. Then again, maybe he was right; maybe it was my lingering presence that was causing the trouble.

I almost groaned with the effort of trying to make sense of it. Why, oh why, was this so difficult?

"If it is understanding we lack," the bard exhorted, "then let us look to the prophecy." Pressing the palms of his hands together, he touched his fingertips to his lips and drew a deep breath. Closing his eyes, he began, speaking with quiet intensity, to declaim the prophecy given me by Gwenllian, Banfáith of Ynys Sci.

I needed no help in recalling the prophecy; I remembered the Banfáith's words as if they were engraved on my heart. Still, each time I heard those stern, unforgiving words spoken aloud, I felt the thrill in my gut. This time it was more than a thrill, however; I felt the distinct tug of a power beyond my ken bearing me along—destiny, perhaps? I do not know. But it was as if I was standing on a seastrand with the tide flowing around me; I could feel its irresistible pull. Events like waves had gathered and now were moving, bearing me along. I could resist—I could swim against the tide—but I would be carried along anyway in the end.

Tegid came to the end of the recitation, saying, "Before Albion is One, the Hero Feat must be performed and Silver Hand must reign."

This last seemed to please both Bran and Cynan immensely. Bran nodded sagely, and Cynan folded his arms across his chest as if he had carried the day. "Silver Hand reigns!" he declared proudly. "And when the Cylchedd is complete, Albion will be united once again under the Aird Righ."

"That is surely the way of it," enthused Bran.

I remained unconvinced, but had run out of arguments. Then Goewyn arrived with one of her maidens bringing our supper, and so I decided to let the matter rest for the time being. If anything were seriously wrong, Professor Nettleton would surely return to tell me so, or send a message to me somehow.

"Let us hope that is the way of it," I agreed reluctantly, and then dismissed them to their own tents and to their rest.

"We will remain vigilant, lord," Bran vowed as he left. "That is all we can do."

"True, Bran. Very true."

He and Cynan filed out, followed by Tegid, who, though he appeared anxious to tell me something, merely gazed at Goewyn for a moment, bade her a good night's rest, and went out, leaving us alone to share our meal and my misery.

"Eat something, husband," Goewyn prodded gently. "A man cannot think or fight on an empty stomach."

She lifted a bowl under my nose. The aroma of boiled meat in thick, salty broth made my mouth water. Taking the bowl in my silver hand, I dipped my fingers in and began eating. My mind turned again to the harsh promises of the prophecy, and I ate in silence, ignoring Goewyn as she sat directly before me.

"Here, my love," she said after a time, drawing me from my thoughts. "For you." I looked up to see her break a small loaf of brown bread in her hands. She smiled, extending half the loaf to me.

A small gesture: her hand reaching out to me—as if she would thwart all the unknown hazards of the future with a bit of broken bread—it was so humble and trifling against such overwhelming uncertainty. Yet, in that moment, it was enough.

The next day we resumed the circuit, and all went as it had before. Nothing terrible happened. The earth did not open before our feet and swallow us whole; the sky did not fall; the sun did not deviate from its appointed course. And, when evening came, the moon rose to shed a friendly light upon the land. All was as it should be.

After a few such uneventful days, I began to persuade myself that the wild pig's disappearance was merely a lingering ripple in the disturbance caused by Simon and Meldron; a simple, small, isolated event, it foreshadowed no great catastrophe. Albion was healing itself, yes, but it would be unrealistic to expect everything to return to normal overnight. Undoubtedly, the healing process would go on for a long time. And after all, my reign was, as Cynan and Tegid implied, a major element of that recovery. How could I think otherwise?

Maffar, sweetest of seasons, had run its course full and fair, and Gyd, season of sun, was well begun before we at last turned the wagons north. I was glad to have made the circuit, but more so now that it was finished. I missed Dinas Dwr and all the friends we had left behind. And I wanted to see what had been accomplished in my absence.

The southern leg of our journey completed, Cynan and Tángwen bade us farewell, but not before I extracted a promise to winter with us in Dinas Dwr. "Favor us with the pleasure of your company. Our hall is a cowbyre compared to yours," I declared. "And it is as cold beside the hearth as on the hilltop when the snow drifts deep. But it would be less wretched if you would deign to share our meager fare."

"*Mo anam*!" Cynan cried. "Do you expect me to refuse such a generous offer? See the cups are filled, brother—it is Cynan Machae at your gate when the wind howls in the roof-trees!"

He and Tángwen returned to Dun Cruach, and we proceeded on to Sarn Cathmail. Once we had set our faces towards home, my impatience knew no bounds. We could not move swiftly enough. Each day's distance brought us no nearer, or so it seemed to me, yet with every step my eagerness increased; like thirst burning in a parched throat, I ached with it.

It was not until the land began to lift and I saw the high hills glimmering in the blue heat haze that I began to feel we were at last returning. On the day I saw Môn Dubh, I could contain myself no longer. I rode ahead, with Goewyn at my side, and would likely have left the others far behind if Tegid had not prevented us.

"You cannot return this way," he said when he had caught up with us. "Allow your people to make ready a proper welcome."

"Just seeing Dinas Dwr again is welcome enough for me," I insisted. "We could have been there by now if you had not stopped us. We will go ahead. Let the rest come along in their own good time."

He shook his head firmly. "One more day, then you will enter your city and receive the welcome due a king. I will send Emyr ahead to prepare the way for you." He turned a deaf ear to my protests and insisted, "We have observed the rite without flaw. Let us complete it likewise."

Goewyn sided with him. "Let it be as your wise bard advises," she urged. "It is only one more day, and your people will be grateful for the opportunity of anticipating the return of their king and welcoming you back in a manner worthy of your rank."

So, Emyr Lydaw was sent ahead to announce our arrival. I spent one more night in a tent on the trail. Like a child on the eve of a celebration, I was too excited to sleep. I lay in the tent, tossing this way and that, and finally rose and went out to walk away my restlessness.

It was dark, the moon high overhead and bright. The camp was quiet. I heard a tawny owl calling, and the answering call of its mate a short distance away. I looked up at the sound and saw a ghostly shape flickering through the treetops. The surrounding hills were softly outlined against a sky of silver-flecked jet. All was dark and quiet and as it should be—except for one small detail: a spark-bright glimmer on the crest of a faraway hill.

I watched for a moment before realizing what it was: a beacon. In the same instant, I felt a chill in my silver hand; a sharp cold stab.

I turned to scan the hilltops behind me, but saw no answering flare. I wondered what the signal fire betokened, and thought to fetch Tegid from his bed to show it to him. But the beacon faded and, with its departure, my own certainty of what I had seen. Perhaps it was nothing more than the campfire of hunters; or maybe Scatha had set watchers along the ridge to warn of our approach.

Stalking the perimeter of the camp, I spoke briefly with the guards at the horse picket, but they had seen nothing. I finished my inspection of the camp and returned to my tent. I lay down on the fleece and fell asleep listening to Goewyn's deep, slow breathing.

I awakened early the next morning, dressed quickly, and proceeded to make a general nuisance of myself by urging everyone to hurry. We were but a day's march from Druim Vran, and with all speed we would reach the lake at sunset and dine at Dinas Dwr that night.

By midday I could see the dark line of Raven Ridge, and I thought we would never arrive. Nevertheless, as the sun began sinking low in the west, we entered the broad plain spreading before the ridgewall. The shadow of the gorsedd mound stretched long across the plain and the looming mass of Druim Vran soared above it.

All along the ridge stood the people, my people, waiting to welcome us home. My heart soared at the sight.

"Listen," said Goewyn, tilting her head. "They are singing."

We were too far away to hear the words, but the voices fell like a fine sweet rain splashing down from on high. I halted on the trail, swivelled in the saddle, and called to Tegid, "Do you hear? What are they singing?"

He rode to join me and halted to listen a moment, then smiled. "It is *Arianrhod's Greeting*," he said. "It is the song Arianrhod sings to her lover when she sees him sailing over the waves to rescue her."

"Is it?" I wondered. "I have never heard that story," I said.

"It is a beautiful tale," Tegid said. "I will sing it to you some time."

I turned my face to the heights and listened to the glad sound. I would not have imagined that the sight of my people standing along the ridgewall and singing their welcome to the valley below could touch me so deeply. My eyes grew misty with tears at the sound; truly, I had come home.

13

The Aird Righ's Mill

"Hie! Hie!" cried Goewyn as she galloped past. "I thought you were eager to reach home!" she shouted.

I lashed my mount to speed and raced after her. She gained the ridgewall before me and, without slackening her pace, flew straight up the track. I followed in a hail of dust and pebbles thrown up by the horses' hooves, but could not catch her. She reached the top first and slipped from the saddle, turning to await me.

"Welcome home, O King," she said.

I threw a leg over the neck of my horse and slid to the ground beside her. "Lady, I claim a welcome kiss," I said, pulling her to me. The crowd came running to meet us, and we were soon pressed on every side by eager well-wishers.

What a glad greeting it was! The tumult was heartfelt and loud, the reception dizzying. We were soon engulfed in a heady whirl of welcome. Scatha appeared in the forefront of the press. She seized her daughter in her arms and held her; Pen-y-Cat hugged me next, clasping me tightly to her, and, taking my hand and one of Goewyn's, she gazed at us with shining eyes and declared, "Welcome, my children, I give you good greeting."

She kissed us both, and held us together before her while her eyes drank in the sight. "I have missed you both," she said. Then, fixing each one of us in her gaze, she asked, "It *is* just the two of you?"

"Still just two," my bride told her mother. She squeezed my hand.

"Well," Scatha allowed, "you are no less welcome. I have longed for you every day."

We embraced again, and I glimpsed the crannog in the lake beyond. "I see that Dinas Dwr has survived in our absence."

"Survived?" boomed Calbha, wading towards us through the crowd to stand before us. The Ravens we had left behind followed at his heels. "We have thrived! Welcome back, Silver Hand," he said, gripping my arms. "You have fared well?"

"We have fared exceedingly well, Calbha," I answered. "The circuit of the land is complete. All is well."

"Tonight we will celebrate your return," Scatha announced. "In the hall, the welcome cup awaits."

Thanks to Tegid's foresight, Scatha and Calbha had had time to prepare a feast for our return. Trailing well-wishers, we made our way down to the city on the lake; in the golden light of a setting sun Dinas Dwr seemed to me a gem aglow in a broad, shining band.

At the lakeshore, we climbed into boats and paddled quickly across to the crannog, where we were welcomed by those who had stayed behind to attend to the preparations.

The tang of roasting meat reached us the instant we stepped from the boats. Two whole oxen and six pigs were dripping fat over pits of charcoal; ale vats had been set up outside the hall, and skins of mead poured into bowls. At our approach, a dozen maidens took up gold and silver bowls and ran to meet us.

"Welcome, Great King," said a dimpled, smiling maid, raising the bowl to me. "Too long have you been absent from your hearth, lord. Drink deep and take your ease," she said prettily, and it melted my heart to hear it.

I accepted the bowl, lifted it to my lips, and drank the sweet, golden nectar. It was flavored with anise and warmed my throat as it slid silkily over my tongue. I declared it the finest drink I had ever tasted, and passed the bowl to Goewyn. The king having drunk, the remaining bowls, cups, and jars could be distributed; this was done at once and the feast began.

No one was happier than I to be back home. I looked long on the hall, and on the happy faces of all those I had left behind. They were my people, and I was their king. I truly felt I had come home, that my absence had pained, and that my return was pleasing.

It was not until I stood before my own hall with the taste of herbed mead in my mouth and the shouts of acclaim loud in my ears that I realized Tegid's wisdom in proposing the circuit. In going out like a king, I had become a king indeed. I belonged to the land now; heart and soul, I was part of it. In some ancient, mystical way, the circuit united my spirit with Albion and its people. I felt my soul expand to embrace those around me, and I remembered all those I had met in the course of my circuit of the land. As I loved those around me, I loved them all. They were my people, and I was their king.

I saw Tegid standing a little distance apart with a bowl to his lips, surrounded by his Mabinogi. He sensed me watching him and lowered the bowl, smiling. The crafty bard knew what had happened. He knew full well the effect circuit and homecoming would have on my soul. He smiled at me over the bowl and raised it to me, then drank again. Oh yes, he knew.

Goewyn pressed the bowl into my hands once more and I raised it to Tegid and drank to him. Then Goewyn and I shared a drink. Garanaw, who had stayed behind to help Scatha train the young warriors, came and greeted me like a brother. We drank together then, and I embarked upon a long round of drinking the health of all my long-absent friends.

Food followed, mounds of bread and cakes, and crackling joints of roast meat, great steaming cauldrons full of leeks, marrows, and cabbages. It was a splendid feast: eating by torchlight under the stars, the night dark and warm around us.

After we had eaten, Tegid brought out his harp and we drifted away on wings of song. Under his peerless touch, the skyvault became a vast Seeing Bowl filled with the black oak water of all possibilities, each star a glimmering promise. Dawn was glinting in the east when we finally made our way to bed, but we slept the sleep of deep contentment.

We bade farewell to Calbha a few days later. He was anxious to return to his lands in Llogres and establish himself and his people before Sollen set in. I did not envy him the work he faced. I made certain he took a large portion of seed grain and meal, and the best of the pigs, sheep and cattle to begin new herds. I gave him everything he would need to see him through the first winter, and we parted with vows of everlasting friendship, and promises to visit one another often. He and the remnant of his tribe left with a dozen wagons piled high with provisions, tools and weapons.

As Calbha had said, Dinas Dwr prospered in our absence. The crops and herds had flourished, the people had plenty and were content. The horror loosed by the Great Hound Meldron was fading, and with it the tainting abomination of his reign.

Having completed the Cylchedd of the land, I was not content to sit on my throne and watch the world go by. Indeed, I was more eager than ever to be a good king. As the warm days passed, I found myself wondering what I might do to benefit my people. What could I give them?

My bard suggested I give them wise leadership, but I had in mind something more tangible: an engineering feat like a bridge, or a road. Neither seemed quite right. If a road, where would it go? And if a bridge, what body of water needed spanning?

I ambled around for a couple of days trying to decide what sort of endeavor would serve the people best. And, as luck would have it, one morning I was walking among the sheds and work huts on the lakeshore when I heard the slow, heavy mumble of the grinding wheel. I turned and lifted my eyes from the path to see two women bent over a massive double wheel of stone. One woman turned the upper stone with a staff while the other poured dried grain into the hole in the center. They saw me watching and greeted me.

"Please continue," I said, "I do not wish to interrupt your work."

They resumed their labor and I watched the arduous process. I saw their slender backs bent and their shapely arms straining to turn the heavy stone. It was hard work for meal which would be eaten in a moment, and there would be more grain to grind tomorrow. When they finished, the women collected the flour from around the stone, using a straw whisk to sweep every last fleck into their bag. They bade me farewell then, and left. No sooner was the grindstone idle, however, than two more women appeared and, taking grain from the storehouse, they also began to grind their flour.

This was no new chore in Dinas Dwr. It had been performed in just this way since before anyone could remember, probably since the first harvest had been gathered and dried. But this was the first time I had seen it as the back-breaking labor it was. And so I arrived at the boon I would give my people. I would give them a mill.

A mill! Such a simple thing, rudimentary really. Yet, a wonder if you do not have one. And we did not have one. Neither did anyone else. So far as I knew there had never been a grain mill in Albion. When I thought of how much time and energy would be saved, I wondered I had not thought of it before. And, after the mill, I could see other, perhaps more exalted ventures. The mill was just the beginning, but it was as good a project as any to begin with.

Returning to the crannog, I called my wise bard to me. "Tegid," I said, "I am going to build a mill. And you are going to help me."

Tegid peered at me sceptically and pulled on his lower lip.

"You know," I explained, "a mill—with stones for grinding grain."

He looked slightly puzzled, but agreed that, in principle at least, a mill was a fine thing to build.

"No, I do not mean a pair of grindstones turned by hand. These stones will be much bigger than that."

"How big?" he wondered, eyeing me narrowly.

"Huge. Enormous! Big enough to grind a whole season's supply of grain in a few days. What do you think?"

This appeared to confound Tegid all the more. "A worthy ambition, indeed," he replied. "Yet, I cannot help thinking that grindstones so large would be very difficult to move. Are you suggesting oxen?"

"No," I told him. "I am not suggesting oxen."

"Good," he remarked with some relief. "Oxen must be fed and—"

"I am suggesting water."

"Water?"

"Exactly. It is to be a water mill."

The bewilderment on his face was wonderful. I laughed to see it. He drew breath to protest, but I said, "It is a simple invention from my world. But it will work here. Let me show you what I mean."

I knelt and drew my knife. After scratching a few lines in the dirt, I said, "This is the stream that flows into the lake." I drew a wavy circle. "This is the lake."

Tegid gazed at the squiggles and nodded.

"Now then." I drew a square on the stream. "If we put a dam at this place—"

"If we make a dam at that place, the stream will flood the meadow and the water will not reach the lake."

"True," I agreed. "Unless the water had a way past the dam. You see, we make a weir with a very narrow opening and let the water out slowly—through a revolving wheel. A wheel made of paddles." I drew a crude wheel with flat paddles, and indicated with my hand how the water would push the paddles and turn the wheel. "Like so. See? And this turning wheel is joined to the grindstone." I laced my fingers to suggest cogs meshing and turning.

Tegid nodded shrewdly. "And as the wheel turns, it turns the grindstone."

"That is the way of it."

Tegid frowned, gazing at the lines in the dirt. "I assume you know how this can be accomplished?" he said at last.

"Indeed," I stated confidently. "I mean, I think so."

"This is a marvel I would like to see." Tegid frowned at the dirt drawing and asked, "But will it not make the people lazy?"

"Never fear, brother. The people have more than enough to keep them busy without having to grind every single seed by hand. Trust me."

Tegid straightened. "So be it. How will you proceed?"

"First we will select the place to build the weir." I stood, replacing my knife in my belt. "I could use your advice there."

"When will you begin?"

"At once."

We left the crannog and walked out along the lakeshore to the place where the stream which passed under the ridgewall flowed into the lake. Then we followed the stream towards the ridge. We walked along the stream, pausing now and then to allow Tegid to look around. At a place about halfway to the ridgewall—where the stream emerged from deeply-cleft banks at the edge of the woods which rose up on the slopes of Druim Vran, the bard stopped.

"This," Tegid said, tapping the ground with his staff, "is the place I deem best for your water mill."

The location seemed less than promising to me. "There is no place for a weir," I pointed out. I had envisaged a flat, calm mill pond, with brown trout sporting in dappled shade—not a steep-banked slope on a hill.

"The weir will be easily dug here," Tegid maintained. "There is wood and stone within easy reach, and this is where the water begins its race to the lake."

I studied the waterflow for a moment, looking back along the course of the stream; I considered the wooded slopes and the stony banks. Tegid was right, it would a good place for a mill. Different from what I'd had in mind, but a much better use of gravity to turn the mill wheel and much less difficulty in keeping the water from flooding the meadow. I wondered what the shrewd bard knew about such things as gravity and hydraulics.

"You are right. This is the place for us. Here we will build our mill."

Work began that same day. First, I had the site cleared of brush. While that was being done, I searched for a way to draw some of my ideas, settling for a sharpened pine twig and a slab of yellow beeswax, and I began educating my master-builder, a man named Huel Gadarn, in the ways of water-powered mills. He was quick as he was clever; I had only to scratch a few lines on the beeswax and he grasped not only the form of the thing I was drawing but, often as not, the concept behind it as well. The only aspect of the procedure he found baffling was how the power of the water wheel was transferred to the giant grinding-stones. But this difficulty owed more to my poor skill in sketching a gear than to any failing on Huel's part.

Next we built a small model of the mill out of twigs and bark and clay. When that was finished, I was satisfied that Huel had all the various elements of the operation firmly under his command. I had no fear that, given time and inclination, Huel the master-builder could build the mill himself. We were ready to proceed.

Once the site was cleared, we could begin excavating the weir. But then it rained.

I spent the first day drawing various kinds of gears. On the second day I started pacing. By the fourth day, which dawned just as grey and wet as the three before it, I was pacing *and* cursing the weather. Goewyn endured me as long as she could, but finally grew exasperated and informed me that no grindstone, however huge, was worth the aggravation I was causing. She then sent me away to do my stalking, as she called it, elsewhere.

I spent a wet, restless day in the hall, listening to idle talk and itching to be at the building site. Fortunately, the next day dawned clear and bright, and we were able, at last—and with Goewyn's emphatic blessing—to begin digging the foundations for Albion's new wonder: the Aird Righ's Mill.

14

Intruders

Through Maffar's long days of warmth and bliss the Year's Wheel slowly revolved. Rhyll came on in a shimmering blaze, but the golden days and sharp, cool nights quickly dulled. The high color faded and the land withered beneath windy grey skies and cold, drenching rain.

Our harvest, so bountiful the previous year, yielded less than anticipated due to the rain. Day after day, we watched the skies, hoping for a break in the weather and a few sunny days to dry the grain. Rot set in before we could gather it all. It was no disaster, thanks to the bounty of the last harvest, but still a disappointment.

Progress on the mill slowed, and I grew restive. With Sollen's icy fingers stretching towards us, I was anxious to get as much finished as possible before the snow stopped us. I drove Huel and his workers relentlessly. Sometimes, if the rainfall was not heavy, I made them work through it. As the days grew shorter, I grew more frantic and demanding. I had torches and braziers brought to the site so that we could work after dark.

Tegid finally intervened; he approached me one night when I returned shivering from a windy day in the rain. "You have accomplished a great deal," he affirmed, "but you go too far. Look around you, Silver Hand; the days are short and the light is not good. How much longer do you think the sky will hold back the snow?

Come, it is time to take your rest."

"And just abandon the mill? Abandon all we have done? Tegid, you are talking nonsense."

"Did I tell you to abandon anything?" he sniffed. "You can begin again as soon as Gyd clears the skies once more. Now is the time for rest, and for more pleasurable pursuits indoors."

"Just a few more days, Tegid. It is not going to hurt anyone."

"We neglect the seasons to our peril," he replied stiffly.

"There will be plenty of time for lazing around the hearth, never fear."

Riding out to the building site early the next morning, I regretted those words. We had worked hard, very hard; but the mill had been begun late in the season and now the weather had turned against us. It was absurd of me to expect men to work in the dark, wet, and cold, and I was a fool for demanding it of them.

Worse, I was becoming a tyrant: self-indulgent, insensitive, obsessive and oppressive. My great labor-saving boon had so far produced nothing but plenty of extra work for everyone.

My wise bard was right. The time-honored rhythm of the seasons, of work and play and rest, served the purpose of balance in the sacred pattern of life. I had tipped the scales too far, and it was time for me to put it right.

The day had dawned crisp, the sunlight thin, but bright; the chill east wind tingled the nostrils with the fresh scent of snow. Yes, I thought as I came upon the vacant site, it was time to cease work for the winter. I dismounted, and walked around, inspecting the excavations, waiting for Huel and his builders to arrive.

Despite the incessant delays, we had made good progress on the construction: a shallow weir had been dug and lined with stone; the foundations, both timber and stone, for the mill house had been established. In the spring, we would quarry the huge grindstones, and set them in place—the mill house would be raised around them. The wheel would be built and then the shafts and gears attached. If all went well, I reflected, the mill would be ready to grind its first grain by harvest time next year.

Preoccupied with these plans, I wandered around the diggings and slowly became aware of a peculiar sound, faint and far away, but distinct in the crisp autumn air: a slow, rhythmic thump—like stones falling onto the earth at regular intervals. What is more, I realized with a start that I had been hearing it for some time.

I glanced quickly towards the ridge trail, but saw no one. I held myself completely still and listened. But the sound was gone now. Intrigued, I remounted my horse and rode up the slope of the ridge and into the wood. I paused to listen. There was nothing but the whisper of the wind in bare branches.

Turning away, I thought I heard the soft thudding pat of running steps on the path ahead—just a hint and then the wind stole the sound away again. Raising myself in the saddle, I called out, "Who is it?" I paused. No answer came. I shouted again, more loudly, "Who is there?"

Lifting the reins, I rode forward, slowly, through the close-grown pines and came upon one of the many tracks leading to the top of the ridge. Following the track, I gained the ridgeway and proceeded along the top of the ridge. Almost at once, I came upon a footprint in the damp earth. The print appeared fresh—at least, rain had not degraded it overnight; a swift search revealed a few more leading into the wood.

I turned from the trail, proceeding cautiously towards the edge of the ridge, and immediately came upon an enormous heap of timber: fallen branches and logs fetched from the wood and thrown into a pile at the very edge of the ridge. The place was well chosen, screened from the trail behind by the trees, yet open to the valley beyond. There was no sign of anyone about, so I dismounted and walked to the woodpile.

Scores of footprints tracked the damp earth, and on closer scrutiny I observed the prints of at least three different people. The immense size of the heap astonished me. It was the work of many days—or many hands. Either way, I did not like it. An intruder had raised a beacon on our very threshold.

I whirled from the beacon-heap and vaulted into the saddle. I snapped the reins and urged my mount to speed, skirted the beacon, and galloped along the ridgeway until I reached a place where I could look down on either side of the ridge: on one side, the valley with its brown fields and the long slate-grey lake with the crannog in the center; on the other side, the gravemound beside the river, and the empty plain spreading beyond.

I released my breath through clenched teeth. I had half-expected to see Meldron's massed war host, risen again, streaming into the valley. But all was still and silent.

Even so, I sat in the saddle for a time, looking and listening. The clouds shifted and the light dimmed. A cold, misty rain began drizzling out of the darkening sky. The wind caught it and sent it swirling. I turned away from the ridgeway and started back down the trail to the lake. I had almost reached the lake path when I met the workmen coming up to the mill.

"Go back to your families," I told them. "Sollen has begun; it is time we took our ease."

The workmen were much relieved to hear me say this. So it surprised me to have Huel instantly appeal against the decision. "Lord," said my master-builder, "allow us but one more day to secure the site against the snows to come. It will save much labor when the sun returns and work resumes."

"Very well," I told him. "Do what you think best. But after today there will be no more work until Gyd."

Leaving them to continue on their way, I returned to the crannog. Tegid was standing at the hearth in the hall, and I sent Emyr to fetch Bran. The bard noticed my agitation at once. "What has happened?" he asked.

I thrust my hands towards the fire. My silver hand glowed with the light of the flames, and my flesh hand began to warm. I looked at the gleaming silver, cold and stiff as a chunk of ice on the end of my arm. Why was it so cold?

"Llew?" Tegid placed a hand on my shoulder.

"There is a beacon on the ridge." I turned to regard him. His dark eyes were intense, but he showed no other sign of alarm. "It is on the ridgeway above the mill."

"Did you see anyone?"

"Not a soul. But I heard a sound—wood thrown onto the heap, I think. And I saw footprints: three men at least, maybe more. Someone has gone to a great deal of effort, Tegid."

Bran arrived just then, and I repeated what I had just told Tegid. The bard stared at the flames, stroking his chin. Bran scowled as he listened and, when I had finished, said, "I will take the warband and search the woods and ridge. If the footprints are fresh, the men cannot have travelled far. We will find those who have done this and bring them back to face you."

The Chief Bard continued to gaze into the flames. Bran was waiting for an answer. "Yes," I told him. "Raise the warband at once. We will begin at the beacon—"

Tegid raised his head. "It is not for you to go," he said softly. I started to object, but he gave a slight shake of his head; he did not like to contradict me in front of Bran. Recalling our previous discussion concerning kings chasing criminals, I understood his hesitation and relented.

"Ready the men," I commanded, and told him where to find the beacon. "You can start there." The Chief Raven gave his assent and made to turn away. I caught him by the sleeve. "Find them, Bran. Track them down, and bring them to me. I would know who has done this and why."

A moment later Bran's voice resounded through the hall as he chose the men who were to accompany him. A group numbering twenty or so left the hall at once—to startled speculation all around.

Turning once more to Tegid, I said, "I will ride with them only as far as the beacon." The bard turned his eyes from the fire and regarded me with a sceptical look. "What are you thinking?" I asked.

"You say it is a beacon," he said. "Why?"

"I know a beacon-pile when I see one, brother."

"That I do not doubt," he replied quickly. "But you assumed an enemy had made it."

"You think otherwise?"

"I think you have not told me all." He had not raised his voice, but his gaze grew keen and accusing. "If there is something I should know, tell me now."

"I have told you all I know—just as it happened," I began, but he cut me off with an impatient twitch of his mouth. I stared hard at him. Why was he behaving like this?

"Think!"

"I am thinking, Tegid!" My voice echoed in the hall. I bit back the words and clamped my mouth shut. Why did I assume an enemy? A beacon is a signal made to be seen from a distance; a beacon is . . . I looked at my silver hand almost touching the flames, and felt the chill still tingling there. And I remembered the last time I had felt such a chill . . .

Raising my eyes, I said, "You are right, Tegid. It happened so long ago I had forgotten. I did not think it important."

"Perhaps you are right. Tell me now."

With that, I told him about the beacon-fire I had seen on the night we camped on the plain below Druim Vran. "I am sorry, brother," I told him when I had finished. "I should have told you then. But the next day we were home, and I guess I assumed the beacon had been lit for our return, and I forgot about it—until now."

"That is not the reason you did not tell me," he stated flatly. "You allowed your impatience to obscure your judgment. In your eagerness to see Dinas Dwr you did not want to believe anything could be wrong, so you hid this from yourself, and from me."

My Chief Bard was most astute. "I am sorry. It will not happen again."

He dismissed my apology with an impatient gesture. "It is done and cannot be undone."

"So, you think we have been watched since our return?"

"What do *you* think?"

"I think it likely."

"And I think it certain."

"But why?"

"That we will learn when Bran returns with those who have been watching."

So we settled back to wait, and I found the waiting hard. I wanted to be out on the trail with my men, dealing directly with the threat instead of sitting in the hall doing nothing. One day passed, and then another. I kept my misgivings to myself. As the third day waned— and still no word from the tracking party—I voiced my mounting anxiety to Tegid. "They should have returned by now. It has been three days."

He did not look up from the basket of leaves he was sorting into a bowl. "Did you hear me?"

"I heard you." He stopped sifting the leaves and raised his head. He was bothered by Bran's absence, too; I could tell. "What would you have me say?"

"They have run into trouble. We should go after them."

"They are twenty worthy warriors," the bard pointed out. "Bran is more than a match for any encounter. Leave it to him."

"Three days more," I said. "If we have heard nothing by then, I am going after them."

"If we have heard nothing in three days," he agreed, "then you can go after them. And I will ride with you."

Nevertheless, I rode to Druim Vran the next day, just to learn if there was anything to be seen from the high ridgetop. Though cold, the day was bright, the clouds high and white. Goewyn rode with me and, though we pursued the ridgeway east a fair distance, we saw no sign of any trouble.

Before starting back, we paused to rest the horses. Sitting together on a rock overlooking the valley below, a fresh wind stinging cheeks and chin, I draped my cloak around us both and held her close as we watched the mist flowing down the hillsides to blanket the glen.

"We should be getting back," I said, "or Tegid will send the hounds after us."

We made no move, however, content to sit and watch the valley fill with thick, grey mist. The light began to fail at last and, although luxuriating in Goewyn's nearness and warmth, I nevertheless forced myself to stand. "It will be dark soon," I said. "We should head home."

"Mmmm." Goewyn sighed and drew her feet under her, but did not stand.

Moving to the horses, I pulled the tether pegs and gathered the reins. "Llew?" Goewyn said. Her voice struck a note that made me turn at once.

"What is it?"

"There is something moving down there—along the river... in the mist."

In three strides I was by her side and gazing into the quickly fading glen. "I do not see anything," I said. "Are you certain?"

She stretched her arm to point out the place. "There!" she said, without taking her eyes from the spot.

I looked where she was pointing. The mist parted somewhat and I saw what appeared to be three dark shapes moving along the river bank. Whether afoot or on horseback, I could not say. I saw only three swarthy, shapeless bulks moving along the riverside... and then the mist took them from my sight.

"They are coming this way," I concluded. "They are coming to Druim Vran."

"Is it Bran, do you think?"

"I cannot say. But something tells me it is not Bran—or any of those with him."

"Who then?"

"That I mean to find out." I reached a hand down to Goewyn and pulled her to her feet. "Ride back to Dinas Dwr and alert Tegid and Scatha. Tell them to assemble a warband, and show them where to come."

Goewyn clutched my arms. "You are not going down there."

"Yes, but only to keep an eye on our visitors." I squeezed her hand to reassure her. "Do not worry, I will not challenge them. Go now—and hurry."

She did not like to leave me alone, but she did as I bade her. I returned to the lookout and gazed into the valley. I caught a fleeting glimpse of the invaders making their way along the river, before the mist closed over them once more.

Mounting my horse, I rode back along the ridgetop the way we had come; since the trail was high, it remained light enough to see well ahead, but Goewyn was already out of sight. I rode until I reached the main track leading down into the glen and started down, encountering the swirling mist about halfway to the valley floor.

I continued on—almost blind in the shifting, all-enveloping vapor—until I reached the bottom, whereupon I stopped to listen. Everything was dead still, the foggy murk muffled all sound—and yet, I thought that if there was anything to be heard I would hear it quite plainly.

Absolutely motionless, I sat in the saddle, straining forward to catch any stray sound. After a while, I heard the light jingle of horses' tack and the hollow clop of horses' hooves, moving slowly. I could get no sense of the distance, but the sound did not seem close. I lifted the reins and urged my mount forward, very slowly, very quietly.

No more than ten paces further on, however, the mist swirled away and I saw a horseman directly in front of me. Ice water trickled down my neck and spine.

A distance of a spear's throw separated us. I halted. Perhaps he would not see me.

The rider came on; I saw him raise his eyes from the track in front of him. His face was but a shadow under his cloak which was pulled up over his head. His hands jerked the reins and his dark mount halted. He called something over his shoulder to unseen companions behind him. I heard his shout, sharp and urgent, but could not catch the words.

The fog moved in again on the fitful wind, and the rider was taken from sight. But just as the mist stole him from view, I thought I saw him turn his horse and bolt off the trail.

Drawing my sword from its place under the saddle, I took a deep breath. "Stop!" I shouted as loud as I could.

"Stay where you are!" In reply I heard only the quick scramble of hooves as the horse galloped away.

Gripping the sword—and wishing I had brought a spear and shield with me—I rode forward cautiously and stopped at the place where the rider had appeared. He was not there, of course, and I could see but a few paces ahead in any case. I waited for a while, and when I heard nothing more, decided to return to the ridge track to await Scatha and the others. That way, I could guard the track if the riders tried to reach it by going around me.

Wheeling my horse, I made my way back to the place where the trail began to rise to the ridge, and took up my position. Daylight had gone by now, and a murky twilight had settled over the glen. Soon fog and darkness would make it difficult, if not impossible, to ride at all. No doubt this was what the three intruders were counting on. I took some small comfort from the fact that what was difficult for one, was difficult for all. Anything that would hinder me, would hinder them as well; I was as much protected by the fog as they were.

I waited, watching and listening. I do not know how long I sat there—the fog, like damp wool, curled and shifted, obscuring and confusing all senses—but I gradually began to imagine that I heard the sound of horses once again. Because of the mist, I could not yet tell from which direction the sound reached me.

It might be the warband coming to join me, I thought, but they could not have had time enough to gain the ridgetop, much less descend. More likely, the invaders, having satisfied themselves that I had gone, were proceeding once more.

Listening with every fiber in me, holding my breath, I strained into the darkening murk for any sound that would tell me which way they would come. The sound of horses grew steadily louder as the intruders drew nearer. I turned my head this way and that, alert to any nuance of motion.

Then, swimming out of the fog: dimly glowing orbs of light... torches, two of them, no more than twenty paces away. I tightened my grip on my sword and shouted, "Stop! Go no further!"

At once the invaders stopped. The torches hung motionless in the air; I could not see anyone beneath the hanging lights, but I could hear their horses breathing and blowing, and the creak of leather as they waited.

Not wishing to show myself just yet, I continued speaking from where I sat. "Stand easy, friends," I called, "if peace is your desire, your welcome is assured. But if it is a fight you want, you will receive a warmer welcome elsewhere. Get down from your horses."

There was a moment's silence before the intruder replied. I heard the impatient stamp of a hoof, and a voice: "We are peaceful men. But it is not our way to obey commands from any man we cannot see."

"Nor is it my way to greet travellers with a sword," I replied sternly. "Perhaps we both find ourselves in unaccustomed positions. I advise prudence."

There was a further silence in which I heard the hiss and flutter of the torches. And then the voice said, "Llew?"

15

Child-Wealth

"Cynan?"

I heard a muttered command, and the movement of a rider dismounting... quick footsteps approaching... then Cynan's four-square, solid form looming out of the fog. His hair, moustache, and cloak were pearly with beaded mist, and his eyes were wide.

"*Clanna na cù!*" he muttered, relief washing over his ruddy features. "Llew! Is it you, brother?" He glanced around, looking for others. "*Mo anam*, man! Are you alone out here?"

"Greetings, Cynan!" I said, replacing the sword and swinging down from the saddle. In two steps I was in his embrace. "I am glad to see you."

"A strange welcome this—if welcome it is." He turned to those with him, a party of ten or so, waiting silently on the trail. "Tángwen! Gweir! It is Silver Hand himself come to greet us!" he called to them.

"If I had known it was you," I told him, "I would have ordered a thousand torches to light your way."

"Who did you think it would be?" he asked, concern quickly giving way to bewilderment. "And what do you think you are doing out on the trail alone, challenging travellers at swordpoint?"

I told him of the intruders Goewyn and I had seen in the valley, and I asked if he had seen anyone.

"Have I seen anyone?" he chuckled, gesturing to the all-obscuring fog. "Man, I have not even seen my own face in front of me since entering the valley. Is it worthwhile searching for them, do you think?"

"We would never find them in this stew. Come along," I turned and started towards my horse, "the fire is bright on the hearth, and the welcome cup awaits! Let us warm ourselves and drink to your arrival." I swung up into the saddle. Cynan still stood looking on. "What? Have you forsworn the bowl?"

"Never say it!" he cried, and hastened back to his mount. He shouted a command to those with him, and I turned my horse and led the way up the trail. We had not ridden far, however, when we were met by Scatha, Goewyn, and a warband of thirty, all carrying torches.

We halted and I explained what had happened. After Goewyn and Scatha had greeted Cynan, Tángwen and their retinue, we continued on our way. The fog thinned as we climbed the ridge, and cleared away completely by the time we reached the top—though the sky remained obscured. It would be a dark night, without moon or stars. I spoke briefly with Scatha and we decided to establish a watch of thirty men in threes along the ridgeway, lest the intruders attempt to cross Druim Vran during the night.

Then we proceeded to the crannog and the hall. Tegid awaited us at the hearth. "Hail, Cynan Two-Torcs! Hail, the beautiful Tángwen!" he announced as we trooped in. I called for the bowl to be brought at once. The hall was crowded, and at Cynan's appearance a chorused cry of welcome went up from all those gathered there.

The bard embraced Cynan warmly, and then turned to Tángwen. She inclined her head, offering only her hands to him. "Greetings, Tegid Tathal," she said, smiling; but the smile, like the greeting, lacked any warmth.

I marked the reaction, but the bowl arrived, frothing with new ale; I took it and pressed it into Cynan's eager hands and the moment passed. Cynan drank deeply and, wiping the creamy foam from his moustache on his sleeve, gave the bowl to his wife. She drank, and passed the bowl on to Gweir, Cynan's battlechief. "Thank you," she said in a low voice.

"I have missed you, my friend," said Goewyn throwing off her damp cloak. She gathered Tángwen in her arms and the two women exchanged kisses.

"And it is good to see you," Tángwen replied. "I have been looking toward this day for a long time." She stretched her hands towards the fire, but I noticed that she still held herself as if she were cold. The rigors of the trail, no doubt—the cold and foul weather had put her on edge.

"We would have arrived earlier," Cynan put in, "but the mist slowed us. Still, I did not care to spend another night on the trail."

"Well, you are here now," Goewyn said, taking Tángwen's cloak from her shoulders. "Come, we will find you some dry clothes."

The women withdrew, leaving us to dry ourselves at the hearth. "Ah, this is good," sighed Cynan. "And here was I thinking we would never arrive."

"I had forgotten you were coming," I confessed.

Cynan threw back his head and laughed. "That I could readily see. Here is Silver Hand, guarding the trail with his sword, challenging all comers. Could you not see it was me, man?"

"Obviously, if I had seen it was you, Cynan," I replied, "I would have let you wander lost in the fog."

"The fog! Do not talk to me about the fog!" he said, rolling his eyes.

"It must be fierce indeed, if it daunts the renowned Two-Torcs," observed Tegid.

"Is that not what I am saying? This cursed mist has dogged us for days. I almost turned back because of it. But then I thought of your excellent ale, and so I asked myself, "Cynan Machae, why spend the season of snows in your own draughty hall, alone and lonely, when—"

"When you could be drinking Llew's ale instead!" I finished the thought for him; he regarded me with a deeply wounded look.

"Tch! The thought never entered my head," Cynan scolded. "It is your friendship I crave, brother, not the fellowship of your vat.

Although, now that you say it, your brewmaster is a very man among men." He raised the bowl again and drank deep and long. "Ahh! Nectar!"

"And I have missed you, too," I told him. Seizing the bowl, I raised it to him. "*Sláinte,* Cynan Two-Torcs!" I drained the bowl—there was not much left in it—and called for it to be filled again. One of Tegid's Mabinogi came running with a jar.

"I would hear a good word about your harvest," Tegid said as the bowl was refilled.

"And I would speak a good word if I could," Cynan replied, shaking his head slowly. "Dismal—that is the word. We could not get the grain out of the field for the rain. And then we lost much. But for last year's bounty, we would be looking at a meager planting."

"It is the same with us," I told him. "A good year that ended badly."

Sharing the bowl between us, we fell to talking about all that had happened since we had last seen one another. Goewyn and Tángwen returned to join us; Tángwen was now dressed in clean, dry robes and her hair was combed and dressed. She appeared relaxed; the strained stiffness had left her and she was more herself.

We moved to the table where food had been laid on the board. We began to eat, and I noticed how the two women talked happily to one another all through the meal. The way they talked and laughed together put me in mind of Goewyn with one of her sisters. Raised in the close companionship of Govan and Gwenllian, Goewyn had had no female friend since her sisters were killed.

Scatha entered the hall as we were eating and approached the place where I sat. She bent near to speak a private word. "The watch is established," she reported. "If anyone tries to cross the ridge we will soon know it."

Nothing more was said about this, and indeed I gave it no further thought. The hall was warm and bright—made all the more so by Cynan's arrival—and the conversation lively. I dismissed intruders from my mind.

Nor did I think ill when Goewyn and Tángwen went riding the

next day. The sentries had watched through the night and the ridge remained clear of fog and mist; they had neither seen or heard anyone. And when the mist cleared in the valley there was no trail to be found. So I let the matter go.

Bran and the Raven Flight returned that same day. The watchers on the ridge saw them enter the valley and brought us word of their return. Tegid, Scatha, Cynan and I rode out to meet them; and though they were filthy and tired from their journey they were in good spirits.

"Hail, Bran Bresal!" I called, eager for his news. "I trust you have had good hunting."

"The hunting was excellent," the Raven Chief replied, "but we failed to corner our quarry."

"Most unfortunate," Tegid remarked. "What happened?"

"We found the trail as it left the valley," Bran explained. "Indeed, it was not difficult to follow. But, though we pursued as far and as fast as we could, we never caught sight of those who made it."

"How many were you tracking?" I asked.

"Three men on horseback, lord," a muddy Alun Tringad answered.

"Tell us everything now," suggested Tegid. "Then we will have no need to speak of it within the hall."

"Gladly," replied Bran, "but there is little enough to tell." He went on to explain how they had followed the trail east all the way to the coast before losing it on the rocky strand. They had ranged north and south along the coast for a time without raising the trail again or seeing any sign of an invader, and so at last turned back. "I hoped to bring you better word, lord," Bran told me.

"You have returned safely," I said. "I am well content."

The days dwindled down, growing colder and darker as if Sollen cramped and compacted them with an icy grip. But the hall remained snug and warm and alive with harpsong and fine companionship. We played games and listened to the old tales; we ate, drank, and took our ease, filling the long cold nights with laughter and light.

The lake froze and the children of the crannog played on the ice. It was on one of those rare days, when the sun flared like a fiery gem in a blue-white sky, that we went out to watch the youngsters. A good many had carved strips of bone and tied them to their buskins. The simple skates worked extremely well, and everyone cheered to see the antics of these intrepid skaters.

Cynan, enraptured by the gliding forms, strolled out onto the frozen lake and allowed himself to be cajoled into trying the skates. He cut such a comical figure that others took to the ice, eager to outdo him, if not in skill, then in absurdity. It was not long before there were more skaters than spectators.

We slipped and slid over the ice, falling over ourselves, and improvising silly dances. A gaggle of young girls clustered around Goewyn, beseeching her to try the bone skates, too. She quickly assented and tied the strips to her feet, then, holding out her hand to me, she said, "Take my hand! I want to fly!"

I took her hand and pulled her around the windswept ice—laughing, her lips and cheeks red from the cold, her golden hair and blue-checked cloak flying. The sound of her laughter, and that of all the other skaters, bubbled up as from a fountain, sun-splashed and lavish, a hymn to the day.

Around and around we twirled, stopping only to catch our breath and collapse into one another's arms. The sun shone bright on the silver lake, and set the snow-crusted hilltops glittering like high-heaped diamond hoards. Such beauty, such joy—it made the heart ache to see it, to feel it.

Cynan's frolics, loudly embellished and featuring spectacular falls, carried the day. We laughed so hard the tears flowed down our cheeks. Nevertheless, I could not help but notice that of all those who had come to watch, only Tángwen refused to join in the fun. Instead, she stood on the boat landing with her arms crossed beneath her cloak and a pained look on her face.

"I think someone does not appreciate our sport," I whispered to Goewyn as I lifted her from her latest spill.

Catching my gaze, Goewyn turned to observe her friend standing alone on the landing. "No," she said slowly, "it is something else."

"Do you know?"

She took my hand and pressed it. "Not now. Later," she said, putting her face close to mine. Goewyn slipped her arms around my neck and pulled me close. "Come here."

A directness in her tone aroused my curiosity. "What?" Her eyes sparkled and her lips curved prettily. "What is it?" I asked suspiciously. "What are you hiding?"

"Well, it will not remain hidden for long. The king's wealth is increasing. Soon everyone will know." She released me and pressed a hand to her stomach.

"Wealth? Child-wealth?" She laughed at my surprise. "A baby! We are going to have a baby!" I threw my arms around her and hugged her tight—then remembered myself and released her, lest I crush the tiny life growing within her. "When? How long have you known?"

"Long enough," she said. "I was waiting for the right moment to tell you, but... well, it is such a splendid day I could not wait any longer."

"Oh, Goewyn, I love you." I put my hand behind her head, held her, and kissed her long and hard. "I love you, and I am glad you did not wait. I am going to tell everyone—now!"

"Shh!" she said, laying her fingertips on my lips. "Not yet. Let it be our secret for a few days."

"But I want to tell."

"Please—just a little while."

"At the solstice then," I suggested. "We will have a celebration like the one last year at Cynan's wedding. And in the middle of the feast we will make our announcement. Does anyone else know?"

"No one," she assured me. "You are the first."

"When will it be—the birth, I mean? When will the child be born?"

Goewyn smiled, stepped into my embrace, kissed me and put her cheek against my neck. "You will have your wife a while longer. The child will be born in Maffar—before Lugnasadh, I think."

"A fine time to be born!" I announced. "Goewyn, this is wonderful! I love you so much!"

"Shh!" she cautioned. "Everyone will hear you." She stepped backward, sliding away on the bone-skates. Holding out her hands to me she called, "Come away, best beloved! I will teach you to fly!"

We flew, and the day sped from us. Short, but brilliant in its perfection, it faded quickly: a spark fanned to life in the midst of gathering darkness. It illumined our hearts with its brave radiance and then succumbed to onrushing night.

As the sun sank below the rim of hills, festooning the sky with streamers of rose and scarlet, a few sickly stars were already glowing in a black eastern sky. Night was spreading over Albion. Dazzled by my love for Goewyn, I saw the darkness and knew it not.

That night we left the hall early. Goewyn took my hand and led me to our bed, now piled high with furs and fleeces against the cold. She loosened her belt and unwound it, then drew her mantle over her head and stood before me. Taking up the cup she had placed beside the fire-ring, she drank, watching me all the while. Her eyes never left mine.

Her body, caressed by the rushlight, was a vision of softly-rounded, intimately melding curves, beguiling, bewildering in its smooth subtlety. She stepped toward me, reached out and tugged the end of my belt free, loosened it, and let it fall. She drew me to her; I felt her body warm against me and, taking a handful of her hair, I held her head and kissed her open mouth. I tasted the rich warmth of honeyed mead on her tongue and passion leapt like a flame within me. I abandoned myself to the heat.

We shared the golden mead and made love that night in celebration of the child to be. The next day Goewyn was gone.

16

The Search

I rose early, but Goewyn had already wakened and dressed. She came to the bed-place, leaned over, kissed me, and said, "I did not want to wake you."

"What are you doing?" I asked, taking her hand and pulling her down on me. "Come back to bed—both of you."

"I promised to go with Tángwen," she said.

"Oh," I yawned. "Where are you going?"

"Riding."

"Would you abandon your husband in his cold, lonely bed? Come back and wait until the sun rises at least."

She laughed and kissed me again. "It will be light soon enough. Sleep now, my love, and let me go."

"No." I raised my hand and stroked the side of her neck. "I will never let you go."

She nuzzled the hand and then took it and kissed the palm. "Tángwen is waiting."

"Take care, my love," I said as she left. I lay in our bed for a while, then rose, dressed quickly and went out. The night-black sky was fading to blue-grey and the stars were dim; away over the encircling hills to the east the sky blushed with blood-red streaks like slashes in pale flesh. There was no one in the yard; smoke from the cookhouses rose in a straight white column. I shivered with the cold and hurried across the yard to the hall.

The hall was quiet, but a few people were awake and stirring. The hearthfire had been stoked and I walked to it to warm myself. Neither Goewyn nor Tángwen was to be seen, no doubt intending to break fast when they returned from their ride.

Garanaw wakened and greeted me, and we talked until the oatcakes came out of the oven and were brought steaming into the hall. Seating ourselves at the board, we were quickly joined by Bran and a few early-rising Ravens, and some of Cynan's retinue. Cynan himself arrived a short time later, noisily greeting everyone and settling himself on the bench. The oatcakes were hot and tasty; we washed them down with rich brown ale.

Talk turned to hunting, and it was quickly agreed that a day spent in pursuit of deer or boar would be a day well spent. "We will savor our supper all the more for the chase," Cynan declared; to which Alun quickly added, "And we will relish the chase all the more for a wager."

"Do my ears deceive me?" wondered Cynan loudly. "Is that Alun Tringad offering his gold?"

"If you can bring back a bigger stag than the one I shall find, then you are welcome to the champion's portion of my gold."

"I would be ashamed to take your treasure so easily," quipped Cynan. "And I never would, were it not advisable to teach you a valuable lesson in humility."

"Then put your hand to it," Alun told him, "and let us choose the men to ride with us. The sooner we ride, the sooner I will claim my treasure. Indeed, I can already feel the weight of your gold bracelets on my arm."

"Unless you hope to lull me to sleep with your empty boasting," Cynan said, "you will soon see a hunter worthy of his renown. Therefore, I advise you to look your last upon your treasure."

Alun stood and called to his brother Ravens, "Brothers, I have heard enough of this haughty fellow's idle talk. Let us show him what true hunters can do, and let us decide now how to divide his treasure among us."

Cynan also stood. "Llew, ride with me, brother," he said, and he called others of his retinue by name. "Come, my friends, the chase is before us, and much good gold for our efforts."

They fixed the time for their return: "At sunset we will assemble in the yard," Alun suggested.

Cynan agreed. "And the Penderwydd of Albion will judge between us who has fared the better—although this will not be necessary, for it will be readily apparent to one and all which of us is the best hunter."

"True, true," Alun affirmed casually. "That they will easily discern."

I glanced quickly around, but Tegid had not entered the hall. It did not matter, there would be time to talk to him later, when we returned from the hunt. The hall buzzed with eager voices as side wagers were laid, odds fixed, and amounts agreed. Snatching up the last of the oatcakes, we burst from the hall and hastened across the ice-bound lake to the cattle pens to fetch the horses. We saddled our mounts and, with much friendly banter, rode out along the frozen lakeside.

Cynan and I led the way, following the hoof tracks Tángwen and Goewyn had left in the new snow. Halfway to the wood, the track left the lakeside, leading away to the ridge. We continued around the lake, however, to the game runs on the long slopes. As soon as we entered the wood, we divided our number—those who rode with Alun went one way, and those of Cynan's party the other.

The sun rose above the rim of the hills and the day was good. There was snow on the game runs, but because of the trees it was not deep. We saw the tracks of scores of animals, but as it had not snowed for several days it was impossible to tell which were fresh and which were older.

We spread ourselves across the run and proceeded deeper into the silent sanctuary of the forest, our spears along our thighs as we pushed through the underbrush. The shadows of the trees formed a blue latticework on the crusted snow. The cold air tingled on the skin of my cheeks, nose and chin. I had spread my cloak around me to

173

capture the heat of the horse and help keep me warm. With a bright, white sun, a clear blue sky, and the company of valiant men, it was a fine day to hunt.

I let those most eager take the lead and settled back to enjoy the ride. We followed the long run as it lifted towards the ridge: crossing a small stream we scared a red deer sheltering in a blackthorn thicket. The hounds would have given chase, but Cynan was after bigger game, and forced them back onto the trail. His patience was rewarded a short time later when we came upon the fresh spoor of a small herd of deer.

"It is still warm," announced Cynan's man as I joined them.

"Good," Cynan said. "Be alert, everyone. The prize is near."

We continued at a swifter pace and soon sighted the deer: three hinds and a big stag. The hounds did not wait to be called back a second time, but sounded the hunting cry and sped to the chase. The stag regarded the dogs with a large, inscrutable, dark eye, then lifted his regal head and belled a warning call to his little clan.

The hinds lifted their tails and bounded as one into the thicket. Only when they were away did the stag follow. Rather than try to force a way through the tangle, we let the dogs run and gave ourselves to the chase.

A glorious chase! The old stag proved a cunning opponent and led us a long and elaborate hunt—through deep woods and up along the high ridge and down again into piney forest. We caught him, in the end, with his back to a stony outcrop at the foot of the ridgewall. His clan had escaped, and he was near dead from exhaustion. Still, he turned and fought to the last.

The sun was little more than a day moon, pale and wan on the horizon, when we finished securing the stag to a litter and turned our horses for home. We had travelled far afield in our fevered pursuit. We were tired, and cold where the sweat had soaked our clothes, but well content with our sport, and hopeful of winning the wager. A fine and regal spectacle of a sky washed pale lavender and gold in a brilliant Sollen sunset greeted us as we emerged from the woods and began making our way along the lake.

Alun Tringad's party had returned ahead of us, and they were waiting for us at the cattle pen when we arrived. Their kill—two fine bristle-backed boars—lay on the snow outside the pen. At the sight of our stag, they began exclaiming over our lack of success.

"One lonely deer, is it?" cried Alun, foremost in the gathering. "With all you hardy men on horseback shaking your spears at it, why, I do not doubt this poor sickly thing expired in fright."

"As sickly as it is," Cynan replied, swinging down from the saddle, "our stag will yet serve to separate you from your treasure." He regarded the wild pigs with a sad, disappointed air. "Oh, it is a shameful thing you have done, Alun, my man—taking these two piglets from their mother. Tch! Tch!" He shook his head sadly. "Why not just give the gold to me now and save yourself the disgrace of having your skill revealed in such a pitiful light?"

"Not so fast, Cynan Machae," replied one of Alun's supporters. "It is for the Chief Bard to tell us who has won the wager. We will await his decision."

"Hoo!" said Cynan, puffing out his cheeks, "bring Tegid by all means. I was only trying to save you the fearful humiliation I see coming your way."

At first sight of our party on the lakeside track, Alun had sent a man to fetch Tegid. A call from one of Cynan's men directed our attention to the crannog. "Here he comes now!" shouted Gweir. "The Penderwydd is coming!"

I turned to see a crowd from the crannog hurrying across the ice towards us. I looked for Goewyn, expecting to see her among them, but neither Goewyn nor Tángwen was there. No doubt they had decided to stay in the warm. Nor did I fault them; I had long been wishing myself out of my sodden clothes and holding a warming jar beside the fire.

A genial hubbub arose as the throng arrived. Everyone exclaimed at the sight of the game, extolling the prowess of the hunters and the success of the hunt—as well they might, for we would eat heartily on the proceeds of our effort for many days.

"Penderwydd!" Alun shouted. "The hunt is finished. Here is the result of our labors. As you can see, we have done well. Indeed, we have bested Cynan and his band, which is clear for all to see. It only remains for you to agree and confirm the inevitable decision."

The Chief Bard withdrew a hand from his cloak and raised it. "That I will do, Alun Tringad. What is clear to you may not be so clear to those who lack your zeal for Cynan's gold. Therefore, step aside and allow someone with an eye unclouded by avarice to view the evidence."

Tegid examined first Alun's kill and then Cynan's. He prodded the carcasses with a toe, inspected the pelts, teeth, tusks, eyes, hoofs, tails, and antlers. All the while, the two parties baited one another with quips and catcalls, awaiting the bard's decision. The bard took his time, pausing now and then to muse over this or that point which he pretended to have discovered, or which had been pointed out to him by the extremely partisan crowd.

Then, taking his place midway between the stag and the two boars, and frowning mightily, he rested chin upon fist in earnest contemplation. All this served to heighten the anticipation; wagers were doubled and then tripled as—from the slant of an eyebrow or the lift of a lip—one side or the other imagined opinion swaying in their favor.

At last, the Chief Bard drew himself up and, raising his staff for silence, prepared to deliver his decision. "It is rightly the domain of the king to act as judge for his people," he reminded everyone. "But as the king took part in the hunt, I beg his permission to deliver judgment." He looked to me.

"I grant it gladly," I replied. "Please, continue."

The crowd shouted for the Chief Bard to proclaim the winner, but Tegid would not be hurried. Placing a fold of his cloak over his head, he said, "I have weighed the matter carefully. From the time of Dylwyn Short-Knife," here the spectators groaned with frustration, but Tegid plowed ahead slowly, "and the time of Tryffin the Tall, it has been in the nature of things to hold the life of a stag equal to that of a bear, and that of a bear equal to two boars." The groan turned from impatience to frustration as the crowd guessed what was coming. "It would appear then," Tegid calmly continued, "that a stag is equal to two boars. Thus, the matter cannot be settled according to the quantity of meat, and we must look elsewhere for a resolution."

He paused to allow his gaze to linger around the ring of faces. There were murmurs of approval, and mutters of protest from many. He waited until they were silent once more. "For this reason I have examined the beasts most carefully," Tegid said. "This is my decision." The throng held its breath. Which would it be? "The stag is a worthy rival and a lord of his kind..."

At this, Cynan's party raised a tremendous shout of triumph.

"But," Tegid quickly cautioned, "the boars are no less lordly. And what is more, there are two of them. Were this not so, I would hold for the stag. Yet, since the difficulty of finding and bringing down *two* such noble and magnificent beasts must necessarily try the skills of the hunter the more, I declare that those who hunted the boars have won this day's sport. I, Tegid Tathal, Penderwydd, have spoken."

It took a moment to unravel what the Chief Bard had said, but then all began wrangling over the decision. Cynan appealed to the beauty of his prize and to various other merits, but Tegid would not be moved: Alun Tringad had won the day. There was nothing for it, the losers must pay the winners. Tegid thumped his staff three times on the ground and the matter was ended.

We returned to the warmth and light of the hall, eager for meat and drink to refresh us, and tales of the hunt to cheer us. Upon entering the hall, I quickly scanned the gathering. Goewyn was nowhere to be seen. I turned on my heel and hastened to our hut.

It was dark and empty, the ashes in the fire-ring cold. She had not been there for some time, perhaps not since early morning. I ran back to the hall and made my way to Tegid; he was standing at one end of the hearth, waiting for the ale jar to come his way.

"Where is Goewyn?" I asked him bluntly.

"Greetings, Llew. Goewyn? I have not seen her," he replied. "Why do you ask?"

"I cannot find her. She went riding with Tángwen this morning."

"Perhaps she is—"

"She is not in the hut." My eyes searched the noisy hall. "I do not see Tángwen, either."

Without another word, Tegid turned and beckoned Cynan to join us. "Where is Tángwen?" the bard said.

I looked at Cynan anxiously. "Have you seen her since this morning?"

"Seen her?" he wondered, raising his cup. He drank and then offered the cup to me. "I have been on the trail since daybreak, as you well know."

"Goewyn and Tángwen went riding this morning," I explained, holding my voice level, "and it appears they have not returned."

"Not returned?" Cynan looked towards the door, as if expecting the two women to enter at that moment. "But it is dark now."

"That is the least of our worries," I said, "if something has happened—"

"If they are here, someone will have seen them," Tegid interrupted calmly. The bard stepped away. A moment later he was standing on the table, his staff upraised. "Kinsmen! Hear me! I must speak with Goewyn and Tángwen. Quickly now! Who can tell me where to find them?"

He waited. People looked at one another and shrugged. Some inquired among themselves, but no one offered any information. Clearly, no one could remember seeing either of the women. Tegid asked again, but received no answer. He thanked the people for their attention, and returned to where Cynan and I waited.

"We will search the crannog," he said. Although he spoke quietly, I could tell the bard was worried. This did nothing to soothe my mounting anxiety.

And then one of the serving maids came to where we stood. "If you please, lords," she said, clutching the beer jar tightly, "I have seen Queen Goewyn."

"Where?" I did not mean to be curt with the young woman. "Please, speak freely."

"I saw the queen in the yard," she said.

I started for the door. Tegid caught me by the arm. "When was this?" he said; the maid hesitated. "Speak up," he snapped. "When did you see her?"

"Early this morning," the maid said, her voice quivering. She realized, I think, that this was not at all what we wanted to hear. "They were laughing as they walked—the two of them, the queen and Queen Tángwen. I think they were leaving the crannog to go riding."

"It would have been dark still," Cynan said. "Are you certain?"

"Yes, lord," the maiden said. "I know who I saw."

"And Tángwen was with her?" Cynan pursued.

"Yes, lord."

"Thank you, Ailla," I said, recognizing the young woman at last; she often served as one of Goewyn's handmaids.

Tegid dismissed her then, and said, "Now we will search the crannog."

On our way from the hall, Tegid snared Gwion, his foremost Mabinog, and whispered something in the boy's ear. Gwion nodded once, and darted through the door ahead of us.

We searched, the three of us, each taking a section of the crannog. It did not take long. I ran from house to house, smacking my silver hand on the doorposts to alert those within, then thrusting my head inside. Most of the huts were empty—the people had gathered in the hall—and in those that were occupied, none of the residents had seen either woman. I also looked in the storehouses. As I hurried to rejoin the others at the hall, I knew that Goewyn was not in Dinas Dwr.

Upon returning to the hall, I met Tegid standing at the entrance with Gwion Bach beside him. "It is not good," Tegid told me bluntly. "I sent Gwion to the stables. Their horses have not returned."

My heart sank and my stomach tightened. "Then something has happened."

Cynan approached, and I could tell from the way he walked—head down, shoulders bunched—that he had discovered nothing and was now more than concerned. "The trail will be difficult," he said, wasting no time. "We will need a supply of torches and a change of horses. I will summon my warband."

"The Ravens will ride with us," I said. "Drustwn can follow a trail even in the dark. I will ready the horses. Go now. Bring them. And hurry!"

17

Night Ride

We took up the trail at the place where I had seen it diverge from the lakeshore track. By torchlight the horses' hoofprints showed a staggered black line across the wide expanse of snow.

Across the valley floor we galloped, thirty strong, including Cynan, myself and the Raven Flight. Tegid stayed behind. He would order matters at Dinas Dwr while we were away and uphold us in our search.

I wrapped the reins around my metal hand and clutched the torch with my flesh hand. The torchflame fluttered in the wind above my head, red sparks sailing out behind me as I raced over the undulating snow. The cold air stung my cheeks and eyes; my lips burned. But I did not stop so much as to draw my cloak over my chin. I would not stop until Goewyn was safely beside me once more.

Upon reaching the heights of Druim Vran the trail became thin and difficult to see. The wind had scoured most of the snow from the ridgetop, but some remained in the sheltered places, and we proceeded haltingly from patch to patch where we could find hoofprints.

It appeared they had ridden eastwards along the ridgeway. The day was good. They had moved toward the rising sun. I imagined the two women making their way happily along Druim Vran with the silver-bright dawnlight in their eyes. We, however, followed in Sollen's deep dark, a starless void above; no moon lit our way. The only light we had was that which fluttered in our hands, and that was fitful indeed.

I refused to allow myself to think about what might have happened to them. I pushed all such thoughts from my mind and held one only: Goewyn would be found. My wife, my soul, would be returned unharmed.

Drustwn pushed a relentless pace. He seemed to know where the tracks would lead and found them whenever he paused to look. Thus we followed the Raven's lead along the ridgeway—deep, deep into the dark Sollen depths on our night ride. We rode without speaking, urgent to our task.

Nor did we stop until the trail turned down into the glen. The facing slope was clear of snow, and though we spread ourselves along the brush-covered decline, we could not recover the trail in the dark. In the end, we dismounted to search the long downward slope on foot.

"It may be that we can find the trail again in the morning," Drustwn suggested when we halted at the bottom of the glen to confer. "It is too easily missed on bare ground."

"My wife is gone. I will not wait until morning."

"Lord," Drustwn said, his face drawn in the torchlight, "daylight is not long away."

At these words I raised my head. Drustwn was right, the sky was already paling in the east. Night had passed me in a blur of torchlight on glittering snow.

"What do you advise?" I asked.

"It is no good thrashing around in the dark. We could destroy the trail without knowing it. Let us rest until there is light enough to see."

"Very well," I agreed. "Give the order. I will speak to Cynan."

Drustwn's call rang out behind me as I wheeled my horse and started back up the line. Cynan had been riding to the right of me when I had last seen him. Several of his men passed me, hurrying to

Drustwn's call. I saw Gweir and asked him where Cynan was, and he pointed to two torches glimmering a little distance away. Cynan and Bran were talking together as they rode to where Drustwn waited. I reined in beside them. "Why has he stopped?" Cynan asked. "Have you found something?"

"We have lost the trail," I answered. "There is no point in going further until sunrise."

"Then it is best we halt," Bran replied.

"No," I told him tersely, "finding them would be best. But this is all we can do now."

"It has been a cold night," Cynan fretted. "They were not prepared."

I made no reply, but at Cynan's remark I realized that I had not considered the women having to spend the night on the trail. It had not occurred to me because I did not for an instant believe that they had merely lost their way. It was possible, of course, but the likelihood of intruders on Druim Vran had led me to assume otherwise.

Now Cynan's words offered a slender hope. Perhaps they had merely wandered too far afield and been forced to shelter on the trail for the night, rather than try to find Dinas Dwr in the dark. Perhaps, one of the horses had been injured, or... anything might have happened.

We continued to where Drustwn and most of the other riders were now waiting. They had quickly gathered brush from the slope and had a fire burning. Others were leading horses to a nearby brook for water. I dismounted and gave my horse to one of the warriors to care for and, wrapping myself in my cloak, sat down on a frost-covered stone.

Shivering in the cold while waiting for the sun to rise, I remembered the beacon. I rose at once. "Alun!" I shouted. "Alun Tringad! Come here!"

A moment later, Alun was standing before me. He touched the back of his hand to his forehead. "Lord?"

"Alun," I said, laying my hand to his arm, "do you recall the beacon we found on the ridge?"

"I do, lord."

"Go to it. Now. And return with word of what you find."

He left without another word, riding back up the slope to the ridgeway. I returned to the rock and sat down again. Dawnlight seeped into a grey-white sky. Darker clouds sailed low overhead, shredding themselves on the hilltops as they passed. Away to the north, white-headed mountains showed above the cloudline. The wind rose with the sun, gusting out of the east. Likely, there would be snow before day's end, or sleet.

I grew restless, rose, and remounted my horse. "It is light enough to see," I told Drustwn bluntly.

Bran, standing with him, said, "Lord Llew, allow us to search out the trail and summon you when we have found it."

"We ride together." I snapped the reins and turned to the slope once more.

We were still searching for the trail when Alun returned. Cynan was with me, and Alun seemed reluctant to speak in front of him. "What did you find, man?" I demanded.

"Lord," he said, "the beacon has been lit."

"When?"

"Impossible to tell. The ashes were cold."

Cynan's head whipped toward Alun at the news. "What beacon?"

I told him quickly about the beacon-pile I had found on the ridge. "It has been burnt," I said.

His jaw bulged dangerously. "*Clanna na cù!*" he rasped through clenched teeth. "Beacons on the ridge and strangers in the glen—and we let them go riding alone!"

He did not blame me for my lack of vigilance, but he did not need to; I felt the sting of his unspoken accusation all the same. How could I have let it happen?

"We will find them, brother," I said.

"Aye, that we will," he growled, slapping the reins against the neck of his mount. He rode off alone.

As if in answer to Cynan's gruff affirmation, there came a blast on the carynx. Drustwn had found the trail. We raced to the place and took up the chase again. The sun was well up and the morning speeding as if on wings. The tracks led across the glen. After we had followed a fair way, it became clear that they had made for the far side of the glen. Why? Had they seen something to entice them on?

Across the glen and up into the low hills beyond, the way was straight; they had ridden directly without turning aside or halting. Why? I wondered. Perhaps they had raced.

I pounced on the idea. Yes, they had raced. That would explain the resolute directness of the trail. I expected that upon reaching the hill, we would find where they had stopped to catch their breath before turning back.

Once across the crest of the first hill, however, this certainty began to fade. The tracks did not alter. The double trail led up the hillside and over—without varying, without stopping.

I paused atop the hill to look back briefly. Druim Vran loomed like a wall behind us, blank and unbreachable, with the glen flat as a floor below. The beacon-fire would have been seen from every hilltop in the realm—though not, I reflected, in Dinas Dwr itself. It might have been lit at any time and we would not have seen it. I turned away and pursued Drustwn's lead, grim urgency mounting within me.

It was in the next valley that we found where the women had stopped.

Drustwn halted, stiffened in the saddle and called Cynan and me to him at once. The rest of the search party were still behind us a little distance. The Raven's eyes were mere slits as he scanned the tracks.

"What have you found?" Cynan demanded.

"They stopped here, lord," he said, stretching a hand towards the marks on the ground.

I looked and saw what had upset him. My heart fell. "How many?" I asked, struggling to keep my voice steady. "How many were there?"

"I make it three or four. Five at most. Not more."

"*Saeth du,*" Cynan muttered. "Five..."

I stared hard at the trampled snow. The confusion of tracks defied explanation. Clearly, the women had met someone. No one had dismounted; there were no footprints among the hoofmarks.

"They rode on that way," Drustwn said, looking to the east. I could see that he was right. I also saw that a decision was required.

I waited until the others had gathered around us, and showed them what Drustwn had discovered. There was much muttering and mumbling over this, but I cut it short. The day was hastening from us. "Garanaw!" I said, calling on the first man to meet my eye. "You, Niall and Emyr will return to Dinas Dwr. Tell Tegid what we have found here, and then gather provisions and supplies. Cynan and I will ride ahead. Make haste and join us as soon as you can."

Cynan was quick to catch the meaning of my words. He immediately ordered Gweir and four of his band to go with the three Ravens to help carry the provisions. He was evidently thinking, as I was, that we might well be on the trail longer than anyone intended. A depressing thought. Neither of us spoke a word of this to the other, however, and as soon as the riders had departed we pressed on.

The muddled tracks soon reconciled themselves: two horses going side-by-side close together—the two women, I assumed—with a rider on either side a little distance apart; one rider to lead the way and another to follow close behind. That was four strangers accounted for. If there were more, we saw no sign.

The trail led eastward, staying on the low ground, winding through the creases between hills rather than crossing them directly. Clearly, they were in no hurry, seeking instead to stay out of sight.

I had no doubt now that the tracks we followed were already a day old. I knew also that we would not find Goewyn and Tángwen sheltering in the heather somewhere, waiting for us to rescue them. They had been taken. Stolen. Abducted.

I still could not face the implications of that. Indeed, I put the thought from me whenever it surfaced, and concentrated instead on pursuing the trail. I would not speculate on what awaited me at the end.

The sallow sun faded as it passed midday and sank towards dusk on its low Sollen arc. We rode on—a long time, I think, because, when I looked again, clouds had closed over the place and the snow that had held off all day began to fall in icy pellets that bounced where they hit.

I imagined the snow striking Goewyn, becoming caught in her hair and eyelashes. I imagined her lips blue and trembling. I imagined her shoulders shaking as she cast anxious glances behind her, searching the empty trail, hoping to see me riding to her rescue.

We stopped at a brook to rest and water the horses. The snow fell in undulating sheets. I knelt and scooped icy water to my mouth, then went to where Cynan stood staring across the narrow strip of black water.

"The tracks continue on the other side," he said, without taking his eyes from the place. "They did not even stop for water."

"No," I said.

"Then we should not stop, either," he snapped. He was worried about Tángwen and the strain was telling on him.

"They have a fair lead on us, brother," I pointed out. "We do not know how long we must ride until we catch them. We must nurse our strength."

He did not like me saying it, but knew I spoke the truth. "How could this happen?" he demanded.

"The blame is mine. I should never have allowed them to go. I was not thinking."

Cynan turned his face towards me; his blue eyes were almost black. "I do not blame you, brother," he said, though his tone was reproach enough. "The deed is done. That is all. Now it must be undone."

When everyone, men and horses, had drunk their fill, we moved on.

The snow stopped just before sundown and the sky cleared slightly in the west. The setting sun flared with a violent red-orange and then plunged behind the lonely hills. The too-short winter day was ended, but we rode on until it grew too dark to see. We made camp in a narrow valley in the windshadow of a broad hill, huddled close to our fires.

We had nothing to eat, so passed a hungry night. It was midday the next day before those who had returned for provisions reached us. By riding through the night, they managed to catch us before sundown. We paused then to eat and feed the horses, before going on.

The trail we pursued led unerringly east. Long before I heard the far-off crash of the sea against the rocky shore I knew the trail would end at the coast. And when, as another sun set on another cold day, we stood on a wind-battered dune looking at the freezing, foam-blown waves, their ceaseless thunder loud in our ears, I knew beyond all doubt that Goewyn no longer remained in Albion.

In the fast-falling twilight, we fanned out along the strand and found tracks in the sand. Hope kindled bright for a moment, but died when we found one of the women's horses: loose, empty-saddled, trailing its reins along the beach. It was Tángwen's horse, and its discovery plunged Cynan into a frenzy of distress.

"Why one horse only?" he demanded, jerking the reins through his fist. "What does it mean?"

"I do not know," I told him. "Perhaps she tried to escape."

"It makes no sense!" he steamed. "None of this makes sense. Even if she tried to escape and they caught her, why would they leave her horse but take the others?" He glared at me as if I were withholding the answers to his questions.

"Brother, I cannot say what happened here. I wish I could."

Too agitated to stand still, he lashed his mount to speed and galloped away along the shore. I was about to follow him up the coast when Drustwn hailed me. He had discovered two long deep grooves in the sand—grooves made by the keels of boats which had been beached above the tideline.

While two of Cynan's men rode to recall their lord, I dismounted and stood over one of the keel-marks and gazed east across the sea towards Tir Aflan. Somewhere beyond those raw waves, hard and dark as slate, my bride awaited rescue.

I turned from the empty sea, my face burning with rage and frustration. Bran Bresal, who had been standing silently beside me, said, "I think they will not be found in Albion."

"Yet, I tell you they *will be found*," I declared. "Send two men back to the crannog. Bring Tegid; I want him with me. Scatha will want to come, but she is to remain to protect Dinas Dwr."

"At once, lord." The Chief Raven wheeled his horse and clattered away over the pebbled shingle.

"Cynan!" I shouted. "Cynan, here!"

A moment later he joined me. "Send men to bring the boats. We will make camp and await them here."

He hesitated, cocking an eye at the sky, and seemed about to gainsay the plan. Instead, he said, "Done."

Cynan wheeled away, calling for Gweir to join him. I pulled the winter fleece covering from my saddle and spread it on the wet shingle. Then, setting my face to the sea as it gnashed the shore, I sat down to begin the long wait.

18

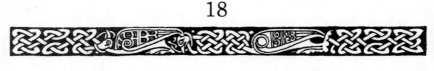

The Geas of Treán ap Golau

We waited three days for the ships to arrive, and then three more. Each day was slow torture. Just after daybreak on the seventh day, four ships arrived from the winter harborage in the south Caledon estuary where Cynan kept them. He commanded the men to stand ready, and then we returned to our camp on the strand to await Tegid's arrival. The bard appeared just before sunset; Scatha, who would not be left behind, rode with him.

"My daughter has been taken," she said by way of greeting, "I mean to aid in her release."

There was no denying her, so I said, "As you will, Pen-y-Cat. May your presence prove a boon to us."

Tegid explained. "As Scatha meant to join us, I summoned Calbha to watch over Dinas Dwr. That is why we could not come sooner."

I was not pleased with this development. "Let us hope your thoughtless delay has not cost the lives of either Goewyn or Tángwen." I turned away and hastened to ready the ships to sail, calling for torches to be lit and for the provisions to be loaded.

"It will be dark soon, and there will be no moon tonight," Bran pointed out, stirring himself from the fretful silence of the last days. "We should wait until morning."

"We have wasted too much time already," Cynan told him. "We sail at once."

Tegid dismounted and hurried to my side. "There is something else, Llew," he said.

"It can wait until we have raised sail."

"You must hear it now," the bard insisted.

I turned on him. "I will hear it when I choose! I have waited on this freezing shore for seven days. Seven days! At this moment I am interested in just one thing: rescuing Goewyn. If what you have to say will accomplish that the quicker, then say it. If not, I do not want to hear it."

Tegid's face became hard; his eyes flashed quick-kindled fire. "And yet you *will* hear it, O Mighty King," he snapped, fighting to control himself.

I made to turn away from him, but he caught me by the wrist of my silver hand and held me. Anger flared hot within me. "Take your hand off me, bard. Or lose it!"

Several bystanders saw what was happening and stopped to watch—Scatha and Cynan among them. Tegid released me, and raised his hand over his head in the way of a declaiming bard.

"Hear me, Llew Llaw Eraint!" he said, spitting the words. "You are Aird Righ of Albion, and thus you are set about by many geasa."

"Taboos? Save your breath," I growled. "I do not care!" I was doubly angry now. He had disobeyed my commands and put us many days behind, and now had the audacity to hinder us further, talking about some ridiculous taboo or other. "My wife is abducted! Cynan's bride is gone! Whatever it takes, I will have them back. Do you understand that? I will give the entire kingdom to obtain their release!"

"The kingdom is not yours to give," the bard declared flatly. "It belongs to the people who shelter beneath your protection. All you possess is the kingship."

"I will not stand here arguing with you, bard. Stay here if that is what you wish. I am leaving."

Holding me with his voice, he said. "I say you cannot go."

I stared at him—speechless with rage.

"The Aird Righ of Albion cannot leave his realm," he announced. "That is the principal geas of your reign."

Had he lost his mind? "What are you saying? I have left before. I have travelled—"

Tegid shook his head, and I grasped his point. Since becoming king, I had never set foot outside Albion's borders. Apparently, this was forbidden me now for some obscure reason. "Explain," I snapped. "And be quick about it."

Tegid simply replied, "It is forbidden the High King to leave the Island of the Mighty—at any time, for any reason."

"Unless I hear a better explanation than that," I told him, "you will soon find yourself standing here alone. I have ordered the ships to sail, and I mean to be aboard the first one when it departs."

"The ships may depart. Your men may depart," he said softly. "But you, O King, may not so much as set foot beyond this shore."

"My *wife* is out there! And I am going to find her." I made to turn away again.

"I say you will not leave Albion and remain Aird Righ," he insisted, emphasizing each word.

"Then I will no longer be king!" I spat. "So be it! One way or another, I am going to find my wife."

If my kingship would bring her back, I would give it a thousand times over. She was my life, my soul; I would give everything to save her.

Scatha stood looking on impassively. I understood now why she had come, and why Tegid had disobeyed my explicit order. She knew that I would not be able to leave Albion, and she assumed that once I understood the problem I would change my mind. But I was adamant.

I glanced at Cynan, who stood pulling his moustache and gazing thoughtfully at me. I raised my hand and pointed at him. "Give the kingship to Cynan," I said. "Let him be Aird Righ."

But Cynan only grunted. "I am going."

"Then give the sovereignty to Scatha," I said.

Scatha also declined. "I am going to find my daughter," she said. "I will not remain behind."

I turned at once to Bran, only to see him reject the offer as well. "My place is by your side, lord," was all he would say.

"Will no one take the kingship?" I demanded. But no eye met mine, and no one answered. It was rapidly growing dark, and I was quickly losing what little remaining dignity I possessed.

Whirling on Tegid as if on an attacker, I said, "You see how it is."

"I see," replied the bard icily. "Now I want *you* to see how it is." With that, he paused, closed his eyes, and took a deep breath. His first words caught me by surprise.

"Treán ap Golau was a king in Albion," Tegid announced. "Three things he had which were all his renown: the love of beautiful women; invincibility in battle; and the loyalty of good men. One thing he had which was his travail: it was the geas of his people that he must never hunt boar. And this is the way of it..."

I glared at him. A story! He meant to tell me a story. I could not believe it. "I do not have time for this, Tegid," I protested.

His head came up, his eyes flew open, and he fixed me with a baleful stare. "One day," he intoned icily, "when the king is out hunting with his warband, there arises a fearful grunting and growling, like that of a wild beast. So great is the noise that it shakes the trees to their roots and the very hills from top to bottom, cracking the rocks and cleaving the boulders. Once, twice, three times, the mighty grunting sounds, each time louder and more terrible than the last.

"King Treán cries to Cet, his wise bard, 'This sound must be silenced, or every living thing in the land will die! Let us find the beast that is causing this din and kill it at once.'

"To this, Penderwydd Cet replies, 'That is more easily said than done, Mighty King. For this sound is made by none other than the Boar of Badba, an enchanted beast without ears or tail, but with tusks the size of your champion's spears and twice as sharp. What is more, it has already killed and eaten three hundred men today, and it is still hungry. This is why it grunts and growls so as to sunder the world.'

193

"When Treán ap Golau hears this he says, 'A boar and a bane it may be, but if I do not stop this beast there will be nothing left of my realm.'

"With that, the king rides to meet the monster and finds it tearing at a broken yew tree to sharpen its tusks. Thinking to take it with the first blow, he charges the Boar of Badba. But the giant pig sees him coming and looses such a horrible growl that the king's horse falls to its knees with fright and Treán is thrown to the ground.

"The enchanted boar charges the fallen king. Treán hefts his spear, takes aim, and lets it fly. Closer and closer drives the boar. The spear flies true, striking the pig in the center of its forehead. But the spear does not so much as crease the boar's thick hide, and it bounces away.

"The boar closes on the king. Treán draws his sword, and slash! Slash! But the solid blade flies to pieces in his hand, while the pig remains unharmed. Indeed, not even a single bristle is cut.

"Down goes the boar's head, and up goes the king. He clings for a moment to the pig's back, but the frenzied beast shakes him off with such a fury that the king is thrown high into the air. The king lands squarely on the yew tree: the splintered trunk pierces his body, and he hangs there, impaled on the yew. And the king dies.

"Seeing this, the Boar of Badba begins to devour the king. The beast tears at the dead king's limbs. He devours the king's right arm and the king's right hand, still clutching the hilt of his shattered sword. The broken blade sticks in the beast's throat, and the Boar of Badba chokes on it and dies.

"The king's companions run to aid the king, but Treán ap Golau is dead." Looking directly at me, Tegid said, "Here ends the tale of King Treán, let him hear it who will."

I shook my head slowly. If, by telling me this tale, he had hoped to discourage me, he would be disappointed. My mind was made up.

"I hear your tale, bard," I told him. "And a most portentious tale it is. But if I must break this geas, so be it!"

Strangely, Tegid relented. "I knew that was what you would say." He paused and, as if to allow me a final chance to change my mind, asked, "Is that your choice?"

"It is."

He bent down and laid his staff on the ground before him, then straightened, his face like stone. "So be it. The taboo will be broken."

The Chief Bard paused and regarded the ring of faces huddled around us in the failing light. Speaking slowly, distinctly, so that none would misunderstand, he said, "The king has chosen, now you must choose. If any man wishes to turn back, he must do so now."

Not a muscle twitched. Loyal to a man, their oaths of fealty remained intact and their hearts unmoved.

Tegid nodded and, placing a fold of his cloak over his head, began speaking in the Dark Tongue. *"Datod Teyrn! Gollwng Teyrn. Roi'r datod Teryn-a-Terynas! Gwadu Teryn. Gwrthod Teryn. Gollwng Teryn."* He ended, turning to face each direction: *"Gollyngdod... gollyngdod... gollyngdod... gollyngdod."*

Retrieving his staff, he proceeded to inscribe a circle around the entire company gathered on the beach. He joined the two ends of the circle together and, returning to the center, drew a long vertical line and flanked it either side with an inclining line to form a loose arrowhead shape—the *gogyrven*, he called it: the Three Rays of Truth. Then he raised the staff in his right hand and drove it into the sand and, taking the pouch from his belt, sifted a portion of the obscure mixture of ash he called the *Nawglan* into each of the three lines he had drawn.

He stood and touched my forehead with the tips of his fingers— marking me with the sign of the gogyrven. Raising his hands palm outward—one over his head, one shoulder high—he opened his mouth and began to declaim:

> *In the steep path of our common calling,*
> *Be it easy or uneasy to our flesh,*
> *Be it bright or dark for us to follow,*
> *Be it stony or smooth beneath our feet,*
> *Bestow, O Goodly-Wise, your perfect guidance;*
> *Lest we fall, or into error stray.*

For those who stand within this circle,
Be to us our portion and our guide;
Aird Righ, by authority of the Twelve:
The Wind of gusts and gales,
The Thunder of stormy billows,
The Ray of bright sunlight,
The Bear of seven battles,
The Eagle of the high rock,
The Boar of the forest,
The Salmon of the pool,
The Lake of the glen,
The Flowering of the heathered hill,
The Strength of the warrior,
The Word of the poet,
The Fire of thought in the wise.

Who upholds the gorsedd, if not You?
Who counts the ages of the world, if not You?
Who commands the Wheel of Heaven, if not You?
Who quickens life in the womb, if not You?
Therefore, God of All Virtue and Power,
Sain us and shield us with your Swift Sure Hand,
Grant us victory over foes and false men,
Lead us in peace to our journey's end.

Through this rite, the bard had sained us—consecrated us and sealed our journey with a blessing. I felt humbled and contrite. "Thank you for that," I said to him.

But Tegid was not finished. He reached into a fold of his belt, withdrew a pale object, and offered it to me. I held out my hand and he gave the object to me. I felt the cool weight in my palm and knew without looking what it was: a Singing Stone. Bless him, he knew I would choose to break the geas in order to save Goewyn, and he meant to do what he could to help me.

"Again, I thank you, brother," I said.

Tegid said nothing, but withdrew two more stones and placed them in my hands. With that, the bard released me to my fate. I tucked the three stones safely into my belt, turned, and ordered the men to board the ships. Everyone raced to be first aboard, and I followed close behind. I had all but reached the water when Tegid shouted. "Llew! Will you leave your bard behind?"

"I would go with a better heart if you went with me," I answered. "But I will think no ill if you stay behind."

A moment later he stood beside me. "We go together, brother."

We waded through the icy surge and were hauled aboard by those waiting on deck. Men took up long poles and pushed into deeper water as the sails flapped, filled, and billowed. Night closed its tight fist around us as the sharp prow divided the waves, throwing salt spray in our faces and spewing sea foam over our clothes.

In the deep dark of a moonless Sollen night I left Albion behind. I did not look back.

The seas were rough, the wind raw and cold. We were battered by rain and sleet, and tossed on every wave as the sea battled our passage. More than once I feared a water grave would claim us, but sailed ahead regardless. There was no turning back.

"What makes you think they have escaped to the Foul Land?" Tegid asked. I stood at the prow, holding to the rail. We had not seen the sun since our departure.

"Paladyr was behind this," I told him, staring at the waves and pounding my fist against the rail.

"Why do you say so?"

"Who else could it be?" I retorted. Nevertheless, his question brought up the doubt I had so far suppressed. I turned my head to meet his gaze. "What do you know?"

His dark brows arched slightly. "I know that no man leaves a trail on the sea."

"The trail leads to Tir Aflan. That is where we banished Paladyr, and that is where he has taken them," I declared, speaking with far more certainty than I felt at the moment. Standing on the shore, there had been no doubt. Now, after two days aboard a heaving ship, I was not so sure. What if they had sailed south, and made landfall at any of a thousand hidden, nameless coves?

Tegid was silent for a time, thinking. Then he said, "Why would Paladyr do this?"

"That much is obvious: revenge."

The bard shook his head. "Revenge? For giving him back his life?"

"For sending him to Tir Aflan," I answered curtly. "Why? What do you think?"

"Through all things Paladyr has looked to himself and his own gain," Tegid countered. "I think he would be content to save himself now. Also, I have never known Paladyr to act alone."

True. Paladyr was a warrior, more inclined to the spear than to subtle machinations. I considered this. "It does not matter," I decided at last. "Whether he acted alone or with a whole host of devious schemers, it makes no difference. I would still go."

"Of course," Tegid agreed, "but it would be good to know who is with him in this. *That* might make a difference." He was silent for a moment, regarding me with his sharp grey eyes. "Bran told me about the beacon."

I frowned into the slate-dark sea.

"Is there anything else you have not told me? If so, tell me now."

"There is something else," I admitted finally.

"What is it?" Tegid asked softly.

"Goewyn is carrying our child. No one else knows. She wanted to wait a little longer before telling anyone."

"Before telling anyone!" Tegid blustered. "The king's child!" Shaking his head in amazement and disbelief, he turned his face to the sea and gazed out across the wave-worried deep. It was a long time before he spoke again. "I wish I had known this before," he said at last. "The child is not yours alone; it is a symbol of the bounty of your reign and belongs to the clan. I should have been told."

"We were not trying to hide it from anyone," I said. "Would it have made a difference?"

"We will never know," he answered bleakly and fell silent.

"Tegid," I said after a while, "Tir Aflan—have you ever been there?"

"Never."

"Do you know anyone who has?"

He gave a mirthless rumble of a laugh. "Only one: Paladyr."

"But you must know something of the place. How did it get its name?"

He pursed his lips. "From time past remembering it has been called Tir Aflan. The name is well deserved, but it was not always so. Among the Learned Brotherhood it is said that once, long ago, it was the most blessed of realms—Tir Gwyn, it was called then."

"The Fair Land," I repeated. "What happened?"

His answer surprised me. "At the height of its glory, Tir Gwyn fell."

"Fell?" I wondered. "How?"

"It is said that the people left the True Path: they wandered in error and selfishness. Evil arose among them and they no longer knew it. Instead of resisting, they embraced it and gave themselves to it. The evil grew; it devoured them—devoured everything good and beautiful in the land."

"Until there was nothing left," I murmured.

"The Dagda removed his Swift Sure Hand from them, and Tir Gwyn became Tir Aflan," he explained. "Now it is inhabited only by beasts and outcasts who prey upon one another in their torment and misery. It is a land lacking all things needful for the comfort of men. Do not seek succor, consolation, or peace. These will not be found. Only pain, sorrow, and turmoil."

"I see."

Frowning, Tegid inspected me out of the corner of his eye. "Yes, you will soon see it for yourself," he said, pointing with the head of his staff to the sea before us. I looked at what appeared to be a dull grey bank of cloud riding low on the horizon: my first glimpse of the Foul Land. "After we have sojourned there awhile, tell me if it deserves its name."

I gazed at the colorless blotch of landscape bobbing in the sea-swell. It seemed dreary, but not more so than many another land mass when approached through mist and drizzle on a sunless day.

Indeed, I wondered after Tegid's description that it did not look more abject and gloomy.

I had come to find Goewyn, and I would go through earthquake, flood, and fire to save her. No land, however hostile, would stand in my way.

But in that I was wildly and woefully naive.

19

Tir Aflan

Easier to carry ships across the sea on our backs than make safe landfall in the Foul Land. The ragged coast was rimmed with broken rocks. The sea heaved and shredded itself on the jagged stumps with a sense-numbing roar. We spent the better part of a day searching along the coast for harborage, and then, as the day sped from us, we happened upon a bay guarded by two rock stack promontories that formed a narrow entrance.

Despite the shelter offered by the headlands, Tegid did not like the bay. He claimed it made him feel uneasy. Nevertheless, after a brief consultation, we concluded that this was the best landfall we had yet seen and the best we were likely to find.

I gave the order, and one by one the ships passed between the towering stacks. Once inside the shelter of the rocks, the water was deathly calm—and deep-hued, darker even than the sea round about. "Listen," Tegid said. "Do you hear?"

I cocked my head to one side. "I hear nothing."

"The gulls have departed."

An entire flock of seagulls had been our constant companions since the voyage began. Now there was not a single bird to be seen.

I stood at the prow as Cynan's vessel passed ours and drew into the center of the bay. Cynan hailed us and pointed out a place where we might land. He was still leaning at the rail, hand extended, when I saw the water in front of his ship begin to boil.

Within the space of three heartbeats it was bubbling furiously. No cauldron ever frothed more fiercely. The water heaved and shuddered; gassy bubbles burst the sea surface, releasing a pale green vapor that curled over the churning water.

The men on board rushed to the rails and peered into the seething water. Exclamations of amazement turned to cries of anguish when out of the troubled water there arose the scaly head of an enormous serpent. Fanged jaws gaping, forked tongue thrusting like a double-headed spear, the creature hissed and the sound was that of ships' sails ripping in a gale.

From behind and a little to one side, I saw the monster with the clarity of fear. Its mucus-slick skin was a mottled green and grey, like the storm-sick sea; its head was flat, its yellow eyes bulged; scales thick and ragged as tree bark formed a ridge along its back, otherwise its bloated body was smooth and slimy as a slug. A steady stream of filmy slime flowed from two huge nostril flaps at the end of its snout and from a row of smaller pits, that began at the base of its throat and ran along the midline of the creature's sinuous length.

If its appearance had been designed to inspire revulsion, the monster could not have been better contrived. My throat tightened and my stomach heaved at the sight. And then the wind-blast of the beast's breath hit us and I retched at the stench.

"Llew!" Tegid appeared beside me at the prow. He pressed a spear into my hand.

"What is that thing?" I demanded, dragging my sleeve across my mouth. "Do you know?"

Without taking his eyes from the creature, he replied in a voice hollow with dread: "It is an *afanc*."

"Can it be killed?"

He turned his face to me, pasty with fright. His mouth opened, but he made no sound. His eyes slid past me to the creature.

"Tegid! Answer me!" I grabbed him by the arm and spun him to face me. "Can it be killed?"

He came to himself somewhat. "I do not know."

I turned to the warriors behind me. "Ready your spears!" I cried. There were five horses in the center of the boat; the sudden appearance of the monster had thrown them into a panic. They bucked and whinnied, trying to break their tethers. "Calm those horses! Cover their eyes!"

A tremendous cracking sound echoed across the water. I turned back to see Cynan's vessel shiver and lurch sideways. Then it began to rise, hoisted aloft on a great, slimy coil. Men screamed as the ship tilted and swayed in the air.

"Closer!" I shouted to the helmsman. "We must help them!"

In the same instant, an eel-like hump surfaced before the prow. The ship struck the afanc and shivered to a halt, throwing men onto their hands and knees. Winding a rope around my metal hand, I leaned over the rail and, taking my spear, drove the blade into the slime-covered skin. Blue-black blood oozed from the wound.

I withdrew the spear and struck again, and then again, sinking the blade deep. On the third stroke I drove the iron down with all my strength. I felt the resistance of hard muscle, and then the flesh gave way and the spear-shaft plunged. The great bloated body twitched with pain, almost yanking my arm from its socket. Black water appeared below me; I released the spear just as Tegid snatched me by the belt and hauled me back into the boat.

Others, quickened by my example, began slashing at the afanc with their weapons. Wounds split the smooth skin in a hundred places. The grey-green seawater soon became greasy with the dark issue of blood. Whether the monster felt the sting of our blades, or whether it merely shifted itself in the water in order to concentrate its attack, I do not know. But the afanc hissed and the wounded hump sank and disappeared. The warriors raised a war cry at their success.

Meanwhile, Cynan and his men, clinging to the rails, loosed a frenzied attack upon the beast's head and throat. I saw Cynan balancing precariously on the tilting prow. He lofted his spear. Took aim. And let fly. He groaned with the effort as the shaft left his hand.

The spear flew up and stuck in the center of the afanc's eye. The immense snaky head began weaving from side to side in an effort to dislodge the spike.

The men cheered.

The praise turned to shouts of dismay, however, as the afanc reared, lifting its odious head high above the water. Its mouth yawned open, revealing row upon row of teeth like sharpened spindles. Warriors scattered as the gaping maw loomed above them. But several men stood fast and let fly their spears into the pale yellow-white throat.

Hissing and spitting, the awful head withdrew, spears protruding like bristles from its neck. The ship, still caught in the afanc's coil, heaved and shook.

We were still too far away to help them. "Closer!" I shouted. "Get us closer!"

Cynan, clinging desperately to the rail, shouted for another spear as the afanc's head rose to strike again.

"Closer!" I cried. "Hurry!" But there was nothing we could do.

The afanc's mouth struck the ship's mast. The crack of timber sounded across the water. The mast splintered and the ship rolled, spilling men and horses into the froth-laced waves.

Amidst the screams of the men, I heard a strange sound, a dreadful bowel-churning sound—thick, rasping, gagging. I looked and saw the top half of the ship's mast lodged sideways in the afanc's throat. The terrible creature was working its mouth, trying to swallow, but the splintered timber had caught in the soft flesh and stuck fast.

Unable to free itself, the afanc lashed its hideous head from side to side, thrashing in the water like a whip. And then, when it seemed the ships would be dashed to bits by the flailing head, the bloated body heaved and, with a last cataclysmic lash of its finless tail, the beast subsided into the deep. The two ships nearest to it were inundated by water and near to foundering, but turned and steered towards the shore. The last ship, swamped in the heavy chop, nearly capsized.

We drove towards Cynan's vessel and aided those we could reach. Even so, three horses drowned and a dozen men had a long, cold swim to shore. We were able to save the damaged ship, but lost the provisions.

When the last man had been dragged ashore, numb with shock and half frozen, we gathered on the shingle, mute, as we gazed out over the now-peaceful bay. We made fast the ships as best we could and then withdrew further up the coast, well away from the afanc's bed, to spend a sleepless night huddled around sputtering fires in a forlorn effort to warm ourselves.

Sleet hissed in the fitful flames and the wet wood sizzled. We got little heat and less comfort for our efforts, and as the sun rose like a wan white ghost in a dismal grey sky, we gave up trying to get warm and began searching the shoreline for signs of Goewyn, Tángwen, and their abductors. Discovering no trace of them, settled for finding our own way inland.

"*Clanna na cù*," grumbled Cynan, mist beaded in his wiry hair and moustache. "This place stinks. Smell the air. It stinks." His nostrils flared and he grimaced with distaste. The air was rank and heavy as a refuse pit.

Tegid stood nearby, leaning on his staff and squinting sourly at the dense tangle of woodland rising sheer from the narrow beach like a grey wall. The strand was sharp with shards of flint. Dead trees lay on the shore like stiffened corpses, shriveled roots dangling in the air. "We should not linger here," he said. "Our coming will be marked."

"All the better," I remarked. "I want Paladyr to know we are here."

"I was not thinking of Paladyr only," the bard told me. "He may be the least of our worries. I sense far worse trouble awaiting us."

"Bring it on," Alun declared. "I am not afraid."

Tegid grunted and turned a baleful eye on him. "The less boasted now, the less you will later regret."

Shortly after, Garanaw returned from his foray up the coast to report that he had found a stream which would serve as a path inland. Cynan proposed a plan to make for the hills we had seen from the ships; from the vantage of height we might discern the lie of the land and espy some sign of the enemy habitation.

The evidence of the hoofprints, beacons, and the grooves of ships' keels left little doubt that Paladyr had the help of others. From the heights we could easily spot the smoke from a campfire or settlement. It was an extremely slender hope resting on the narrowest of chances, but it was all we had. So, we pursued it as if we were sure of success.

Drustwn returned from a survey of the coast to the south. "The land rises to steep cliffs. There is no entry that I could see."

"Right. Then we go north. Lead the way, Garanaw."

We moved off slowly, following Garanaw's lead. Bran and the other Ravens walked with him, Cynan and his warband followed them in ragged ranks, and Tegid, Scatha and I came next, followed by six warriors leading the horses in a long double line. The wood lining the shore was so close-grown and thick there was no point in riding. We would have to go on foot, at least until the trail opened somewhat.

The stream Garanaw had seen turned out to be a reeking seepage of yellow water flowing out of the wood and over the stony beach to slide in an ochre stain into the sea. One sniff and I decided that it was the run-off from a sulphur spring. Nevertheless, the water had carved a path of sorts through the brush and undergrowth: a rough, steep-sided gully.

With a last look at the dead white sky, we turned and headed inland along the ravine. Undermined trees had toppled and lay both in and over the gully, making progress tortuous in the extreme. We soon lost sight of the sky; the ceiling above was a mass of interwoven limbs as close and dense as any thatch. We advanced with aching slowness through a rank twilight, our legs and feet covered in vile-smelling mud. The only sound to reach our ears was the cold wind bawling in the bare treetops and the sniffling trickle of the stream.

The horses refused to go into the wood, and we had barely begun when we were forced to stop while a score or more of the animals were blindfolded. Calmed in this way, the lead animals proceeded and the rest allowed themselves to be led.

We toiled through the day, marking our progress from stump to broken stump of fallen trees. We ended the day exhausted and numb from slipping and sliding against the sides of the gully, and climbed from the defile to make camp. At least there was no shortage of firewood, and soon there were a good many fires ablaze to light that dismal day's end.

Tegid sat a little apart, bowed over his staff. His thoughts were turned inward, and he spoke no word to us. I thought it best not to intrude on his musings, and left him to himself.

After resting, the men began to talk quietly to one another, and those in charge of the provisions stirred to prepare supper. I sat with Scatha, Bran and Cynan, and we talked of the day's progress—or lack of it.

"We will fare better tomorrow," I said, without much conviction. "At least, we can do no worse."

"I will not be sorry to get out of this putrid ditch," Cynan grumbled.

"Indeed, Cynan Machae," Alun said, "the sight of you struggling through the muck is enough to bring tears to my eyes."

Scatha, her long hair bound in tight plaits and tucked under her war cap, scraped mud from her buskins with a stick as she observed, "It is the stench that brings tears to *my* eyes."

Our gloom lightened somewhat at that, and we turned our attention to settling the men and securing the camp for the night. We ate a small meal—with little appetite—and then wrapped ourselves in our cloaks and slept.

The next day dawned wet. A raw wind blew from the north. And though it was cold enough there was no snow—just a miserable damp chill that went straight to the bone and stayed there. The following day was no different, nor was the one after that. We slogged along the bottom of the defile, threading our way over, under, and around the toppled logs and limbs, resting often, but stopping only when we could no longer drag one foot in front of the other.

The ground rose before us in a steady incline, and by the end of the third day we had all begun to wonder why we had not reached our destination.

"I do not understand it," Bran confessed. "We should have gained the top of this loathsome hill long since."

He stood leaning on his spear, mud and sweat on his brow, breecs and cloak sodden and filthy—and the rest of the noble Raven Flight were no better. They looked more like fugitives of the hostage pit than a royal warband.

None of us had shaved in many days, and all of us were covered in reeking mud. I would have given much to find a suitable trickle or pool to wash away some of the muck. But both this and the summit eluded us.

I turned to Tegid and complained. "Why is it, Tegid? We walk a fair distance every day, but have yet to come in sight of the top."

The bard's mouth twisted, as if with pain, as he said, "You know as much as I do in this accursed land."

"What do you mean? What is wrong?"

"I can see nothing here," he muttered bitterly. "I am blind once more."

I stared at him for a moment, and then it came to me what he meant. "Your *awen*, Tegid—I had no idea..."

"It does not matter," he said bitterly, turning away. "It is no great loss."

"What is wrong with him?" asked Cynan. He had seen us me talking, and had joined me just as the bard flung away.

"It is his awen," I explained. "It is no use to him here."

Cynan frowned. "That is bad. If ever we needed the sight of a bard, it is here in Tir Aflan."

"Yes," I agreed. "Still, if wisdom fails, we must rely on wits and strength alone."

Cynan smiled slowly. He liked the sound of that. "You make a passable king," he replied, "but you are still a warrior at heart."

We made camp in the dank wood and rose with the sun to renew our march. The day was a struggle against tedium and monotony but least it was not so cold as previous days. In fact, the higher we climbed, the warmer the air became. We welcomed this unexpected benefit and persevered; we were rewarded in the end by reaching the top of the hill.

Though the sun had long since given up the fight, we dragged ourselves over the rim of the hill to a level, grassy place. A sullen twilight revealed a large, flat clearing. We quickly gathered firewood from the forest below and built the fire high. Bran cautioned against this, thinking that the last thing we needed was a beacon to alert any enemy who happened to be near. But I judged we needed the light as well as the warmth, and did not care if Paladyr and his rogues saw it.

As my wise bard had already warned, however, Paladyr was the least of our troubles—as the shouts of alarm from the pickets soon proved.

20

The Siabur

In the time-between-times, just before dawn, the horses screamed. We had picketed them just beyond the heat-throw of the campfire, so the flames would not disturb them. As we were in unknown lands, Bran had established a tight guard on the animals and around the perimeter of the camp as well.

Yet the only warning we had was the sudden neighing and rearing of the horses—quickly followed by the panicked shouts of the sentry.

I had my spear in my hand and my feet were already moving before my eyes were fully open. Bran was but a step behind me and we reached the place together. The guard, one of Cynan's men, stood with his back to us, his spear lying beside him on the ground.

The man turned towards us with an expression of mystified terror. Sweat stood out on his brow and his eyes showed white. His teeth were clenched tight, and cords stood out on his neck. Though his arms hung slack at his sides, his hands twitched and trembled.

"What has happened?" I asked, seeing no evidence of violence.

By way of reply the warrior extended his hand and pointed to an angular lump nearby. I stepped nearer and saw that what, in the cold light, appeared to be nothing more than a outcrop of rock...

Bran pushed forward, and knelt for a closer look. The Raven

Chief drew a long, shaky breath. "I have never seen the like," he said softly.

As he spoke, I became aware of a sweetly rancid smell—like that of spoiled cheese, or an infected wound. The scent was not strong but, like the quivering guard, I was overcome with a sudden upwelling of fear.

Get up! Get out! a voice cried inside my head. *Go! Get away from here while you can.*

I turned to the guard. "What did you see?"

For a moment he merely stared at me as if he did not understand. Then he came to himself and said, "I saw...a shadow, lord...only a shadow."

I shivered at the words but, to steady my own trembling hand, bent down, picked up the sentry's fallen spear, and gave it to him. "Bring Tegid at once."

Roused by the commotion, others had gathered around. Some murmured uneasily, but most looked on in silence. Cynan appeared, took one look and cursed under his breath. Turning to me, he said, "Who found it?"

"One of your men. I sent him to fetch Tegid."

Cynan stooped. He reached out his hand, thought better of it and pulled back. "*Mo anam!*" he muttered, "it is an unchancy thing."

Tegid joined us then. Without a word, he stepped to the fore. Scatha followed on his heels.

"What has happened?" asked Scatha, taking her place beside me. "What..." She took in the sight before her and fell silent.

The bard spent a long moment studying the misshapen heap before him, prodding it with the butt of his staff. Turning away abruptly, he came to where Bran, Cynan and I stood. "Have you counted the horses?" he inquired.

"No," I said. "We did not think to—"

"Count them now," Tegid commanded.

I turned and nodded to two men behind me; they disappeared at once. "What happened? What could..." I strained for words, "what could do this?"

211

Before he could answer, someone shouted from the hillside below. We hurried at once to the place and found a second display just like the first: the body of a horse. Though, like the first, it scarcely resembled a horse any more.

The dead animal's hide was wet, as if covered with dew, the hair all bunched and spiky. An oddly colorless eye bulged from its socket, and a pale, puffy tongue protruded through the open mouth. But the remains were those of a creature starved to death whose corpse has collapsed inward upon itself—little more than skin stretched across a jumble of sharp-jutting bone.

The horse's ribs, shoulder blades, and haunches stood out starkly. Every tendon and sinew could be traced with ease. If we had starved the hapless beast and left it exposed on the hilltop all winter the sight would have been no more stark. Yet, as I knelt and placed my hand against the animal's bony throat, the sensation was so uncanny my hand jerked back as if my fingers had been burned.

"The carcass is still warm," I said. "It is freshly killed."

"But I see no blood," Scatha observed, pulling her cloak high around her throat.

"Och, there is not a drop of blood left in the beast," Cynan pointed out.

Appalled by the wizened appearance of the animals, it had not occurred to me to wonder why they looked that way. I considered it now. "It looks as though the blood has been drained from the carcass," I said.

"Not blood only, I think," Bran mused, answering my own thought. So saying, he lifted the point of his spear and sliced into the belly of the dead horse. There was no blood—no bodily fluid of any kind. The organs and muscle tissue were dry, with a stiff, woody appearance.

"*Saeth du*," Cynan grunted, rubbing his neck. "Dry as dust."

Tegid nodded grimly, and glanced around the long slope of hillside as if he expected to see a mysterious assailant escaping through the trees. There was little to be seen in the thin early morning light; the mist-draped trunks of trees, and a thick hoarfrost covering grass and limbs and branches bled the color from the land until it looked like ... like the stiff and bloodless carcass before us.

The horse lay where it had fallen. Aside from a few strange, stick-like tracks around the head of the carcass, I could see no prints in the frosty grass. Nor were there any tracks leading away from the kill.

"Could an eagle do this?" I wondered aloud, knowing the notion absurd as the words left my lips. But nothing else suggested itself to me.

"No natural-born creature," Bran said; he held his chin close to his chest. A good many others were unconsciously protecting their throats.

"Well?" I asked, looking to Tegid for an answer.

"Bran is right," the bard replied slowly. "It was no natural creature."

"What then?" demanded Cynan. "*Mo anam*, man! Will you yet tell us?"

Tegid frowned and lowered his head. "It was a *siabur*." He uttered the word cautiously, as if it might hurt his tongue. I could tell by the way he gripped his staff that he was badly shaken.

The men returned from counting the horses. "Two tens and eight," was their census.

"Thirty-three men," I remarked, adding, "and now we have horses for twenty-eight. Great. Just great."

"This siabur," Scatha wanted to know, "what manner of creature is it?"

Tegid grimaced. "It is one of the *sluagh*," he told us reluctantly. He did not like speaking the name aloud.

Ghost? Demon? I tried to work out the meaning of the word, but could get no further than that.

"The Learned call them siabur. They are an order of spirit beings that derive their sustenance from the lifeblood of the living."

"Blood-sucking spirits?" Cynan blustered, his tone forced and his voice overloud. He was holding fear at bay the best way he knew, and only half succeeding. "What is this you are telling us?"

"I am telling you the truth." Tegid jerked his head around defiantly, as if daring anyone to gainsay him.

"Tell us more, brother," Bran urged. "We will hear you."

"Very well," the bard relented, flicking a cautionary glance in Cynan's direction. "The siabur are predatory spirits—as you have seen with your own eyes. Upon finding their prey, they take to themselves a body with which to make their attack, devouring the very blood as it flows."

I did not blame Cynan for his disbelief; Tegid's description was incredible. But for the two dead horses, sucked dry and cast aside like withered husks, I would have dismissed it as little more than whimsy. Clearly, there was nothing remotely fanciful about it. And Tegid stood before us solemn and severe.

"Nothing like this is known in Albion," said Scatha. "Nothing like this..."

"That is because the Island of the Mighty remains under the protection of the Swift Sure Hand," Tegid said. "It is not so in Tir Aflan."

"What can be done?" I wondered aloud.

"Light is their enemy," the bard explained. "Fire is light——they do not like fire."

"Then tonight we will bring the horses within the circle of the campfire," Cynan suggested.

"Better than that," I replied. "We will build a circle of fire around the entire camp."

Tegid approved. "That will serve. But more must be done. We must burn the carcasses of the horses and the ashes must be scattered in moving water before the sun sets."

"Will that free us from the siabur?"

"Free us?" Tegid shook his head slowly. "It will prevent them from inhabiting the bodies of the dead. But we will not be free until we set foot in Albion once more."

No one was willing to touch the dead horses, and I had not the heart to compel any man to do what I myself abhorred. So we heaped a mound of firewood over the unfortunate beasts and burned them where they lay. The carcasses gave off an excess of thick, oily black smoke with the same rancid cheese smell I had marked earlier.

Tegid made certain that every scrap of hide and bone was burned, and then raked the coals and gathered the ashes in two leather bags. After that we turned our attention to finding a stream or river into which we could strew the ashes.

This proved more difficult than anyone imagined.

Tegid considered the turgid seepage in the ravine unacceptable for our purposes, and we were forced to look elsewhere. Leaving Bran in charge of the camp, Tegid, Scatha, Cynan and I set off in the bright light of a dour, windswept morning in search of a stream or brook. We soon discovered that the hilltop we were camped upon was not a natural hill at all.

Scatha first tumbled to the fact that the plain on which we stood was strikingly flat for a natural plateau, and furthered this observation by remarking the peculiar regularity in the curve of the horizon. We rode a fair portion of the circumference just to make certain, and found as we expected that the rim of the plateau formed a perfect circle.

Despite this evidence, Tegid remained hesitant and withheld judgment, until he had examined the center. It took considerable effort just to *find* it; it was no simple matter to quarter a circle that large. But Tegid lined out a course and we followed it. After a lengthy survey we found what we were looking for: the broken stub of a massive pillar stone.

So immense was the thing, we had failed to recognize the hill for what it was: a gigantic mound, ancient beyond reckoning, raised by human hands. Sheer size obscured its true nature. But the presence of the pillar stone removed all remaining doubt. The mound was the *omphalos*, the symbolic center of Tir Aflan. Judging by the size of the circular plateau, it was something in the order of twenty to thirty times larger than the sacred mound of Albion on Ynys Bàinail.

Tegid was thunderstruck. He knelt in the long grass with his hands resting on his thighs, staring blankly at the bare hump of weather-worn rock protruding from the ground. Cynan used his sword to hack away some of the turf while Scatha and I looked on. The wind gusted fitfully around us and the horses whickered uneasily. I noticed that though the grass was long and green, the horses refused to eat more than a few mouthfuls.

Cynan sliced with the edge of his sword, and rolled away grass and earth in a thick mat. Then he dug with his hands. When he had finished, a portion of grey stone lay exposed to view. The flat, smooth surface of the stone was incised with lines deep-cut and even—the remains of the saining symbols originally carved into the pillar stone.

We all stared at the peculiar marks and struggled to imagine how the great standing stone would have appeared to those who had built the mound and raised it. A relic of the remote past, before the Fair Land declined, the broken stone seemed to defy understanding even as it commanded veneration. It was as if we were confronted by a presence that both overwhelmed and beguiled. No one spoke. We just stood looking on...

Tegid was first to shake off the unnatural fascination. Rising slowly, he staggered and made an arc in the air with his staff. "Enough!" he said, his voice thick and sluggish. "Let us leave this place."

As he spoke, I felt a sudden and virulent resentment at his suggestion. I wanted only to be allowed to remain as I was, quietly contemplating the broken pillar stone. Tegid's voice reached me as a grating annoyance.

"Llew! Cynan! Scatha!" he shouted. "We must flee this place at once."

Into my mind came an image of Tegid lying on the ground bleeding from his nose and mouth; I could feel his staff in my hands. I was seized by an urge to strike the bard down with his own staff. I wanted to punish him for disturbing me. I wanted to make him bleed and die.

"Llew! Come, we must—"

His face swam before me, concern creasing his brow. I felt his hands, grasping, clawing...

"Llew!"

I do not remember moving—nor raising my silver hand at all. I saw a shimmering blaze out of the corner of my eye and felt a jolt in my shoulder. And then Tegid—lurching, falling, hands clutching his head...

Bright red blood on green grass, and Tegid's staff in my hands...

... and then Cynan's arms were around me and I was struggling in his grasp as he lifted my feet off the ground.

"Llew! Let be!" Cynan's voice was loud in my ear. "Peace, brother. Peace!"

"Cynan?" I said, and felt myself returning as if from a great distance, or emerging from a waking dream. "Release me. Put me down."

He still held me above the ground, but I felt his grip loosen somewhat. "It is over, brother," I reassured him earnestly. "Please, put me down."

Cynan released me and together we knelt over Tegid, who was lying dazed on the ground, bleeding from a nasty gash over his temple.

"Tegid?" I said. His eyes rolled in his head and came to rest on me. He moaned. "I am sorry," I told him. "I do not know what happened to me. Can you stand?"

"Ahhh, I think so. Help me." Cynan and I raised him between us, and held him until he was steady on his feet. "That metal hand of yours is harder than it looks—and quicker," he said. "I will be better prepared next time."

"I am sorry, Tegid. I do not know what came over me. It was... uh, I am sorry."

"Come," he replied, shaking off the assault, "we will speak no more of it now. We must leave here at once."

Cynan handed Tegid his staff, and threw me a wary glance. "The horses have strayed. I will bring them," he said, but seemed reluctant to leave.

"Go," I said. "I will not attack Tegid again." Still, he hesitated. "Truly, Cynan. Go."

As Cynan indicated, the horses had strayed. Indeed, they had wandered far across the plain and were now some distance from us. "They must have bolted," I observed, watching Cynan stride away. "But I do not remember it."

Wiping blood from his face with the edge of his cloak, Tegid squinted up at the sky and announced, "We have lingered here longer than we knew."

"What do you mean?" I asked, following his gaze skyward. I tried to gauge the position of the sun, but the bright morning had faded and thick clouds now gathered overhead. How long had we stood there?

"The day has passed us," the bard declared. "It will be dark soon."

"But that cannot be," I objected. "We dismounted only a few moments ago."

He shook his head gravely. "No," he insisted, "the day is spent. We must make haste if we are to reach camp before dark." He called to Scatha and started off after Cynan.

Scatha made no move to join us. Her spear lay on the ground beside her. I retrieved the weapon, and put my hand on her arm. "Scatha?" The skin was cold and hard beneath my touch—more like stone than living flesh. "Tegid!" I shouted.

He was beside me in an instant. "Scatha!" He shouted her name loud in her ear. "Scatha! Hear me!" He shouted her name once and again, but her eyes stared emptily ahead—wide and eerily intent, as if she were transfixed by something that demanded all her attention.

When she did not respond, Tegid groaned deep in his throat and, dropping his staff, seized her by the arms and turned the unresisting Pen-y-Cat bodily away from the stone. He shook her, but she did not respond.

"Let us take her away from here," I suggested. "Maybe—"

The bard's hand flicked out and struck her cheek. The sound of the slap shocked me, but brought no response from Scatha. He slapped her again, and shook her hard. "Scatha! Fight it, Scatha. Resist!"

His open palm connected and her head snapped back. I could

trace the print of his hand on her cheek. He shook her and raised his hand to strike again.

"No!" I said, catching his wrist. "Enough. It is enough. It is not working." On a sudden inspiration, I suggested: "Here, I will carry her."

Without waiting for Tegid's assent, I swept Scatha into my arms and began moving away from the stone. Her body, at first rigid, relaxed as soon as I lifted her feet off the ground and turned my back on the broken stone.

She moaned softly, and closed her eyes. In a moment, tears slipped from under her lashes to slide down the side of her face. I stopped walking and put her down. She leaned heavily against me. "Scatha," I said, "can you hear me?"

"Llew... oh, Llew," she said, drawing a shaky breath. "What is happening?"

"It is well. We are leaving this place. Can you walk?"

"I feel so—lost," she said. "A pit opened at my feet—I stood at the edge and I felt myself falling. I tried to save myself, but I could not move... I could not scream..." She raised her fingertips to her reddened cheek. "I heard someone calling me..."

"This place is cursed," Tegid said. "We must go from here."

Supporting her between us, we began walking to where Cynan was laboring to catch the horses. They were skittish and he was having difficulty getting close enough to grab the dangling reins. We watched as he stole closer, lunged, grabbed—only to have the horse shy, buck, and run away. Cynan picked himself up off the ground and stamped his foot as the horses galloped further out of reach.

"It is no use," he said, as we drew near. "The stupid beasts are frightened and flee at shadows. I cannot get near them."

"Then we must walk back to camp," Tegid replied, moving off.

"What about the horses?" I asked. "We cannot—"

"Leave them."

"We need our weapons, at least," I maintained. Scatha had kept her spear, but Cynan and I had left ours beneath our saddles when we dismounted.

"Leave them!" the bard shouted, turning to confront us. His voice resounded emptily over the plain. "Believe me when I say that this mound is no safe place for us after dark. Our only protection lies within the circle of the fire."

He turned away again and began striding through the grass with long, swinging steps. Cynan, Scatha and I followed. Tegid was right; the level expanse of the circular plain was unbroken by any feature we could use to advantage. There were no trees, no rocks, no hollows for hiding.

I glanced back at the stump of stone behind us, and saw the eastern sky dark with fast-approaching night. How odd, I thought—I had never known daylight to fade so swiftly.

And with the advance of darkness, there arose a distant, wailing whine, like the howl of the wind in high mountain peaks—but there were no mountain peaks nearby, and it was not the wind I heard.

21

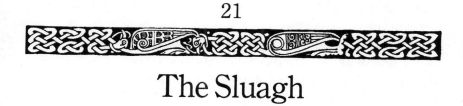

The Sluagh

Darkness overtook us as we hastened from the broken pillar stone. I do not think that even with our horses we could have reached the camp before nightfall. The way back was farther than I remembered it, and the weird twilight came on with unnatural speed. Horses could not have outrun it. Also, with the swiftly-deepening night, the eerie wail increased, as if the source of the uncanny sound were drawing relentlessly nearer.

Tegid kept one eye on the sky as we hurried along. As soon as he saw we could not reach camp before night overtook us, he announced, "We must make for the nearest slope. There we can find fuel for a fire at least."

"That is well," Cynan agreed. "But where is it? I can see nothing in this murk."

Tegid's plan was a good one; the banks of the mound were thickly forested, and firewood abounded. But how could we be certain which way to go when we could not see two steps in front of us?

"We should be near the edge of the plain," Tegid said. The pillar stone marked the center and we have been moving away from it—"

"Aye," allowed Cynan, "*if* we have not been making circles around it instead."

Tegid ignored the remark, and we rushed on. We had not

advanced more than a hundred paces, however, when Scatha halted.

"Listen!"

I stopped, but heard only the weird wailing sound which, apart from growing slightly louder, had not altered in any significant way. "What is it?"

"Dogs," she said. "I thought I heard dogs."

"I hear nothing," said Cynan. "Are you cert—" The bark of a dog—short, quick, unmistakable—cut him off.

"This way! Hurry!" shouted Tegid, darting ahead.

No doubt the bard thought we were right behind him, following in his footsteps. But I turned, and he had already melted into the darkness. "Tegid, wait! Where are you? Cynan?"

A muffled answer reached us. "This way ... follow me ..."

"Tegid?" I called, searching the darkness. "Tegid!"

"Where have they gone?" Scatha wondered. "Did you see?"

"No," I confessed. "They just vanished."

The dog barked again—if dog it was.

"It is closer," Scatha said, and the bark was immediately followed by another, a little further off and to the left.

"Yes, and there are more than one." I glanced this way and that, but could see nothing in any direction to guide us. Darkness had penetrated all, obliterated all. "We'd better keep moving."

"Which way should we go?" Scatha wondered aloud.

"Any way will be better than standing here," I replied. I put out my hand and grabbed hold of Scatha's cloak; she took the end of mine. "We will stay together," I told her. "Hold tight, and keep your spear ready."

Clutching one another's cloaks, we proceeded into the formless dark. I did not for a moment entertain any false hopes of eluding the beasts behind us. But I thought we might at least find a place to make a stand if we reached the slope of the mound before the creature on our trail reached us.

We went with as much speed as we dared. It is unnerving running blind. Every step becomes a battle against hesitation, against fear. And the steps do not grow easier with success. Indeed, the fear grows with every step until it becomes a dominating force.

But for Scatha's presence beside me, I would have halted every few steps to work up my courage. But I did not care to appear weak or fainthearted in her eyes, so I braced myself for the inevitable bone-breaking fall—and ran on.

All the while, the barking of the dogs grew louder and more insistent as they drew nearer. Their numbers seemed to have increased as well, for I thought I could make out at least five individual voices—at least, there were more than the two we had heard before.

Whether we would ever have reached camp this way, I will never know. Likely it was as Tegid had said—that darkness held no safety for any creature alone on the mound, and fire offered the only protection. We did, however, reach the rim of the plain and fell sprawling over one another as the ground tilted away beneath us without warning.

I fell, half-tumbling, half-sliding down the unseen slope, and landed on my side, knocking the breath from my lungs. It was a moment before I could speak. "Scatha!"

"Here, Llew," she replied, catching her breath. "Are you all right?"

I paused to take stock. My jaw ached, but that was from clenching my teeth as we ran. "I seem to be in one piece."

From the plain directly above us came the sudden swift rush of feet through the grass—as that of an animal making its final rush on its prey.

"Quick!" I yelled. "Down here!"

Diving, falling, rolling, down and down the slope we slid, until we came to rest in a sharp-thorned thicket. I made to disentangle myself, but Scatha said, "Shh! Be still!"

I stopped thrashing around and listened. I could still hear the dogs, but it sounded as if we had somehow managed to put a little distance between us and our pursuers. I was for moving on while we had a chance, but Scatha advised against it. "Let us stay here a moment," she urged, pushing deeper into the thicket.

Following her example, I wormed my way into the prickly

embrace of the bush and settled down beside Scatha to wait. "Do you still have your spear?" I asked.

"Yes."

"Good," I said, and wished yet again that I had remembered to retrieve my spear when we dismounted. And then I wished for a flint and striker to make a fire—if not that, then at least a single firebrand to light our way. But neither wish appeared likely to be granted.

Yet, as we sat in the inky darkness, waiting for we knew not what, the accursed night loud with the barking of the dogs, I imagined that my silver hand began to shine. The merest gleam at first, the faintest wink of a shimmer. I raised my hand to my face . . . the gleam vanished. I lowered my hand and it returned.

I craned my neck to look up and, to my surprise, glimpsed a pale eye peering back at me: the moon. Cloud-wrapped, a cold, wan and waxy blur in the Sollen-black sky, and fitful as a ghost, it gave me heart nonetheless, and I willed the light to stay.

The dogs were right above us on the plain. They were almost upon us. I expected them to be at our throats at any moment . . .

Scatha shifted. The glint of her spearblade pricked the gloom as she crouched forward to meet the attack. I felt around me for a stick to use as a club, but found nothing.

Meanwhile, the sound of pursuit had risen to a pitched din. The dogs were all around us, their cry deafening. I drew a last deep breath. *Come on,* I thought, *do what you will.* Amidst the baying I discerned the quick scatter of feet tearing through the undergrowth, and then, as quickly as it had grown, the sound began to dwindle away. Clasping one another's hands, we held ourselves deathly still, hardly daring to believe we had escaped. Only when the sound had diminished to a distant echo did we relax.

The moonlight grew stronger. I could see the glimmer of Scatha's eyes as she gazed steadily up the slope towards the plain. She felt my stare, turned her face towards me and smiled. In that moment, she looked just like Goewyn. My heart clutched within me. She must have sensed my distress, for she said, "Are you hurt?"

"No, I was thinking of Goewyn."

"We will find her, Llew." Her tone offered certainty, warm and confident. If there was any doubt at all in her heart or mind, she kept it buried deep within her, for I heard no trace of it in her voice.

It was now light enough to distinguish broad shapes on the slope. We waited, listening. I became cold sitting still so long. "We should move on," I said at last. "They might come back."

"I will go first," Scatha said, and began slowly disentangling herself from the thorns. She crept from the thicket and I followed, stepping free of the prickly branches to discover that we stood on the edge of an overgrown wood. In the faint moonglow, I could just about make out the rim of the circular plain a short distance above.

"The sky is clearing somewhat. We may be able to see the camp from up there," I said, thinking that if we could not find Tegid, we might at least locate the camp.

Scatha agreed and we climbed slowly back up the slope, gained the rim, and stood gazing across the plain. I had hoped to see the yellow fireglow from the camp—the ruddy smudge of the blaze reflected on the low clouds, at least—but there was nothing. I thought of shouting for Tegid and Cynan, then thought better of it. No sense in alerting the dogs.

"Well," I said, "if we stay close to the edge, we should reach camp eventually."

"We can also retreat to the wood if need be," Scatha pointed out.

Quickly, silently, like two shadows stealing over the dull grey field, we fled. Scatha, spear ready in her hand, led the way, and I maintained a constant lookout behind, scanning the plain for any sign of the camp, or of Tegid—I would have been delighted to find either. We ran a fair distance, and I became aware of a spectral flicker out of the corner of my eye. Thinking I had seen the campfire, I stopped walking and turned... but if I had seen anything it was gone.

Scatha halted when I did. "I thought I saw something," I explained. "It is gone now."

A moment later, it was back.

We had hardly put one foot in front of the other when I saw the strange flittering shimmer once again—just on the edge of sight. And as before, I stopped and turned to look.

"There is something out there," I told Scatha.

"I do not see anything."

"Nor do I. But it was there."

And again, as soon as we began walking, the glimmering image returned. This time, I did not stop, nor did I look directly at it. Rather, I let the subtle shifting glow play on the periphery of my vision while I tried to observe it to learn what it might be.

All I could perceive, however, was a fickle gleam in the air—as if the chill moonlight itself had thickened and congealed into elongated strands and diaphanous filaments that streamed through the night-dark air, rippling and waving like seaweed under water.

Yet, each time I turned my head, thinking to catch a glimpse, the phantoms vanished. There was, I decided, a phenomenon at work similar to the erratic light of certain stars which are clearly discernable when the eye is looking elsewhere, but which disappear completely when an attempt is made to view them directly.

We walked along and I soon observed that the amorphous shapes were not confined to the plain; they swarmed the air above and on every side. Whichever way I turned my head, I glimpsed, as if on the very edge of sight, the floating, curling shapes, merging, blending, wafting all around us.

"Scatha," I said, softly. She halted. "No—keep walking. Do not stop." We resumed, and I said, "It is just that the shapes—the phantoms seem to be gathering. There are more of them now, and they are all around us. Can you see them?"

"No," she said. "I see nothing, Llew." She paused for a moment and then said, "What do they look like?"

Bless you, Pen-y-Cat, I thought, for not thinking me mad. "They look like . . . like shreds of mist, or spider's webs drifting on the breeze."

"Do they move?"

"Constantly. Like smoke, they are always blending and changing shape. I find that if I do not look at them directly, I can see them."

We walked on and after a while I began to discern that the

phantom shapes were coalescing into more substantial forms, thicker, more dense. They still merged and melted into one another, but they seemed to be amassing substance. With this change, I also felt my silver hand begin to tingle with the cold—not the hand itself, but the place where the metal met flesh.

I thought this an effect of the cold night air, then reflected that cold weather had never affected me in that way before. Indeed, my metallic hand had always seemed impervious to either heat or cold. Always, that is, except once: the day I discovered the beacon.

I puzzled over this as we ran along. Could it be that my metallic appendage, whatever other properties it possessed, functioned as some sort of warning device? Given the fantastic nature of the hand itself and how it had come to attach itself to me, that seemed the least implausible of its wonders. Indeed, everything about the silver hand suggested a more than passing affinity with mystery and strange powers.

If my silver hand possessed the ability to alert its owner of impending danger, what, I wondered, did its warning now portend?

So absorbed had I become in these thoughts, that I ceased attending to the shifting shapes on the edge of my vision. When I again observed them, I froze in mid-step. The phantoms had solidified and were now of an almost uniform size, though still without recognizable form; they appeared as huge filmy blobs of congealed mist and air, roughly the size of ale vats. Something else about them had changed, too. And it was this, I think, that stopped me: there was a distinct awareness about them, almost a sentience. Indeed, it was as if the phantom shapes seemed eager, or excited—impatient, perhaps.

For, as I hastened to rejoin Scatha, I sensed an agitation in the eerie shapes—as if my movement somehow frustrated the phantoms and threw them into turmoil. A strange and unsettling feeling overcame me then, for it seemed that the wraiths were aware of my presence and capable of responding to it.

Meanwhile, the frosty tingling in my silver hand had become a definite throbbing chill, striking up into my arm. I quickened my stride and drew even with Scatha. "Keep moving," I told her. "The phantoms know we are here. They seem to be following us."

Following was not the precise word I wanted. The things were all around us—in the air above and on the ground on every side. It was more that we were traversing a dense and hostile wood where every leaf was an enemy, and every branch a foe.

Without slackening her pace, she raised her spear and indicated a patch of darkness to the right. "I see the glow of a fire ahead."

A dull yellow glow winked low on the horizon. "It must be the camp," I said, and an icy realization washed over me. That explains their agitation, I thought. The phantoms do not want us to reach camp. "Hurry! We can make it."

The words were hardly out of my mouth when Scatha threw her arm across my chest to stop me. In the same instant, a sweetly gangrenous stink reached my nostrils—the same as I had smelled coming from the dead horses. The gorge rose in my throat.

Scatha recognized the odor, too. "Siabur," she cursed, all but gagging on the word.

I heard a soft, plopping sound and saw a bulbous shape fall onto the ground a few paces ahead of us. The sickly-sweet stink intensified, bringing tears to my eyes. The round blue-black blob lay quivering for a moment, and then gathered itself like a bead of water on a hot surface. At the same time, it seemed to harden, for it stopped trembling and began to unfold its legs from around a bulging stomach. Its head emerged, beaded with eyes on top and a crude pincer mouth below.

I understood then what I had been seeing. The wraiths were those creatures Tegid called the sluagh. And now, by means of whatever power they possessed, the things had gathered sufficient strength to take on material form as a siabur. The immaterial had solidified, and the form it took was that of a grotesquely bloated spider. But a spider unlike any I had ever seen: green-black as a bruise in the moonlight, with a hairy distended belly and long spindly legs ending with a single claw for a foot, and freakishly large—easily the size and girth of a toddling child.

The immense body glistened with a liquid ooze. The siabur made a slobbering sound as it dragged its repulsive bulk over the grass.

"It is ghastly!" breathed Scatha, and with two quick strides she was over it, her spear poised. Up went her arm, and then down. The spear pierced the creature behind its grotesque head, pinning it neatly to the ground. The siabur squirmed, emitting a bloodless shriek; its legs twitched and its mouth parts clashed.

Scatha twisted the spear; the fragile legs folded and the thing collapsed in a palpitating heap. She raised the spear and drove it into the creature's swelling middle. A noxious gas sputtered out and the loathsome thing seemed to melt, its body losing solid form and liquefying once more into a blob that simply dissolved, leaving a foul-smelling blotch glistening on the grass.

My feet were already moving as the siabur evaporated. I caught Scatha by the arm and pulled her away. I heard the sound of another soft body fall just to the right, and another where we had been standing a moment before. Scatha twisted towards the sound. "Leave it!" I shouted. "Run for the camp."

We ran. All around us the night quivered with the sound of those hideous bloated bodies plopping onto the ground. There were scores, hundreds of the odious things. And still they kept coming, dropping out of the air like the obscene precipitation of a putrid rain.

The stench fouled the air. My breath came in ragged gasps that burned my throat and lungs. Tears flowed down my cheeks. My nose ran freely.

The long grass tugged at our feet as if to hinder us. The plain was alive with crawling siabur heaving their gross shapes over the ground, scrabbling, struggling, straining to get at us. Their thin legs churned and their drooling mouths sucked. They would swarm us the moment we halted or hesitated. And then we would become like the horses we had seen that morning: dry husks with the lifeblood sucked from our bodies.

Our path grew difficult and running became hazardous as we were forced to dodge this way and that to avoid the scuttling spiders. My silver hand burned with the cold.

A siabur appeared directly in my path and I vaulted over it. As my feet left the ground, I felt a cold weight between my shoulder blades—long legs groped for my neck. Its touch was the stiff cold touch of a dead thing. I flailed with my arms, dislodged the creature, and flung it to the ground where it squirmed and shrieked.

Another took its place. The dead cold weight clasped my shoulder, and I felt a sharp, icy bite at the base of my neck. An exquisite chill spread through me from the neck and shoulders down my back and sides and into my thighs and legs. I stopped running. The darkness became close, suffocating. My face grew numb; I could not feel my arms or legs. My eyelids drooped; I longed for sleep... sleep and forgetting... oblivion.... I would sleep—but for a small voice crying out very far away. Soon that voice would be stilled....

Hearing my shout, Scatha whirled around and, with a well-placed kick, detached the siabur from my neck. A quick jab of her spear pierced the spider through its swollen sac. The wicked thing wriggled, then dissolved into jellied slime and melted away.

My vision cleared and my limbs began to shake. I felt Scatha's hands lifting me. I tried to get my feet under me, but could not feel my legs. "Llew, Llew," Scatha crooned softly. "I have you. I will carry you." She helped me stand. I took two wobbly steps and pitched onto my face. The siabur rushed in at once—they could move with startling speed. I kicked out and struck one. It squealed and scurried out of the way, but two more charged me. Their claw-tipped legs snagged the cloth of my breecs as I thrashed on the ground.

Scatha stabbed the first one as it clawed at me and, with a quick backward chop, sliced the second in half. Then, planting her foot, she pivoted to the side and skewered two more as they scuttled nearer. A third tried to evade her, but she pierced the swell-bellied thing, lifted it on the point of her spear and flung it hissing into the air.

Using all her strength, Scatha hauled me upright and drove me forward once more. Tottering like an old man, I stumbled ahead. Moving helped; I regained the use of my limbs and was soon covering ground quickly again. We bolted for the edge of the plain and the wooded slopes below, where I hoped we might more easily elude them. A cluster of siabur tried to cut off our escape, but Scatha's inspired spearwork cleared the way and we reached the slope to a chorus of sharp angry squeals.

We gained the edge and plunged down the slope. The air was clean and I gulped it down greedily. My vision cleared and my nose and lungs stopped burning. Upon reaching the first fringe of the wood, I glanced back to see the siabur boiling over the brim of the plain in a vile, throbbing flood. Although I had expected pursuit, my heart sank when I saw their number: the scores and hundreds had become thousands and tens of thousands.

They flowed down the slope in an enormous pulsating avalanche, shrieking as they came. There was no stopping them, and no escape.

22

Yellow Coat

My heart sank. The hideous cascade of siabur inundated the wooded slope. We could not long evade them; there were just too many.

Scatha appeared at my shoulder. "Take this," she said, thrusting a stout branch into my hand. Ever resourceful, Pen-y-Cat had found me a weapon—suitable for spiders at least.

Taking the branch, I glanced back towards the hillside. The spiders were not coming as fast as before. Their movements were sluggish and they clumped together in an awkward press. "I think they are stopping."

"They are tiring," observed Scatha. "We can outrun them. This way! Hurry!" Scatha began pushing deeper into the brushy tangle.

I took two steps and screamed as pain shot up through my arm, stabbing into my shoulder. "Aghh!"

Scatha's hands were on me. "Are you hurt, Llew?"

"My hand—my silver hand... ahh, oh, it is so cold." I stretched my hand towards her. "Do you feel it?"

Scatha touched the metal gingerly at first, then grasped it firmly. "It is not cold at all. Indeed, it is warm as any living hand."

"It feels like ice to me. It is freezing."

Turning back to the hillside above us, the siabur had halted their advance and were drawing together into heaving, throbbing piles.

The stench reached our nostrils as a gush of fetid air. Though the moonlight was not strong, I could see their misshapen bodies glistening in lumpen knots as they writhed and wriggled with a sound like the mewing and sucking of kittens at the pap.

And then, rising up out of one writhing heap: the head and forelegs of a hound—a monstrous, flat-headed cur with huge pointed ears and long, tooth-filled jaws. Its coat was a sodden mess of pitch black hair, and its eyes were red. The ugly head thrashed from side to side as if struggling to free itself from the spider mass, which had become an oozy quagmire of quivering bellies and twitching legs.

I watched in sick fascination as the beast clawed its way free, pulling its short back and hindquarters up and out of the stinking, squirming muck. But the hellhound was not escaping, it was being born of the abhorrent couplings of the siabur. Even as this thought took form in my mind, I saw another head emerging and beside it a third and, a short distance away, the snout and ears of a fourth.

"Run!" Scatha shouted.

The first hound had almost freed itself from its odious womb, but I could not tear my eyes from the loathsome birthing.

Scatha yanked on my arm, pulling me away, her voice loud in my ear. "Llew! Now!"

From higher up the slope I heard a slavering growl and the rush of swift feet. Grasping my club and without looking back, I lowered my head and darted after Scatha. She led a difficult race, lunging, bounding, ducking, springing over fallen branches, and swerving around tall standing trunks. I followed, marvelling at the grace and speed with which she moved—flowing through the tangled thickets and trees with the effortless ease of a flame.

The unnerving sound of their weird spectral baying assured me that the first hound had been joined by the other three. They had raised the blood-call—cruelly fierce, baleful, unrelenting—a sound to make the knees weak and courage flow away like water. I risked a fleeting backward glance and saw the swarthy shapes of the beasts gliding through the undergrowth, their eyes like live coals burning in the moonglow. We could not outrun them; and with but one spear between us, neither could we fight them. Our only hope was to keep ahead of them.

We ran for what seemed like an eon. I could hear the demon dogs tearing through the brush behind me. From the noise they were making, I judged that they were gaining ground on us and that there were more of them than before.

Chancing another backward look, I saw that the hellhounds were indeed very much closer now. Three or four more had joined the pack with others, no doubt, on the way. The sound of their baying blood-call cut through me, raising the hair on my scalp.

When I turned back, Scatha had disappeared.

"Scatha!" I cried. What if she had fallen?

I ran to the place where I had last glimpsed her, but she was not there, and nowhere to be seen. I could not stay and look for her, nor could I leave her.

"Scatha! Where are you?"

"Here, Llew!" came the answer—close at hand, but I could not see her.

A howl broke into a snarl as the foremost hellhound closed on me. I turned to meet the beast, putting my back to the nearest tree and holding my makeshift weapon before me, ready to strike. I could reckon to get in at least two good blows before the other hounds arrived. What I would do after that, I did not know.

The creature attacked with breathtaking speed. I braced myself to receive the weight as it sprang...

The butt end of a spear shaft descended directly before my face. "Take hold!" a voice cried from above.

I dropped the club, seized the spear with my flesh hand and jumped, swinging my legs up towards the boughs above. Hooking a branch with one knee, I caught another with my metal hand. A hair's breadth beneath me the hound's jaws closed with the force of a sprung trap. Clutching for dear life to the shaft of the spear, I felt myself lifted higher. "Let go the spear, Llew," my savior told me. "There is a branch beside you."

But I could not release my grip on the spear—the instant I did so, I would plummet to the ground. Another hound had joined the first and both were leaping at me, jaws snapping, teeth cracking.

"Let go, Llew."

I looked to the right and left. If I released the spear I would fall and be torn apart by the hounds.

"Llew! I cannot help you if you do not let go."

I hesitated, dangling dangerously close to the snarling creatures below. A third hound bounded over the backs of the other two and snagged my cloak in its teeth, almost tearing my grip from the spear, and dragging me down with its weight.

"I cannot hold you!"

Clinging to my cloak, the hellhound tugged furiously, trying to pull me from my precarious roost. The fabric of my cloak began to give way. A second hound caught a corner of the cloak and began to yank, its forelegs lifted off the ground. My grip on the spear began to slip as I was dragged down yet further. More hounds had reached the tree and were leaping at me, trying to snag a piece of my dangling cloak.

"Llew! Let go!"

Grip failing, slipping backward bit by bit, cloak pulled tight against my neck to choke me, there was nothing for it but to let go of the spear and try for a more secure handhold on the unseen branch.

"I cannot hold you!"

I released the spear and flung my hand out. The weight of the hounds jerked me down. But my hand closed securely on a branch and I quickly wrapped my arm around its sturdy length and held fast.

Scatha was there beside me, trembling with the effort of supporting my weight on the end of her spear. "I might have dropped you," she said.

"I could not see the branch," I replied through clenched teeth.

Kneeling on the branch beside me, Scatha leaned low and thrust down with the spear. A rabid snarl became a squalling yelp and the weight on my cloak decreased by half. Another quick thrust of the spear brought another bawl of pain and I was free. I fumbled with the brooch pin and somehow managed to unfasten the brooch and let the cloak fall free.

I pulled myself upright and climbed higher into the tree. Below were no fewer than eight hellhounds—some leaping frantically in the air, others running insanely around the tree, and at least two trying to scale the trunk by their claws. One of these managed to reach a fair height but, gripping the branch with one hand, Scatha leaned down and stabbed the creature in the throat. It fell yelping to the ground, landed on its spine and thrashed around, furiously biting itself as the black blood gushed from its wounded throat.

The beast died and, like the spiders, simply dissolved into a shapeless mass that quickly evaporated leaving nothing but a glutinous residue behind. But there were a dozen or more dogs running beneath the tree now. They sprang at us, clashing their teeth and snarling. Often one would try to climb the tree, whereupon Scatha would spear it, and it would fall back either wounded or dead. The dead quickly dissolved and disappeared, but were just as swiftly replaced by others.

We were trapped, clearly, and I began to think that by sheer strength of numbers the hounds would bring down the tree. Just watching the swirling, vicious chaos of their frenzy made me fearful and weary. Scatha, too, felt the futility of fighting them; for, although she still gave good account of herself with her spear when opportunity presented, I noticed that she seemed to be losing heart. Gradually, her features lost all expression, and her head drooped.

I tried to encourage her. "We are safe here," I told her. "The camp is near. The warriors will hear the hounds and come in force to rescue us."

"If they are not themselves under attack," she replied bleakly.

"They will find us," I said, doubt undercutting my words. "They will rescue us."

"We cannot escape," she murmured.

"They will find us," I insisted. "Just hold on."

Nevertheless, it soon began to look as if Scatha was right. The monstrous hounds did not tire, and their numbers, so far as I could tell, continued to increase. Scatha eventually ceased striking at them with her spear. Instead, we edged higher into the tree and sat staring hollow-eyed at the frenzy, growing gradually numb from the cold and the continual shock of the baying, snarling, howling cacophony below.

Watching the moonglint on teeth and claws, and the dizzy tracery of red-glowing eyes, my mind began to drift. The gyrating black bodies seemed to merge into one savage torrent like a raging cataract, fearful in its wrath. And I wondered what it would be like to join that swirling maelstrom, to become part of that horrific turbulence. No intent but chaos, no desire but destruction. What defiance, what strength, what abandon—to give myself over to such fury.

What would happen to me? Would I die? Or would I simply become one of them, primal and free? Knowing no limits, no restraint, a creature of naked appetites, feral, possessed of a savage and terrible beauty—what would it be like to act and not think, to simply *be*—beyond thought, beyond reason, beyond emotion, alive to sensation only...

I was startled from my dire reverie by the sudden shaking of the branch beside me. Scatha, eyes fastened on the tumult raging around the trunk of the tree, was standing on the limb, teetering back and forth, her arms outflung to keep her balance. She had dropped her spear.

"Scatha," I called. "Do not look at them, Scatha! Take your eyes off them."

I continued speaking as I cautiously crept closer along the branch until I was sitting beside her. Standing slowly, I put my arm around her shoulders to steady her. "Let us sit down again, Pen-y-Cat," I said. She yielded to this suggestion, and allowed herself to be guided to a sitting position on the branch. "That is better," I told her. "You had me worried, Scatha. You might have fallen."

She turned blank, unseeing eyes on me and said, "I wanted to fall."

"Scatha, hear me now: what you feel is the sluagh—they are doing this to us. I feel it, too. But we must resist. Someone will find us."

But Scatha had turned her gaze once more towards the howling, boiling mass beneath us. Desperate for some way to distract her, I fought the urge to return to my own contemplation of the turmoil below, and scanned the surrounding wood for some hopeful sign.

To my astonishment, I saw the faint glow of a torch moving down the slope.

"Look! Someone is coming. Scatha, see—help is on the way!"

I said this mostly to divert Scatha's attention, but I took heart myself. There was no logical reason to believe that rescue had come, but a multitude of reasons to assume that some fresh horror had found us instead.

Indeed, my hopes were all but extinguished when Scatha said, "I see nothing. There is no torch."

It was true—the glow was not a torch. What I had seen, burnished by hope into bright-gleaming flame, appeared now to be nothing more than a dull moonstruck yellow glow. It moved steadily through the wood towards us, however, and I gradually became aware that it moved to a sound of its own—difficult to hear above the snarling, growling, hellhound yowl, but distinct from it all the same.

"Listen... can you hear it?"

Scatha listened for a moment, turning her eyes away from the maelstrom below. "I... um, I hear... barking," she concluded uncertainly.

"That is it," I assured her. "Barking, exactly—the same as we heard before the siabur appeared."

Scatha regarded me sceptically, as well she might, considering how we had fled in terror of the sound upon hearing it. Odd to find comfort in it now. And yet, I did take comfort in it. I peered intently through the close-grown wood as the strange yellow glow wafted through the trees. The barking sound grew as the glow drifted, and there could be no doubt that it was the same that we had heard earlier.

My silver hand, which had long since become a chunk of ice on the end of my arm, began to tingle. A moment later, I glimpsed several smooth white shapes racing through the underbrush towards us.

"Something is coming!" I gasped.

The warming tingle quivered up into my arm as three sleek

white dogs broke through the undergrowth and drove straight into the impossible turmoil of hounds beneath our tree. White as new snow from snout to tail—except for their ears which were bright, blood red—the dogs were smaller and leaner than the black hellhounds, but swifter of foot and just as fierce.

I expected them to be torn apart in an instant, but to my amazement the hellhounds reacted as if they were being scalded alive. They reared on hind legs, leapt in the air, and scrambled over one another in a desperate struggle to escape the onslaught of the newcomers. And, as soon became apparent, with good reason.

The red-eared dogs charged in a frenzy of bared teeth, each seizing a hound by the throat, ripping furiously, and then lunging to another kill. The stricken hounds whined and crumpled, decaying into shapeless jelly and vanishing within moments.

Like lightning shattering the stormcloud, the three white dogs routed our assailants, killing with keen efficiency and striking again. Within moments of their arrival, dozens of their opponents were dead and hellhounds were fleeing for cover, clawing one another to get away. Soon the wood rang to the sound of the dogs' triumphant howls as they pursued the retreating hounds into the wood.

"They are gone," Scatha said, releasing her breath in a rush.

I opened my mouth to agree, and then I saw him: standing almost directly below us and looking in the direction the dogs had gone. He was wearing a long yellow coat with sleeves and a belt. It was this coat I had seen moving through the trees like a will-o'-the-wisp.

He stood for a moment without moving, and then he raised his face to look into the branches where Scatha and I were hiding. I almost fell from my perch. Peering up at me was easily the ugliest man I had ever seen: big-faced, gross in every feature, his long nose ending in a fleshy hook, and his mouth the wide thick-lipped cleft of a frog. Ears like jug handles protruded from under a thick pelt of wild black hair, and large wide-spaced eyes bulged balefully from beneath a single heavy ridge of black brow.

He held my gaze for the briefest instant, but long enough for me to know that he saw me. Indeed, he lifted his hand in farewell just before he stepped from beneath the branch and disappeared into the wood once more.

Only after he had gone could I speak. "I have seen that face before," I murmured. Once, long ago . . . in another world.

I felt a hesitant touch on my arm. "Llew?"

"It is over," I told her. "The dogs belonged to him."

"Who?"

"The man in the yellow coat. He was just there. I saw him; he—" I broke off. It was no good insisting. Clearly, Scatha had not seen him. Somehow that did not surprise me.

"We can go now," I told her, and began easing my weight from the branch.

I lowered myself to the lowest branch and prepared to drop to the ground. Just as I released my hold, Scatha called from above, "Wait! Listen!"

But her warning came too late. I landed awkwardly and fell rolling on my back. As I did so, I heard something big and heavy crashing through the wood. I jumped to my feet, searching wildly for Scatha's fallen spear, wishing I had saved the club.

"Llew!" Scatha called. "There—behind you!" The spear lay a few steps behind me. I ran to it, picked it up, and whirled to meet . . . Bran and Alun Tringad, swords drawn, along with twenty or more torch-bearing warriors.

"Over here!" I cried. "Scatha! It is Bran! We are saved!"

Bran and Alun advanced warily, as if I might be an apparition.

"Here I am!" I shouted again, lowering the spear and hurrying to meet them. "Scatha is with me."

"Llew?" the Chief Raven wondered, lowering his sword slowly. He glanced at Alun, who said, "I told you we would find them."

"We were returning to camp and lost our way," I explained quickly. I hurried back to the tree and called to Scatha. "You can come down now. It is safe."

Scatha dropped from the branch and landed catlike on her feet.

"Are Cynan and Tegid with you, too?" Alun asked, peering up into the branches.

"We became separated," I replied. "I do not know where they went."

"They did not return to camp last night," Bran said.

"How did you know where to find us?"

"We heard the dogs," Bran explained. "They circled the camp, and Alun saw someone—"

"Three times they circled the camp," Alun put in eagerly. "The fellow with them beckoned us to follow."

"I did not see anyone," stated Bran firmly. "I saw only the dogs."

"This fellow," I asked Alun, "what was he wearing?"

"A long mantle with a broad belt," Alun replied readily.

"And the mantle—what color?"

"Why, dun colored it was. Or yellow." Alun allowed. "Difficult to tell in the dark, and he carried no torch."

"And the dogs?"

"White dogs—" said Bran.

"With red ears," added Alun Tringad. "Three of them. They led us here."

"You heard nothing else?"

"Nothing else, lord," Alun answered.

"The baying of hounds perhaps?" I prodded. "Here in this very place?"

Bran shook his head. "We heard only the dogs," he declared. "And there were but three of them."

"And the man," Alun maintained.

"Yes, there was a man—the man in the yellow coat," I confirmed. "Scatha did not see him, but I did."

"I saw only the dogs," Scatha said with relief. "But that was enough." I noticed she said nothing about the hellhounds or the spiders. But then, neither did I.

23

Crom Cruach

Tegid and Cynan had in fact returned to camp before us and were waiting for our arrival. The sun broke above a grey horizon as we entered the still-smoldering circle of the protective fire. Upon stepping across this threshold of ashes, I was overcome with exhaustion. My legs became leaden and my back ached. I stumbled and almost fell.

Tegid grabbed my arm and steered me to a place at the campfire. "Sit," he commanded, and called to a nearby warrior. "Bring a cup!"

I stood swaying on my feet, unable to make the necessary movement. The ground seemed very far away.

Cynan, none the worse for lack of a night's sleep, hastened to Scatha's side, put his arm around her shoulders, and brought her to where I stood.

"Sit, brother," the bard urged. "You are dead on your feet."

I bent my knees and promptly collapsed. Scatha, dull-eyed and pale from our all-night ordeal, crumpled beside me.

The cup arrived. Tegid pressed it into my hands and helped me raise it to my lips. "What happened to you?" he asked as I drank.

The ale was cold and good, and I all but drained the cup before recalling that Scatha was thirsty too. I passed the cup to her as I replied, "We lost you in the dark. We called for you—we could not have been more than ten paces apart. Why did you leave us?"

"But we heard nothing," Cynan declared, mystified. "Not a sound."

"No?" It did not surprise me in the least. "Well, when we could not find you, we made for the edge of the mound."

"We were chased by hounds," Scatha said, shivering at the all-too-fresh memory.

"Then the dogs came and drove the hounds away," I told them simply. "Bran and Alun arrived a few moments after that and brought us back."

"Tell me about the dogs," Tegid said, kneeling before us.

"There were three of them—long-legged and lean, with white coats. They came through the wood and drove the others away."

Scatha supplied the details I had neglected. "The hounds had red ears and there was a man with them. I did not see him, but Llew did."

"Is this so?" the bard asked, raising his eyebrows.

Before I could reply, Alun answered, "It is so. I saw him, too. He was wearing a yellow mantle and running with the dogs."

Bran confirmed Alun's report. "I saw the dogs; they circled the camp three times and then led us to the very place where Llew and Scatha were hiding."

Tegid shook his head slightly. "What of the hounds?" he said.

I did not want to speak of them. I saw no point in planting yet more fear in the warriors' hearts—there was enough already.

"Well," I said slowly, "there is not much to tell. They were big, ugly beasts. Fierce. If Bran and Alun had not come when they did we would not be here now."

"The man with the dogs, you mean. He saved you. We came after." said Alun, dragging the facts before us once more.

"The point is," I said, "we could not have survived much longer."

"The hounds," Tegid persisted, "tell me about them."

"They were just hounds," I replied.

"They were sluagh," Scatha informed him.

Tegid's eyes narrowed. He did not ask how we knew this, but accepted it without comment. For this, I was grateful.

"The same as attacked our horses?" Cynan demanded.

"The same," Tegid replied. "The sluagh change bodies to suit their prey."

"Changelings!" Cynan shook his head and whistled softly between his teeth. "*Clanna na cù*. It is a fortunate man you are, Llew Silver Hand, to be drawing breath in the land of the living this morning."

Tegid said nothing, his expression inscrutible. I could not guess what he was thinking.

But Cynan was eager to talk. "After you and Scatha wandered away in the dark," he volunteered, "we found a grassy hollow and settled there to wait until sunrise. Oh, but the night was black! I could have seen no less if I had been struck blind. By and by the sky began to pale and the sun came up. We came on to the camp then. Indeed, we were no great distance away—but did we ever see the fire? No, we never did."

Tegid rose abruptly. "This mound is cursed. We cannot stay another night here."

"I agree. Send out scouts—two parties of four each, one to ride east and the other west around the perimeter of the mound. If they see any sign of an encampment two are to keep a lookout, and two are to return here at once."

"But they must not be long about it," Tegid added. "We will leave at midday."

"It shall be done," the Raven Chief said, rising to leave.

"I will send Gweir to lead one of the parties," Cynan offered, "and they will return the swifter."

Bran and Cynan moved off to begin organizing the scouts. I lay down to rest until the scouting party returned. But I did not bear the waiting easily, for I fell into an anxious reverie over Goewyn. Where was she? What was she doing at this moment? Did she know I was searching for her?

I entertained the idea of building a tremendous signal fire to let her captors know that we were here. In the end, I decided against the notion, however. If they did not know, we might yet surprise them; and if Paladyr and his thugs knew already, it would be better to keep them guessing our intentions.

Near midday, Tegid came with some food for me. He placed the bowl beside my head and squatted at my side. "You should eat something."

"I am not hungry."

"It is not easy to fight demons on an empty stomach," he told me. "Since you are not sleeping, you might as well eat."

I raised myself on one elbow, and pulled the bowl toward me. It was a thick porridge of oats flavored with turnip and salted meat. I lifted the bowl and sucked down some of the mush. Tegid watched me closely.

"Well, what is on your mind, bard?"

"How are you feeling?"

"Tired," I replied. "But I cannot rest. I keep thinking of Goewyn."

"Goewyn will not be harmed."

"How can you be so certain?"

"Because it is you they want, not her. She is the bait in the trap."

Tegid spoke frankly. His calm manner allowed me to speak my deepest fear: "If that is true, they might have killed her already." My heart skipped a beat at the thought, but it was spoken and I felt the better for it. "We would not know it until we walked into the trap and by then, of course, it would be too late."

Tegid considered this for a moment, then shook his head slowly. "No." His tone was direct and certain. "I do not think that is the way of it." He paused, looking at me, studying me—as if I were an old acquaintance newly returned and he was trying to determine how I had changed.

"What is it, bard?" I said. "You have been inspecting me since I walked into camp this morning."

The corner of his mouth twitched into an awkward smile. "It is true. I want to hear more about this man with the white dogs—the man with the yellow mantle."

"I have told you all I know."

"Not all." He leaned towards me. "You know him, I think."

"I do not know him," I stated flatly. Tegid's look of reproof was quick and sharp. "I have seen him before," I confessed, "but I do not know him. It is not the same thing."

"Where did you see him?"

Anger spurted up like bile into my mouth. "It is nothing to do with any of this. Leave it."

But the bard did not desist. "Tell me."

Tegid's probing was making me remember my life in the other world and I resented it. I glowered at him, but complied. "It was not in this worlds-realm," I mumbled. "It was before, when I was with Simon—Siawn Hy—in the other place; he had gone into the cairn, and I was waiting for him to come out. I saw the man nearby."

"Describe this cairn," said Tegid. And when I had done so, he asked, "Did you also see the white dogs?"

"Yes, I saw the dogs—white with red ears. But they were with someone else—a farmer, I think—oh, it was all so long ago, I cannot remember. They were all there, I think."

The bard was silent for a long moment; at length he mused, "He was the same."

"Who was the same?"

"With the dogs or without them, it makes no difference," Tegid announced cryptically. When I asked for explanation, he said: "Yellow Coat is usually seen with the dogs, it is true. But you saw the dogs and you saw him—together or apart, it makes no difference."

"Bard, make plain your meaning."

"*Crom Cruach, Tuedd Tyrru, Crysmel Hen*—he goes by many names and in many forms," he said, his voice falling a note. "But in all he remains who he is: Lord of the Mound."

Tegid spoke the name and I felt a clammy hand at my throat. "I do not remember any mound," I said.

"When a warrior sees the Washer at the Ford," Tegid said, "he knows that death is at hand."

I had heard stories of this sort before. Typically, a warrior going into battle arrives at a river ford and sees a woman—sometimes sometimes wonderfully fair, sometimes brute ugly—washing bloodstained clothes in the water. If he asks whose clothes she is washing, the Morrigan will tell him that they are his own. By this the warrior knows his doom is near. I considered this, then asked, "Is it the same with Yellow Coat?"

"Only those whose affairs concern Crom Cruach may see him," Tegid replied with typical bardic ambiguity.

"Does it mean death?" I demanded bluntly.

He hesitated. "Not always."

"What does it mean then?"

"It means that Crom Cruach has acknowledged you."

This explanation fell somewhat short of full elucidation, and Tegid appeared reluctant to expand further. "Is this connected with me breaking my geas?" I asked.

"Rest now," Tegid said, rising. "We will talk later."

I finished my meal and tried to sleep. But Tegid's dark insinuations and the bustle of the camp kept me awake. After a time I gave up and joined the waiting men. We talked idly, avoiding any mention of the disturbing events of the previous night. Cynan tried to interest the warriors in a wrestling match, but the first grappling was so half-hearted that the game was abandoned.

The morning passed. The sun, almost warm, climbed through its low southern arc, trailing grey clouds like mouldered grave-clothes. Just before midday, the first scouting party returned to camp to report that they had discovered no sign of the enemy. The four who had ridden east, however, did not return.

We waited as long as we dared, and longer than was wise. Tegid kept one wary eye on the sun, and muttered under his breath while he stumped around impatiently. Finally, he said, "We cannot stay here longer."

"We cannot desert them," Cynan said. "Gweir was leading. I will not leave my battlechief and warriors behind."

The bard frowned and fumed a moment, then said, "Very well, we will go in search of them."

"What if it is a trap?" put in Bran. "Perhaps that is exactly what Paladyr expects us to do."

"Then we will spring his trap and be done with it," Tegid snapped. "Better to face Paladyr and his warband than spend another night on this accursed mound."

"True," agreed Bran.

"Then we ride east," I said.

We rode across the plain following the trail of the missing scouts through the coarse grass—granting the stubbed pillar stone a wide leeway—and reached the eastern rim as daylight dwindled. We stood looking out across the treetops at the land beyond: all brown and mist-faded grey, what we could see of it below the low-hanging clouds.

"This is where the trail ends," Bran said, his voice low.

"Ends?" I turned to look at him. His dark aspect was made darker still by the thick black beard he was growing; he seemed to be slowly changing into a raven.

He pointed to a trodden place in the grass; the snow was well trampled with hoofprints, but there was no sign of a skirmish of any kind. "The scouts stopped here, and here the trail also stops. They might have gone down into the wood," he said doubtfully.

"But you told them not to do that."

"Yes. I told them."

We started down the long wooded slope. The dense wood made our going difficult. We had not ridden far, however, when we were forced to dismount and blindfold the horses. As before, the animals stubbornly refused to be ridden into the wood, and we had to lead them on foot in order to continue. Even so, this did not slow our progress much, the undergrowth was so thick and the tangle so impenetrable.

Bran led, ranging the Ravens on either side of him in the hope that we might raise the trail of the missing scouts. But by dusk we had not seen a single footprint, much less any sign of a trail. We moved with maddening slowness, hacking a halting path through the underbrush with our swords. And despite this exertion, I noticed that the further down the slope we went, the colder it got—so that by the time we began looking for a likely place to camp, we were all wrapped chin to heel in our cloaks, and our breath hung in frosty clouds above our heads.

We made camp under a great gnarled oak beneath whose twisted limbs we found a reasonable clearing. Brushwood was gleaned from round about and heaped into three sizeable piles from which we would feed three good fires. Tegid lit each fire himself, saying, "With three, if one goes out there are always two with which to rekindle it."

"Are you thinking the fires will fail?" I wondered.

"I am thinking that it is dangerous to be without a fire at night," was his reply. Accordingly, we appointed men to tend the fires through the night just to make certain they did not falter.

The night passed cold, but uneventful, and we awakened to nothing more sinister than a dull dogged rain. The next day brought no change, nor did those that followed. We pushed through an endless succession of barbed thickets dense as hedge, hauling ourselves over fallen trunks, wading through mud and mire, scrambling over and around great rocks. By day we shambled after one another in a sodden procession; by night we did our best to dry out. With every step the air grew colder so that by the fifth day the rain changed to snow. This did nothing to improve our progress, but the change was welcome nonetheless.

We walked in silence. Scatha, grim-faced and morose, spoke to no one; nor did Tegid have much to say. Cynan and Bran addressed their men in terse, blunt words, and only when necessary. I could find nothing to say to anyone, and slogged along as mute and miserable as the rest.

The slope flattened so gradually that we did not realize we had finally left the mound until we came to a slow-moving stream fringed with tall pines and slender birches. "It will be easier going from now on," Bran observed.

Although we had not been attacked by the sluagh again, I felt a rush of relief wash over me once the mound was left behind. I sensed we had also left behind its preying spirits. We rested under the pines and followed the stream all the next day. The trees were old and the branches high; the undergrowth thinned considerably, which made the going easier. Gradually, the stream widened to become a small,

turgid river which wound between mud-slick banks among the
exposed roots of the pines. From time to time, we glimpsed a
desultory sun through breaks in the close-grown branches overhead.

As daylight faded in a dull ochre haze, we reached the end of the
wood at last and looked out upon a wide valley between two long
rock-topped bluffs. Snow covered the valley floor, but the snow was
not deep. The river took on new life as it flowed out from the wood
over a rocky bed. There were few trees to be seen, so we decided to
stay the night at the edge of the wood where we would be assured of
fuel for the fires. We spent all the next morning amassing firewood
and loading the horses with as much as they could carry. Still,
despite a late start, we made fair progress and by day's end had
travelled further than we had any day since coming to Tir Aflan.

The sun remained hidden behind a solid mass of low, swart cloud
for the next few days as we traced a course along the river, stopping
only to water the horses and to eat and sleep. The weather continued
cold, but the snow fell infrequently, and never for long. We saw
neither bird nor beast at any time; neither did we see any track save
our own in the thin snow cover.

For all we knew, we were the only people ever to penetrate so far
into the Foul Land. This impression lasted for a long while—until we
began seeing the ruins.

At first it seemed that the bluff-top on the left-hand side of the
valley had simply become more ragged with impromptu heaps of
stone and jagged, toothy outcrops. But, as we pushed further down
the length of the valley, the bluffs sank lower and closer to the valley
floor to reveal the shattered remnants of a wall.

We looked on the ruined wall with the same mixture of dread and
fascination we had experienced on encountering the mound. Day
succeeded day, and with every step the wall grew higher and more
ominous: snaking darkly along the undulating ridgetop above us,
gapped where the stone had collapsed and slid down the sheer
bluffsides into broken heaps below. On the sixth day we came in
sight of the bridge and tower.

The tower sat on a bare hump of rock at a place where the valley narrowed. The remains of a double row of demolished columns stumbled across the valley floor and river to the facing bluff opposite. We proceeded to the huge round segments lying half-buried in the ground—like the sawn trunks of megalithic trees—sinking into the land under their own bulk and an enormous weight of years. Here we halted.

At some time in the ancient past, the river must have been a roaring torrent spanned by a great bridge—a feat for giants. And guarding the bridge at one end, a bleak, brooding tower. The same questions were on every man's mind: who had raised the tower? What lay beyond the wall? What did they keep out? Curiosity grew too much to resist. We halted and made camp among the half-sunken columns. And then Cynan, Tegid, the Ravens and I scaled the bluffside.

The tower was stone, comprised of three sections raised in stepped ranks. There were odd round windows, like empty eye sockets staring out across to the other side. At ground level was a single entrance with a gate and door unlike any I had ever seen: round, like the windows; and the door was a great wheel made of stone, not wood, banded with iron around its rim and set into a wide groove. The surface of the gate and door were covered with carved symbols which were now too weathered to comprehend. The remains of a stone-flagged road issued from the gate and ended where the bridge had once joined the bluff. Judging from the width of the road, the bridge would have been wide enough for horsemen riding four abreast.

The wall joined the tower level with its first rank, easily three times a man's height. There was no way in, except through the round gate, and there was apparently no way to budge the great stone door. But Alun and Garanaw grew inquisitive and began examining the gate. It was not long before they put their shoulders to it, and between the two of them got it to move.

"It will roll," cried Alun. "Help us clear the groove."

The track in which the stone rolled was choked with rock debris. In no time, with the help of Emyr, Drustwn, and Niall, they succeeded in removing the grit and stone. And then they turned their attention to the door itself. The five Ravens gave a mighty heave and pushed.

To everyone's amazement the stone rumbled easily aside, revealing a darkened chamber beyond.

After warily poking their heads inside, they reported that they could see nothing. "We need torches," Tegid advised, and at a nod from their chief, Emyr and Niall scrambled back down the cliff to fetch a bundle each. We waited impatiently while Tegid set about lighting them. But soon the torches were kindled and distributed and, with pulses pounding, we passed through the imposing gate and into the strange tower.

24

The High Tower

Cautiously, shoulders hunched, walking on the balls of our feet, prowling like thieves desperate not to wake the sleeping occupants, we entered the dark tower.

The air was damp and smelled of earth and wet stone like that inside a cave. And even with the torches, it was dark as a cave. Gradually, however, as our eyes became adjusted to the fluttering light, we began to pick out individual features in the darkness.

We stood in a single large chamber, two or three times larger, for all I could tell, than any king's great hall. There was a single row of stone pillars through the center of the room supporting the floor above. Huge iron rings were fixed in the pillars at various heights.

"Here!" called Drustwn from a little way ahead. "Look here!"

In a jumbled heap, as if tossed aside in a moment's wrath, were a score of bronze chariots, their wheels warped and poles bent or broken, the metal green with age. The high, circular sides of the chariots appeared to be wicker, but were in fact triangular strips of bronze woven together, immensely strong for their weight.

Lying a little apart from the chariots was a small pyramid of large discs, stacked one atop another. And beside this, a pile of oversized axeheads—unusual in that they consisted of a short stout blade on one side balanced by a blunt spike on the other. There must have been several hundred of these and as many discs which, on closer inspection, turned out to be bronze shields.

Bran pulled one of the shields from the stack, causing a dusty avalanche. He lifted the round device by the rim and held it before him; it was huge, much larger than any the men of Albion used, and plain. Its only markings appeared on the center boss: a few curious symbols worked in raised bronze around the simple image of a peculiar thick-bodied serpent.

"Whoever carried this was a stronger man than me," Bran remarked, replacing the shield, and retrieving his torch.

We continued our examination but, aside from a neat row of short, heavy bronze thrusting spears, we found nothing else in the lower chamber, and took our search up a flight of stone steps to the next level.

The round windows in the center of each of the four walls allowed some light to enter the large, square room, the floor of which was littered with helmets and war caps—high crowned and rising to a slight point at the top, all of bronze, and all with a bronze serpent coiled around the rim with its flat head raised upon the brow. Alun picked one up and set it on his head, but it was made for a man twice his size. There were perhaps two hundred or more of these serpent-crested helmets scattered on the floor, but nothing else in the room.

On the floor above we discovered a great stone table set with huge bowls of silver and bronze, with one gold vessel among them. The silver was black and the bronze green, but the gold was good as the day it was made; it gleamed dully in the light of our torches. Also on the table were three piles of coins in the rotted remains of leather bags. The coins were silver and gold. The silver coins were little more than black lumps, but the gold shone bright. We took up some of these and looked at them.

"Here is their king," said Tegid, holding a coin before his eyes. "I cannot read his name."

The coin showed the image of a man as if etched by a precocious child. The man clasped a short spear in one hand and a spiked axe in the other. He was bareheaded and his hair was long, curling down to his shoulders; he wore beard and moustache almost as long. His chest was bare—he bore no torc or other ornament—but he wore what appeared to be striped breecs or leggings, and tall boots on his feet. Words in strange letters clustered like wasps around his head, but they were impossible to read.

We each took a handful of the coins to show the others, and Cynan took the gold bowl. "For Tángwen, when I see her," he said.

Beside the table stood a large iron tripod bearing a huge bronze cauldron. Beneath the cauldron was a ring of fire-blackened stones, and inside it the baked, brick-hard shards of the last meal. But the outside of the cauldron was what caught my eye. The surface was alive with activity: warriors in chariots charged around the bottom of the cauldron lofting spears, long hair trailing in the wind; on the next tier above, narrow-eyed men on horses galloped, brandishing swords and spears; above these were ranks of warriors on foot, shoulder to shoulder, bearing round shields and helmets such as we had seen in the lower chamber; on the highest tier a number of winged men were running, or perhaps flying, and each bore a serpent in his right hand and a leafy branch in his left. The rim of the cauldron was a scaly serpent with its tail in its mouth.

"The Men of the Serpent," Tegid said, indicating the warriors.

"Do you know of them?"

"Their tale is remembered among the Derwyddi but, like the song of Tir Aflan, we do not sing it." I thought he would not say more but, gazing at the cauldron, he continued, "It is said that the Serpent awoke and with a mighty war host subdued the land. When there were no more enemies to conquer the Serpent Men fell into disputes and warring among themselves. They destroyed all they had built, and when the last of them died, the Serpent crawled back into the underworld to sleep until awakened again."

"What awakens it?" I asked.

"Very great evil," was his only reply.

Strewn about the room were objects of everyday use: more cups and bowls; many short, bone-handled swords fused to their scabbards; a few round shields; a collection of small pots, flasks, and boxes carved of a soft reddish stone—all of them empty; several long, curved spoon-shaped ladles and long-handled forks for getting meat and broth from the cauldron; numerous axeheads; knives of various sizes; a mask of bronze showing the glowering face of a bearded warrior with a great flowing moustache, elaborately curled hair, and a serpent helmet on his head, his mouth open in full cry; four very tall lampstands, one in each corner, bearing stone-carved oil lamps.

Underneath one of the shields, Emyr found a curious object—a circlet of small shield-like discs linked together around a protruding conical horn. Turning it this way and that, he announced, "I think it is a crown." Like most of the other objects we had seen, it was made of bronze and, when he put it on his head, it was shown to have been made for a much larger head.

"*Mo anam,*" muttered Cynan, trying the crown himself, "but these serpent men were giants."

"Look at this!" called Garanaw, holding his torch to the far wall.

We crossed to where he stood and saw a painting on the wall. It was well done, and no doubt brightly colored at one time. And though the colors had faded to an almost uniform grey-brown, leering out at us was the face of a serpent man, fleshy lips curved in a mocking smile, pale reptilian eyes staring with frozen mirth, his mouth open and forked tongue extended. A mass of coiled curls wreathed the face, and below the chin it was still possible to make out the winged torso and a raised hand grasping a black serpent which coiled around the arm.

We turned from the painting and Niall called our attention to an iron ladder set in a recess of one wall. The ladder rose through the stone ceiling to the roof above. He climbed it and then called down for us to follow. There was nothing on the roof, but the view was breathtaking. Looking to the south, far below us in the riverbed among the fallen columns, lay our camp, men and horses gathered near the grey thread of moving water.

To the west rose the gigantic hump of the mound, its top lost in the low-hanging cloud, and to the east only the river flowing on between its rock-bound bluffs. To the north, behind the high stone wall stretching away to the east and west, lay an endless series of low, snow-covered hills, rising and falling like white sea waves in a frozen ocean.

The size and emptiness of the landscape, like that of the dark tower and its objects, made us feel small and weak, and foolish for trespassing where we did not belong. I scanned the rolling hillscape for any sign of habitation, but saw neither smoke nor any trail by which we might go. "What do you think, bard?" I asked Tegid, who stood beside me.

"I think we should leave this place to its dire memories," he answered.

"I am all for it, but where do we go from here?"

"East," he replied without hesitation.

"Why east? Why not south or west?"

"Because east is where we will find Goewyn."

This intrigued me. "How do you know?"

"Do you remember when Meldron cast us adrift?"

"Mutilated and left to die in an open boat—could I ever forget it?"

"In exchange for my eyes, I was given a vision." He made it sound as if he had merely traded one pair of breecs for another.

"I remember. You sang it in a song."

"Do you remember the vision?"

"Vaguely," I said.

"I remember it." He closed his eyes as if he would see it anew. He began to sing, and I listened, recalling the terrible night that vision had been given.

Softly, so that only I would hear, Tegid sang of a steep-sided glen, and a fortress on a shining lake. He sang of an antler throne adorned with white oxhide and established high on a grass-covered mound. He sang of a burnished shield with the black raven perched on its rim, wings outspread, raising its raucous song to heaven. He sang of a beacon-fire flaming the night sky, its signal answered from hilltop to hilltop. He sang of a shadowy rider on a pale yellow horse, riding out of the mist which bound them; the horses' hooves striking sparks from the rocks. He sang of a great warband bathing in a mountain lake, the water blushing red from their wounds. He sang of a golden-haired woman in a sunlit bower, and a hidden Hero Mound.

Some things I recognized: Druim Vran, Dinas Dwr, my antler throne; the golden-haired woman in the bower was Goewyn on our wedding day. But other things I did not know at all.

When he had finished, his eyes flicked open again and he said, "This land has a part in my vision. I did not know it before coming here to this tower."

"You mentioned no tower in your vision—was there a tower?"

"No," he confessed, "but this is the land. I know it by the feel and taste and smell." His dark eyes scanned the far hills, rising and falling one behind another to the edge of sight and beyond. "In this worlds-realm a mighty work waits to be accomplished."

"The only mighty work I care about is rescuing Goewyn before—" I broke off abruptly. The others were not listening, but they were close by.

"Before the child is born," Tegid finished the thought for me.

"Before anything happens to *either* of them."

"We will journey in hope, and trust the Swift Sure Hand to guide us."

"A little guidance would not go amiss right now," I confessed, gazing out at the trackless waste of hills and empty sky.

"Llew," he said, "we have ever been led."

We left the roof, retreating back through the tower to the gate. Tegid advised us to close the door, so we rolled the stone back to its place. Then we climbed down the bluff to rejoin our waiting warband. We showed them the coins we had found and they wanted to go back up and get the rest, but Tegid would not allow it. He said further disturbance would not be welcome.

They let it go at that. The tower had a dolorous air, and even those who had not been inside felt the oppressive sadness of the place. Besides, it was already getting dark and no one wanted to risk being caught outside the fire-ring after nightfall.

That night we listened to the plaintive cry of the wind tearing itself on the broken stones of the wall on the bluffs high above. I slept ill, my dreams filled with winged serpents and bronze-clad men.

Twice I wakened and rose to look at the tower—a brooding black bulk against a blacker sky. It seemed to be watching us, perched on its high rock like a preying bird, waiting to unfold its wings of darkness and swoop upon us. I was not the only one bothered by bad dreams; the horses jigged and jittered all night long, and once one of the men cried out in his sleep.

We continued on our way the next day, listening to the wind hiss and moan through the valley. The snow fell steadily and drifted around our feet; we pulled our cloaks over our heads, bundled our saddle fleeces around our shoulders for warmth, and slogged through the weary day. The scenery altered slightly, but never really changed—always when I lifted my head there were the sheer bluffs and the wall looming ragged and dark above.

For five days it was the same—cold and snow and deep starless nights filled with wailing wind and morbid dreams. We struggled through each day, riding and walking by turns, shuddering with cold, and huddling as close as possible to the fires at night. And then, as the sixth day neared its end, we saw that the bluffs had begun to sink lower and the river to spread as the valley opened. Two days later we came to a place where the bluff ended and the wall turned to continue its solitary journey north over the endless hills. Rising before us was the dark bristling line of a forest.

Seeing it, like a massive battlehost arrayed on the horizon, my spirit quailed within me. Tir Aflan was a wasteland vast beyond reckoning. Where was Goewyn? How would we ever find her in this wilderness?

"Listen, bard, are you sure this is the way?" I demanded of Tegid when we stopped to water the horses. We had left the wall behind and were drawing near the leading edge of the forest, but there was still no clear sign that we were going in the right direction.

Tegid did not reply at once, and did not look at me when he did. "The forest you see before us is older than Albion," he said, his dark eyes scanning the treeline as he rolled his ashwood staff between his palms.

"Did you hear me?" I demanded. "Is this the way we are to go?"

"Before men walked on Albion's fair shores, this forest was already ancient. Among the Learned it is said that all the world's forests are but seedlings to these trees."

"Fascinating. But what I want to know is, do you have even the haziest notion of where we are going?"

"We are going into the forest," he answered. "In the forest of the night, we all find what we seek—or it finds us."

Bards!

25

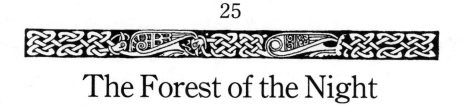

The Forest of the Night

Taking the river as our only guide, we passed into the forest. The snow, which had drifted deep in the exposed valley, was but scant under the trees. And such trees!

There were trees of every kind: along the river were stands of silver birch, willows of various types, thickets of elder, blackthorn, hawthorn, hazel and holly; and on the broad meads stood great groves of oak, chestnut, hornbeam, lime, elm, sycamore, plane, walnut, ash, larch, and others; on the high ground there were evergreens: fir and pine and spruce in abundance, as well as cedar and yew. Lichen and moss flourished, making every trunk and branch look as if someone had slathered it in thick, grey-green plaster.

I could well believe that the forest was ancient. The moss-bound branches were bent and the trunks bowed by ages of years beyond counting, eons of accumulated leafmould cushioned the forest floor, dry grass like wisps of unkempt hair clustered in elderly hanks around massive curving roots. The trees were old.

And big! The river, wide and deep as it entered the forest, seemed to dwindle to the size of a mere brook beneath those massive boles. Some of the larger limbs stretched from one bank clear across to the other, arching over the river like huge arboreal snakes.

We moved in a world of outsize proportions. And the further into the forest we penetrated, the smaller and more vulnerable we felt—shrinking in our own eyes. In the shadows of those ancient trees we were not men at all, but insects: insignificant, powerless, futile.

Dismaying though it was to be a mere insect, more unsettling by far was the silence.

As we entered the forest, the sound of the world beyond faded, and it diminished further with every step until we could hear nothing at all—not even the wind. No alien birdcall reached our ears, no tick of leafless branch, or creak of sagging limb. Our own footfalls were muffled in the spongy leafmould, and the river flowed mute in its slime-slick bed.

I was speculating whether the cold had stolen my hearing, when Cynan called out, "*Mo anam*, brothers! But this quiet is not natural among men of noble clans. What do we fear that we dare not raise a pleasant tune when and where we please?"

When no one answered him, the red-haired hero began to sing, roaring out the words as if he were bending horseshoes with them. Full-throated, his head thrown back, he sang:

> *Hie, up! Rise up, brave and dauntless friends!*
>   *The sun is red on gorsey hill,*
>   *and my black hound is straining to the trail.*
> *Hie, up! Rise up, bold and doughty men!*
>   *The deer do run on heathered brae,*
>   *and my brown horse is tending to the trace.*
> *Hie, up! Rise up, raven-haired lady fair!*
>   *A kiss before I join the chase,*
>   *A kiss before I fly . . . Hie!*

It was a valiant effort, and I admired him for it. He even succeeded in rousing some of the men for a time, but no one had the heart to sustain it. This angered Cynan, who sang on alone for a time out of sheer stubbornness. But eventually even Cynan's brash spirit was stifled by the vast, all-absorbing silence of the forest.

Thereafter we pursued our way with hushed steps, dull in sense and dispirited. The forest seemed to prey upon our minds and hearts, stirring our fears, bringing doubt and dread to the surface where they could wear away at us with their corrosive power. I suspected that we were being watched, that in the forest around us, hidden from sight, the enemy waited.

In the lattice-work of limbs high over us, in the shadow-choked darkness beyond the river trail, behind every trunk and bole, cold eyes watched and cold hands waited. I imagined a multitude of winged serpent-men clutching their short bronze thrusting spears, eyeing us with icy reptilian malice. I imagined that they moved as we moved, matching us stride for stride, gliding with the silence of snakes in the silence of the forest.

I told myself that my fears were mere inventions of my mind, but I watched the shadows all the same.

Night stole secretly over the forest, and it marked little change. In this place, ever dark and preternaturally still, daylight was a weak and alien presence. *Coed Nos*, Forest of the Night, is what Tegid had called it, and he was right. The sun might boldly pursue its diurnal course, might rise and set in blinding flames that caught the outside world alight; but we had entered Night's own realm and the sun had no power in that place.

We made camp by the deep-flowing river and banked the fires high. If I hoped fire would offer us some comfort, I was deceived. The forest seemed to suck the warmth and light, the very life, from the flames, making them appear pale and wan and impotent. We sat with faces close to the tepid blaze and felt the stealthy silence hard at our backs.

I could not rest. I could not eat or speak to anyone, but every few moments I must turn my head and peer over my shoulder. The feeling was strong—I was certain of it—we were being stalked. Others felt it too, I think; there was no talk, no genial exchange around the fire as there usually is when men gather after a long day's journey. It seemed that if we could not overcome the all-subduing silence, we preferred to sink into it, to let it cover us and hide us from the things that stalked the shadows.

We made a miserable night of it. No one slept; we all lay awake, gazing into the crowded tangle of limbs and branches faintly illumined by our feeble fire. That does not mean, however, that we did not dream. We did. And I think each man among us was visited by queer, disturbing nightmares.

Sitting hunched over my knees, staring hollow-eyed into the limb-twisted darkness, I saw a faintly glimmering shape that resolved itself into a human form as it approached: a woman, slender, clad in white. Goewyn?

I jumped to my feet.

Goewyn!

I ran to her. She was shivering, her arms were bare and cold, and it was clear that she had been wandering in the forest for many days. She must have escaped from her captors and fled into the forest.

"Goewyn! Oh, Goewyn, you are safe," I said, and reached out to take her hand, forgetting that my metal hand would be cold against her skin. I touched her with it and she cried out.

"I am cold, Llew," she whimpered.

"Here, take my cloak," I said, drawing it from my shoulders. "Put it around you. Come to the fire. I will warm you," I said, and thrust my silver hand into the flames of the campfire.

In a moment, the metal warmed and I turned and took Goewyn's hand in mine. The metal was too hot and it seared into her flesh. Acrid smoke flared up, stinging my eyes. Goewyn screamed and pulled away, but the skin stuck to the metal and came off as she jerked her hand from my grasp. And not the skin only—the burned muscle stuck too.

Screaming in agony, she raised her hand before her face, but only bones were left. Without the muscles or ligaments to hold them together they separated and fell to the ground and were lost in the snow. Goewyn clutched her stub of arm and screamed.

I stood in a panic of indecision, wanting to comfort her, but not daring to touch her for fear that my touch would maim. Tegid ran to us. He took Goewyn by the shoulders and began shaking her violently. "Be quiet!" he shouted. "Be quiet! They will hear you!"

But she could not control herself. Tears flowed from her eyes and she sobbed, holding her arm. Tegid kept shouting at her to be quiet, that she would alert the enemy.

Bran came running with his sword. Without a word to anyone, he struck Goewyn. She turned toward him and he thrust the blade into her heart. He pulled it out again and a scarlet stain flowed down her white mantle. She turned and cried out. "Llew! Save me!"

But I could not move. I could do nothing to save my beloved. She fell, scattering drops of blood from her wound. She lay on her back and raised her arm toward me. "Llew..." she gasped, her voice already fading. My name was the last word on her lips.

Her warm blood seeped from the wound, melting deep into the white-drifted snow. And the snow began to melt—and went on melting. Soon I could see green showing through the snow; grass was growing, growing up where the blood melted the snow.

I raised my eyes to look around. I was not in the forest any more. Tegid and Bran had departed and left me standing alone on a hilltop above a stream; across the stream stood a grove of slender silver birches. I watched as the snow melted from the sides of the hill and hundreds of yellow flowers appeared. The clouds parted, revealing a bright blue sky and a warming sun.

When I turned back, Goewyn was gone, but there was a slight mound in the place where she lay—little more than a grassy hump of earth. Upon this mound a cluster of white flowers grew: a yarrow plant had sprouted where Goewyn lay.

With tears in my eyes, I turned away and stumbled down the hill to the stream where I knelt and bathed my face in the clear cold water. While I was washing there, I heard a voice coming from the birch grove—a melody falling light as birdsong. I rose and splashed across the stream and entered the grove.

I stepped softly through dappled green shadows and passed among the slender white birch trees, following the song. I came to a clearing and paused. In the center of the clearing in a pool of golden sunlight stood a bower made of birch branches; the song was coming from the bower.

My senses quickened. I moved cautiously from the cover of the trees and entered the meadow. At my approach the singing stopped. I saw a movement from within the green-shadowed interior, and I, too, halted.

A woman clothed in green and yellow emerged. Her hair was softly golden in the sunlight, falling around her face and, with her head bent, I could not see who it was. She stepped gracefully from the arbor and cupped her hands to the sun as if she would gather in sunbeams like water. And then, though I had not moved or even breathed, she turned to me and said, "Llew, there you are. I have been waiting for you. Why do you tarry so?"

At this she pulled back the hair from her face. I gaped in disbelief. She laughed at my distraction and said, "Well, where is my welcome kiss?" And oh, her voice was sweet music to my ear.

"Goewyn?"

She held out her arms to me. "I am waiting, best beloved."

"Goewyn, you are dead. I saw you die."

"Dead?" She said the word as gently as a butterfly lighting on a petal. Still smiling—her lips formed a delicious curve that swept into the fold of her soft cheek—she lifted her chin in mock defiance. "I am done with dying," she said. "Now, where is my kiss?"

I stepped willingly into her embrace and felt her warm lips on mine and a taste like honey on my tongue. I crushed her to me, kissing her mouth and cheek and neck, holding her tight lest she slip like bright sunlight through my fingers.

"I thought I had lost you," I told her, tears of joy welling in my eyes. I breathed in the warm living scent of her as if I could breath her in with it, make her part of me. "Never leave me, Goewyn."

She laughed softly. "Leave you? How could I ever leave you? You are part of me now, as I am part of you."

"Tell me, again. Please, tell me you will never leave me."

"I will never leave you, my soul," she whispered. "I love you for ever ... for ever ..."

"Llew? What are you doing?"

The voice was Tegid's. I turned on him with some exasperation.

"Can you not see what I am doing? You are not wanted here. Go away."

"Llew, come back to the fire. You have been dreaming."

"What?"

Tegid's face grew dim, as if a cloud had passed overhead, blotting out the sun.

"Come back to camp with me," he said. "You have been walking in your sleep."

With these words, the sun-favored clearing vanished. I looked around and saw that I was back in the forest and it was night. The leafy bower was gone, and Goewyn was nowhere to be seen.

I spoke to no one for two whole days after that. Heartsick, discouraged and embarrassed, I avoided all my companions. If any command was required, Cynan or Bran saw to it and gave the order.

We pushed deeper into the forest. The trees grew larger, their great entwined limbs and interlaced branches imprisoning the light, making our passage dim and, if that were possible, even more silent. If we had been sewn in leather sacks it could not have been closer or more stifling than Coed Nos had become.

An air of malignant weariness emanated from the twisting roots and boles around us; languor seeped like an ooze from the soft leafmould under our feet. Lethargy, like the grey lichen that covered everything, clung to our limbs, bleeding strength with every step.

We rode single file, heads down, shoulders bent. Those on foot went ahead so that no one should be left behind. Tegid feared that if anyone fell back, we would never see them again. Cynan and Bran took it in turn to lead, changing every time we stopped to rest and water the horses. They did their best to keep a steady pace and keep the men moving despite the torpor.

Even so, we seemed not so much to journey as to view a slowly-revolving trail. We moved, but did not advance; we proceeded, but never arrived. We staggered steadily forward toward a perpetually receding destination. Day passed day, and we gradually lost track of the days. We slept little, talked less, and drove ourselves relentlessly on.

Food became scarce. We had hoped to hunt in the forest—at least to encounter game we might take along the way. If there was game in the forest, we never saw it, nor crossed any animal trail. Our dried meat gave out, and we subsisted on old bread and ale, soaking the crusts in our cups to soften them. When the ale ran out, we used water from the river. The bread became moldy and unfit to eat, but we ate it anyway. There was nothing else. And when the bread was gone, we boiled the precious little grain we had left with roots and bark that Tegid found to make a thin gruel. The horses ate the grey lichen which we harvested from the trunks with knives and swords, and bound into bales for them. It was food ill-suited for such noble beasts, but at least there was an unending supply of the stuff and they ate it readily enough.

We grew long-bearded, and sallow-skinned from lack of sunlight. But we bathed regularly in the river—until the men began to encounter leeches whenever they entered the slow-flowing water. Thereafter, we left off bathing altogether and contented ourselves with washing only.

Cynan grew restive. As the days progressed, he urged us to greater speed and complained with increasing regularity that we were not making enough effort to get clear of the forest.

"Be easy, brother," Bran advised. "Nothing will be gained by pushing too hard."

"It is taking too long," Cynan grumped. "We should have come through this forest long ago."

"Do not lose heart," I told him. "We will come to the end soon."

Cynan turned on me. "My wife is taken, too! Or have you forgotten? I tell you she is no less a queen than your precious Goewyn!"

"I know, brother," I soothed. "Please, be—"

"You think I do not care for my wife?" he challenged. "You think, because I say nothing, that I do not speak her name in my heart with every step?"

"I am sure you do, Cynan. Calm yourself. We will find them both." I put my hand on his arm. He knocked it away, glared at me, and then stormed off.

Some time later—two days or ten, I no longer knew—we stepped from the forest into a clearing bounded by the high rock bluffs of the river. And in the center of the clearing on the left bank stood a city, ruined and deserted, carved into the red stone bank. I call it a city, though closer scrutiny soon revealed that it was a single structure: an enormous palace with hundreds upon hundreds of dwelling places, halls, walls, columns, courts, and shrines, all heaped together in a haphazard jumble of red stone.

We came upon it suddenly and stood blinking in the light of a faded day. It was the first we had seen of the sky for days uncounted, and all we could do was to stand and stare, our hands shielding our sore eyes. And then, quivering with the shock of the sun and sky and easy air, we crept cautiously forward—as if the strange red palace were a mirage that might vanish if we glanced away.

But the structure was solid stone from the countless pinnacles of its high-peaked rooftops to its many-chambered foundations. Most of the columns were broken and the roofs collapsed; the round eye-socket windows stood empty and unlit. However, by far the greater part of the palace remained intact. Carved figures of animals and birds were placed in the pediments, but we saw no human figures represented. The edifice had been constructed to front the river. Indeed, a single round entrance like that of the high tower, but larger by far, opened onto a terrace which ended in a wide sweep of steps descending directly to the black water. The stone-carved walls flowed in curves, bending into one another like limbs, merging without joints or straight lines. This gave the place a disturbingly organic quality which Cynan identified at once. "Aye, see it lying there—like a great red lizard asprawl on the riverbank."

"Indeed," agreed Alun Tringad. "It is a sleeping lizard. Let it lie."

Nothing moved; no sound could be heard among the rubble. The red palace was as lifeless and deserted as the tower we had seen before, and just as old. And yet, whatever power preserved the structure had not entirely abandoned it. For clearly the palace still exerted dominion over the forest, or else the red stone would have been overgrown long ago. Something yet lingered which prevented the vegetation from invading and reclaiming the clearing and its deserted edifice, root and branch.

At the far end of the terrace, the broken remains of what appeared to be a wide, stone-paved road led from the city at an angle away from the river. Tegid observed the red palace for a long time, and then counselled us to move on, saying, "It is an evil place. We will find nothing but misery here."

Alas! We should have heeded his wise counsel.

26

Yr Gyrem Rua

Even in the short time we had been contemplating the ruin, daylight began to dwindle; it would be dusk soon, and night followed swiftly. We would have to find a place to make camp, and I was determined not to spend another night in the forest. So we decided to pass by the palace to the road beyond and see where it might lead.

In two tight lines, we moved out onto the terrace. Strange to feel solid rock under foot, stranger still to hear the hollow echo of hoofs after the smothering silence of the forest. We crept slowly across the wide terrace, every step ringing in our ears, reverberating from a hundred angled walls.

Bran, leading the procession, reached the center of the terrace—midway between the river steps and the gaping entrance to the palace. I saw him look to this door, turn, and stop. He raised his hand for those behind him to halt. "I saw something move in there," he explained as Cynan and I joined him.

I looked to the entrance—round as a wheel, and five times the height of a man, it was also dark as a pit; I could not imagine how he saw anything inside.

"Let us move on," I said, and was still looking at the empty doorway when we heard the cry: plaintive, pitiable, the wail of a lost and frightened child.

"*Mo anam,*" muttered Cynan, "there is a babe in there."

We stared at one another for a moment, wondering what to do. "We cannot pass by and leave the poor thing," Cynan said. "It is not right."

Loath as I was to agree with him, I conceded to a quick investigation. "It must be swift indeed," Tegid warned. "It will be dark soon. We dare not linger."

Leaving Scatha and the rest to guard the horses, Bran, Emyr, Garanaw, Tegid, Cynan and I prepared torches and crept toward the red palace, watching the vacant entrance as we drew nearer. We saw nothing and the cry did not come again.

At the threshold, we paused to light the torches and entered an enormous, empty hall. Surprisingly, the room was many times larger on the inside than it appeared from the outside. The reason for this, Tegid immediately discovered. "It is all one," he pointed out. "There is but a single chamber."

All the hundreds of windows which, on the outside, appeared to open onto separate rooms, served to shed light on this single gigantic chamber. Even so, there was precious little illumination, just enough to see that we stood on a ledge with wide, shallow steps leading down to a floor somewhere below. Neither the floor below nor the roof above could be seen from where we stood, and the light of our torches did little to challenge the darkness of the place.

The air inside the hall was dank and cold—colder than outside. We stood and listened, our breath hanging in clouds around us. Hearing nothing, we started down the steps, shoulder to shoulder, torches held high. Each step stirred an echo that flitted like a bat into the darkness.

"A cheerless house, this," muttered Bran, his voice ringing in the vast emptiness.

"Even with a blaze the hearth would be cold," added Emyr.

"Still, I would welcome a fire now," Garanaw said. "The darkness here is dark indeed."

Six steps down, we came onto a wide landing, and then six more to another landing, and a final six to the floor, which was covered with six-sided glazed black tiles. The tiles glistened with moisture and made a slick surface for our feet as we moved slowly to the center of the hall where the firepit would be.

"Your hopes for a welcome fire are in vain, Garanaw," remarked Tegid. "There is no hearth."

No hearthstone, no fire-ring, nor even a brazier such as we had seen in the tower. The room, as far as we could tell, was devoid of any furniture whatsoever. Instead, where the hearth would have been, there was a mosaic picked out in small red, white and black tesserae depicting the same winged serpent emblem we had seen in the tower. The serpent here, however, was less stylized and somewhat more lifelike: sinuous red coils shimmering in the torchlight, red eyes glaring, reptilian wings spread behind its flat head. And there was a word spelled out in red tiles beneath it, which I took to be the creature's name.

I looked at the image traced upon the floor and my silver hand sent a warning tingle up my arm.

My eyes were better adjusted to the dark now, and I saw that the great room was oval-shaped, its many-peaked roof supported by rows of tapering columns whose tops were lost to the blackness above. Directly opposite the entrance door across the expanse of floor, a second round doorway, nearly as large as the first, opened into the smooth rockface of the bank.

We proceeded warily across the room to this second doorway, which proved to be the opening of a cave—elaborately dressed with fine finished stone without, but nothing more than a ragged rock tunnel inside. It came to me that the whole palace was but a façade built to conceal or, more likely, to enshrine this single cave entrance.

"Well," said Cynan, eyeing the tunnel doubtfully, "we have come this far. Will we turn back without seeing what lies beyond?"

Up spoke Tegid. "Do you yet wonder what lies beyond?"

"Enlighten us, bard," Cynan said. "I cannot guess."

"Can you not? Very well then, I will tell you. It is the creature whose image we have seen since coming to the Foul Land."

"The beast set in the floor back there?" wondered Cynan,

gesturing to the empty hall behind us.

"The same," said Tegid. "It is in my mind that this hole leads to the lair of the beast. *Yr Gyrem Rua* is its name."

"The Red Serpent?" murmured Cynan. The warriors glanced around warily. "Do you know this beast?"

"Unless I am much mistaken," the bard replied, "the creature within is that which the Learned call the Red Serpent of Oeth." He hesitated. "Some call it Wyrm."

"Wyrm..." Bran muttered, glancing over his shoulder.

Sick dread broke like a wave over me; I understood now why the palace consisted of just one room, and why the bronze men of the high tower revered the image of the serpent: it was their god; they sacrificed to it. And this was Yr Gyrem Rua's shrine and sanctuary.

"Let us leave this place while we may," urged Bran.

With that, we turned from the door, retreating back across the floor but three paces when the cry sounded again—the thin, tremorous whimper of a forlorn and miserable infant.

"The child has wandered in there," gasped Cynan, hurrying back to the cave entrance. Peering inside, he put his hands to his mouth and called to the child, waited, and when he received no reply, started into the tunnel.

I snatched him by the cloak and pulled him back. "You cannot go in there alone."

"Then come with me, brother."

I turned back to the others. "Stay here," I said. "We will take a quick look inside."

Trembling in every limb, Cynan and I started down the tunnel, the light of our torches flickering on the damp red stone. We moved cautiously on, but encountered little more than a strong smell: musty and somewhat sweet, but with a ripe gamey taint, like rancid oil or fat.

Fifty paces more and I saw a glistening mass lying on the floor of the passage. My metal hand went suddenly cold and I stopped in my tracks.

"What is that?" breathed Cynan, gesturing with his torch.

I stepped closer and held my torch nearer. My stomach tightened and my mouth filled with bile. I gagged and choked.

Lying in a pool of vomitus on the floor before us was the undigested head of one of our missing scouts. The flesh was badly corrupted, the face horribly marred; even so, I recognized the man.

Cynan made to brush past me, but I swung towards him and put my hand in the center of his chest. "Brother, no . . . It is Gweir."

He strained forward, anger, sorrow and disbelief battling across his features. He glanced over my shoulder. "*Saeth du!*" he cursed and turned away.

There was nothing to be done for Gweir, so we moved on, the odor growing more potent with every step. In a little while the passage turned and widened out somewhat, forming a low grotto. The stench hit me full force as I stepped into this inner chamber; it rocked me back on my heels, but I choked back the bile and staggered ahead. Cynan entered quickly after me.

In the center of the grotto was a hole in the rock floor. The rough edges of the hole were smoothed to an almost polished luster. It was not difficult to guess how the rough stone had gained its glassy sheen.

Scattered on the floor of this hateful chamber were various body parts of our missing warriors and their mounts: a foot still in its buskin, a mangled horse's head and several hooves, jawbones, human and animal teeth, the stripped rib cage and spine of a horse. There were other, older bones, too, skulls and broken shanks scoured clean and brown with age—sacrificial victims of a distant age.

I could not bear the sight and turned away. The eerie child-like whine sounded again, rising from the depths below, and I realized it was the Wyrm itself, not a child, that made the cry. Tightening my grip on the torch, I stepped towards the hole. A blade of ice stabbed up into my arm.

Cynan caught me by the shoulder. "Stay back," he barked in a harsh whisper, pulling me roughly away. "We can do nothing here."

We retraced our steps to the great hall. Tegid saw the grim set of our faces and asked, "Well? Did you find the child?"

Cynan shook his head, "There was no child," he answered, his

voice a low growl in his throat. "But we have found the serpent...
and our missing scouts as well."

Tegid swallowed hard and bowed his head as we described
what we had seen. "The evil which has slept untold ages has
awakened," the bard said when we had finished. "We must leave
this place at once."

The sky outside had lost all color and light. Bran wasted no time
moving the men along. We hurried towards the road beyond the
palace. The first warriors reached the far end of the terrace, and
paused to allow the rest of the party to assemble before moving on.
It was then the Wyrm struck.

The attack came so swiftly and silently, that the first we knew of
it was the choked-off scream of the man it seized and carried away.
Hearing the man's dying shriek, I spun around in time to see a
sinuous shape gliding into the dusky shadows.

A heartbeat later, we were all racing back across the terrace to
where the others had halted. "Did you see?" they shouted. "The
Wyrm! It took Selyf!"

I shouted above the clamor. "Did anyone see where it went?"

The Wyrm had attacked and vanished once more into the
shadows without a trace. "We cannot go that way," Bran concluded,
staring in the direction of the road. "We will have to go around."

I peered around doubtfully. On one hand, the river, itself as silent
and deadly as a serpent; on the other, the red palace and its evil
occupant. Behind loomed the forest, rising like a massive,
impenetrable curtain. Turning towards the forest with great
reluctance, I said, "This way; we will try to find another path."

"What about Selyf?" Cynan demanded. "We cannot leave him
behind."

"He is gone," Bran said. "There is nothing to be done for him."

Cynan refused to move. "He was a good man."

"And will it help Selyf if we all join him in the pit?" Bran asked.
"How many more good men must we lose to the Wyrm?"

My sympathies lay with Cynan, but Bran was right—fleeing
made the best sense. "Listen to him, brother," I said. "What benefit

to Tángwen if you are not there to rescue her? The serpent could return at any moment. Let us go from here while we have the chance."

Leaving the terrace, we entered the forest, pausing only long enough to light torches, before moving on. Bran led, with myself and Cynan behind, keeping the river to our backs. We worked our way into the undergrowth in an effort to skirt the palace. The further we moved from the river, the more tangled and close-grown the wood became. We slashed and hacked with our swords, and forced our way, step by step, until we reached a rock wall rising sheer from the forest floor.

"It is the same bank from which the palace is carved," said Bran, scratching away the moss with his blade to reveal red stone beneath.

Raising our torches, we tried to gauge the height of the bank, but the top was lost in the darkness and we could not see it. "Even if we could climb it," Cynan pointed out, "the horses could not."

Keeping the rock bank to our right, we continued on, moving away, always away, from the palace. When one torch burned out, we snatched up another brand from the snarl of branches all around us. Time and again, we stopped to examine the bank and, finding neither breach nor foothold, we moved on. A late-rising moon eventually appeared and poured a dismal glow over us. Now and then, I glimpsed its pale face flickering in the wickerwork of branches overhead.

"I see a clearing ahead," called Bran from a few paces on.

"At last!" It seemed as if we had walked half the night and had yet to discover any way we might cross the stone bank. I signalled for the rest of the men to stop while Bran and I went ahead to investigate the clearing. Shoulder to shoulder, we crept slowly forward, pressing ourselves against the rock bank. We entered the clearing to see the red palace directly before us and, a little distance to the right, the darkly glimmering river.

"We have come full circle," I remarked. Indeed, we were standing just a few paces from where we had started.

"How is it possible?" wondered Bran.

"We must have become confused in the dark. We will go the other way."

Retracing our steps, we informed the others of the mistake, and struck off once more. Again, we kept the rock bank hard at the right hand so that we would not go astray. The moon reached the peak of its arc and began descending. We pressed relentlessly on, arriving after another long march at yet another clearing. Bran and I stepped together from the shielding edge of the wood into the open: the palace stood directly before us, and off to the right, the dark river.

I took one look and called for Tegid. "See this, bard," I said, flinging out my hand, "it makes no difference which way we go, we return to this place in the end. What are we to do?"

Tegid cocked an eye to the night sky and said, "Dawn is not far off. Let us rest now, and try again when it is light."

We gathered at the edge of the clearing near the river and set about making a rough camp. We lit fires, established a watch, and settled down to wait for sunrise. Cynan wrapped himself in his cloak and lay down. I had just spread a saddle fleece on the ground and sat down crosslegged, a spear across my knees, when Tegid leapt to his feet.

He froze. Listening.

A faint, rippling sound reached me. It sounded like a boat moving against the riverflow. "It is coming from the water," I whispered. "But what—"

"Shh!" Tegid hissed. "Listen!"

Faintly, as in the far-off distance, I heard the nervous whicker of a horse; it was quickly joined by another. Cynan rolled to his feet, shouting, "The horses!"

We flew through the camp towards the horse picket. I felt a sharp icy stab of pain in my silver hand and in the same instant saw, outlined against the shimmering water, a monstrous serpent, its upper body raised high off the ground and great angular head weaving slowly from side to side. The enormous body glistened in the faint moonlight; the head, armored with horned plates, swung above three tremendous coils, each coil the full girth of a horse, and a stiff forked tail protruded from between the first and second coil.

Two long, thick, back-swept ridges ran down along either side of its body from just below the ghastly swaying head.

A trail of water led up from the river. Obviously, the creature had more than one entrance to its den. It had come up from the river close to the horses, no doubt intent on gorging its fearsome appetite on horseflesh. The horses, terrified, bucked and reared, jerking on their picket lines and tethers. Several had broken free and men were trying to catch them.

The Wyrm seemed keenly fascinated by the commotion, its plated head swerving in the air, eyes gleaming in the firelight. I saw the plunging horses and the campfires...

"Help me, Cynan!" I shouted. Dashing forward, I speared one of the lichen bales with which we fed the horses, and ran with it to the nearest fire. I thrust the bale into the flames and lofted the spear. Then, with the courage of fear and rage, I ran to the serpent and heaved the flaming spear into its face.

The missile struck the bony plate below the monster's eye. The Wyrm flinched, jerking away from the fire.

I whirled away, shouting to those nearby. "Light more bales!" I cried. "Hurry! We can drive it away."

Cynan and two other warriors bolted to the stack of fodder, skewered three bales and set them ablaze. Cynan lunged to meet the Wyrm, raising a battle cry as he ran.

"*Bás Draig!*" he bellowed. The two warriors at his side took up the cry. "*Bás Draig!*"

Returning for another spear and bale, I saw Scatha running towards me. "Rally the warband!" I shouted. "Help Cynan drive the serpent away from the horses." Turning to Tegid, I ordered, "Stay here and light more bales as we need them."

Bran and Alun, having seen my feat, appeared with bales ablaze. I quickly armed myself again and joined them; together we charged the Wyrm. Scatha and the warband had taken up a position on the near side, midway between the serpent and the river—dangerously close to the creature, it seemed to me. They were already strenuously engaged in trying to attract the beast's attention and draw it away from the camp.

I made for a place opposite them, thinking that if the serpent turned towards them, we three would be well placed for a blind-side attack. Upon seeing our approach, the Ravens, flying to meet us with weapons alight, sent up a shrill war cry, distracting the serpent. Scatha and her band saw their chance and rushed forward, weapons low and shields raised high. They struck at the huge coils, driving their blades into the softer skin of the belly between the scales. The huge snaky head swung towards them.

"Now!" I shouted, sprinting forward. My silver hand burned with a freezing fire.

Scatha's band stood fearless to the task, jabbing their spears into the Wyrm's side. The annoyed beast lowered its head and loosed a menacing hiss. As the awful mouth cracked open, I heaved the shaft with all my might. The unbalanced missile fell short, striking the creature on the underside of its mouth with a great flurry of sparks, but no hurt to the creature at all. As my first missile fell harmlessly away, I was already running for another.

Alun had no better luck with his throw. But Bran, seeing how we had fared, managed to compensate for the top-heavy spear with a well-judged, magnificent throw. The serpent, aware of our presence due to our first clumsy attempts, swung towards Bran, hissing wickedly.

As soon as the great wide mouth opened, Bran's spear was up and in. The Ravens cheered for their chieftain. But the serpent gave a quick shake of its head and dislodged the barb and fire bale.

I thought that Bran, like Cynan and me, would return to Tegid for another fire bale. Instead, he simply bounded forward and took up the shaft I had thrown. He impaled the fiery bale and prepared for another throw.

Perhaps the beast anticipated Bran's move. More likely, Yr Gyrem Rua, enraged by our attack, struck blindly at the closest moving shape. I glanced around just in time to see the huge horny head swing down and forward with breathstealing speed just as Bran's arm drew back to aim his throw.

The serpent's strike took the Raven Chief at the shoulder. He fell and rolled, somehow holding on to his weapon. He gained his knees as the Wyrm struck again, raising the spear in both hands as the head descended so that he took the blow on the shaft instead. The spear with its flaming head fell one way and Bran was sent sprawling the other. The serpent drew back and tensed for another strike.

The Ravens leapt forward as one man to save their chieftain. Alun, reached him first and, taking up the fallen weapon, flung it into the serpent's face while the others dragged Bran to safety.

"Alun! Get out of there, man!" Cynan cried.

Diving sideways, Alun hit the ground, rolled, and came up running. But instead of retreating to the campfire with the others, he stooped to retrieve the spear Bran had thrown.

I saw him do it and shouted. "No! Alun!"

27

Battle Awen

The Wyrm struck. Alun whirled, throwing the flaming bale at the same time. The throw grazed the serpent's jaw and bounced away as the head descended, knocking Alun off his feet and throwing him onto his back.

I seized a spear Tegid had readied and ran to Alun's defence. Garanaw and Niall heard my shout, turned, and ran to his aid. Scatha's warriors redoubled their attack. They drove in close, stabbing fearlessly. Scatha, by dint of sheer determination, succeeded in forcing a spear into a soft place between two scales on the serpent's side. With a mighty lunge, she drove the blade in. I saw the shaft sink deep into the beast's flesh, and I heard her triumphant cry: "*Bás Draig!*"

Spitting with fury, the red serpent hissed and the long neck stiffened; the two ridges on the side of its body bulged, then flattened into an immense hood, revealing two long slits on either side and two vestigial legs with clawed feet. The legs unfolded, claws snatching, and suddenly two great membranous wings emerged from the side slits behind the legs. These huge bat wings shook and trembled, unfurling like crumpled leather, slowly spreading behind the Wyrm in a massive canopy.

Scatha gave the embedded spear another violent shove. The

serpent hissed again and swivelled its head to strike, but Scatha and her warrior band were already retreating into the darkness.

Meanwhile, Garanaw and Niall pulled Alun away. And I took advantage of the momentary lapse to position myself for another throw. Cynan, flaming spear streaking the night, ran to my side. As its evil head turned, the Wyrm's mouth came open with an angry, rasping, seething hiss.

"Ready? . . . Now!" I cried, and twin trails of fire streaked up into the monster's maw. Cynan's spear struck the roof of the serpent's mouth and fell away causing little hurt; mine hit on one of the long fangs and glanced away. I ran back to the campfire. "Give me another spear," I demanded. "Hurry!"

"It is not working," Tegid began. "We must find another way to—"

"Hurry!" I shouted, grabbing the firebrand from his hand and setting it to the nearest bundle. I took up a spear and plunged it into the bale. "Cynan! Follow me!"

Scatha had seen us return for more bales and understood that we meant to try again. As we flew once more to our positions, she launched another attack on the Wyrm's side. This time both she and one of the warriors with her succeeded in forcing spears between the thick scales. Two other warriors broke off their attack and leaped to Scatha's side, adding their strength to help drive the shaft deep into the serpent's flesh.

Scatha's success inspired the Ravens, who raced to repeat the feat on the opposite side. Drustwn and Garanaw charged in close, working their weapons into a crack between scales. They, too, succeeded in wounding the beast.

Yr Gyrem Rua screamed and flapped its enormous wings; its forked tail thrashed from side to side like a whip.

Cynan and I took up our positions. Placing the butt of the spear in the palm of my metal hand, I stretched my other hand along the shaft as far as I could reach. As the Wyrm's head veered towards me once more, I crouched low, my heart racing. The flames flared; sparks fell on my upturned face and singed my hair.

"Come on, you bloated snake," I growled, "open that ugly mouth!"

The massive neck arched. The hideous head tensed high above me. I saw the fireglint in a hard black glittering eye.

With a shout of "Die, dragon!" Cynan took his place slightly behind and to the left of me. The serpent shrieked, and the sound was deafening; its awful wings arched and quivered, and clawed feet raked the air. My stomach tightened. I clenched my teeth to keep from biting my tongue.

"Strike!" I taunted. "Strike, Wyrm!"

The enormous mouth opened—a vast white pit lined with innumerable spiked teeth in a triple row. Two slender fangs emerged from pockets in the upper mouth. The blue-black ribbon of a tongue arched and curled to a frightful screech.

And then the awful head swooped down.

I saw the fangs slashing towards me. My body tensed.

"Now!" cried Cynan. His spear flashed up over my shoulder and into the descending mouth. "Llew!"

I hesitated a rapid heartbeat longer, and then heaved my flaming missile with every ounce of strength I possessed. My metal hand whipped up, driving the missile into a high, tight arc.

Cynan's spear pierced the puffy white flesh and stuck fast. My spear flashed up between the two fangs, over the teeth, and into the throat.

The red serpent recoiled. Its mouth closed on the shaft of Cynan's spear, driving the spearhead even deeper into the soft skin and forcing the mouth to remain open. The creature could not close its mouth to swallow, which would have allowed it to quench the flames now searing its throat.

The Wyrm began thrashing violently from side to side. With great, slow strokes, the terrible wings beat the air. Burning lichen rained down on our heads. The lethal tail slashed like forked lightning, striking the ground with killing clouts.

"Run!" Cynan shouted, pulling me away.

We fled to the fire where the Ravens now stood shouting and

cheering. Bran lay on the ground bleeding from a wound on the side of his head. Alun sat slumped beside him, white-faced, a foolish, dazed expression on his face.

Blood oozed from Bran's head, and Alun's eyelids fluttered as he fought to remain conscious. Rage seized me and spun me around. I saw the winged serpent slam down its head as if to bite the earth. The force of the blow splintered the spear holding open its mouth. The huge jaws closed, the throat convulsed, and up came my spear with the smoldering bale still attached.

Wings beating a fearful rhythm, the serpent slowly lifted its flat head and upper body, loosed its coils and began half-flying, half-slithering away. Our campfire guttered in the gale of its retreat.

"It is fleeing!" shouted Drustwn, lofting his spear in triumph.

"Hie-e-ya!" crowed Emyr with a jubilant whoop. "Yr Gyrem Rua is defeated!"

"The Wyrm is conquered!" Cynan shouted. He grabbed me and clasped me to his chest. I saw his mouth move, but his voice had become the irritating buzz of an insect. His face creased with concern; sweat gleamed on his skin in the firelight. The glint of each bead became a needle of stabbing light, a naked star in the frozen universe of night. The ground beneath my feet trembled, and the earth lost all solidity.

And I felt my spirit expand within me; I was seized and taken up, as if I were no more than a leaf released from a branch and set sailing on a sudden gust of wind. My ears pounded with the bloodrush; my vision hardened to a sharp, narrow field: I saw only the winged serpent—scales gleaming blood red in the shivered light of our fire, grotesque wings stiffly beating, lifting that huge body to the freedom of the night sky. I saw the Red Serpent of Oeth escaping; all else around me dimmed, receded, vanished.

A hand grasped my shoulder, and then two more laid hold to my arms. But Ollathir's battle awen burned within me and I would not be held back. Power surged up in a mighty torrent. Like a feather in a flood, lightly riding the currents, upheld by them, I became part of the force flowing through me. The strength of the earth and sky was mine. I was pure force and impulse. My limbs trembled with pent energy demanding release. I opened my mouth and a sound like the bellow of the battlehorn issued from my throat.

And then I ran: swift as the airstream in the wind-scoured heights, sure as the loosed arrow streaking to its mark. I ran, but my feet did not touch the earth. I ran, and my silver hand began to glow with a cold and deadly light, the etchwork of its cunning designs shining like white gold in the Swift Sure Hand's refining fire. My fist shone like a beam of light, keen and bright.

A gabble of voices clamored behind me, small and confused. But I could not be bound or deflected. Can the spear return to the hand that has thrown it?

I was a ray of light. I was a wave upon the sea. I was a river beneath a mountain. I was hot blood flowing in the heart. I was the word already spoken. The Penderwydd's awen was upon me and I could not be contained.

The serpent's bulk rose like a curving crimson wall before me, and I saw Scatha's spear buried mid-shaft in the creature's side. Grasping the shaft with my silver hand, I pulled myself up. My flesh fingers found a crack between scales and my foot found the spearshaft. One quick scramble and I reached the serpent's back.

Solid beneath me, but fluid, like a molten road undulating slowly over the land, the red beast fled, fell wings stroking the air. Moving with the quickness of a shadow and the deftness of a stalking cat, I skittered over the sinuous backbone, over scales large as paving stones. A notched ridge down the center of the creature's back made good footing as the earth dropped away below. The foul beast had gained the air, but I heeded it not.

With the uncanny skill of a bard's inspiration I climbed towards the vile creature's head, and passed between the buffeting wings. Keen-eyed in the night, I glimpsed a fold of skin at the base of the serpent's skull and, above it, a slight depression where the spine met the skull; thin skin stretched tight over soft tissue.

The Wyrm's body stiffened beneath me as it rose higher. Mounting to the bulging mound of muscle between the two wings, I planted myself there and, raising my silver hand high, I smashed it down hard.

The metal broke the skin and slipped under the ridge of bone at the base of the serpent's skull. I stabbed deep, my metal hand a thrusting blade—cold silver sliding as in a sheath of flesh, plunging, piercing, penetrating the red serpent's cold brain.

A blast like the windscream of a Sollen gale rent the night. The wingbeats faltered as the immense leathery wings struggled to the sprung rhythm of a suddenly broken cadence.

"Die!" I shouted, my voice the loud carynx of battle. "Die!"

I slammed my fist deeper, metal fingers grasping. My arm sank past the elbow and my fingers tightened on a thick, sinewy cord. Seizing this cord, I ripped up hard and my fist came out in a bloody gush. The left wing faltered and froze. The Wyrm slewed sideways, plunging deadweight from air. I clung to the bony rim of scales and held on as the earth rushed towards me.

My feet struck the ground with an abrupt bone-rattling jolt. I rolled free and stood unshaken. The Wyrm convulsed, recoiling, rolling over and over, wrapping itself in itself, pale belly exposed in twisted loops.

The Red Serpent began striking its underbelly. The poisoned fangs slashed again and again, sinking into the exposed flesh. I laughed to see it, and heard my voice echo in the empty depths of the nearby shrine.

Once more I felt the hands of men on me. I was encircled in strong arms and lifted off my feet. Laughing, I was hauled from the path of the writhing serpent. I glimpsed men's faces in the darkness, eyes wide with awe, mouths agape in fright and wonder as they carried me away from the writhing Wyrm and out of danger.

The death throes of Yr Gyrem Rua were harrowing to behold. The serpent screamed—curling, twisting, spinning, crushing itself in its own killing coils, clawed feet raking the soft belly, battered wings rent and broken. The forked tail lashed and stung, striking the earth in a violent frenzy.

The Wyrm's paroxysms carried it to the portal of the palace

shrine. The tail smashed into the stone, loosened the ancient pillars and knocked them from their bases. Chunks of stonework began falling from the time-worn façade. The serpent spun in a knot of convoluted wrath, shattering the forecourt of the obnoxious temple, which began to crumble inward like an age-brittle skull. The dying serpent squirmed, beating against the hard shell of its cavern sanctuary. Red stone crashed and red dust rose like a blood mist in the moonlight. The frenzy gradually began to ease as the life-force ebbed. The movements became languid and sluggish; the sibilant shrieks dwindled to a pathetic strangled whine, its last cry a monstrous parody of a child in distress.

Slowly, slowly, the potency of its own poison began to work its deadly effect. Even so, the red Wyrm was some time dying. Long after the thrashing had stopped, the forked tail twitched and a broken wing stump stirred.

As I stood watching, my eyesight dimmed and my limbs began to twitch. The trembling increased. I fastened my teeth onto my lower lip and bit hard to keep from crying out. I wrapped my arms around my chest and hugged myself tight to keep my limbs from shuddering.

"Llew! Llew!" a sharp voice assaulted me.

Pain exploded in my head. I felt hands on me. The taste of blood filled my mouth; words bubbled from my bleeding tongue and I prated in a language unknown to those around me. Faces clustered tight over me, but I did not know them—faces without identity, familiar strangers who stared in anguish. My head throbbed, pounding with a fierce and steady ache, and my vision diffused, dwindling to vague patterns of light and dark, shapes with no clear features.

And then I tumbled over the edge into senselessness. I felt waves of warm darkness lapping over my consciousness and I succumbed to oblivion.

I awoke with a start as they laid me on the ground beside the fire. The awen had left me—like a gale that has passed, leaving the rain-soaked grass flattened in its wake. I struggled to sit up.

"Lie still," advised Tegid. Placing his hands on my chest, he pressed me down on the oxhide.

"Help me stand," I said; my words slurred slightly as my wooden tongue mumbled in my mouth.

"All is well," the bard insisted. "Rest now."

I had no strength to resist. I lay back. "How is Bran?"

"Bran is well. His head hurts, but he is awake and moving. Alun is unharmed—a scratch; it will heal."

"Good."

"Rest now. It will be daylight soon and we will leave this place."

I closed my eyes and slept. When I woke again the sun was peeping cautiously above the trees. The men had struck camp and were ready to go. They were waiting for me to rise, which I did at once. My arms and shoulders were stiff, and my back felt like a timber plank. But I was in one piece.

Tegid and Scatha hovered nearby. I joined them and they greeted me with good news. "We have scouted the high road beyond the shrine," Scatha reported, "and it has been used recently."

A spark of hope quickened my heart. "How recently?"

"It is difficult to know for certain," the bard answered.

"How recently?" I demanded again.

"I cannot say."

"Show me."

"Gladly." Scatha, haggard and near exhaustion, smiled and her features relaxed. "All is ready. You have but to give the command."

"Then let us go from here," I said. "It is a hateful place and I never want to see it again."

We passed the ruined temple to reach the road. Little of the shrine remained intact. Scarcely one stone stood upon another; it was all a jumble of red rubble. In a twisted mess amidst the debris, lay the wrecked body of Yr Gyrem Rua. A single broken wing fluttered in the wind like a tattered flag. The venom of its bite was quick about its grisly work of dissolving the muscled flesh; decay was already far advanced. The stink of the decomposing Wyrm brought tears to our eyes as we rode quickly past.

While it stood, the temple had hidden much of the road which could now be seen stretching out straight and wide, leading on through the forest and away from the river. It was, as Scatha had said, a proper high road: paved with flat stone, fitted together so closely and with such cunning that no grass grew between the joins.

"Show me the evidence of its use," I said as Tegid reined in beside me.

"You will see it just ahead," he replied. We continued on a short distance and stopped. Tegid dismounted and led me to the side of the road. There, nestled like round brown eggs in the long grass, I saw the droppings of perhaps three or four horses. A little way beyond, the grass was trampled and matted where a camp had been established. There was no evidence of a fire, so we could not tell how long ago the travellers had sojourned there. Nevertheless, I reckoned it could not have been more than a few days.

We returned to our horses, remounted, and moved out upon the high road with a better heart than at any time since entering the Foul Land.

28

On the High Road

Once on the high road, we journeyed with something approaching speed—a mixed blessing, as it soon exposed the loss of our horses. Those on foot could not keep pace, and we were constantly having to halt the mounted column to allow the stragglers to catch up. Thus we were obliged to rotate the men, foot-to-saddle, with increasing frequency as the swifter pace began to tell.

At the end of the day, we had travelled a fair distance. Since we planned to camp right on the road itself, we pushed on until it became too dark to see more than a few hundred paces ahead. There were stars shining in the sky and, though still cold, the air seemed not so sharp as on other nights. This served clear notice that time was passing. The weather was changing; Sollen was receding and Gyd would soon arrive.

I begrudged the time—every passing day was a day without Goewyn and empty for the lack. I felt an urgency in my spirit that nothing, save the light in Goewyn's eye, could appease. I was restless and craved the sight of my beloved. The infant was growing now within her, and I wondered if it had begun to show. I repeated her name with every step.

As Cynan and I walked together, taking our turn on foot, I asked, "Do you miss Tángwen greatly?"

His head was bent low. "My heart is sore for yearning, I miss her so much."

"You never say anything," I prodded gently.

"It is my heartache. I keep it to myself."

"Why? We share this pain together, brother."

Cynan swung his spear shaft forward, rapping the butt sharply on the stone, but kept his eyes fixed on the road. "I keep it to myself," he said again, "for I would not grieve you with my complaint. Bad enough that Goewyn is stolen; you do not need my troubles added to your own."

He would say no more about it, so I let the matter rest. His forbearance humbled me. That Cynan could forswear the very mention of his own hurt lest it increase mine, shamed me; doubly so, since I had scarcely given *his* suffering a second thought. How could I be worthy of such loyalty?

That night we came to the end of the little grain that remained, and it was a sorry meal.

"The sooner we leave this accursed forest, the better," grumbled Bran Bresal. We sat at council around the fire while the men ate, wondering what to do. "It cannot go on for ever."

"Nor can we," I pointed out. "Without meat and meal, we will soon grow too weak to travel."

"We have meat on the hoof," Scatha suggested delicately. "Though every horse we take means that another warrior must walk."

"I have never eaten horsemeat," Cynan muttered. "I do not intend to start now."

"I have eaten horse," said Tegid. "And I was glad to. It warmed the belly and strengthened the hand to the fight."

I remembered the time Tegid meant: the flight to Findargad in the mountains of northern Prydain. Then, as now, it was winter. We were pursued by the Coranyid, Lord Nudd's demon host, while making our way to Meldryn Mawr's high stronghold. Freezing, starving, we fought our way step by faltering step to the safety of the fortress. We were not freezing this time; but the starving had begun.

"Nothing good can come of eating a horse," rumbled Cynan, pressing his chin to his chest. "It is a low endeavor."

"Perhaps," agreed Scatha, "but there are worse."

I stirred at the sound of footsteps, and Emyr appeared, anxious and uneasy. He spoke directly to Tegid. "Penderwydd, it is Alun. I think you should come and see him."

Rising without a word, Tegid hurried away.

"What has happened to him?" asked Cynan, jumping to his feet. Bran had risen at Emyr's approach and was already following.

We fell into step with Emyr. "Garanaw found him sitting back there," the Raven said, indicating the road we had that day travelled. "He took his turn walking, but he did not join us when we stopped to make camp. Garanaw rode back to look for him."

Alun sat slumped by the campfire. The other Ravens hovered near, quietly apprehensive. They did not speak when we joined them, but gathered close as Tegid stooped before their stricken swordbrother.

"Alun," began the bard, "what is this I hear about you taking your ease by the road?"

Alun's head came up with a smile, but there was pain behind his eyes, and his skin glowed with a mist of perspiration. "Well," he replied in a brave tone, glancing around the circle of faces above him, "I have not been sleeping as well as I might—what with one thing and another."

Scatha knelt beside him. "Where is the hurt, Alun?" she asked, and put her hand on his shoulder. The touch, though gentle, brought a gasp from the Raven. The color drained from his face.

Gently, she reached to unfasten the brooch that held his cloak. Alun put his hand over hers and shook his head slightly. "Please."

"Let us help you, brother," Tegid said softly.

He hesitated, then closed his eyes and nodded. Scatha deftly unpinned the cloak and loosened the siarc. Alun made no further move to hinder her, and soon the shoulder was exposed. A ragged welt curved over the top of the shoulder towards the shoulder blade.

"Bring a torch," the bard commanded, and a moment later Niall handed a firebrand forward. Tegid took the torch and, stepping behind the seated Alun, held the light near.

"Oh, Alun!" sighed Scatha. Several of the Ravens muttered, and Bran looked away.

"Fine brave warriors you are!" complained Alun. "Has no one seen a scratch before?"

There was a small rip in the siarc, and little blood; indeed, the scratch itself had already scabbed over. But the flesh beneath was red and swollen, with a ghastly green-black tinge.

Tegid studied the shoulder carefully, holding the torch near and probing gently with his fingertips. Then he placed his hand flat against the swollen shoulder. "The wound is hot to the touch," he said. "It is fevered."

Scatha reached a hand to Alun's head and pressed her palm to his brow. She withdrew it almost at once. "You are roasting, Alun."

"Perhaps I have been sitting too near the fire," he laughed weakly. "And here I thought I was cold."

"I will not lie to you, brother," Tegid said, handing me the torch and squatting before Alun once more. "It is not good. The wound has sickened. I must open it again and clean it properly."

Alun rolled his eyes, but his exasperation was half-hearted and mingled with relief. "All this fuss over a scratch?"

"Man, Alun, if that is a scratch only," said Cynan, who could contain himself no longer, "then my spear is a pot sticker."

"Bring fresh water—and clean cloths, if you can find any," Tegid ordered impatiently. Cynan left at once, taking Niall with him. "I need a knife," the bard continued, "and I need it sharp."

"Mine will serve," said Bran, pushing forward. He drew the blade from its place at his belt, and handed it to Tegid.

The bard tested the edge with his thumb and gave it back, saying, "Strop it again. I want it new-edged and keen."

"And hold the blade to the firecoals when you have finished," I instructed. Bran raised his eyebrows at this, but I insisted.

"Do it," said the Raven Chief, handing the knife to Drustwn, who hastened to the task. Tegid turned to the remaining Ravens. "Gather moss, and spread oxhides and fleeces; prepare a bed."

"I will not need a bed, certainly," Alun grumbled.

"When I am through," Tegid replied, "*one* of us will be glad of a place to lay his head. I will use it if you will not." He nodded to Garanaw and Emyr, who turned and disappeared at once.

Scatha and I retreated a little apart. "I mislike the look of this," Scatha confided. "I fear the serpent's poison is in him."

"If the poison was in him, he would have been well and truly dead by now," I pointed out. "Help Tegid, and come to me afterwards."

Thus, I set about keeping myself and the rest of the men busy until Tegid and Scatha had finished. The horses were picketed and the fires banked high; Cynan and I positioned the guards and saw the men settled to sleep before returning to the fire to wait.

I dozed, and after a while Cynan nudged me awake. "Here now! He is coming."

I yawned and sat up. "Well, bard?"

Tegid sat down heavily. Fatigue sat like a burden on his shoulders. Cynan poured a cup of water and offered it to him. "If I had a draught of ale," Cynan said, "I would give it to you. As soon as I get another, it is yours."

"And I will drain that cup," Tegid replied, gazing at the fire. He drank and, setting the cup aside, pressed his eyes shut.

"What of Alun?" I asked again.

Ignoring me, Tegid said, his voice cracking, "The wound was but a scratch—as Alun said. But it has sickened, and the sickness has spread into the shoulder and arm. I cut into the wound and pressed much poison out of the flesh. I bathed the cut with water and wrapped it with a poultice to keep the poison draining."

"Yet he will recover," Cynan declared flatly, willing it to be so.

"He is sleeping now. Scatha will sit with him through the night. She will rouse us if there is any change."

"Why did he let it go untended?" I asked. "He should have said something."

Tegid rubbed his face with his hands. "Alun is a brave man. He thought the hurt but small, and he did not wish to slow us.

Until he collapsed on the road, I do not believe he knew himself how ill he had become."

I asked the question uppermost in my mind. "Will he be able to travel tomorrow?"

"I will examine the wound again in the morning; I may see more by daylight. A night's sleep can do much." He rubbed his face again. "I mean to see what it can achieve myself."

With that, he rolled himself in his cloak and went to sleep.

We did move on the next day. Alun seemed to be stronger and professed himself much improved. I made certain that he did not walk, and Tegid gave him healing draughts which he made with the contents of the pouch at his belt. In all, Alun looked and acted like a man on the mend.

So we journeyed on—growing more footsore and hungry by the day, it is true, but more determined also. Two days later, we noticed that the forest was thinning somewhat. And two days after that we came to the end of the forest. Despite the lack of food, our spirits soared. Just to see blue sky overhead was a blessing.

And though the land beyond the forest rose to bald hills of rocky and barren peat moor—as wide and empty as the forest had been dense and close—the warriors began to sing as we stepped from the shadow of the last tree. Tegid and I were riding at the head of the column and we stopped to listen.

"They have found their voices at last," I remarked. "I wonder how long it has been since such a sound was heard in Tir Aflan?"

Tegid cocked his head and favored me with one of his prickly sidelong glances.

"What have I said now?"

He straightened, drew a deep breath, and turned to look at the road ahead—stretching into the hill-crowded distance. "All this by the Brazen Man is come to pass," he intoned, "who likewise mounted on his steed of brass works woe both great and dire."

It was the Banfáith's prophecy, and I recognized it. With the recognition came an arrow-pang of regret for Gwenllian's death. I saw again the dusky shimmer of her hair and her bewitching emerald eyes; I saw her graceful neck and shoulders bent to the curve of a harp, her fingers stroking the strings, as if coaxing beauty from thin air.

"Rise up, Men of Gwir!" I said, continuing the quote just to show Tegid that I remembered. "Fill your hands with weapons and oppose the false men in your midst!"

Tegid supplied the final section: "The sound of the battleclash will be heard among the stars of heaven and the Great Year will proceed to its final consummation."

To which, I replied: "Bring it on. I am ready."

"Are you?" the bard asked.

Before I could reply, we heard a shout. "Tegid! Llew! Here!"

I swivelled in the saddle and saw Emyr running towards us along the side of the road. I snapped the reins and urged my mount forward to meet him. "Come quickly!" he said. "It is Alun."

We raced back along the high road to where two riderless horses waited. A cluster of men stood at the roadside, the Ravens among them. We pushed through the press and found Alun lying on the ground. Bran and Scatha bent over him, and Cynan was saying, "Lie still, Alun. You are ailing, man. It is no shame to tumble from the saddle."

"I fell asleep," Alun protested. "That is all. I fell asleep and slipped off. It is nothing. Let me up."

"Alun," said Tegid, hunkering down beside him, "I want to look at your shoulder."

"But I am well, I tell you." Alun's insistence fell somewhat short of absolute conviction.

I motioned to Cynan, who leant his head towards me. "Move the men along. We will join you as soon as we have finished here."

"Right!" said Cynan loudly. He rose and began turning men around. "It is for us to move on. We can do nothing for Alun— standing over him like trees taken root. The road grows no shorter for stopping."

Reluctantly, the warriors moved along, leaving us to examine Alun's wound. Tegid deftly unfastened the brooch and drew aside the cloak. The siarc beneath was caked with dried blood.

"You have been bleeding, Alun," observed Tegid, his voice dry and even.

"Have I?" wondered Alun. "I did not notice."

Tegid proceeded to draw aside the siarc, pulling it carefully away from the skin. A sweet smell emanated from the wound as the cloth came free. The whole shoulder and upper back were inflamed and discolored now, the flesh an ugly purple with a grotesque green-black cast. The scratch Tegid had opened was raw and running with a thin yellow matter.

"Well?" said Alun, twisting his head around to see his injury.

"I will not lie to you, Alun," Tegid's tone was solemn. "I do not like this." The bard pressed his fingers to the swollen flesh. "Does that hurt?"

"No." Alun shook his head. "I feel nothing."

"You should," replied Tegid. He turned to Bran. "Take Garanaw and Emyr, and ride back to the forest. Cut some long poles and bring them to me. We will make a *cadarn* for him."

Alun twisted free and struggled up. "I will not be dragged behind a horse on an infant's bed," he growled. "I will ride or walk."

The bard frowned. "Very well," he agreed at last, "we will spare you that. But you will endure my medicine before I let you take the saddle again."

Alun smiled. "You are a hard man, Tegid Tathal. Hard as the flint beneath your feet."

"Leave us the horses," Tegid instructed. "We will join you when I have finished."

Bran and I left Tegid and Scatha there, and returned to the column. "Tegid is worried," Bran observed. "He does not want us to know how bad it is." He paused. "But I know."

"Well," I replied lightly, doing my best to soothe the Chief Raven, "Tegid has his reasons. No doubt it is for the best."

We took our places at the head of the line with Cynan. And though the men continued to sing, the good feeling had gone out of it for me.

The day ended in a dull, miserable drizzle. A cold wind whined across the rocky wastes and made us glad of the firewood we had collected to bring with us upon leaving the forest. The wind, mournful and cold though it was, made a welcome change from the stifling close silence and dead air of the forest. So we did not begrudge the chill and damp.

We ate thin gruel, mostly water, boiled with handfuls of a sort of coarse, spiky grass which we pulled from side of the road. The grass lent a stimulating aromatic quality to the brew, and served to flavor it somewhat, although it added little bulk. The water, collected from small rock pools, was far better than that which we got from the river. Some of the warriors scouted the nearest braes for mushrooms, but found none.

Tegid and Scatha watched over Alun through the night. At dawn I went to them to see how the patient had fared. The bard met me before I came near Alun. "I do not think he should travel today."

"Then we will camp here," I said. "We could all use the rest, and the horses have grass enough to graze. How is he?"

Tegid frowned; his dark eyes flicked away from me, and then back. "It is not well with him."

"But he will recover," I asserted quickly.

"He is strong. And he is not afraid of a fight. Scatha and I will do all that can be done to heal him." He paused. "Meat would help as much as rest."

"Say no more. I will see to it."

I chose one of the smaller horses, though not the youngest whose meat might have been more tender. But I was not choosing for culinary value; I wanted to keep the more experienced war horses as long as possible. Bran approved the choice, and Garanaw helped me slaughter the poor beast.

Cynan insisted he would have nothing to do with either killing or eating horses. He kept muttering, "It is not fitting for a king of Caledon to devour his good mount, his helpmate in battle."

"Fine. Then just hold your tongue when the stew starts bubbling and the smell of roasting meat tempts your nostrils."

Despite the cold, Garanaw and I put off our cloaks, siarcs, breecs and buskins. We led the animal a little apart and made the swordthrust as quick and painless as possible. The horse fell without a cry, rolled onto its side and died. We skinned it quickly and spread the hide on a nearby rock. Then we began the grisly task of hacking the carcass into suitable joints. We were covered in blood when we had finished, but we had a fair amount of good meat stacked on the hide.

Niall, Emyr and Drustwn, meanwhile, busied themselves preparing spits on which to roast the meat. Garanaw and I distributed the meat to the men, saving the choice pieces for Tegid's use. Shivering with cold by the time we had finished, we knelt beside a peaty pool and washed away the blood, dressed again, and hurried to warm ourselves while the meat cooked.

Soon the wind carried the smoky-sweet aroma throughout the camp, dispersing any lingering qualms about our meal. When the meat was done, it did not look or smell much different from beef; and the men consumed it happily—not to say greedily. I could see Cynan's resolve wavering, but I knew if I asked him again, he would say no again out of stubborn pride.

Scatha came to his rescue. She collected a double portion and sat down crosslegged beside him. "I always told my Mabinogi," she began, chewing thoughtfully, "that a warrior's chief task is to stay alive and remain fit for battle. Any warrior who fails to do all he can to achieve this aim is no help at all to his kinsmen."

Cynan frowned and thrust out his chin. "I remember."

"I taught you to find birds' eggs and seaweed and—" she paused to lick the juice from her long fingers, "and all such that might make a meal for a hungry warrior away from his lord's hearth."

The broad shoulders bunched in a tight shrug, but the frown remained firmly fixed.

"That is why I make certain to serve horsemeat to all my brood," Scatha continued casually.

The red head turned slowly. "You served us horsemeat?"

"Yes. I find that one taste and it—"

Some of those sitting near overheard this conversation and grinned. No one dared laugh aloud. Cynan's chagrin was genuine, but wonderfully short-lived.

Scatha raised a portion of roast meat and offered it to him. Cynan took it between his hands and stared at it as if he expected it to reproach him. "Never let it be said that Cynan Machae spurned the learning of his youth."

So saying, he lifted the meat to his mouth and bit into it. He chewed grimly and swallowed, and the subject was never mentioned again. We slept well content that night, our stomachs full for the first time in many days. But my sleep was cut short. Tegid came to me and jostled me awake. The wind had risen during the night and was blowing cold from the north.

"Shh!" he cautioned. "Come quickly and quietly."

He led me to where he and Scatha had made a place for Alun between two small fires, one at his head and the other at his feet. Bran stood beside her, leaning on his spear, his head lowered. Scatha had a rag in her hand, and a bowl of water in her lap; she was bathing Alun's face. His eyes were closed and he was lying very still.

Tegid bent over the ailing warrior. "Alun," he said softly, "Llew is here. I have brought him as you asked."

At this, Alun's eyes flickered open and he turned his head. The vile purple stain of the rotten wound had reached the base of his throat. "Llew," Alun said, his voice little more than a whispered breath, "I wanted to say that I am sorry."

"Sorry? Alun, you have nothing to be sorry about," I replied quickly. "It is not—"

"I wanted to help you rescue Goewyn."

"You will, Alun. You will recover. I am counting on you."

He smiled a dry, fevered smile. His dark eyes were glassy and hard. "No, lord, I will not recover. I am sorry to leave you one blade less." He paused and licked his lips. "I would have liked to see the look on Paladyr's face when you appeared. That is one fight I will be sorry to miss."

"Do not speak so, Alun," I said, swallowing hard. My throat

ached and my stomach knotted.

"It is well with me," the Raven said, reaching towards me with his hand. I took it and felt the heat burning in him. "But I wanted to tell you that I have never served a better lord, nor known a king I have loved more. It is my greatest regret that I do not have another life, for I would gladly give you that as well." He swallowed and I saw how much it hurt him. "I was ever keen for the fight, but never raised a blade in malice. If men speak of me in aftertimes, I would have that remembered."

My vision blurred suddenly. "Rest now," I told him, my voice cracking.

"Soon ... I will rest soon," he said; his dry tongue licked dry lips. Scatha raised his head and tilted a little water into his mouth.

He gripped my hand almost desperately. "And remember me to Goewyn. Tell her it would have been the chief pleasure of my life to have fought Paladyr for her freedom. She is a treasure of Albion, Llew, and if you had not seen that at last, I would have married her myself."

"I will tell her, Alun," I said, almost choking on the words. "When next I see her."

He swallowed and a spasm of pain wracked him. When he opened his eyes again, some of the hardness had gone—he was losing the fight. But he smiled. "Ahh, it is enough. It is sufficient." He looked from me to Bran. "I am ready now to see my swordbrothers."

Bran raised his head, nodded, and hastened away at once. Alun, still gripping my hand, though less tightly now, held me. "Lord Silver Hand," he said, "I would make but one last request."

"Anything," I said, tears brimming in my eyes. "Anything, Alun; speak the word and it is yours."

"Lord, do not bury me in this land," he said softly. "Tir Aflan is no honorable place for a warrior."

"I will do as you ask," I assured him.

But he clutched desperately at my hand. "Do not leave me here alone. Please!" he implored; and then added more gently, "please." He swallowed and his features clenched with pain. "When you are finished here, take me back with you. Let me lie on Druim Vran."

That such a noble warrior should have to beg so broke my heart. Tears began rolling down my cheeks and I smeared them away with my sleeve. "It will be done, brother."

This cheered him. "My heart belongs in Albion," he whispered. "If I may not see that fair land again, I will go easier knowing that my bones return."

"It will be done, Alun. I vow it."

His hand relaxed and fell back. Scatha gave him another drink. Bran returned just then, bringing the rest of the Raven Flight with him: Garanaw, Emyr, Drustwn and Niall. One by one, they knelt at the side of their swordbrother and made their farewells. Bran roused Cynan, too, who made his way to Alun's side. All the while, Tegid stood looking on, head bent low, watching with mournful eyes, but saying nothing.

Bran was the last, speaking earnestly and low; he placed his hand on Alun's forehead, then touched his own in salute. When he rose, he announced, "This Raven has flown."

29

Fly, Raven!

Somber in his brown cloak, Tegid scanned with dark eyes the far hillscape. Dun-colored, but for the bleached white rocks, endlessly austere and desperately empty—nothing but sparse heather and peat bogs surrounding outcropped stones rising like bone-bare islands in a rusty sea—the moorland stretched vacant and forlorn as far as the eye could see. Humps of barren hills, hunched like shoulders, jostled one another to the horizon in all directions.

He did not look at me as I came to stand beside him. "You should not have promised Alun to take him home."

"I made a vow, bard. I mean to keep it."

His lips pressed into a thin, disapproving line. "We cannot travel with his body, and there is no way to return him to Albion. We must bury him here."

Regarding the dismal moorland waste, I replied, "Alun deserves better, and he will have it."

"Then I suggest you think of a way."

"What about burning the body? I know it is not the most honorable way, but it could be done with dignity and respect."

Tegid turned his frown on me, thinking. I understood Tegid's reluctance: burning a corpse was reserved only for enemies, outcasts, and criminals. "It is not unknown in Albion," he admitted finally.

"There have been times when such a thing was necessary."

"Might this be one of those times?" I queried lightly. "Our need is on us."

"Yes," the bard relented, "our need is on us and we are bound by a king's vow. This is such a time. But, the fire must be tended properly so that the bones are not burned. For they must be gathered and preserved. I will see to it."

"And when we return to Albion," I added, "they will be buried on Druim Vran."

"So be it."

"Good. We will gather wood to make the pyre."

I sent eight men with extra horses back to the forest to collect the required timber. They rode under Bran's command because, once I had explained what I intended doing, the Chief Raven insisted on leading the party himself. "It is not necessary, Bran. Another can serve in this."

"If Alun's body is to be burned," he replied stiffly, "then I will choose the wood myself. Alun saved me from the Red Wyrm, it is the least I can do for him."

Since he would have it no other way, I gave him leave to go. The forest was no great distance behind us, and the horses were fed and rested; the party would, I reckoned, return by dusk the next day. The day was young yet, and they left as soon as the horses were saddled. We saw them away—sending them with the small amount of horsemeat we had left over.

I watched them out of sight, and then turned reluctantly to the task of choosing another horse for the slaughter.

The wood-gatherers returned early the next morning out of a sodden mist. The moorland squelched to a soggy drizzle brought by a fresh easterly breeze which had replaced the cold northern wind in the night. The damp moors appeared decidedly bleak and miserable in the leaden grey light.

We greeted them, and sent them to warm themselves by the fire. I ordered men to unburden the horses and release them to graze, and then joined Bran at the fire. The Raven Chief gave a terse report.

"The land is dead," he said, shaking out his cloak. "All was as we saw it before. Nothing has changed."

I called for some of the stew we had prepared the previous day, and left them to their meal. Meanwhile, Tegid and I set to work preparing the pyre for Alun's cremation. The wood had been dumped in a heap beside the road, and the bard was busy sorting it according to length when I joined him. When the ordering was finished, we carried armloads of selected timber to a large flat rock nearby and began stacking the wood carefully.

I fell in with the task and we worked together without speaking, carrying and stacking, erecting a sturdy wooden scaffold limb on limb. It was good work—the two of us moving in rhythm—and it put me in mind of the day Tegid and I had begun building Dinas Dwr. I held that memory and basked in its warm glow as we labored side by side. When we finished, the pyre stood on its lonely rock like a small timber fortress. Some of the men had gathered as we worked and now stood looking dolefully at the finished pyre.

Tegid observed them standing there and said, "When the sun sets we will light the fire."

The mist cleared as the day sped from us and the sky lightened in the west, allowing us a dazzling glimpse of golden light before dusk closed in once again. I turned from the setting sun to see the warriors coming in twos and threes across the moor to the rock where Tegid and I waited.

When all had gathered, Alun's body, which had been covered and sewn into an oxhide after his death, was brought by the Ravens and laid carefully upon the pyre. Tegid kindled a fire nearby and prepared torches, giving one to each of the remaining four Ravens and Bran.

The bard mounted the rock and took his place at the head of the pyre. He raised his hands in declamation. "Kinsmen and friends," he called loudly, "Alun Tringad is dead; his body lies cold upon the pyre. It is time to release the soul of our swordbrother to begin its journey through the High Realms. His body will be burned, but his ashes will not abide in Tir Aflan. When the fire has done its work, I will gather the bones and they will return with us to Albion for burial on Druim Vran."

Then, placing a fold of his cloak over his head, the Chief Bard raised his staff and closed his eyes. After a moment, he began to chant gently, tunelessly, a death dirge:

> *When the mouth shall be closed,*
> *When the eyes shall be shut,*
> *When the breath shall cease to rattle,*
> *When the heart shall cease to throb,*
> *When heart and breath shall cease;*
>
> *May the Swift Sure Hand uphold you,*
> *And shield you from evil of every kind.*
> *May the Swift Sure Hand uphold you,*
> *And guide your foot along the way,*
> *May the Swift Sure Hand uphold you,*
> *And lead you across the sword-bridge,*
> *May the Swift Sure Hand shield, lead, and guide you*
> *   Across the narrow way*
> *By which you leave this world;*
>
> *And guard you from all distress and danger,*
> *And place the pure light of joy before you,*
> *And lead you into Courts of Peace,*
> *And the service of a True King*
> *   In Courts of Peace,*
> *Where Glory and Honor and Majesty*
> *   Delight the Noble Kin for ever.*
>
> *May the eye of the Great God*
> *Be a pilot star before you,*
> *May the breath of the Good God*
> *Be a smooth way before you,*
> *May the heart of the Kingly God*
> *Be a boon of rich blessing to you.*
>
> *May the flames of this burning*
> *Light your way . . .*
> *May the flames of this burning*
> *Light your way . . .*
> *May the flames of this burning*
> *Light your way to the world beyond.*

So saying, the Chief Bard summoned the Ravens. One by one they stepped forward—Garanaw, Emyr, Niall and Drustwn—each bearing a torch which he thrust into the kindling at the base of the pyre. Bran came last and added his torch to the others. The fire ruffled in the wind, caught, and began climbing towards Alun's body lying so still on his rough wooden bed.

Like those around me, I watched the yellow flames licking up through the latticework of wood to caress the cold flesh of my friend. Grief I felt for myself: I would never again hear his voice lifted in song, nor see him swagger into the hall. I would miss his preposterous bragging, his bold and foolish challenges—like the time he challenged Cynan to a day's labor plowing land and felling and hauling timber, nearly ruining himself with the exertion, and all for a golden trinket.

I felt the tears welling in my eyes, and I let them fall. It was good to remember, and to weep for what was lost and could not be again.

Farewell, Alun Tringad, I said to myself as the fire hissed and cracked, mounting higher. *May it go well with you on your journey hence.*

A voice, hoarse with grief, rent the silence: "Fly, Raven! Try your wings over new fields and forests; let your loud voice be heard in lands unknown." Bran, his noble face shining with tears in the firelight, drew back his arm and lofted his spear skywards. I saw the tip glint in the cold starlight and then it disappeared into the darkness—a fitting image of release for the spirit of a warrior.

The flames grew hot; I felt the heat-sheen on my face and my cloak steamed. The flame-crack grew to a roar; the light danced, flinging shadows back into the teeth of the ever-encroaching darkness. In a little while, the pyre collapsed inward, drawing the hide-covered corpse into the fierce golden heart of the funeral fire, there to be consumed. We watched long—until only embers remained, a glowing red heap upon the rock.

"It is done," Tegid declared. "Alun Tringad has gone." Whereupon we turned and made our way back to camp, leaving Tegid to perform the tasks necessary for reclaiming the bones from the fire.

I found myself walking beside Bran. I thought his farewell apt and told him so. "It was a fitting farewell to a Raven who has gone."

Bran cocked his head to one side and regarded me as if I had suggested that I thought the moon might sleep in the sea. "But Alun has not gone," Bran observed matter-of-factly, "he has only gone on ahead."

We walked a little further, and Bran explained: "We have made a vow, we Ravens, to rejoin one another in the world beyond. That way, if any of us should fall in battle, there is a swordbrother waiting to welcome us in the world beyond. Whether in this world or the next, we will still be the Ravens."

His faith in this arrangement was simple and marvellous. And it was absolute. No shadow of doubt intruded, no qualm shadowed the bright certainty of his confidence. I, who had no such assurance, could only marvel at his trust.

We departed the next morning at dawn. Mist gathered thick, making our world blurred and dull. The sky, dense as wool to every horizon, drooped like a sodden sheepskin over our heads. As the unseen sun rose towards midday, the wind stiffened, rolling the mist in clouds across the darkening moor.

We moved in a ragged double column, shivering beneath our wet cloaks. The horses walked with their heads down, noses almost touching the ground, hooves clopping hollow on the stone-paved high road.

Wet to the skin, my hair plastered to my scalp, I stumped along on numb feet and longed for nothing more than to sit before the fire and bake the creeping cold from my bones. So Tegid's abrupt revelation, when it came, caught me off guard.

"I saw a beacon last night."

My head whipped around and I stared up at him, incredulous that he had not bothered to mention it before. He did not look at me, but rode hunch-shouldered in the saddle, squinting into the drizzle: soggy, but unconcerned.

Bards!

"When the embers had cooled," he continued placidly, "I gathered Alun's bones." My eyes flicked to the tidy bundle behind his saddle wrapped in Alun's cloak. "I saw the beacon-flare when I returned to camp."

"I see. Any particular reason why you bring this to my attention now?"

"I thought you might like to hear a good word." At this, my wise bard turned his head to look down on me. I glared up at him, water running down my hair and into my eyes. "You are angry," he observed. "Why?"

Frozen to the marrow, having eaten nothing but horsemeat for days, and heartsick at Alun's death, the last thing I expected or wanted was my Chief Bard withholding important information from me. "It is nothing," I told him, heaving my anger aside with an effort. "What do you think it means?"

"It means," he replied with an air that suggested the meaning was obvious, "we are nearing our journey's end."

His words filled me with a strange elation. The final confrontation would come soon. Anticipation pricked my senses alert; my spirit quickened. The dreariness of the day evaporated as expectation ignited within. The end is near: let Paladyr beware!

We pressed our way deeper into the barren hills. The peat moors gave way to heather and gorse. Day followed day, and the road remained straight and high; we travelled from dim grey dawn to dead grey dusk, stopping only to water the horses and ourselves. We ate only at night around the campfire when we could cook the flesh of yet another horse. We ate, bitterly regretting the loss with every bite; but it was meat, and it warmed an empty belly. No one complained.

Gradually, the land began to lift. The hills grew higher and the valleys deeper, the descents more severe as the hill-country rose towards the mountains. One day we crested a long slope to see the faint shimmer of snow-topped heights in the distance. Then cloud and mist closed in again and we lost the sight for several more days. When we saw them again, the mountains were closer; we could make out individual peaks, sharp and ragged above darkly streaming clouds.

The air grew clearer; and though mists still held us bound and blind by day, nights were often crisp and clear, the stars sharp and bright as spearpoints in a heaven black as pitch. It was on such a night that Tegid came to me while I slept beside a low-burning fire.

"Llew..."

I came awake at the touch of his hand on my shoulder.

"Come with me."

"Why?"

He made no answer, but bade me follow him a little way from camp. A late moon had risen above the horizon, casting a thin light over the land. We climbed to the top of a high hill, and Tegid pointed away to the east. I looked and saw a light burning on a near-distant ridge and, some way beyond it, another. Even as we watched, a third light flickered into existence further off still.

Standing side by side in the night, straining into the darkness, my bard and I waited. The wind prowled over the bare rock of the hilltop, like a hunting animal making low restless noises. In a little while, a fourth fire winked into life like a star alighting on a faraway hill.

I watched the beacons shining in the night, and knew that my enemy was near.

"I have seen this in my vision," Tegid said softly, and I heard again the echo of his voice lifted in song as the storm-frenzied waves hurled our frail boat onto the killing rocks.

The wind growled low, filling the darkness with a dangerous sound. "Alun," Tegid said deliberately and slow, choosing his words carefully, "was the only one among the Ravens to see Crom Cruach."

At first I did not catch his implication. "And now Alun is dead," I replied, supplying the answer to the bard's unspoken question.

"Yes."

"Then I am next. Is that what you mean?"

"That is my fear."

"Then your fear is unfounded," I told him flatly. "Your own vision should tell you as much. Alun and I—we both saw Yellow

Coat. And we both fought the serpent. Alun died, yes. But I am alive. That is the end of it."

Indicating the string of beacons blazing along the eastern horizon, he said, "The end is out there."

"Let it come. I welcome it."

The sky was showing pearly grey when we turned to walk back down the hill to the camp. Bran was awake and waiting for us. We told him about the beacons and he received the news calmly. "We must advance more warily from now on," he said. "I advise we send scouts to ride before us."

"Very well," I concurred. "See to it."

Bran touched the back of his hand to his forehead and stepped away. A little while later, Emyr and Niall rode out from the camp. I noticed that they did not ride on the hard surface of the road, but in the long grass beside it. They would go less swiftly, but more silently.

So it begins at last, I thought.

I followed them a short distance from camp and watched the riders disappearing into the pale dawn. "The Swift Sure Hand go with you, brothers!" I called after them; my voice echoed in the barren hills and died away in the heather. The land seemed unsettled by the sound. "The Swift Sure Hand shield us all," I added, and hastened back to camp to face the day's demands.

30

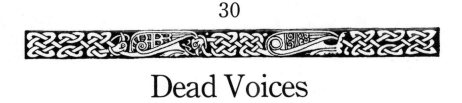

Dead Voices

The hills grudgingly gave way to an endless expanse of rock waste—all sharp-angled, toppling, sliding, bare but for tough thickets of thorny gorse. The land tilted precariously all around, yet the road held firm and good. Rain and wind battered us; mist blinded us for days without end. But the road held good.

And with each day's march the cloud-shrouded mountains drew nearer. We watched the wind-carved peaks rise until they crowded the horizon on every side—range upon range, summit upon summit fading into the misty distance. Brooding, fierce, and unwholesome, they were no kindly heights, but loomed stark and threatening over us: white, like splinters of shattered bone or teeth broken in a fight.

Enough grass grew along the roadside to keep the horses fed, and the horses fed us. This meant losing another mount every few days, but the meat kept us going. We drank from mountain runnels and pools, numbing the ache of hunger with cold water.

Gyd, Season of Thaws, drew ever nearer, bringing wet gales to assail us. The snow on the lower slopes began melting and filling the gorges, gullies and rock canyons with the icy run-off. Day and night, we were battered by the sound of water gushing and smashing, gurgling and splashing, as it rushed to the lowlands now far behind us. Mists rose from deep defiles where waterfalls boomed; clouds hung low over crevices where fast-flowing cataracts clattered and echoed like the clash of battle-crazed warbands.

The bleak monotony of naked rock and the harshness of the wind and crashing water bore constant reminder—if any was needed—that we journeyed through a hostile land. The higher we climbed among the shattered peaks, the greater grew our trepidation. It was not the wind that screamed among the ragged crowns and smashed summits; it was fear, raw and wild. We lay shivering in our cloaks at night and listened to the wind-voices wail. Dawn found us ill-rested and edgy to face the renewed assault.

Twice during each day's trek, we met with the scouts—once at midday, and then again when they returned at dusk. The Ravens took it in turn to carry out the scouting duty, two at a time, rotating the task among their number so that each day saw a fresh pair ride out. One day, Garanaw and Emyr returned as we were making camp for the night beneath a high overhanging cliff.

"There is a better place just beyond the next turn," Emyr informed us. "It is not far, and it would prove a much better shelter should the wind and rain come up in the night."

As we had not yet unsaddled the horses or lit the fires, we agreed to move on to the place they suggested. Garanaw led the way and, when we arrived, said, "This is as good a shelter as these bare bones provide."

Cynan heard this and replied, "Broken bones, you mean. I have seen nothing for days that was not fractured to splinters."

Thus, the mountains became *Tor Esgyrnau*, the Broken Bones. And what Cynan said was true; through naming them, they became less threatening, less frightening—however slightly. At least, we began looking on them with less apprehension than previously.

"That is the way of things," Tegid offered when I remarked on this a few days later. "Among the Derwyddi it is taught that to confer a name is to conquer."

"Then get busy, bard. Find a name with which to conquer Paladyr. And I will shout it from the crown of the highest peak."

Later, as darkness claimed the heights, I found him standing, peering into the gloom already creeping over the lowlands behind. I stared with him into the distance for a moment, and then asked. "What do you see?"

"I thought I saw something moving on the road down there," he replied, still scanning the twisted ribbon.

"Where?" I looked hard, but could make out nothing in the murk. "I will send someone back to see."

Tegid declined, saying, "There is no need. It is gone now—if anything *was* there. It might have been a shadow."

He walked away, but I stayed, staring into the dull twilight, searching the darkness for any sign of movement. We had climbed a fair distance into the mountains and, though the days were slightly warmer now, the nights were still cold, with biting winds sweeping down from the snow-laden peaks above. Often we woke to frost on our cloaks, and the day's melt frozen during the night to make the road treacherous until the sun warmed the stone once more.

For warmth we burned the hard-twisted knots of gorse trunks we hacked from their stony beds with our swords. They burned with a foul smell and gave off an acrid, oily smoke, but the embers remained hot long after the fire had gone.

We reached a high mountain pass and crossed the first threshold of the mountains. I looked back to see the land dull and shapeless behind us; a bleak, treeless, mist-obscured moor, colorless, sodden and drear. It was good to leave it behind at last. I stood long, looking at the road as it stretched into the distance. Ever since Tegid's suggestion that we might be followed, I had spent a fair amount of time looking back, and this time even managed to convince myself that, yes, there was something, or someone, back there—very faint and far in the distance. Or was it only the fleeting shift of mist or cloud shadow?

Up among the barren peaks, the wind whined and howled, swooping down to tear at our flesh with talons of ice. The gale was unrelenting, save for the chance protection afforded by a rock or wall as the road twisted and wound its tortured way along—sometimes no more than a footpath clawed from the mountainside, little wider than a scar. Everyone walked, for we dared not risk a fall on such a treacherous trail.

Since we could no longer ride, we loaded all the horses with as much hard-scrabble gorse as they could carry. Each animal looked like a walking furze hillock bouncing along. We went more slowly than I would have liked. Still, but for the road, we could not have made the climb at all.

On and on we went, dragging ourselves blue-lipped and shivering from one march to the next, cringing, tears streaming from our eyes as the wind and cold pared us to the bone. We grew hard as leather and sharp as knives. We grew hungry, too, with a fierce and gnawing desire no feast could satisfy. It was a longing to be healed as much as filled, a yearning to return to Albion, and allow the sight of its fair hills and glens to salve our ravaged hearts. It was *taithchwant*, the profound hunger for home.

But I could not go home. I would sooner abandon my life than my beloved. My enemy's head would adorn my belt before I turned my steps towards Druim Vran; my wife would stand once more beside me, before I turned my face towards Dinas Dwr. My queen would return with me to Albion, or I would not return at all.

At dusk, the first night after crossing the mountain threshold, we sensed a change in the mood of the land. But it was not until two nights later, when we had penetrated deep into the mountain fortress, that the change began to make itself felt. Where the lowland moors had been bleak and broody, the mountains were threatening; where the forest had been forbidding, the mountains were menacing. And it was not merely the threat of plunging from the narrow road to die broken on the rocks below. There was a wary malevolence aprowl among the peaks, a dark power that deemed our presence an invasion and reacted accordingly.

On the third night we finally understood the nature of our adversary. The day's march had gone well; we had made good progress and had found a suitable refuge for the night in a deep divide between two peaks. Solid rock walls rose sheer from the roadside, the surface raked jagged as if the road had been hacked through the mountain with a dagger; the peaktops were lost in cloud above us. Here the wind could not reach us so easily, thus the place provided a welcome respite and made as good shelter as could be found in those bare crags.

We huddled close to the fires, as always, but that night as the gale rose to its customary shriek, we heard in the wind-wail a new and chilling note. Tegid, ever alert to the subtle shifts and shades of light and sound, was first to perceive it. "Listen!" he hissed.

The talk, low and quiet around the fire, ceased. We listened, but heard nothing—save the icy blast tearing itself on the naked peaks of Tor Esgyrnau.

I leaned close. "What did you hear?"

"Did and do," Tegid said, cocking his head to one side. "There—again!"

"I hear the wind," Bran volunteered, "but nothing more."

"Nor will you if you keep drowning it with your own voice."

We waited a long while. When the sound did not come again, I asked, "What did it sound like?"

"A voice," he said, hunching his shoulders more tightly. "I thought I heard a voice. That is all."

The way he said it—curt and dismissive—made me curious. "Whose voice?"

He poked a loose ember back into the campfire with the tip of his staff, but made no reply.

"Whose voice, Tegid?"

Cynan and Bran, and several others sitting near, looked on with increasing interest. Tegid glanced around, and then back to the fire quickly. "The storm is rising," he said.

"Answer me, bard. Whose voice did you hear?"

He drew a breath, and said the name I least expected to hear. "Ollathir's," he replied softly. "I thought I heard Ollathir."

"Ollathir? He has been dead for years. He is—"

"Well I know it!"

"But—"

"You asked me whose voice I heard," he replied, speaking angrily and low. "And I am telling you the truth. I thought I heard Ollathir, Chief Bard of Albion, long dead in his grave."

The words were still hanging in the air when Bran leapt to his feet. "I heard it!" He stood over us, his face in shadow. "There! Do you hear?" He paused. "And again! But it is not your Ollathir—it is Alun Tringad!"

Cynan turned a baleful eye towards me. "There is something uncanny here, I feel." His voice was a wary whisper, as if he feared being overheard.

The fire creaked and ticked, and the wind cried. Then Cynan himself rose slowly to his feet, placing a finger to his lips. "No... no..." he said, his voice little more than a sigh, "it is not Alun I hear, it is..."—amazement transformed his features in the firelight—"Cynfarch... my father!"

Soon the whole camp was in turmoil, as everyone succumbed to the eerie voice of a dead friend or kinsman. Everyone, that is, except me. I heard only the wild wind-wail, but that was unnerving enough. For as night wore on the gale raked more fiercely at the unseen peaks and fell shrieking from the heights. We could only cower closer to the fires and hold our hands over our ears.

And then even the fires were taken from us. The wind screamed down between the walls like a rushing waterfall. The campfires flattened, guttered, and went out. Plunged into a chill darkness churning with the gale and the cries of dead friends and loved ones, the men began scrambling for their weapons.

"Tegid!" I shouted, trying to make myself heard above the wind-roar. "Someone is going to get hurt if we do not act."

"I fear you are right," agreed Cynan. "It is most unchancy in the dark."

"What do you suggest?" replied Tegid. "I cannot stop the wind!"

"No, but we can stop the men from running amok."

At that, he jumped up onto a nearby rock and raised his staff. "*Aros! Aros llawr!*" he shouted in the bullroar voice of command. "Stay! Stand your ground. It is not the voices of the dead!" he cried. "Some treachery is upon us. But do not be deceived. Take courage!"

"They are calling us!" someone shouted. "The dead have found us! We are doomed!"

"No!" I told them. "Listen to our Wise Bard: we have all lost friends and loved ones. Our thoughts are with them, and so you imagine you hear their voices. It is a trick of the wind and storm. Nothing more."

"Do you not hear them yourself?" another frightened voice demanded.

"No, I do not. I hear only the wind," I told them sternly. "It is raw and wild, but it is only the wind. Sit down, all of you, and we will wait it out together."

This seemed to calm the men. They drew together, some with weapons at the ready, and crouched shoulder to shoulder to wait. And, gradually, the gale died down and the eerie assault ceased.

We rekindled the fires and slowly relaxed and settled down to sleep, thinking the trouble was ended. Wishful thinking, as it turned out: the ordeal was just beginning.

31

Bwgan Bwlch

We had just settled to our rest when the eerie sounds began again, but not voices alone. This time, the dead also appeared.

As the wind dropped, fog descended from the icy altitudes—a strange, ropy mist that ebbed and flowed in rippling tidewaves. Grey as death and cold, the elusive vapor stole along the bare rockface of the wall and slid over and around the rubble at the roadside, groping and curling like tendrils. The sentries were the first to see it and raised a tentative alarm. They were concerned but uncertain, as there was no clear danger.

"No, no," I told Niall who apologized for waking me, "this night was never meant for sleeping. What is happening?"

His face, deep-shadowed in the fitful light, screwed into a squint as he peered beyond me into the darkness. "A fog has come up," he said, paused, and glanced back to me. "It has an evil feel, lord. I do not like it."

I rose and looked around. The fog had crept thick, forming a solid cover on the ground beyond the ring of light thrown out by our campfires. If it had been a living creature, I would have said it seemed reluctant to come into the light. Probably it was just the heat of the flames, creating a margin of space around us. Yet, it seemed almost sentient, the way it snaked and coiled as it thickened.

"It is watching us," Niall whispered.

He was not the only one to feel that way. Very soon the unnatural vapor had formed a weird landscape almost man-height around us. Queer shapes bulged up from the mass only to melt back into it again. Men began to see things in the grey billows: floating limbs, heads, torsos, ethereal faces with empty eyes.

The horses did not like the fog; they raised such a commotion with their jerking and jigging and whinnying that I ordered them to be blindfolded and brought within the fire-ring. They liked that scarcely better, but allowed themselves to be pacified.

Our fears, however, could not be so easily allayed. I ordered the men to arm themselves and to stand shoulder to shoulder and shield to shield. We took what comfort we could in the heft of our weapons and the nearness of our swordbrothers, watching helpless as the spectral display continued.

Disembodied heads mouthed silent words; detached arms gesticulated, legs twitched, and other body parts melded and separated in monstrous couplings. Grasping hands reached out from the mass and beckoned to us, melted and reformed as toothless sucking mouths. I saw a huge lidless eye split into smiling lips, and then dissolve into a puckered fistula.

"*Clanna na cù!*" Cynan growled under his breath.

Tegid, hovering near, whispered, "Something is stirring here that has slept for ages. The ancient evil of this land has awakened, and its minions stalk the land once more."

Cynan turned his face, sweating despite the cold. "What could do that?"

"Could it be Paladyr?" I wondered. "Could he have done something to rouse this—this evil power, whatever it is?"

"Perhaps," Tegid allowed. "But I think it is a thing more powerful than Paladyr alone—a presence, maybe. I do not know. I feel it here." He pressed his fist to his chest. "It is a sensation of deep wickedness. I do not think Paladyr capable of such hatred and malice." He paused, thinking, and added, "This is more like..."

The ghostly shapes formed and congealed, altering in subtly

suggestive ways. Watching this silent, shifting dance of the macabre put me in mind of Lord Nudd's Demon Host at the Battle of Dun na Porth at Findargad. "Lord Nudd," I said aloud. "Prince of Uffern and Annwn."

"From the tale of Ludd and Nudd?" wondered Cynan.

"The same."

At mention of the name, I began to feel an almost hypnotic effect. Whatever hostile power animated the fog, it was beginning to exert a fell authority over us. I was drawn to it, coaxed, beckoned. Fascinated, my spirit yearned towards the billowing panoply of mutating forms.

Come to me, the fog seemed to say. *Embrace me, and let me comfort you. Your struggle can be over; your striving can end. Sweet release. Oh, your release is near.*

The sly seduction of this insinuation proved potent indeed to a band of bruised and exhausted warriors. Long on the trail in a harsh and hostile land, there were those among us who had begun to weaken. One young warrior across the circle from me threw down his shield and staggered forth. I called to his companions who hauled him back.

He was no sooner returned to the fold than another warrior, a man named Cadell, gave a cry, dropped his weapons, and made to dash into the fog. Thinking quickly, those on either side of him grabbed him by the arms and restrained him.

Cadell resisted. He dug in his feet and shook off those holding him. Turning, he made to run into the fog. A nearby warrior tripped him with the butt of a spear. His kinsmen were on him in a moment, dragging him back to the line. As if overcome by a gigantic strength, kicking and flailing with his arms, Cadell sent his holders flying. Screaming terribly, he staggered to his feet, turned, and lumbered towards the fog once more.

Calling for Bran's aid, I darted after him. He had reached the fog, which seemed to surge towards him in an embrace, curling around his wrists and ankles. I felt a cold exhalation emanating from the undulating fog as I put my hand on the warrior's shoulder—it was like touching a damp rock.

Cadell twisted around me, flinging out his arm. His flying elbow caught me on the point of the chin and I was lifted off my feet and thrown back; I thought my head had come off. I rolled onto my knees, black stars spinning in dark circles before my eyes.

I shook my head fiercely. My assailant was once again staggering into the fog. I stood on unsteady legs and launched myself at him. I did not try to turn him again, nor did I try to restrain him; it was too late for that. I simply sprang, raising my silver hand and bringing it sharply down on the nape of his neck.

The warrior stiffened and threw out his arms. He raised his head and screamed, then toppled backwards like a felled tree. He hit the ground and lay still.

Fearing I had killed him, I stooped over Cadell and pressed my fingertips against his throat. The instant I touched the body it began jerking and trembling—all over, head to foot, all at once—as if he were dancing in his sleep. His eyelids snapped open and his mouth gaped wide; his clawed fingers clutched at me, grasping for my throat.

I swung my silver hand hard against the side of his head. He convulsed and I heard a gurgle low in his throat. The breath rushed out of his lungs and with it something else: a transparent, formless shape like a flying shadow. It brushed me as it fled and I felt a sick, slimy chill and an aching, piercing emptiness—as if all the loneliness and misery in all the world were gathered into a swiftly fleeing distillate of woe. In that fleeting touch, I felt the creature's mindless anguish, and knew what it was to be a tortured animal, able to feel pain, but unable to fathom its cause or reason. My heart felt as if it would burst with the utter desolation of that sensation.

And then hands seized me, pulling me to my feet. The despair passed as swiftly as it had come. "I am myself," I told them, and looked down at the body before me. To my surprise, the man opened his eyes and sat up. The warriors hastened us both back to the safety of the circle.

I had no sooner returned to my place beside Tegid and Cynan when the eerie spirit voice beckoned once more:

Come to me. Oh, come and cast away your care. Let me hold you and comfort you. Let me free you from your pain. Come to me ... come to me ...

"Hold, men! Stand your ground!" I shouted. "Do not listen!"

"It is gaining strength." Tegid said, glancing all around. "Our fear is feeding it, and we are losing the will to resist." He spun away, tugging me with him. "There might be a way ... Help me!"

"Cynan, you and Bran take over," I ordered as I hastened to follow. "Whatever happens, stand firm."

The squat twisted stems of the gorse bushes we burned for warmth were not large enough to serve, but our spear shafts were made of ashwood. Working quickly, we cut the blades from three shafts and Tegid had me hold them while he dipped into the pouch at his belt for the Nawglan, the Sacred Nine, as he called it.

Taking the specially-blended ashes, he sprinkled a portion into the palm of his right hand and then rubbed it the length of the bladeless shafts, each in turn.

"There," he said when he finished. "Now let us see if they will stand."

It was not possible to drive the wooden shafts into the stone-paved road, of course. But we tried wedging the ends between cracks in the stones. "This would have been easier with the blades still attached," I complained.

"There can be no metal in this rite," the bard replied. "Not even gold."

We persevered, however, and eventually succeeded in wedging the three spear shafts into cracks: one standing upright, two on either side inclined at a slight angle to form a loose arrowhead shape—a gogyrven. Gathering live coals on the inner rim of a shield, we placed a small pile of embers around each standing shaft. Taking up the hem of his cloak, Tegid quickly fanned the embers into a flame that licked slowly up the slender poles.

Holding his staff in both hands over his head, the bard began walking rapidly around the blaze in a sunwise direction. I could hear him muttering something under his breath in the Taran Tafod; I was not supposed to hear or know what he said.

"Hurry, Tegid!" I urged.

At the completion of the third circuit, the bard stopped, faced the blazing gogyrven and said, "*Dólasair! Dódair! Bladhm dó!!*"

The words of the Dark Tongue resounded in the pass, echoing up the sheer rock divide. Extending the staff vertically, Tegid began to speak the words of a saining rite.

Gifting Giver!
You whose name is very life to them that hear it, hear me now!
Tegid Tathal ap Talaryant, Chief Bard of Albion, I am.
See me established in the sunwise circle;
hear my entreaty.

Earth and sky, rock and wind, bear witness!
By the power of the Swift Sure Hand, I claim this ground
and sain it with a name: Bwgan Bwlch!

> *Power of fire I have over it,*
> *Power of wind I have over it,*
> *Power of thunder I have over it,*
> *Power of wrath I have over it,*
> *Power of heavens I have over it,*
> *Power of earth I have over it,*
> *Power of worlds I have over it!*

> *As tramples the swan upon the lake,*
> *As tramples the horse upon the plain,*
> *As tramples the ox upon the meadow,*
> *As tramples the boar upon the track,*
> *As trample the forest host of hart and hind,*
> *As trample all quick things upon the earth,*
> *I do trample and subdue it,*
> *And drive all evil from it!*

> *In the name of the Secret One,*
> *In the name of the Living One,*
> *In the name of the All-Encircling One,*
> *In the name of the One True Word, it is Bwgan Bwlch,*
> *Let it so remain as long as men survive*
> *To breathe the name.*

So saying, the Chief Bard brought his staff down with a loud crack upon the rocks. He turned to me. "It is done. Let us hope it is enough."

The writhing mist shuddered and drew inward upon itself, as if contracting under a hail of blows; or as if it were a creature cowed by fire, but reluctant to allow its prey to escape. The mutations rippled through the churning mass with ever-increasing frequency.

Returning to my place in the front rank, I lofted my spear and called aloud:

"In the name of the Secret One, In the name of the Living One, In the name of the All-Encircling One, In the name of the One True Word, this place is Bwgan Bwlch!"

Bran, standing next to me, took up the words, calling out in a clear, strong voice. Soon others were shouting them, too, raising a chant against the malignant spirit bubbling like a foul froth all around us. We chanted and the fog churned with ghastly half-formed shapes whose origins could scarcely be guessed.

I saw an eyeless face with a swine's snout and goat's ears; a grasping hand became a five-headed cat before dissolving into the form of a gross, grinning mouth that opened to reveal a huge, bloated toad for a tongue. A pair of emaciated bovine haunches mutated into a coiled snake before disintegrating into a scattering of scuttling cockroaches.

I saw a horse's head on the body of an infant; the infant torso stretched into a pair of thin scabby stork shanks with the long skeletal feet of a rodent. An immense belly swelled and split, spilling out blind lizards before dissipating into a clutch of palpitating reptile eggs which merged to become two slack-jawed haglike heads...

"Louder!" I shouted, taking heart that our chanting seemed to be producing some effect. "Sain the ground! Claim it!"

The men redoubled their efforts. The voices of the warriors, so long pent by Tir Aflan's dismal hush, swelled to fill the troubled pass; their voices raced up the sheer rock walls to strike the icy heights. Indeed, it seemed as if by the vigor of shouting alone we might drive the wicked *bwgan* spirit from its roost.

With blinding swiftness, the ghastly metamorphoses became instantaneous. Bizarre shapes blurred together in a fantastic stream of mutating forms—changing too fast now to be recognized as anything but hazy images of vaguely human and animal shapes.

I heard Tegid's powerful voice lifted above the rest. On his lips a song, the words of the saining rite. Man by man, we added our voices to Tegid's and the song soared up strong and loud, and the bwgan shrank before the sound. We sang:

> *Power of fire I have over it,*
> *Power of wind I have over it,*
> *Power of thunder I have over it,*
> *Power of wrath I have over it,*
> *Power of heavens I have over it,*
> *Power of earth I have over it,*
> *Power of worlds I have over it!*

The bard's saining song drove into the vile spirit like the thrust of a flaming spear, a gogyrven of song. The fog began to fade and dissipate, vanishing as we watched.

> *As tramples the swan upon the lake,*
> *As tramples the horse upon the plain,*
> *As tramples the ox upon the meadow,*
> *As tramples the boar upon the track,*
> *As trample the forest host of hart and hind,*
> *As trample all quick things upon the earth,*
> *I do trample and subdue it,*
> *And drive all evil from it!*

At the precise moment of its fading, the bwgan revealed itself as a huge hulking thing, a beast with the immense hairy body of a she-bear, its hind legs those of an ox, and its front legs those of an eagle. Its tail was the long, naked, hairless cauda of a rat, but its head and face were disturbingly human—flat-featured, big-lipped, with huge, pendulous ears, round, staring eyes and a thick protruding tongue.

In the name of the Secret One,
In the name of the Living One,
In the name of the All-Encircling One,
In the name of the One True Word, it is Bwgan Bwlch,
Let it so remain as long as men survive
To breath the name.

And then, growing transparent as the mist dissipated, the bwgan vanished.

The mountain pass echoed with the resounding cheers of the warriors, who sent their song spinning up into a night sky suddenly splashed with bright burning stars.

"We have done it!" cried Cynan, happily slapping every back he happened upon. "We have beaten the bwgan beast!"

"Well done, men!" shouted Bran. "Well done!"

We were all so busy praising one another that we did not at first hear the thin wail coming from the peaks above. But Tegid heard it. "Silence!" he called. "Silence!"

"Silence!" Cynan shouted, trying to quiet the men. "Our bard is speaking!"

"Listen!" Tegid said, lifting a hand towards the darksome peaks.

As the jubilation of the men died away, I heard a bloodless and mournful shriek—like that of a great predatory bird—far away, and receding swiftly, as the unclean spirit passed out of the world of men.

I looked to Tegid. "Bard?"

"That is the bwgan," Tegid explained with satisfaction. "It is searching for a new home among these broken peaks. If it finds no home before sunrise, it will die." Throwing high his hands, he cried, "Behold! A new day is dawning in Tir Aflan."

Turning as one, we saw the sun was rising in the east. We watched it rise—hungry for it, like men too long away from the light. Soon a shaft of clear light touched the narrow pass and filled it, expelling any lingering shadows with the force of its radiance. The rocks blushed red-gold; the peaks glowed, every one a gem.

"That evil spirit will not return here," the bard continued. "This ground is sained now, reclaimed for humankind."

"We have conquered indeed!" Bran Bresal shouted.

It was a happy moment, a blessed relief to look upon that new day. Yet even in the midst of such celebration I could feel the deep melancholy despair of the land reasserting itself once more. We might have recovered one mountain pass among a myriad others but, as the inexorable tide of grief flowed back, I understood that no mere saining rite could banish the long ages of torment and misery. It would, I reflected, take something more than a song to redeem Tir Aflan.

We struck camp and journeyed on. It was not long before dark clouds gathered to obscure the sun. The day, so brightly begun, sank into gloom once more—a gloom made all the more palpable for the glory of the dawn we had witnessed. I felt it—we all did—as a wound in the chest, a hole through which the soul leaked away like blood.

Five days, two horses and three mountain passes later, we stood together, wind-wracked and wrapped in our tattered cloaks, staring dully at a peculiar dark pall of cloud hanging over the wide bowl of a valley far below us.

"A very odd-looking cloud," I observed.

"It is smoke," replied Tegid. "Smoke and dust and fear."

32

Strangers

I gazed into the valley. The road showed as a narrow scar winding down the mountainside to lose itself in the pall of smoke and dust. My whole body leaned towards the sign in anticipation: direct evidence of human habitation. The end of our journey was near. I felt no fear.

"Why do you say fear?" Cynan asked Tegid.

"See it rising on clouds of smoke and dust," the bard replied, extending his hands and spreading his fingers, "see it casting a shadow over this unhappy land. Great distress lies before us, and great fear." Tegid lowered his hand and his voice. "Our search has ended."

"Goewyn is there?"

"And Tángwen?" Cynan asked with eager impatience. "*Mo anam*, brothers! Why do we delay? Let us hasten to free them at once." He looked quickly from one to the other of us. "Is there anything to prevent us?"

Had it been left to Cynan we would have raised the battle call of the carynx then and there, and stormed the valley by force. But Bran's cooler head prevailed. "Paladyr is surely awaiting us," he said, harking back to the beacons we had seen. "It is likely he knows our strength, but we do not know his. It would be well to discover our enemy's might before beginning battle."

"Then come," I told him. "You and I will spy out the land."

"I will go with you," Cynan offered quickly, starting away at once.

I placed my silver hand in the middle of his chest. "Stay, brother. Bran and I will go. Ready the warband and await our return."

"My wife is taken also," he growled. "Or have you forgotten?"

"I have not forgotten. But I need you to prepare the men," I replied, adding, "and to lead them if anything should happen and we do not return." Cynan scowled, but I could see him weakening. "We will not be gone long, and we will hasten back as soon as we have learned what we need to know."

Cynan, still glowering, relented. "Go, then. You will find us ready when you return."

Bran quickly readied two horses and as we mounted Tegid took hold of the reins and stopped me. "You asked me what could rouse the ancient evil of the Foul Land," he said.

"Do you know the answer now?"

"No," he confessed, "but this I know: the answer will be found down there." The bard indicated the smoke-dark valley.

"Then I will go and put an end to this mystery," I told him.

Bran and I started down into the broad valley. The road was lined with enormous boulders all the way. We thought to ride to the level of the smoke haze, then leave the horses where we could reach them at need. We would continue on foot to get as near as we could.

We made our way silently, every sense alert. Bran carried his spear, and I my swordblade naked against my thigh. But we heard nothing save the hollow clop of our horses' hooves on the road, and saw only the smoke gently undulating like a filthy sea swell. Down and down we went, following the sharp switchback of the road as it uncoiled into the valley. I watched the smoke sea surge as we descended to meet it.

In a little while we dismounted and led the horses off the road to tether them behind a rock. A little grass growing at the base of the boulder would keep the animals occupied until we returned. We then proceeded on foot, all but blind in the haze. The acrid smoke burned our eyes, but we remained watchful and proceeded with all caution, pausing every few paces to listen. Having come this far, we could not allow a moment's carelessness to ruin our cause.

We flitted from rock to rock, scanning the road below before moving on. After a while, I began to hear a drumming sound, deep and low, like an earth heart beating underground. The rhythmic rumble vibrated in the pit of my stomach and up through the soles of my feet.

Bran heard it, too. "What is that?" he asked when we stopped again.

"It is coming from the valley." The smoke pall was thinning as we descended, and I saw that we would soon drop below it. "Down there." I pointed to a large, angular boulder jutting up beside the road. "We should be able to see better from there."

We made for the boulder, pursuing the sinuous path as it slid down and down. The humming, drumming sound grew louder. In a little while we reached the rock and paused to rest and survey the land below.

The smoke cloud formed a ceiling above us, thick and dark. And, spreading below us, a vista of devastation: the entire bowl of the wide valley was a vast, denuded pit; rust-red mounds of crushed rock formed precarious mountains teetering over tier upon tier of ragged trenches and holes gouged into a rutile land, deep, angry red, like violent gashes in bruised flesh.

Plumes of foul smoke rose from scores of vents and holes, and from open fires burning on the slopes of slag heaps. And rising with the smoke, the stink of human excrement mingled with that of rotting meat and putrid water. The smell made our throats ache.

Crawling over this hellish landscape, swarming the slag heaps and plying the trenches, were thousands of men and women—thronging like termites, delving like ants, toiling away like tireless worker bees—more insect than human. Half-naked and covered in dust and mud and smoke, the wretches struggled under the enormous burdens upon their backs; scaling rickety ladders and clinging to ropes, they toiled with dull but single-minded purpose, hoisting leather bags and wicker baskets filled with earth, and then bearing them away. Squalid beyond belief, the valley squirmed with this teeming, palpitating tumult.

Gazing out over the desolate valley, straining to comprehend the methodical, meticulous thoroughness of its devastation, we could only gawk in dismay. I felt sick, disgusted by the horrific extent of the destruction.

"Maggots," muttered Bran under his breath, "feeding on a rotten corpse."

A fresh-running stream had once passed through the center of the vale. But the stream had been dammed at the further end of the valley and the waters backed to make a narrow lake, now choked with scum and rust-hued mud. Beyond the dam a column of orange-brown smoke issued from an enormous chimney in puffing gusts to the rhythm of the deep pounding earthbeat. The smoke rolled slowly, relentlessly from the stack to add to the heavy canopy of filth hanging over the whole vale.

It took me some moments to work out that I was looking at a crude strip mine. The earthmovers and loaders working this mine were human: bemired, befouled and bedraggled men, women and children.

"It is a mine," I lamented.

Bran nodded woodenly. "They are digging for iron, do you think?"

"Probably. But I want a closer look."

We crept from our hiding place and continued picking our way down. The road curved away from the valley, rimming an inner bend in the mountains. At one place the rock wall climbed steeply on the left-hand side of the road and fell sharply on the right. Water from above seeped down the cliff, gathered in a shallow pool and flowed across the road to splash away below. This small stream had washed loose silt and mud from the cliff above to form a bed. As we crossed this stream, I caught sight of something in the mud that stopped me in midstep.

I halted, putting out my hand to Bran. He froze, spear at the ready, looking quickly around for danger. Seeing nothing, he turned to me. I pointed to the muddy track at my feet. The Raven Chief looked long at it, then bent for a closer inspection.

"Do you know what made this?" he asked.

"I do," I told him. Blood throbbed in my temples, I felt dizzy and sick. "It is a..." I paused, searching for words he would understand. "It is a wheel track," I said at last.

Kneeling, Bran pressed his fingertips into the intricate lacework in the mud. "It is no wheel track that I have ever seen."

"It was made by a—" Before I could say another word, I heard an oddly familiar rumble. "Hurry! We must get off the road."

Bran heard the sound, but made no move. He frowned, cocking his head to one side as he listened, unaware of the danger. Snatching the Raven Chief by the arm, I yanked him to his feet. "Hurry! We must not be seen!"

We sprinted across the road and flung ourselves down the slope. An instant later, I saw a streak of yellow and the dull glint of dark glass as the vehicle passed directly over our heads with a rush. It slowed as it came to the stream; there came the sound of gears grinding as it downshifted, the engine roared—a gut-clutching, alien sound—and the vehicle cruised on.

We pressed our faces flat to the dirt and held ourselves deathly still. The vehicle drove on. When it had gone, Bran raised his head, a stricken expression on his face.

"It was a kind of wagon," I explained. "It comes from my world. That is what made the tracks."

"An evil thing, certainly," he said.

"It has no place here," I replied, rising. "Come on. We must hurry before it returns."

We climbed back onto the road and hurried on. Bran kept looking back to see if any more of these strange wagons were coming at him. But the road remained empty, and I could see nothing moving on it down below.

The appearance of the vehicle shocked and disturbed me more than I could say. But I had no time to consider the implications. It was more crucial than ever now to learn the enemy's strength and position. I ran headlong down the road, dodging behind rocks, pausing to catch my breath and lurching on. Bran ran behind me and we entered the valley, staying well out of sight behind the slag heaps and rock piles.

A tainted rain began to fall. It left black-rimmed spots where it splashed onto my skin. The laborers took no notice. The red dust slowly turned to red mud, transforming the valley into a vast oozy quagmire. Yet the workers toiled on.

Bran and I crept under an overhanging boulder and settled down to watch. The first thing that struck me, after the shock of the desolation and the presence of *Dyn Dythri*, the outworld strangers, was the relentless labor of the miners. They worked as driven slaves, yet I could not see anyone compelling them. There were, as far as I could see, no overseers, no taskmasters. There was no one directing the frenzied toil. Slaves under an invisible lash, then, the mudmen struggled and strove, sinking under their burdens, floundering in a thick stew of ordure and sludge and soot.

The poor, ignorant brutes, I thought, and wondered who, or what, had so enslaved them.

There was a track made of cut logs thrown across the mire on the far side of the valley. I watched as men fought their way up from the pits and trenches to stumble along this track towards the dam. The track crossed the dam and descended out of sight behind it in the direction of the smokestack. This seemed to be the workers' destination.

I considered whether the impetus for the wretches' toil might derive from the object of that labor, rather than any external force or threat. Perhaps they were enslaved by some deep passion within themselves. Maybe they *wanted* to work like beasts of burden. Lacking any other explanation, I decided they must be prisoners of their own rapacity.

"I want to see what is behind the dam," I told Bran. Slowly, carefully, we began making our way around the slag heap. We had not crept more than a dozen paces when we came face to face with two mudmen digging into the mire with crude wooden shovels. They looked at us with dull eyes, and I thought they would raise a cry at seeing intruders. But they merely bent their backs and proceeded with their work without so much as a backward glance as we pushed past and continued on our way.

This was the way of it elsewhere, too. There were so many slaves about that it was impossible not to be seen by some of them; but when we were seen, our presence went unremarked. On the whole they took no notice of us, or if they did, they appeared not to care. If they showed no fear, neither did they show any interest. Their labor was, apparently, all-absorbing; they gave themselves to it completely.

"Strange," concluded Bran, shaking his head slowly. "If they were beasts I would not work them so."

Upon reaching the dam, we skirted the track and kept to an upper path so that we could observe the ground below from a distance. The chimney we had seen was part of an untidy complex of structures. Attached to the largest of these buildings was the spewing smokestack, and from this came the ceaseless dull rumble of heavy machinery. Into this main building trudged an endless succession of miners lugging their burdens in one portal and emerging with empty bags and baskets from another.

My spirits, already low, sank even further. For, if there had been any uncertainty before, every last particle of doubt crumbled away before the belching smoke and rumble of heavy machinery. There was no sign of Paladyr or any warriors; nor of any place large or secure enough to hold hostages—except the factory, and I doubted we would find them there.

"Goewyn and Tángwyn are not here," I told Bran. "Let us return to camp." I saw the question on his face, so before he could ask, I added, "The Dyn Dythri have come in force to plunder Tir Aflan. We will tell the others what we have seen and make our battle plan."

Bran and I turned away to begin making our long way back to where the warband waited. We had almost gained the cover of the smoke layer when I heard the hateful rumble of the vehicle returning.

My mind raced ahead. "That rock!" Whirling, I pointed to a place in the road behind us. A large rock marked the bend: there Bran and I could hide. Upon reaching the place, we flattened ourselves behind the rock and waited for the thing to pass.

I heard the motor race as the driver downshifted into the bend. The vehicle's tires squelched on the wet stone a few short paces from where we hid. The sound ground away, dropping rapidly as it receded into the valley. We waited until we could no longer hear it, and then crept back onto the road. We retrieved the horses and stopped to catch our breath. The valley spread far behind and below us, dull red in the sullen rain like a wound oozing blood.

Bran got to his feet and mounted his horse. "Let us leave this, this *cwm gwaed*," the Raven Chief said bleakly. "It sickens me."

"Cwm Gwaed," I muttered, Vale of Blood. "The name is fitting. So be it." Bran made no reply, but turned his horse onto the road and his back to the valley.

Upon reaching our encampment, we were met by two anxious warriors, Owyn and Rhodri, who ran to greet us with the news, "Strangers are coming!"

Rhodri added, "Cynan and Garanaw have gone down to meet them."

I slid from the saddle, scanning the camp. "Where is Tegid?"

"The Penderwydd is watching from the road," Owyn said. "He said to bring you when you returned. I will show you."

Rhodri took the horses, and Owyn led us a short distance away from camp to a lookout where we could gaze down upon the road rising to meet the pass where we had made our camp. Tegid was there, and Scatha with him, watching, as the warriors had said, a group of horsemen approaching in the distance.

The bard turned his head as we took our places beside him. "Who is it?" I asked. "Do you know?"

"Watch," was all he said.

In a moment, I was able to pick out individual riders, two of whom were smaller and slighter than the others. One of these wore a white hat or headpiece. Closer, the white hat proved to be hair. The man raised his face towards the place where we stood and the sun flared as it caught the lenses at his eyes.

"Nettles!" I shouted. My feet were already running to meet him.

33

Return of the Wanderer

Professor Nettleton urged his horse to speed when he saw me running down the slope to meet him. Gaunt and haggard from his journey, his broad smile measured his relief. I reached up and swept him from the saddle in a fierce embrace. "Nettles! Nettles!" I cried. "What are you doing here? How did you know how to find us?"

The old man grinned, patting my arm and chuckling. "King Calbha sent three stout warriors with me, and Gwion led the way."

At this I glanced at the others, observing them for the first time. Flanked by Cynan and Garanaw were three warriors, looking none the worse for their journey, each leading a packhorse loaded with provisions and, on a fourth, Tegid's young Mabinog, Gwion Bach.

"How did you find us?" I asked, shaking my head in amazement. "I cannot believe you are here."

"Finding you was simplicity itself," the professor replied. "We had but to sail east. Once ashore, we simply followed your trail." He lifted a hand in the young Mabinog's direction. "Gwion has a special gift in that regard," he explained. "We would have been lost many times over without his guidance."

I turned as the others gathered around us. "Is this true, Gwion? You followed our trail?"

"It is so, Lord Llew," the boy replied.

"Well," I told them, "however you have fared, your journey is at an end. You have found us. But you will be tired. Come, rest, and tell us what news you bring. We are all eager to hear how you have fared and what brought you here."

We returned together, talking eagerly to one another about the rigors of the journey. "See here!" I called as we came into camp. "The wanderer has returned."

Scatha and Tegid hailed the travellers, greeting them with astonished admiration. All the warriors gathered around to acclaim their feat, not least because they had seen the provision-laden packhorses and could almost smell the food awaiting them.

"Gwion tracked us," I told Tegid, clapping a hand to the boy's shoulder.

The Mabinog drew himself up and answered with an air of immense satisfaction. "Where you have walked," he replied, "there is a trail of light. Day or night, we merely followed the *Aryant Ol*. The Radiant Way led us to you."

"Well done, lad," said Tegid proudly. "I will hear more of this later." Looking to the others, he said, "You have all faced great hardship and danger. The need must be great to have brought you here. Why have you come?"

Gwion and the warriors looked to Nettles, who answered, "It was at my insistence, Penderwydd. Lord Calbha warned me about Tir Aflan. With every step I feared we would arrive too late."

He paused, turning his bespectacled eyes to me. "It is Weston and his men," he said, licking his lips. He had travelled far with this news burning in him. "They have succeeded in creating a veritable gateway from our world to this. They have learned how to move machinery through the breach and they have devised systems for exploiting the land—diamonds, or something equally valuable."

"Not diamonds," I corrected. "Some kind of precious metal, I think." I explained quickly about the chimney and the machinery, which indicated a smelting process. Then I related to Tegid and the others what Bran and I had discovered in the valley.

Nettleton listened, a pained expression on his face. When I had finished, he said, "It is even worse than I thought. I had no idea..." He fell silent, considering the enormity of the crisis.

"Come," I said, thinking to make it easier for him. "Sit down. Rest yourself, and we will talk."

But he resisted, putting his hand on my arm as if to hold me back. "There is something else, Llew. Siawn Hy is alive."

I stared. "What did you say?"

"Simon is alive, Lewis," he said, using my former name to help drive the point home. "He and Weston are working together. They have been from the beginning."

As he spoke the words, I felt the certainty fall like a dead weight upon me. It was Siawn Hy, not Paladyr, who sought revenge through Goewyn's abduction. Paladyr might have had a hand in the deed, but Siawn Hy was behind it. Siawn's poisonous treachery was at work once more in this worlds-realm.

"Llew?" the professor asked, studying me carefully. "Did you hear me?"

"I heard you," I replied dully. "Siawn Hy alive—that explains much."

"Afer their initial contact," the professor continued, "Weston furnished Simon with information in exchange for funding arranged through Simon's father. It was Simon's ambition to set himself up as king—he even boasted about it. But you thwarted him in that. Indeed, you succeeded where he failed," Nettles stressed. "I do not think he will forgive you that."

"No," I mused. "I do not think he will."

I stepped away from him and, raising my voice, I addressed the warriors. "Unload the provisions and prepare a feast of welcome. Then look to your weapons. Today we ready ourselves and take our ease. Tomorrow we meet the enemy." As the warriors dispersed to their various tasks, I summoned Cynan, Bran and Scatha, saying, "We will hold council now and lay our battle plans."

Darkness had long claimed the camp by the time we finished; the stars shone down hard flecks of light in the black skybowl of night. We had spent the remainder of the day in deliberation, pausing only to share a most welcome meal of bread, salt beef and ale, prepared from the provisions brought for us. That night, while the warband slept, I walked the perimeter of the camp, my thoughts returning time and again to the meaning of the professor's revelation.

Simon, badly wounded by Bran's spear, had fallen across the threshold to be rescued by some of Weston's men. They had rushed him to hospital, where he had spent a lengthy convalescence. "Immediately upon his release," Nettles explained when we had a moment together, "Simon disappeared. And shortly after that the activity began in earnest."

"How did you find out?"

"I have been keeping an eye on the entire operation. Also, I had help." He leaned forward. "Do you remember Susannah?"

At his mention of the name, a face flickered in my memory: a keen-eyed firebrand of a young woman with brains and pluck for any challenge. Yes, I remembered her.

"Susannah has been a godsend," Nettles informed me soberly. "I have told her everything. I do not know how I could have managed otherwise."

He grew grave. After a moment, he said, "It was after Simon disappeared again that I began noticing the signs. I knew something had to be done. The damage is fearful."

"Damage?"

"The damage to the manifest world. There are," he hesitated, searching for the right word, "there are *anomalies* breaking through. Aberrations appear almost daily. The Knot, the Endless Knot, is unravelling, you see. And the manifest world is diminishing; the effect is..."

His eyes were intense behind his round spectacles, imploring, entreating, willing me to understand. "That is when you decided to come back," I suggested.

"Yes, and when Calbha told me that Goewyn had been abducted

and taken to the Foul Land, I feared I had returned too late." Professor Nettleton's voice grew stern and insistent. "They must be stopped, Llew. They are manipulating forces they do not understand. If their violation continues, they will destroy literally *everything*. You cannot imagine..."

With this warning reverberating through my mind, tolling like a bell of doom, I stalked the silent camp through the night's cold. The end was near, I could feel it approaching with the speed of the dawn. Tomorrow, I would meet my enemy and, with the aid of the Swift Sure Hand, I would defeat him. Or die.

The valley appeared as Bran and I had left it, a red gash in the belly of the land. The smoke hung like a sooty ceiling over all, shutting out what little light might have come from the pale and powerless sun. I imagined, for a moment, that sunlight penetrating the fog and burning away all the filth and corruption. Oh, but it would take something stronger than sunlight to reverse the devastation that met our sight.

The scum-filled lake, lethally still beneath the shroud of smoke, lay like a tarnished mirror. The stench of the lake and from the wounded land hurt our lungs and stung our eyes. The men must accustom themselves to this before going nearer.

"The Dyn Dythri are there," I told them, pointing with my speartip to the dam and chimney. Cynan, Bran, Scatha, Tegid and Nettles stood with me; the warband was assembled behind us. "I do not know how many strangers have come, but it may be that they know we are here and will be ready for us."

"Good," grunted Cynan. "Then men will not say we defeated a sleeping foe."

Scatha observed the valley, studying it in detail, green eyes narrowed to attentive slits. "You described it well. But it will be difficult to walk that slope. I think we should use the path," she said, indicating the track on the left-hand side of the lake which the mudmen used to trundle their burdens to the compound behind the dam.

"The slaves will not hinder us," I said. "There is no need to avoid them. They will not fight."

"I do not see any of the strangers, nor their *olwynog tuthógi*," Bran said, and some of the men laughed. But it was nervous laughter; there was no real mirth in it.

I turned to address them, using the words I had pondered during my long, sleepless night. "Kinsmen and friends, we have journeyed far and endured much that would have daunted lesser men." There was a general murmur of approval at this.

"Today," I continued, "we will face a most deceptive and cunning enemy. Deceptive, for his weapons are those of cowardice and guile. Cunning, for he is shrewd in malice and devious in hostility. He will appear to you a weak and unworthy foe, unlike any you have met in battle. His weapons will appear low and inferior, but do not be deceived. For they can kill at a distance, without warning. You must be wary at all times—for when the foeman stands far off, then is he most dangerous."

The men looked at one another in bewilderment, but I went on. "You must understand," I told them. "Heed me well. The enemy we face today will not stand against you. They will run and they will flee. They will fight from hiding." This brought sneers of contempt.

"Hear me now!" I continued. "You must not be deceived. Do not expect skill, neither expect honor. Instead, expect confusion and cowardice—for these are sturdy shields for a foe who understands neither valor nor courage."

The warriors acclaimed this outright, raising their voices in hoots of derision.

"Their strength is not in numbers, but in rapacity and lust for destruction. The enemy will destroy swiftly, without thought or remorse. Pity will not restrain him, nor will mercy stay his hand. He feels no shame."

There were calls and shouts of scorn for such a worthless foe, but I raised my silver hand for silence. "Listen to me! We do not fight today for honor; there is no glory to be won. We fight only for survival. We are few, but we stand between this foe and the ruin of our world. If we fail, Albion will fall beneath the shadow of evil and desolation that has overcome Tir Aflan.

"We fight today for the freedom of those held captive to the foe: for Goewyn and Tángwen, yes, but no less for those who do not yet know their danger.

"Therefore, let us advance with shrewdness and cunning. We must use stealth where we would take the battleground openly, if by stealth and concealment, even flight, we may save ourselves to fight again."

The warband did not like this. They grumbled against such cowardly tactics, but I held firm. "Cling to pride and we will perish. Cherish dignity and we will die."

"We *will* fight today," I told them, "but we must survive the fight. For, if we fail, Albion will fall. And once Albion has fallen, all the pride and dignity in this worlds-realm will not restore it."

There were no shouts or grumbles now. My words had found the mark and taken hold.

I paused before concluding. "Listen, brothers. If I have learned anything in my time among you, it is this: true honor lives not in the skill of weapons or the strength of arms, but in virtue. Skill fades and strength fails; virtue alone remains. Therefore, let us put off all that is false. Let us prefer instead the valor of virtue, and the glory of right."

I had spoken my heart, but could they understand? It appeared I had misjudged the moment. The warriors did not understand; I had lost them, and perhaps the battle as well.

Yet even as doubt began to grow, I heard a small clicking sound. I turned my head towards the sound and saw Bran, eyes level and hard, tapping the shaft of his spear on the rim of his shield. Click, click, click...

The Raven Flight quickly joined him; Scatha and Cynan soon followed. Click! Click! Click! And, by twos and threes, the rest of the warband joined in. Click! Click! Click! The sound became a rattle, and grew to an ominous thunder as the ashwood shafts struck the metal rims. CRACK! CRACK! CRACK!

It mounted to a crashing climax and then stopped so abruptly I could hear the final report echoing away across the valley. And then we turned and descended into Cwm Gwaed, the Vale of Blood.

34

The Trap

Sinuous as a snake, the road twisted down into the valley. Though I had entered it before, I felt the shock afresh—like a fist in the throat. It was still early morning, but the mudmen were already teeming like maggots over the slag heaps and swarming the trenches. The high chimney spewed its noxious emissions into the air beyond the dam to the dull thunder of hidden machinery.

Those with me gazed glass-eyed and dumbstruck at the enmired misery around them. Unable to comprehend the mindless ardor of the toiling wretches, the warriors simply stared and moved on.

We had divided the warband into three divisions each under the command of a battlechief; Scatha, Cynan and I each led a band on foot. The Raven Flight alone was mounted, leaving Bran to range the battleground at will wherever need was greatest. As for the rest, I judged horses would not help us; without them we could make better use of the cover provided by the holes and heaps of crushed rock. Tegid, Gwion and Nettles had stayed behind to look after the other horses. As in the battle against Meldron, the Chief Bard meant to oversee the fight and uphold us in the bardic way.

Cynan's warband descended to the valley floor and worked its way towards the dam along the shore of the polluted lake; I led those with me on the upper road; Scatha and her warriors approached by way of the path on the far side of the lake, doing their best to blend into the pocked and mottled landscape. Bran advanced behind us, out of sight; when I paused to look back I could not see the Raven Flight anywhere.

The first shot came without warning. I heard the whine of a bullet and the dry ricochet on the hillside below us. A moment later the report echoed from below like the crack of a splitting tree trunk. I motioned to the men to lie down on the road. Several more shots dug into the hillside. Over-anxious, undisciplined, our foe could not wait for us to come into range and had opened fire prematurely. This gave us a prime opportunity to fix the enemy's position and assess their numbers without risk to ourselves.

Wisps of white smoke from their guns betrayed the enemy's placement along the top of the dam. I scanned the valley and the far side of the lake to see that Scatha and Cynan had halted and were marking the place as well. The enemy had seen us on the road, as I intended, but had not thought to look elsewhere.

"Such stupidity should be rewarded," I muttered to the man nearest me.

"Then let us be generous, lord," the warrior replied dryly.

The bullets chunked harmlessly into the rock waste below us for a time, and then the shooting tapered off. I signalled to the men to keep low, and we advanced once more, slowly, listening for the bullet's whine and watching for the tell-tale white puff that revealed an enemy gunman. I took heart from the fact that, as yet, the gunmen still concentrated all their attention on us; they had so far failed to notice Scatha and Cynan working their way ever closer below them.

If I could keep the enemy occupied but a little longer, it would allow the others a more protected approach.

Raising my hand, I halted my warriors. We were by now nearly within range of the guns. "Keep down!" I told those with me. "And wait for my command."

Then I stood and, lofting my spear and shield, I began to yell. "Cowards!" I shouted. "Leave your hiding places and let us fight like men!"

I knew the enemy would not understand me. It was to encourage my own warband that I cried my challenge in Albion's tongue. "Why do you crouch like vermin in your holes?" I taunted. "Come out! Let us do battle together!"

My simple ruse worked. The enemy opened fire. The bullets dug into the slag-covered hillside below me, throwing up dust and splinters—but falling well short of the target. They were using small arms—handguns and light rifles. Larger caliber weapons would have carried further, and with far greater accuracy.

"Where is your battlechief?" I called loudly, my voice echoing back from the blank face of the dam. "Where is your war leader? Let him come and meet me face to face!"

This brought a further heated and wasteful volley from the dam. The warriors with me laughed to see it. I summoned them to rise, now that I knew it was safe to do so. And taking my lead, they too challenged the enemy to come out and fight like true warriors. The gunfire beat like a staccato tattoo, and the white smoke drifted up from behind the dam.

"How many did you count?" I asked the nearest warrior.

"Three fives," he replied.

His tally matched my own. I would have thought that fifteen men with guns could have defeated three score with spears—and we were far fewer than that. But without more battle-cunning than these fifteen had so far demonstrated, their weapons would not win the day.

Scatha, sharp as the blade in her hand, was not slow to turn our diversion to advantage. In two rapid, ground-eating advances, she and her warband reached the dam, crossed it and descended the other side. Cynan followed her lead, disappearing behind the dam while we jeered and danced like madmen, drawing the enemy's fire.

All through this commotion, the mud-covered slaves toiled away, scarcely pausing to raise their dull heads as the bullets streaked above them. Were they so far gone that they no longer knew or cared what was happening around them?

The gunfire eventually ceased. But by then the trap was set.

"Now we must find a way to draw them out of hiding so that Scatha and Cynan can strike," I said, thinking aloud.

"The battlelust is on them," said the warrior next to me. "They are greedy for the kill."

"Then let us see if their greed will make them foolish. We will form the shield line." I gave the order and the warriors took their places beside me. We formed a line, shoulder-to-shoulder, and began slowly to advance along the road.

"Raise shields!" I called, and we put our shields before us, rims overlapping. We continued walking.

The enemy gunmen held their fire. We had advanced as far as we dared, and still they did not shoot.

"Halt!" I raised my silver hand. The bluff had not worked; we had not drawn the enemy into the open. Any nearer and a well-aimed shot might easily penetrate our oak-and-iron shields.

"Cowards!" I called down to the dam. We were close enough now to see the shallow holes the men had dug along the top of the dam. "False men! Hear me now! We are the *Gwr Gwir*! Leave your hiding holes and we will show you what true warriors can do!"

At this, the warriors began striking their shields and taunting the hidden foe. The clash of spear upon shield became a rattling roar. The gunmen could not resist such obvious targets: they began firing again. The bullets struck the stone flagging at our feet. I ordered the line to move two paces back.

The temptation proved too strong—they were drawn from cover at last—all fifteen of them, shouting as they came.

The initial volley tore into the stones a few paces ahead of us. One warrior turned away a glancing shot off the pavement; a slug struck the bottom of my shield. I felt the wood shiver as it ripped through. It was time to retreat.

"Back!" I cried. "Three more paces."

The line fell back and halted; the jeering catcalls continued. Seeing that we would come no closer, the enemy gunmen attacked.

They had no sooner abandoned their hiding holes than Scatha and Cynan materialized out of the drifting smoke behind them. The gunmen were neatly trapped.

They whirled in sudden panic, shooting wildly. Two of their number went down—victims of their own incompetence. One of Cynan's men took a shot through his shield and fell. The gunman paid for his last act as a streaking spear sank to its shaft in his belly. The man fell to the ground writhing and screaming.

At this single casualty the fight went quickly out of the rest and they began crying surrender and throwing down their weapons.

"It is over!" I shouted. "Let us join our swordbrothers!"

We hastened down the road to the top of the dam. I cast a quick backward glance for the Ravens, but they were still nowhere to be seen. What could be keeping them?

"Splendid, Pen-y-Cat! Well done, Cynan!" I called. Scanning the throng of warriors, I was surprised to see the man who had been shot standing in the forerank once more. His shield had a chunk bitten out of the upper left quadrant, he was pale and bleeding just below the shoulder, but he was clear-eyed and undaunted.

The wounded gunman was not so fortunate. The spear had done its work. The man lay silent now, and quite still.

I detailed my warband to dispose of the enemy guns. "Gather their weapons," I told the warriors. "Cast them into the lake."

Scatha and Cynan had lined up the twelve remaining gunmen in a row. "Where is Weston?" I demanded, using their own speech.

No one made bold to answer. I nodded to Cynan. He stepped swiftly forward, striking the nearest man in the center of the chest with the butt of his spear. The man dropped like a stone, and lay rolling on the ground, eyes bulging with pain, mouth agape, unable to breathe.

"I ask you again: where is the man called Weston?"

The prisoners glanced anxiously at one another, but made no reply. Cynan moved along the line. He stopped and raised his spear again. The man cringed. "Wait! Wait!" he screamed, waving his hands.

Cynan paused, his spear still hovering.

"Well?" I demanded. "Speak."

"Weston is at the mill," the man sputtered, gesturing wildly in the direction of the smokestack behind him. "They are guarding the mill."

"How many are with him?" I asked.

"Three or four, I think," the man replied. "That's all."

"Is there anyone else?"

The man grew reticent. Cynan aimed the butt of his spear once more.

"No!" he replied quickly. "No one else. I swear it!"

I looked towards the cluster of buildings below the dam. Weston with three or four gunmen holed up in the mill. Rooting them out could prove a difficult and costly undertaking. I raised my silver hand, summoning four warriors to take the gunmen away. "Bind them fast," I ordered. "Guard them well. See that they do not escape."

I summoned Scatha and Cynan to join me, and related what I had learned. "What do you suggest?" I asked.

Cynan spoke first. "The lives of these strangers are not worth the risk of noble warriors," he said with arch disdain.

"Even so, we have taken the men: we cannot allow their leader to go free." I turned to Scatha. "What say you, Pen-y-Cat?"

Scatha was gazing thoughtfully at the smoking chimney. "Smoke will cure fish. It may also cure these foemen."

It was a simple matter to scale the chimney and stuff down a few cloaks to block the flue. Before long, smoke was pouring from every crack in the crudely constructed building.

We advanced, crossing the compound warily. As we neared, I heard a door slam and a motor sputter to life, and a moment later a van broke from hiding behind the building and flew past us. The startled warriors stared aghast as the yellow vehicle, wheels churning up dust and gravel, sped away. Some of the closer warriors heaved stones as it passed, breaking two side windows, but the van gained the road, turned, and raced away, climbing from the valley by another route.

"We will never catch them on foot," I observed, watching the vehicle disappear into the hills. Turning to Cynan, I ordered, "Send men to bring the horses." To Scatha, I said, "We will follow them. If Nettles is right, they will lead us to Siawn Hy and Paladyr."

We hurried on, following the vehicle's trail. It soon became apparent that it was a well-used track. Wary of ambush, I sent scouts ahead on either side of the advancing warband. We hastened along the ascending track, which soon turned away from Cwm Gwaed and began climbing into the mountains once more.

I called a halt at the crest of a hill near a small stream. "We will rest here and wait for the horses," I told them.

As we made to leave the valley, I turned and looked back one last time. "Where is Bran?" I wondered aloud. "What can have happened to him?"

"You need have no worry for Bran," Scatha said. "He will be where he is most needed."

"You are right, Pen-y-Cat," I agreed. "But I would that my War Leader rode with me."

The words were scarcely out of my mouth when we heard the sound of gunfire coming from the other side of the hill. Flying to the hilltop, we looked down to see the yellow van trapped in a narrow defile and stranded halfway across a shallow rock-filled stream. Circling the stalled vehicle were Bran and the Ravens on horseback, shouting and flourishing their spears. Two men were firing indiscriminately from the broken windows of the vehicle.

We hastened to their aid, calling on the Ravens to retreat. The four in the van would be easy to deal with, and I did not want any of my warriors hit by a stray shot. Leaving the vehicle, they came to where we had taken up position, just outside the rifle's lethal range.

The gunfire continued for a few moments and then stopped.

"I did not see you ride from the valley," I told Bran. "I wondered what had become of you."

"Paladyr attacked the camp as soon as we left," the Raven Chief informed me. "We rode to Tegid's aid and drove the enemy away. We pursued, but lost them in these hills. When we saw the *tuthóg-ar-rhodau* fleeing I thought to prevent their escape."

The van's engine whined, there came the sheering whir of

grinding gears and the vehicle jounced across the stream, wheels spinning, and fled the valley.

"Follow," I told Bran, "and keep them in sight, but do not try to stop them and do not go too near. Their trail is clear; they cannot escape. I have sent men for the horses; we will join you as soon as they arrive."

The Raven Flight flew off in pursuit, and as we made our way back up the hill to await the arrival of our horses, we were greeted by the dull drumming of hoofbeats coming from the other side of the hill. "Tegid is here with the horses," I told Cynan, and a moment later the first rider appeared over the crest of the hill directly above us.

But it was not Tegid who appeared, lofting a spear as he crested the hill; and the warriors mounted on horses behind him were strangers.

We had blundered into a trap.

35

Tref-gan-Haint

"Paladyr!" I shouted, halting in mid-step.

The enemy hesitated, hovering on the crest of the hill. There came the clear call of the battlehorn, loud and strong. And then they plummeted down the hillside in an avalanche of pounding hooves and whirring blades. We had only an instant to raise our weapons and they were on us. Scatha took measure of the situation at once. "We cannot fight them here!" she cried, whirling away. She dashed towards the stream: "Follow me!"

Cynan, spear lofted high, bellowed at his warriors to join him as he followed Scatha's lead. I did the same, and we ran for high ground on the other side of the stream, the battlehorn blaring loud in our ears and the dull thunder of hooves shaking the ground beneath our feet. Two of our warriors were ridden down from behind, and we lost another to an enemy spear. But our feinting flight had not been anticipated and we succeeded in gaining the high ground before Paladyr, over-eager for an easy victory, could stop us.

Though we were on foot against a larger force of mounted warriors, we now held a superior position: the horsemen would have to fight uphill on steep and treacherous terrain. Scatha's unfailing battle sense had not only saved us, but given us a slight advantage.

"They are hungry for it!" shouted Cynan, watching the horses struggle up the loose scree of the mountainside. "Come, brother, let us feed our impetuous guests!"

Ducking under his upraised shield, he darted forward, slashing a wide swath before him with the blade of his spear, cutting the legs from under the nearest horse. The beast screamed, plunged, and spilled its hapless rider on the ground. Cynan struck down swiftly with his spear before the foeman could roll free of his thrashing mount.

Cynan threw back his head and loosed a wild war whoop of terrible delight. Two more enemy riders fell to his swift spear before they could turn aside. I dispatched another using Cynan's trick, and when I looked around I saw that Scatha had succeeded in unseating three of the foemen in as many swift forays.

The first clash lasted but a few heartbeats. Gaining no clear benefit for his efforts, Paladyr soon signalled his men to break off the attack. They withdrew to the far side of the stream to regroup.

"This Paladyr is no fool," observed Cynan. "He knows when to retreat, at least."

Looking across the stream, I saw Paladyr, naked to the waist, face and chest daubed with blue warpaint, the muscles of his back and arms gleaming with sweat. He clutched a bronze spear and shield, and was shouting at his men, upbraiding them for their carelessness and incompetence. There was no sign of Siawn Hy among them, but this did not surprise me.

"He is not a fool," I agreed, "but he is impulsive. That may prove his undoing."

"Who is with him?" wondered Cynan.

I studied Paladyr's warband. They were a raw-looking crowd, armed with ancient bronze weapons like those we had seen in the ruined tower. Their shields were small and heavy, their spears short, with blunt heads. Some wore helmets, but most did not. And only a few carried swords as well as spears. They moved awkwardly—as if they were unused to riding and uncertain of themselves. No doubt they had expected to overwhelm us in the first rush; and now they faced a more determined adversary than anticipated.

It came to me that this was not so much a trained warband as a gang of ill-disciplined cutthroats. They were mercenaries, chosen perhaps from among the laborers slogging through the mud in the valley beyond. Though they had horses, it was obvious that they were not accustomed to fighting on horseback: their first disastrous sally proved as much.

"Llew!" shouted Scatha, hastening towards me. "Did you see him?"

"No," I replied. "Siawn Hy was not with them. But what do you make of the rest?"

"It seems to me that Paladyr has tried to stitch himself a warband from very poor cloth," she replied.

"That is just what I was thinking," I told her. "And it will soon unravel in his hands."

"A boast? From Llew?" crowed Cynan, scrambling back up the hillside. "Brother, are you feeling well?"

"Never better," I told him.

The blare of the carynx signalled a second attack and the enemy clattered across the stream once more. This time Paladyr ranged his men along a line and they advanced together, hoping to spread our thin defence and separate us.

Scatha had other ideas. She called the warbands together and formed them into a narrow-pointed wedge. Unable to climb the steep mountainside and strike at us from the flank, the horsemen had no choice but to meet the point of the wedge head on.

They rode at us yelling and screaming, trying their best to frighten and scatter us. But we stood firm and hewed them from their saddles as quickly as they came within striking distance. Eight enemy riders went down before they could even wheel their horses to retreat. And Paladyr was forced to break off the attack once more.

As the enemy turned tail and fled back across the stream, I summoned the battlechiefs to me. "It seems they lack the will to press the attack."

"*Clanna na cù*, what a poor foray," Cynan sneered, thrusting out his chin. "I would be shamed to lead such ill-suited warriors."

"Yes, and Paladyr is a better war leader than this—or once was. I do not understand it."

"Their inexperience is against them," I observed. "They dare not challenge us, so they seek to harry us and wear us down."

"Then they will be disappointed," Scatha said, quickly scanning the hillside. "If they offer no better assault than we have seen, we can stand against them all day."

"We would not have to stand here at all if we had our horses," Cynan said.

"Then let us take theirs," Scatha suggested. "We would make better use of them than they do."

Swiftly we devised a plan to liberate as many of the foemen's horses as possible in the next clash. And it might have worked. But, just as Paladyr's warband crossed the stream and started up the hillside to engage us once more, the Ravens arrived. One fleeting glimpse of the Raven Flight swooping in full cry down the mountainside, and the cowardly enemy scattered. They splashed across the stream to disappear around the far side of the slope. Bran would have offered pursuit, but I called him back.

"I would rather you stayed with us," I told him. "What did you find ahead?"

A strange expression flitted across the Chief Raven's face. "There is a settlement, lord," he said. "But unlike any I have seen before."

"Is it safe?" wondered Cynan. "It could be another trap."

"Perhaps," the Raven Chief allowed. "But I think not."

"Why do you say that?" asked Scatha.

By way of reply Bran said, "I will show you. It is not far."

Calling to Drustwn and Garanaw, I commanded, "Tegid and the horses should have been here by now. Ride to meet them, and bring the horses to us at the settlement. We will await you there." To Bran, I said, "Show us this place you have found."

"It is this way," Bran said, wheeling his horse, and began to lead us up the mountainside and along a ridgeway. The remaining Ravens took up a position well behind, guarding the rear, lest

Paladyr and his band return and try to take us unawares. But the enemy did not return.

A short distance along the ridge, the trail turned and began descending towards a steep-sided valley. A muddy river wound its slow way along the floor of the valley, and at the nearer end, hard against the ridge, a crude holding had been erected. The few larger, more substantial structures were made from rough timber: the rest appeared cobbled together, a patchwork of bits and pieces. A small distance beyond the settlement, a narrow lake gleamed dully in the foul light.

We descended into the valley and entered the town on the single street of hard-packed earth, passing between the patched-together, tumbledown shanties jammed one on top of the other and leaning at all angles. At a wide place before one of the larger dwellings, we halted. A row of rickety stalls had been thrown up along the side of the street facing the building, and a mud-caked stone well stood between them. We stopped here to wait for Tegid and the horses.

We had seen no one since our arrival and, but for the garbage and dung scattered around, I would have thought the place long abandoned. But as soon as it became clear that we meant to stay, the hidden population began to creep forth. Like vermin crawling from the cracks and crevices they emerged, hesitantly at first, but with increasing boldness. Hobbling, scuttling, dragging battered and deformed limbs, they scrambled into the square. In no time at all we were besieged by a tattered rabble of beggars.

They swarmed us with outstretched hands and open mouths, mewing like sick animals for food and cast-offs—though we had none to give. Like the mudmen working the mines, they were dull-looking with dead eyes and slack expressions. More brute than human, they stood splay-legged and slump-shouldered, abject in their misery. Beggars are unknown in Albion, so the warriors did not understand at first what the grasping mob wanted of them. They shrank from the outstretched hands, or pushed them away, which only increased the clamor.

Cynan and Bran watched the press warily and with increasing unease, but said nothing. "We should move on," Scatha said, "or there may be trouble."

"When they see we have nothing to give them," I replied, "they will leave us alone."

But I was wrong. The beggars became more insistent and demanding. They grew belligerent. Some of the women swaggered up to the warriors and rubbed themselves against the men. The warriors reacted with predictable revulsion and chagrin. But the whores were persistent as they were blatant. They wheedled in shrill voices, and clutched at the warriors.

"Llew," Scatha pleaded, "let us leave this ... this *Tref-gan-Haint* at once."

"You are right," I relented. "We will go on to the lake and await the horses there."

The beggars began wailing at our departure, shrieking terribly. The women, spurned and roundly rejected, followed, shouting abuse and scorn. One of them, little more than a girl, saw my silver hand and ran to me. She fell on her knees before me, seized my hand, and began caressing it.

I gently tried to disengage my hand from her grasp, but she clung to me, pulling on my arm, dragging me down. She moaned and pouted, and rubbed her lips over my metal hand.

"I have nothing for you," I told her firmly. "Please, stand up. Do not shame yourself this way."

But she made no move to release me. Taking her by the wrist, I peeled her hand from mine and made to step over her. When she saw I meant to leave her, she leapt at me with a raking swipe of her fingernails. I jerked my head away and she fell in the dirt where she lay writhing and pleading. I stepped over her and moved on. She kicked and cursed me, her sharp voice gradually dissolving into the general uproar around us.

I moved through the crowd, leading the warband away. Hands clutched at my arms and legs. Voices whined and cried. I pushed ahead, eyes level, looking neither right nor left. What could I give them? What did they want from me?

We entered the cramped, stinking street once more, and continued to the end where the refuse heaps of the shanty town smoldered and burned with a noisome smoke. There were beggars here, too, pawing through the garbage and filth for any overlooked morsels.

Scrawny, long-legged dogs nosed in the filth. One man, naked, his skin black from the smoke, lay half-covered in garbage; he struggled onto an elbow and hailed us obscenely as we passed. His legs were a mangled mess of open sores. The odious dogs hovered around him, dashing in now and then to lick at the man's oozing wounds. Turning away from this ghastly sight, I was met by another. I saw two dogs fighting over a carcass—little more than a shred of putrid flesh clinging to a rotting skeleton. With a sudden sick shock, I realized the remains were human. The gorge rose in my throat and I turned my face away.

Tref-gan-Haint, Scatha had called it, city of pestilence, place of defilement. Diseased and dying, it was a cankerous sight and filled the air with the stench of a rotting wound. This, I reflected, was the fate awaiting the slaves when their usefulness was over. They ended their days as beggars fighting over scraps of garbage. The thought grieved me, but what could I do? Swallowing hard, I walked on.

Beyond the settlement a small distance, we came to the shallow lake from which the stream issued, and found it slightly more tolerable. Although the strand was sharp shards of flint, the water was clean enough. No one followed us from the town so we had the lake to ourselves and hunkered down on the hard shore to wait.

I dozed, and fell into a light sleep in which I dreamed that Goewyn had found us and now stood over me. I awoke to find Bran sitting beside me, and no sign yet of the horses. I rose, and Bran and I walked back along the flinty shore together. A dirty yellow sun was lowering in the western peaks, and stretched our shadows long on the rocky strand.

"Where is Tegid?" I wondered aloud, gazing towards the blighted town and the ridge beyond. "Do you think he ran into Paladyr?"

"It is possible. But Drustwn and Garanaw know where to find us," Bran pointed out. "If there was any trouble, they would have summoned us."

"Still, I do not like this," I told him. "They should have reached us by now."

"I will go and find out what has happened," Bran offered.

"Take Emyr and Niall with you. Send one of them back with word as soon as you find out anything."

Bran hastened to his horse, mounted, summoned the remaining Ravens, and the three rode away at once. I watched them out of sight, and then called Scatha and Cynan to me. "I have sent Bran to see what has become of Tegid and the others."

"It is growing late," Scatha said. "Perhaps we should try to find better shelter elsewhere."

"Darkness will be our only shelter tonight, I fear." Looking to the ridge, I scanned the heights, but saw no sign of anyone returning. What could have happened to Tegid and Nettles?

The sun sank in an ugly brown haze, and a turgid twilight gathered. As the sun departed, the thin warmth vanished; I felt the mountain chill seeping out of the air and creeping up out of the ground. Mist rose from the lake and night vapors began threading down the mountainsides in snaking rivulets.

The men had foraged for wood on the stony slopes around the lake, and the little they found was kindled and set alight as night fell, making small campfires that sputtered fitfully and gave little light. We were hungry, having had nothing to eat since early morning; we eased the pangs with lake water. It tasted flat and metallic, but it was cold, and it quenched our thirst.

Dusk deepened in the valley. The sky held a faint glimmer of dying light, and the mist off the lake and slopes thickened to a fog. I walked restlessly along the flinty strand, alert to any sound of our returning horses. Apart from the liquid lap and lick of the water and the occasional bark of a dog in the distance, I heard nothing.

I stood for a long time, waiting, listening. A red moon floated low over the mountains, peering like an eye down through the fog and mist, casting a dismal pall of ruddy light over the lake and slopes.

At length, I turned and walked back to the campfires glowing soft in the fog-haze. I passed the first fire and heard the men talking quietly, their voices a gentle mumble in the mist. But I heard something else as well. I stopped and held my breath...

A thumping sound, low and rhythmic as a heartbeat, sounded in the darkness—thump... thump... thump. Because of the fog and mist, the sound seemed to come from everywhere at once. Cynan heard it as well and joined me. "What can it be?" he asked softly.

"Shhh!"

We stood motionless. The sound grew gradually louder, gaining definition. Thump-lump... thump-lump... thump-lump... To resolve itself into the slow, loping gallop of a horse, coursing along the flinty strand.

"We have a visitor," I told Cynan.

The pace quickened as the horse drew near, approaching from the far end of the glen away from Tref-gan-Haint. My pulse quickened with the speed of the horse and my silver hand sent an icy tingle up my arm.

"I will bring a torch," Cynan said, darting away at once.

I walked a few paces further along the shore towards the sound. My metal hand burned with an icy cold. The rider was nearer than I knew. All at once, I saw him: a rider on a horse pale as the fog itself, charging out of the swirling mist, the horse's iron-shod hooves striking sparks from the flint as they came.

The rider was armored head to heel in bronze; it gleamed dully in the ruddy moonlight. His helmet was plumed and high-crested; a strange battlemask covered his face. He carried a long bronze spear; a small round bronze shield lay on his thigh. His feet were shod in bronze war shoes, and on his hands were gauntlets covered with bronze fish-scales. The high-cantled saddle was ornamented with round bronze bosses. The horse was armored, too; a bronze warcap with long, curving horns was on its head. Bronze breastplates and greaves graced both horse and rider.

Although I had never seen the rider before, I would have recognized him. The Banfáith had warned me long ago, and even in the dead of a foggy night I knew him: it was the Brazen Man.

36

Clash By Night

The Brazen Man drove straight at me. I dodged to the side at the last instant, and he pulled back hard on the reins. The horse reared, its legs fighting the air. The man raised his hand and I made ready to deflect a blow. Instead of a sword, however, I saw he held a knotted sack. He turned his bronze-clad face towards me, blank and staring; and though I could not see his eyes behind the burnished mask, I felt the force of his hatred as a heatblast on my flesh. My silver hand burned with frozen fire.

The mysterious rider swung the sack once around his head and loosed it. The bag struck the ground and rolled to my feet. Then, with a wild, triumphant cry, the rider wheeled his horse and galloped back the way he came.

Cynan ran to me with a burning brand he had pulled from the fire. "Was it Paladyr?"

I shook my head slowly. "No," I told him. "I do not think it was Paladyr..."

"Who then?"

I looked at the knotted sack lying on the strand. Cynan stooped and picked it up. I took it from him. There was something round and bulky but not too heavy in the bottom. I loosened the knot, opened the sack, and peered in, but could not see the contents clearly.

"Here," I said, lowering the bag to the ground and spreading the opening wide. Cynan held his torch closer. I looked again and instantly wished I had not.

Professor Nettleton's pale, bloodless face stared up at me. His glasses were gone and his white hair was matted with clotted blood. I closed my eyes and shoved the sack away. Cynan took it from me.

Scatha, holding a sword in one hand and a firebrand in the other, hastened to us. "Is it...?" Her question faltered.

"It is the white-haired one," Cynan told her. "Llew's friend."

"I am sorry, Llew," she said after a moment. Her voice was grave, but I could tell she was relieved that it was not her daughter.

"What do you wish me to do with it?" asked Cynan.

"Put it with Alun's ashes for now," I told him, sick at heart. "I will not bury it in this place."

"Alun's... the ashes are with Tegid," Scatha reminded me.

I heard her, but made no reply. My mind boiled with questions. Why had this been done? A challenge? A warning? Who would do such a thing? How had he been taken? What did it mean? I stared into the swirling fog willing the answers, like the bronze-clad rider, to appear.

The Brazen Man! The words whizzed like arrows straight to my heart. I heard again the Banfáith's voice speaking out the dire prophecy:

All this by the Brazen Man is come to pass, who likewise mounted on his steed of brass works woe both great and dire. Rise up, Men of Gwir! Fill your hands with weapons and oppose the false men in your midst! The sound of the battleclash will be heard among the stars of heaven and the Great Year will proceed to its final consummation.

"Llew?" Cynan said, touching me gently on the arm. "What is it, brother?"

I turned to him. "Rouse the men. Hurry!"

Scatha stood looking at me, her forehead creased with concern. In the fluttering firelight she looked just like Goewyn. "Arm yourself, Scatha," I told her. "Tonight we fight for our lives."

Cynan alerted the men with a shout and Emyr blew a long,

withering blast on the carynx. Within two heartbeats the camp was a chaos of men running and shouting, arming themselves to meet the foe already swarming onto the strand. Like phantoms they appeared out of the fog—rank on rank, scores of them, an enemy war host arrayed in bronze battlegear.

A spear was thrust into my hand. I could not find a shield, so grabbed a brand from the fire and ran to take my place in the front rank of warriors, Scatha on my right hand, Cynan on my left. We stood with our backs to the lake and leaned into the battle.

They fell upon us in a rush, as if they would drive us into the lake with one great push. But our warriors were battle-hardened men, skilled in close fighting; all had faced the Great Hound Meldron. After the shock of surprise had passed, they fell to with a fierce delight. To a man, they were sick of Tir Aflan, sick of the deprivation and hardship, and eager to lash out at the enemy who had caused them so much misery.

As before, the enemy, though well-armored, were ill-matched to fight real warriors. But there were more of them now than we had faced earlier in the day, a good many more.

Absorbing the initial onslaught, the warriors of Albion leapt like a quick-kindled flame, striking swift and hot, searing into the onrushing foe. The resulting clash threw the attacking enemy back on their heels. Heartened by this early success, Emyr loosed a shattering blast on the battlehorn, and the warriors of Albion answered the call with rousing shout. The battlecry of Albion's warriors echoed along the flint shore, driving into the enemy like a fist.

Scatha, hair streaming, cloak flying, whirled into the enemy line; sword in one hand, firebrand in the other—a Morrigan of battle!—she struck, throwing off sparks and killing with every stroke. The enemy fled before her as before a flaming whirlwind.

Cynan called the cream of Caledon's warriors to him and began hewing a swathe wide enough to drive a chariot through from the water's edge to the top of the strand.

I threw myself into the confused mass between the two battlechiefs, striking with my spear, slashing, stabbing. The spearhead blushed red in the torchlight, and I scanned the churning floodtide of the enemy for the brazen rider. But my silver hand had lost its uncanny chill, and by this I knew he was not near.

Two bronze-clad foemen sprang into my path, brandishing swords above their heads. Their eyes glinted under their horned helmets, and their teeth flashed above the rims of their shields as they shouted a jeering battlecry. Ignoring their blades, I sliced the air in front of their noses with the blade of my spear, and they halted. Spinning the shaft of my spear, I struck aside first one sword, then the other. Then... Crack! Crack! Two sharp raps of the spear butt and both helmets flew off as heads snapped backwards, and the foemen toppled like statues.

Step by step, we hacked our way up the shingle away from the lake, advancing over the bodies of the slain enemy. We fought well. We fought like champions. And the battle settled into a grim and desperate rhythm.

We battled through the night. Sometimes we gained the top of the shingle and made a stand. Sometimes the enemy rallied and we were forced back. Once, we stood in water to our knees, hacking with battle-blunted blades at our armored enemy. But Scatha, moving through the chaos with the grace and poise of a dancer, pierced deep into the heart of the enemy line with a small force of warriors. Rather than face her fearful wrath, the foemen fell back and the advance collapsed.

As the night drew on, the enemy grew disheartened. Fatigue set in. They moved in their heavy bronze armor with a curious lumbering gait. Their shields and weapons wavered in shaky arms; unable to lift their feet, they stumbled back and forth over the flinty strand. Desperate, they lurched at us. We struck. They fell before our skill. The bodies of the wounded and slain began to stack like felled timber around us, yet they would not retreat.

"Whatever it is that drives them," Cynan observed, drawing a bloody hand across his sweaty face, "they fear it more than they fear us."

We had stopped to catch our breath, and leaned on our spears, shoulders heaving with the effort of drawing air into our lungs. "They fear their lord," I told him.

"Who is that?"

"The Brazen Man."

"Brazen coward if you ask me," Cynan snarled with contempt. "I have not had a glimpse of him since the fight began."

"True. He has not yet taken the field."

"Yet? Yet? His war host is being slaughtered. If he thinks to wear us down, he has waited for nothing."

It was true; the weary foe was everywhere falling to the skill and experience of our vastly superior warriors. Darkness and surprise had done their worst, and we had conquered; now we were conquering their numbers as well, slowly, relentlessly paring them down and down.

It came to me that they had no need of a war leader, because the enemy's only plan had been to overwhelm us. They strove to surround us, engulf and smother us; or, failing that, to drive us into the lake by sheer irresistible press of numbers. We fought against a foe lacking any subtlety or craft, an enemy whose only hope lay in dragging us down by brute force alone.

The Brazen Man did not care how many of his men fell to us, because he did not care about his men at all. They were simply fodder to our scything blades. He sent them into battle in wave after heedless wave, trusting to the grim attrition of battle to wear us down. When finally we were too few to resist, he would swoop down from his hidden perch and claim the victory.

Watching the hapless foemen struggling to raise their weapons, my heart softened towards them. They were blind, ignorant and confused; they were stumbling in the dark, bleeding and dying. And, most cruelly of all, they did not know, would never know, why.

These men were not our true enemies; they were puppets only, pawns in the hands of a pitiless master. Their deaths were meaningless. The slaughter had to be stopped. I lowered my spear, straightened and looked around.

The sky was showing grey in the east; red streaks hinted at a raw sunrise. We had fought the whole night to no purpose or advantage. It was insane, and it was time to stop. Turning once more to the battleline, I saw the bronze warriors standing flat-footed, their heads bowed under the weight of the helmets, unable to lift their arms. With long bold strides, I advanced towards them. The blunt spears in their hands struggled up as they stumbled backwards.

"Llew!" shouted Cynan, running after me.

I reached out and seized the nearest spear, and yanked it from the foeman's numb fingers. I threw the spear down on the ground and grabbed another. The third enemy made a clumsy stab at me with a sword. I caught the blade with my silver hand and twisted it easily out of his hand. It was like disarming children.

"Enough!" I shouted. "It is over!"

All along the lakeside, men stopped and turned to gawk at me. I disarmed two more warriors, snatching weapons from limp hands. I brandished my spear and lifted my voice. "Men of Tir Aflan!" I called, my voice carrying along the strand. "Throw down your weapons, and you will not be harmed."

I gazed along the battleline. The fighting had shuddered to a halt and men were gaping stupidly at me. Scores of exhausted foemen swayed on their feet, unable to lift their weapons any more.

"Listen to me! The battle is over. You cannot win. Throw down your weapons and surrender. Stop your fighting—there is nothing to fear."

The enemy stared stupidly at me. "I do not think they understand," said Cynan coming up behind me.

"Perhaps they will understand this," I replied. Raising my own spear, I threw it down on the rocky strand. I motioned for Cynan to drop his weapon as well. He hesitated. "Do it," I urged. "They are watching."

Cynan tossed his spear on top of mine and we stood together unarmed, surrounded by bewildered warriors. I raised my silver hand and said, "Listen to me! You have fought and suffered and many have died. But you cannot win and now the fighting must stop. Throw down your weapons, so that the suffering and dying can end." My voice resounded over the strand. They watched, but no one answered.

"You fight for your lives," I continued. "Men of Tir Aflan! Surrender! Throw down your weapons, and I will give you your lives. You can walk away free men."

This caused a stir. They gaped in wonder, and murmured their amazement to one another. "Is it true?" they asked. "Can it be?"

Extending my hand towards a nearby warrior, I beckoned him. "Come," I told him. "I give you your life."

The man glanced around awkwardly, hesitated, then stumbled forward. He took two steps, but his legs would no longer hold him and he fell forward to lie at my feet. Reaching down, I caught him under the arm and raised him. I took his sword from his hand and tossed it aside. "You are safe," I told him. "No one will harm you now."

I heard a clatter on the rocks as a shield slipped from the grasp of one who could not hold it any longer. The man sank to his knees. I strode to him, raised him and said, "You are safe. Stand there beside your kinsman."

The man took his place beside the first and the two stood trembling in the dim dawn light, not quite believing their good fortune.

The onlookers may have expected me to kill the defectors. But seeing I had not harmed the first two, a third decided to risk trusting me. I welcomed him, and two more stepped forward, laying their weapons at my feet. I welcomed them also and told them to stand with the others. Another defector stepped forward, and then three more.

"Cynan! Scatha!" I turned and beckoned them to help me. "Get ready! The flood is upon us!"

Weapons and armor clattered to the stony shingle all along the lake; the battle-weary foemen could not shed it fast enough. After their initial hesitancy, they gave themselves up freely and with great relief. Some were so overcome, they wept at their unimaginable good fortune. Their long nightmare was over; they were rescued and released.

When we had disarmed the last adversary, I turned to my own warriors standing silent behind me. I looked at their once-fine cloaks, now journey-worn and dirty; I looked at their once-handsome faces, now gaunt and grim, ravaged by want and war. They had given up health and happiness, given up wives, children, kinsmen and friends, given up all comfort and pleasure.

Staunch to the end, they had supported me through all things, and stood ready still to serve, to give their lives if I asked. Battered and bleeding, they stood as one, weapons at the ready, waiting to be summoned once more. Truly, they were the Gwr Gwir, the True Men of Albion.

Raising my silver hand, I touched the back of my hand to my forehead in silent salute. The warriors responded with a shout of triumph that sent echoes rippling across the lake and up into the surrounding hills.

I released them to their rest, whereupon they turned to the lake to drink and to bathe. I stood for a moment watching my ragged warriors lower their exhausted bodies into the water. "Look at them," I said, pride singing through me like a song of exultation. "With such men to support him, any man might be king."

Cynan, leaning on his spear, thrust out his chin, "They would not support just *any* man. Nor would I," he said, and touched the back of his hand to his forehead.

The lake proved a blessing. We waded into the chill, mist-covered water and bathed our aching limbs. The water revived and refreshed us, washing away the blood and grime of battle. I felt the cold thrill of the water on my flesh and remembered another time when, after my first battle, I had bathed like this and felt reborn.

The good feeling proved short-lived, however. Bran and the Ravens had still not appeared by the time the sun had risen well above the surrounding hills.

"I do not like this at all," I told Cynan and Scatha plainly. "Something has happened to them or they would have returned long ago."

"I fear you are right," Scatha agreed.

"We are finished here," Cynan said. "We can go back to Cwm Gwaed to look for them."

I surveyed the armored men sitting splay-legged on the strand. "We will talk to some of these." I indicated the huddled men. "Perhaps they can tell us something."

"That I doubt," Cynan replied. "But I will do it if you think best."

I turned to Scatha who, having washed the soot and blood away, now appeared less like the Morrigan and more like Modron, the Comforter. She had plaited her hair and brushed her cloak, and, from the way the surrendered warriors followed her with their eyes, I thought she might more easily succeed than we in loosening reluctant tongues.

"I will entrust this task to you, Pen-y-Cat," I told her. "I am certain they would rather confide in you than in Cynan Two-Torcs here."

So we watched as she moved among the former enemy warriors, stopping now and then, bending near one or kneeling beside another, speaking earnestly, looking into their eyes as they answered. I noticed she put her hand on their shoulders in the way of a wife or mother, addressing them with her touch as much as with her voice.

In a little while, Scatha returned. "There is a caer near here. Some of them have been there. They say that the Brazen Man keeps captives there."

"Are Tángwen and Goewyn there?" asked Cynan eagerly.

Scatha turned to him, her expression grim. "They do not know. But it is known that the Dyn Dythri often go there, and the *rhuodimi* come from there."

"Roaring things?" wondered Cynan.

The vehicles and machines, I thought. "Then that is where Siawn Hy is waiting, and that is where we will find Goewyn and Tángwen. And," I quickly added, "unless I am far wrong, that is where Tegid and the Ravens are now captive as well."

Scatha agreed. "But there is something else: they say the caer is protected by a powerful enchantment. They are terrified of the place."

We turned our backs to the lake and marched east, following the directions we had been given. A gap, unseen from the shore, opened in the hills; we passed through to find ourselves on a broad plateau. The sea lay before us, green and restless under a mottled grey sky. And on the cracked summit of a rocky headland jutting out into the wave-worried sea stood a crumbling stone fortress. Much like the high tower we had seen before, the caer stood lonely and forsaken on its bare rock, a relic of a forgotten age.

"The Brazen Man has taken that for his stronghold," Scatha said. We had paused to survey the land beyond the pass and, aside from the ruined fortress and a scattering of stone huts in which the warriors had been housed, the land was empty. The defectors had described the place well.

Nevertheless, we approached the fortress slowly, watching for any sign from the ragged walls. I walked first, with Scatha and Cynan leading the Gwr Gwir; unwilling to be left behind, the defeated foe followed at a distance. As we passed onto the promontory, I saw the tracks of heavy vehicles pressed into the soft turf. Many rhuodimi had passed this way. The entrance to the special gate Professor Nettleton spoke of must lie somewhere near by, but I could not see it.

The sea heaved and sighed around the roots of the headland; the wind moaned over the ruins. Great chunks of fallen stone were sunk deep into the thick green moss below once-soaring battlements. We stood gazing at the toppled walls, searching for any sign of life.

"Arianrhod sleeps in her sea-girt headland," I said, thinking aloud, as I looked at the broken gate, black with age and hanging half off its hinges.

To which Scatha replied, "Only the chaste kiss will restore her to her rightful place."

Cynan cast a sidelong glance at us. "Well?" he demanded impatiently. "Are we to stand here waiting all day?"

"No, but first we must see if there is another entrance to this place," I said.

"It will be done." Cynan gestured to Owyn and three other warriors, who disappeared around the near corner of the stone curtain on the run.

They reappeared on the far side a short while later. "There is no other entrance," Owyn said.

"Did you see anyone?" Scatha asked.

"No one," the Galanae warrior answered.

"Then we will go in." I raised my spear in silent signal and the warband, ranged behind me, moved towards the gate.

As we passed under the shadow of the wall, a voice called out. "Stop! Come no closer!"

My head swivelled to the broken battlement. The Brazen Man stood above and to the left, leering bronze mask in place and spear in hand, gazing down upon us.

"Your war host is defeated!" I shouted. "Throw down your weapons and release your captives. Do this at once or you will certainly die."

The bronze warrior tilted back his head and laughed, an ugly, hateful sound. I had heard it before.

The laughter stopped abruptly. "You do not rule here!" he shouted angrily. Then, softening in almost the same breath, he said, "If you want your bride, come and get her. But come alone."

He vanished from the wall before I could answer.

"I mislike this," Cynan grumbled.

"I do not see that we have any other choice," I pointed out. "I will go alone."

Scatha objected. "It is a foolish risk."

"I know," I told her. "But it is a risk we must take for Goewyn's sake."

She nodded, put her hand beneath her cloak and withdrew a slender knife. She stepped close, reached behind me and tucked it into my belt. "I armed you once, and I do so again, son of mine. Save my daughter."

"That I will do, Pen-y-Cat," I replied. She embraced and kissed me, then turned away quickly, taking her place at the head of the warband.

I took two steps towards the gate.

"Wait!" Cynan came to stand beside me. "You will not go alone while Two-Torcs draws breath," he said firmly. "My wife is captive, too, and I am going with you."

He took a step towards the door. "We can dispute the matter, or we can rescue our wives."

There would be no dissuading him, so I agreed, and we advanced together through the gate and into the courtyard beyond.

Dry weeds poked up through the cracks of the paved yard; they shifted in the wind like long white whiskers. Fallen stone lay all around. Arched doorways opened off the courtyard, revealing black, empty passages beyond. At the far end of the yard, opposite the gate, stood a steep-peaked building; the roof was collapsed and curved rooftiles littered the yard like dragon scales. A short flight of stone steps led up to a narrow wooden door. The door, twice the height of a man, stood open.

A chill shivered up through my silver hand. "He is near," I whispered to Cynan.

We moved steadily, stealthily, up the steps, paused, then pushed the door open wide. Instantly we were assailed by the stench of rotting meat mingled with urine and excrement. The outside door opened into a dark vestibule thick with filth. The severed heads of two unfortunates were nailed to the lintel above a low inner door. The doorposts were smeared with blood.

Stepping cautiously through the low door, we passed into the hall beyond. "I have been waiting," a voice said. "We have all been waiting."

37

The Hero Feat

Torches illumined the single great room, casting a thin, sullen light that did little to efface the deep-shadowed darkness. In the center of the room stood the Brazen Man. The torchlight flickering over the facets of his bronze mask made it seem as if his features were continually melting and reforming.

Behind him were two doors barred and bound with iron. As I looked, Goewyn's face appeared at the small window of one door, and Tángwen's at the other. Neither woman cried out, but both stood gripping the bars of their prisons and watching us with the astonished yet fearful expressions of captives who have long ago abandoned hope of release, only to learn that hope has not abandoned them.

My first thought was to run to Goewyn and pull that prison apart with my bare hands. I wanted to take her in my arms and carry her away from that stinking hellhole. I stepped towards the Brazen Man. "Let them go," I said.

"You did not come alone," the man said ominously.

"My wife is captive, too," Cynan spat. "If you have harmed her, I will kill you. Let her go."

"*Your* wife?" the bronze-clad warrior queried. "She might have shared your bed, but Tángwen was never wife to you, Cynan Machae."

"Who are you?" Cynan demanded, pushing past me into the room. The sword in his hand trembled in his clenched fist, he gripped it so hard.

"You want them freed?" the Brazen Man shouted suddenly, taking a swift sidestep. "Free them yourselves." He put out his hand and extended a bronze-mailed finger, pointing to a spot on the floor surrounded by torches. "Do what you will."

I looked where he pointed and saw two keys in an iron ring lying on the stone-flagged floor. Glancing quickly at the cell doors, I saw that they had been recently fitted with new brass locks.

With a nod to Cynan, we moved forward cautiously. My silver hand began to throb with cold, sending sharp pains up my arm. I gritted my teeth and stepped closer, spear ready. The keys had been placed in the center of a knotwork design, the figure outlined on the floor in lines of fine black ash and bits of bone—the ash of burnt sacrifice, I supposed. The braziers burned with a bitter smoke.

"What is it?" Cynan wondered. "Do you know?"

The sign was a crude parody of the *Môr Cylch*, the Life Maze, but it was backwards and broken, the lines haphazard, erratic. All the elegance and beauty of the original had been willfully marred.

"It is a charm of some sort," I told Cynan.

"I am not afraid of a mark on the floor," he sneered.

Before I could stop him, Cynan pushed past me and stooped to grab the keys. Upon entering the circle, however, he was gripped by an instant paralysis, caught and unable to move. "Llew!" he cried, through quick-clenched teeth in a frozen jaw. "Help me!"

I glanced at the bronze-clad man. His eyes glittered hard and black behind the brazen mask. "Oh, help him, yes." The brazen snake almost hissed. "By all means, do help him." Then he laughed.

I knew the laugh. I had heard it too many times before not to recognize it now. He laughed again, and removed every last crumb of doubt, confirmed every suspicion.

"Enough, Simon!" I shouted. "Let him go."

Lifting a bronze gauntlet to his chin, the man lifted the metal mask and took off the helmet. The face was pale, deathly pale, and thin, wasted. The flesh seemed almost transparent; blue veins snaked beneath his eyelids and the skin of his throat. He looked like a ghost, a wraith, but there was no mistaking the set of his chin, nor the hatred smoldering in his eyes.

"Siawn Hy," he corrected, and stepped closer. My silver hand throbbed; icy spikes stabbed into my flesh.

"I made that for you," Siawn said, indicating the circle on the floor. "But I like it better this way. Just you and me. Face to face."

He stood before me and drew the bronze-mailed glove from his left hand, then slowly raised it to his forehead, palm outward. It was a bardic gesture—I had seen Tegid do it many times—but as he turned his hand I saw on the palm, carved into the very flesh, the image of an eye.

Siawn loosed a string of words in a tongue I did not know. I could not take my eyes from the symbol carved into the flesh of his palm. The skin was thickly scarred, but the cuts were fresh and a little blood oozed from the wound.

He spoke again, and the muscles in my arms and legs stiffened. My back and shoulders felt like blocks of wood. Locked in this strange seizure, I could not move. The spear fell from my fingers and clattered on the floor; my limbs grew instantly rigid. More words poured from Siawn's mouth, a dizzying torrent to drown all resistance, a dark chant of wicked power. My breath flowed from my mouth and lungs. Cynan, immobile beside me, made a strangled, whimpering noise.

Someone screamed my name—Goewyn, I think. But I could not see her. I could not close my eyes or look away. The evil eye drew all thought and volition to itself; it seemed to burn itself into my mind as Siawn Hy's words swirled around me, now buzzing like insects, now rasping like crows. My breath became labored, halting; but my vision grew keen.

The ancient evil of Tir Aflan... this was how Siawn Hy had awakened it, and he now wielded it as a weapon. But there existed a power far more potent than he would ever know.

Goodly-Wise is the Many-Gifted, I thought, *who upholds all that call upon him. Uphold me now!*

In the same moment, I felt the Penderwydd's sacred awen quicken within me. Like the unfurling of a sail, my spirit slipped its constricting bonds. A word, a name formed on my tongue and I spoke it out: "Dagda ... Samildanac ..."

Up from my throat it came, leaping from my tongue in a shout. "Dagda Samildanac!"

Searing bolts of icy fire streaked from my silver hand, up my arm and into my shoulder. Whatever the source of the power Siawn possessed, it could not quench the cold fire aflame in my silver hand: the smooth silver surface glowed white; the intricate-patterned mazework of the Dance of Life shone with a fiery golden light.

Siawn's voice boomed in my ears as he moved closer, barking the words. I saw the hideous eye carved into the flesh of Siawn's palm as he reached to touch me with it, to mark me with that hideous symbol.

"By the power of the Swift Sure Hand, I resist you," I said, and raised my silver hand, pressing my palm flat against his.

He screamed, jerking his palm away from mine. Threads of smoke rose from the wound on his hand. Air flowed back into my lungs, and with it the smell of burning flesh. Siawn Hy staggered backwards moaning, cradling his injured hand. The red wound on his palm had been obliterated, the obscene stigmata cauterized; in place of the evil eye was the branded imprint of the Môr Cylch, the Life Maze.

Suddenly free, I leapt to Cynan's aid, knelt beside him, drew a deep breath and blew the black ash away, breaking the power of the charm. Cynan fell forward onto his arms and sprang quickly to his feet. "Brother, that was well done!"

I grabbed the keys. "Watch him!" I commanded Cynan.

"Gladly!" Cynan raised his sword and advanced on the stricken Siawn, pressing the blade into the base of his throat.

I ran to the iron-bound doors, thrust a key into the first lock and turned. The lock gave grudgingly and I pulled with all my might; the hinges complained, but the door swung open. Goewyn burst from her prison and caught me in a crushing embrace. I kissed her face and lips and neck, and felt her lips flitting over my face. She kept repeating my name over and over as she kissed me.

"You are free, my love," I told her. "It is over. You are safe now. You are free."

I held her to me again, and she gave a little cry and pulled away. Her hands went to her stomach, now swelling noticeably beneath her stained and filthy mantle. I put my hand to the softly rounded mound to feel the life within.

"Are you well? Did he hurt you?" I had refused the thought of her suffering for so long that belated concern now overwhelmed me.

Goewyn smiled; her face was pale and drawn, but her eyes were clear and glowing with love and happiness. "No," she said, cupping her hand to my face. "He told me things—terrible things." Tears welled up suddenly in her eyes and splashed down her cheeks. "But he did not hurt me. I think Tángwen is safe, too."

Cynan, holding Siawn Hy at the point of his sword, turned at the mention of his wife's name. The swordpoint wavered as his eyes shifted to the door of her cell. Wrapped in Goewyn's embrace, glancing over her shoulder, I saw the door swing open. Cynan's first response was elation. And then the full significance of the unlocked cell hit him.

The joy on his face turned sickly and died. His eyes grew wide with horror.

"Treachery!" he cried.

The door to Tángwen's cell banged open and armed men charged out of its dark depths and into the room. Cynan was already moving towards them, sword raised. Siawn reacted with blinding speed: his foot snaked out and Cynan pitched forward. He hit the stone floor with a crack; his blade flew from his grasp and skittered across the floor.

A heartbeat later, four men were on his back and four more, with Paladyr chief among them, came for me. I thrust Goewyn behind me, shielding her with my body and drawing the knife Scatha had given me. But I was too late. They were on me. Paladyr's blade pricked the skin of my throat.

Two more foemen caught Goewyn and held her by the arms. Just then, Tángwen, smug with victory, emerged from her cell. "One should always be careful who one marries," Siawn said, as Tángwen came to stand beside him.

"What I did, I did for my father and for my brothers," Tángwen exulted. "They rode with Meldron and you cut them down. The blood debt will be satisfied."

Siawn, still cradling his branded hand, stalked forward, laughing. He came to stand before me, his face the terrible, twisted leer of a demon. He spat a command to one of his minions and the man disappeared into the shadows somewhere behind me. "So, you begin to see at last."

"Let the others go, Siawn," I said. "It is me you want. Take me and let the others go."

"I have you, friend," he jeered. "I have you all."

Just then there arose a commotion from the far corner of the room. A door opened behind me—I could not see it, but I heard the hinges grind—and in shuffled Tegid, Gwion, Bran, and the Ravens, handbound all of them, with chains on their feet and a guard for each one. Tegid's face was bruised and his clothing torn in several places; Bran and Drustwn could not stand upright, and Garanaw's arm dangled uselessly at his side. My proud Raven Flight appeared to have been battered into bloody submission. Behind them came Weston and four other strangers, looking frightened and very confused.

Upon seeing me, Bran cried out and struggled forward; the other Ravens shouted and turned on their captors, but all were clubbed with the butts of spears and dragged back into line.

"You see?" Siawn Hy gloated. "You never fully appreciated me, did you? Well, you have underestimated me for the last time, *friend*." The word was a curse in his mouth.

"Listen to me very carefully," I said, speaking loudly and fighting to keep my voice calm. "My warband is waiting at the gate. They are invincible. If anything happens to any of us, you will die. That is a fact."

If Siawn Hy cared, he did not show it; my words moved several of his warriors, however. Paladyr's sword relaxed.

"It is true, lord," he said. "We cannot hope to defeat them."

Siawn waved aside the remark. "But I am not interested in defeating them," he replied casually. "I am only interested in defeating Silver Hand."

"Then let the others go," I said again. "Once they are free, I will command the warband to allow you safe passage. Without my word, none of you leave this place alive."

"Listen to him, lord," Paladyr said; an note of uncertainty had come into his voice.

"What is he saying?" demanded Weston, his voice an almost incoherent babble in my ears. He started forward. "I demand to know what is going on! You said there wouldn't be any trouble. You said it was all under control."

"Get back!" Siawn snarled in the stranger's tongue. "I gave you what you wanted. Now it is *my* turn. That was the agreement."

"Some of my men have been killed," Weston whined. "What am I supposed to do ab—"

"Shut up!" Siawn growled, cutting him off with a chop of his hand. He turned to me once more. "If I let the others walk free, you will give us all safe conduct to leave—is that right?"

"I give you my word," I vowed. "But they go free first."

"No, Llew," Goewyn pleaded softly. "I will not leave you."

Siawn chuckled. "Oh, I am enjoying this."

"The warband is waiting," I told him. "They will not wait for ever."

"Do you think I care about any of that?" he mocked. "I will not be ordered about by my own prisoner." He brought his face close to mine, breathing hard. The veins stood out on his neck and forehead. "Your word is nothing to me! *You* are nothing to me. I have had nothing but grief from you ever since you came here. But that is about to end, old friend."

He backed away from me. "Do it!" he yelled.

"What do you want us to do, lord?" Paladyr asked.

"Kill him!" Siawn cried.

Paladyr hesitated.

"Do it!" Siawn shouted again.

Paladyr's head whipped around; he glared at Siawn. "No." He lowered the blade and stepped aside. "Let the others go free, or they will kill us."

"Paladyr!" The voice was Tegid's; the bard had waited for precisely this moment to speak. "Hear me now! You claimed naud and Llew gave it," he said, reminding Paladyr that he owed his life to me. "He did not lie to you then; he is not lying now. Release us all and you will not be harmed."

"Silence him!" screamed Siawn Hy. I heard a crack and Tegid slumped to the floor.

"I gave you your life, Paladyr," I said.

"He is lying!" insisted Siawn. "Kill him!"

Paladyr shook his head slowly. "No. He is telling the truth."

"Siawn Hy!" I said. "Take me, and let the others go." To show I meant what I said, I turned the knife in my hand, took the blade and offered him the handle.

"Oh, very well," snarled Siawn Hy. He snatched the knife and half-turned away. Then, with a quick, cat-like movement, he lunged into me. The blade came up sharp and caught me in the center of the chest just below the ribs. I did not even feel it go in.

Goewyn screamed and fought free. She ran two steps towards me, but Paladyr turned and caught her by the arm, and held her fast.

I looked down to see the sharp blade biting into my flesh. With a cry of delight, Siawn thrust the knife deeper. I felt a burning sensation under my ribs and then my lung collapsed. Air and blood sputtered from the wound. Siawn forced the blade deeper still and then released it. The three men holding me stepped away.

My legs grew suddenly weak and spongy. I lifted my foot to take a step and the floor crashed up against my knees. My hands found the knife hilt, grasped it and pulled. It felt as if a beacon-fire had been lit in my chest and was now burning outwards. I flung the knife from me.

Blood, hot and dark, welled from the wound, spilling over my hands. A dark mist gathered at the periphery of my vision, but I was conscious of everything around me: Siawn staring at me with wicked glee; Cynan fighting with all his might, still pinned to the ground by Siawn's men; Paladyr grim and silent, clutching Goewyn's arm.

My throat tickled and I opened my mouth to cough, but could not. My breath rasped in my throat. My mouth was dry—as if the fire in my chest was devouring me from within. I gasped, but could get no air. A strange, sucking sound came from my throat.

I put out my hand to support myself, but my elbow buckled and I rolled onto my side. Goewyn jerked her arm from Paladyr's grasp and ran to me. She gathered me in her arms. "Llew! Oh, Llew!" she wept, her warm tears falling onto my face. "Llew, my soul..."

I gazed up at her face. It was all I could see now. Though she wept, she was beautiful. A flood of memory washed over me. It seemed as if all I had endured in her pursuit was nothing—less than nothing—beside her. I loved her so much, I ached to tell it, but could not. The burning stopped, and I felt instead a chill numbness in my chest. I tried to sit up, but my legs would not move. Instead, I raised my hand to Goewyn's face and stroked her cheek with trembling fingertips.

"Goewyn, best beloved," I said; my voice came out as a dry whisper. "I love you ... farewell ..."

Goewyn, tears streaming from her eyes, lowered her face to mine. Her lips, warm and alive, imparting a final sweet caress, was the last sensation I knew.

Darkness descended over me. Though my eyes continued to stare, I could see nothing for the black mist that billowed over and around me, swallowing me down and down. It seemed that I was floating and falling at the same time. I heard Goewyn weeping, saying my name, and then I heard a roaring crash like that of the sea rolling in upon a far-off shore.

The sound grew until I could hear nothing else. It grew so great that I thought my head would burst with the pressure of the noise. For one terrible instant I feared the sound would consume me, obliterate me. I resisted, though how I resisted, I do not know. I could not move, could not speak or see.

But when I thought I could not bear it any more, the sound stopped abruptly and the dark mist cleared. I could see and hear again, more clearly than I ever had before. I could see, but now saw everything from slightly above and outside my normal view. I saw Goewyn bent over me, cradling my still body in her lap, her shoulders heaving as she wept. I saw Siawn and Tángwen looking on, their faces flushed with a hideous gloating pride. I saw Paladyr standing a little apart, subdued, his arms hanging limp at his sides. I saw the Ravens and Tegid, stunned and staggered at the atrocity they were powerless to prevent.

I saw Cynan lying on the floor, enemies kneeling on his back as he raged against my death. I felt sorry for him. His wife had betrayed us all to Siawn, had deceived us from the beginning; he would bear the burden of that shame for the rest of his life, a fate he did not deserve. Through all things he was my good friend; I would have liked to bid him farewell. Peace, brother, I said, but he did not hear me.

Siawn turned and ordered his men to bind Cynan. Then he turned to Paladyr. "Pick up the body and carry it outside," he commanded.

Paladyr stepped forward, but Goewyn clutched me tighter and screamed, "No! No! Do not touch him!"

"I am sorry," he mumbled as he bent over her.

"Take her!" shouted Siawn. Two of his minions scurried forward, grabbed Goewyn and tore her from me. Shouting, crying, she fought them, but they held her tight and pulled her away.

Paladyr knelt and gathered my corpse into his arms. Straining, he lifted my limp body and held it.

"Follow me!" Siawn Hy barked. He turned on his heel and started from the room, taking a torch from a nearby sconce as he passed.

At the vestibule, Siawn paused and let Paladyr pass. "They are waiting for their king," he smirked. "They shall have him."

Paladyr carried me out of the hall, across the empty courtyard, and out of the gate to the warband gathered beyond. Behind him came Siawn and Tángwen, followed by Cynan and Goewyn, both with a guard on either arm, though the fight had gone out of Cynan, and the guards had to support Goewyn to keep her upright. Tegid and the Ravens marched boldly forth, quickly recovering something of their dignity and mettle. Lastly came Weston and his hirelings, edging their way with fearful and uncertain steps.

The emerging procession provoked a quick outcry among the waiting warriors, but the sight of my lifeless body shocked them to silence. Scatha made to run to her daughter, but Siawn shouted, "Stop! No one move!"

Then Siawn ordered Paladyr to lay my body on the ground. Brandishing his torch, he stood over me. "Here is your king!" he crowed, his voice raking at the shattered warband.

"Siawn Hy!" Scatha shouted. "You will die for this! You and all your men."

But Siawn only laughed. "Do you want him? I give him to you. Come! Take him away!"

Scatha and two warriors stepped forward slowly. Siawn allowed them to approach and, as they neared, he pulled a flask from behind his bronze breastplate and quickly doused me with the contents. And then, as they stooped, their hands reaching for me, Siawn lowered the torch and touched it to the liquid glimmering on my skin.

A ball of bright yellow flame erupted with a whoosh. The heat was instant and intense. The fire spread swiftly wherever the liquid had penetrated. My clothing burned first and then my flesh.

Goewyn screamed, and fought free of her captors. She would have thrown herself upon the flames, but they caught her again and hauled her back.

Siawn looked on my burning corpse with an expression of immense satisfaction. He had been planning his revenge for a long time, and he savored the moment to the full. Cynan, mute, immobile, did not look at the flames, but at his treacherous bride standing haughtily beside Siawn.

The layers of cloth burned away from my body. The skin of my face and neck began to shrivel and smoke as the flames licked over them. The fire crackled and fizzed as the fat from my flesh ignited. My hair burned away, and my siarc and breecs. My belt, because it was wound around my waist in several layers, was slower to burn. But as the first two layers of my belt were consumed, there appeared three round lumps.

Siawn, glancing down, saw the lumps and stared more closely. A strange light came into his eyes as he recognized the stones Tegid had given me to carry into Tir Aflan. Singing Stones, three of them, glowing white as miniature moons in the fire. Three Singing Stones within easy reach.

38

Bright Fire

Siawn Hy could not resist them. Despite the flames, he edged close and, quick as a striking snake, snatched up one of the song-bearing stones. He raised it with a wild shout of triumph. "With this stone, I conquer!"

The stone was hot and as he held it high, his cry still ringing in the air, the milk-white rock turned translucent as ice and melted in his hand. Siawn stared as the liquid rock ran through his fingers and down his upraised arm like water.

He bent to retrieve another stone, braving the flames once more. His fingers flicked out and closed on another of the precious stones; but as he made to withdraw it, the liquid rock ignited. Flames engulfed his hand and raced up his arm along the molten trail of the previous stone.

Siawn jerked back, still clenching the second stone. He held the flaming hand before his face. With a blast of pure white light the stone in his fist burst into a thousand pieces, scattering flaming fragments far and wide in a rain of shimmering white fire.

Each fragment melted and began to burn with a wonderful incandescence.

The third stone, still resting on my stomach, melted and the liquid stone began flowing like silver honey, like shining water. It covered my burning corpse, and quickly seeped out onto the ground around me. Like a fountain it flowed, increasing outwards of itself, pouring up from my body, spreading and spreading in bright-shimmering waves. And where the melted stone touched one of the flaming fragments, it burned with flames of shining white.

Men drew back from the fire, and many ran. But there was no escape. The flames were swift as they were bright. They raced before the wind of their burning, gathering greater speed as the fire kindled other fires and mounted, leaping towards the sky. The grass burned and the earth and rocks. The air itself seemed to ignite like touchpaper. Nothing was spared, nothing escaped the all-devouring white fire.

Everyone, friend and enemy alike, fell before the all-engulfing flames. Siawn, standing nearest, was the first to succumb; he crumpled into a writhing heap. Tángwen rushed to him, and was caught as the flames raced towards her, igniting her cloak and mantle; her hair became a fiery curtain. Seeing this, the guards dropped their weapons and ran, but the fire was swifter than their feet.

Cynan and Goewyn fell to the flames. Cynan alight from heel to head, staggered towards Goewyn to protect her, but she slumped to the ground before he could reach her, and after a few steps he expired.

Bran and the Ravens were caught, along with Tegid and Gwion. Their feet chained, they could not run, so turned to face the flames unafraid. Not so the enemy warriors guarding them. They stumbled over one another in their haste to flee. But the fire streaked like lightning along the ground and ignited them. At first they wailed in fear and agony, but their voices were quickly drowned in the roar of the onrushing blaze.

On and on it sped, inundating all of Tir Aflan in a rolling flood of bright silver-white fire, that consumed all it touched with a keen and brilliant flame. The grass and rocks blazed. And as the conflagration spiralled higher and higher, leaping skyward in dazzling plumes, igniting the very air, there came a sound like a crystal chime. It was the voice of the inferno, belling clear and clean. And it rang with a song, the matchless Song of Albion:

Glory of sun! Star-blaze in jeweled heavens!
Light of light, a High and Holy land,
Shining bright and blessed of the Many-Gifted;
A gift for ever to the Race of Albion!

Lifted high on the wings of the wind, the cleansing fire streaked through the sky, kindling the clouds and gloom-laden vapors, scouring the heavens. Grey and black turned to glowing blue and then to white. The airy firmament glowed with a light more brilliant than starlight, brighter and more radiant than the sun. The Song rang through the heights and raced on:

Rich with many waters! Blue-welled the deep,
White-waved the strand, hallowed the firmament,
Mighty in the power of the One,
Gentle in the peace of great blessing;
A wealth of wonders for the Kinsmen of Albion!

Reaching the shore, the fire sped out across the sea. From wave-top to wave-top, leaping in liquid tongues, spreading over the sea-well. The sea began to boil, and then flashed from turgid green to jade and then the color of white gold in the crucible. The waters became molten flame and the great, glowing sea resounded like a bell to the Song, blending its deep-voiced toll to the high tone of the heavens. And the Song raced on:

Dazzling the matchless purity of green!
Fine as the emerald's excellent fire,
Glowing in deep-clefted glens,
Gleaming on smooth-tilled fields;
A Gemstone of great value for the Sons of Albion!

Down the broad headland the bright fire flew, a towering wall of blistering, shimmering flame, raking the wasted valleys of Tir Aflan, flashing across the wasted expanse of moorland. The filth-crusted settlement exploded at the first touch of flame; the mudmen in the mines saw the flames streaking towards them and threw themselves into their pits. But the cunning flame-fingers searched out the dark, small places and set them ablaze, streaking across the mud, scorching the earth, turning every boulder in Cwm Gwaed into a pillar of fire. And the Song raced on:

> *Abounding in white-crowned peaks, vast beyond measure,*
> *the fastness of bold mountains!*
> *Exalted heights—dark-wooded and*
> *Red with running deer—*
> *Proclaim afar the high-vaunted splendor of Albion!*

The mountaintops round about sprouted crowns of silver-white flame, blazing like titanic beacons. Each mountain became a fiery volcano; rock and snow, moss and ice fed the ravenous fire. Heatwaves flowed out in every direction. The mountains' stone skin turned glassy and their stony hearts glowed white. Sheets of flame danced among the stars. And the Song raced on:

> *Swift horses in wide meadows!*
> *Graceful herds on the gold-flowered water-meads,*
> *Strong hooves drumming,*
> *a thunder of praise to the Goodly-Wise,*
> *A boon of joy in the heart of Albion!*

> *Golden the grain-hoards of the Great Giver,*
> *Generous the bounty of fair fields:*
> *Redgold of bright apples,*
> *Sweetness of shining honeycomb,*
> *A miracle of plenty for the tribes of Albion!*

> *Silver the net-tribute, teeming the treasure*
> *of happy waters; Dappled brown the hillsides,*
> *Sleek herds serving*
> *the Lord of the Feast;*
> *A marvel of abundance for the tables of Albion!*

Following the rivers and streams, setting the myriad waterways alight, stretching across the Foul Lands with fingers of fire, the bright flames flew, striking deep into the heartland of Tir Aflan, kindling the fields and meadows. Marshlands steamed and then smoldered, then became lakes of fire. Reeds and grasses, gorse thickets and gnarled trunks, whole forests burst into flowering flame. By blade and twig the hungry fire devoured the wasted heartland. And the Song raced on:

> *Wise men, Bards of Truth, boldly declaring from*
> *Hearts aflame with the Living Word;*
> *Keen of knowledge,*
> *Clear of vision,*
> *A glory of verity for the True Men of Albion!*

> *Bright-kindled from heavenly flames, framed*
> *of Love's all-consuming fire,*
> *Ignited of purest passion,*
> *Burning in the Creator King's heart,*
> *A splendor of bliss to illuminate Albion!*

Silver-white columns of fire danced and leapt—high, high, burning with the intensity of ten-thousand suns, scourging both the land below and the heavenly places above, filling the black void of night with blazing light. And the Song raced on:

> *Noble lords kneeling in rightwise worship,*
> *Undying vows pledged to everlasting,*
> *Embrace the breast of mercy,*
> *Eternal homage to the Chief of chiefs;*
> *Life beyond death granted the Children of Albion!*

> *Kingship wrought of Infinite Virtue,*
> *Quick-forged by the Swift Sure Hand;*
> *Bold in Righteousness,*
> *Valiant in Justice,*
> *A sword of honor to defend the Clans of Albion!*

> *Formed of the Nine Sacred Elements,*
> *Framed by the Lord of Love and Light;*
> *Grace of Grace, Truth of Truth,*
> *Summoned in the Day of Strife,*
> *An Aird Righ to reign for ever in Albion!*

No one could stand before the ferocity of the fire. The frail human frame vaporized in the heat, flesh and bone dissolved, spilling their molecules into the fiery atmosphere. The All-Encompassing Song raced on and on in ever-widening rings of purifying fire.

And everything touched by the holy fire was scoured, consumed, melted, reduced to the very core elements, and then further reduced to atoms. The released atoms ruptured, fused, and recombined in new elements of being. Deep in the white-hot heart of the fire, I saw the Swift Sure Hand moving, gathering unformed matter and molding it into pure new forms.

I alone saw this, and I saw it with the eye of the True Aird Righ, the sacred, eternally self-sacrificing king. I saw it with the unblinking eye of the Everliving One, whose touch quickens the insensate soul, who swallows death in life. Out of the molten heat, I saw the foul land of Tir Aflan recast, reshaped, and in fire reborn.

Nothing escaped the refining fire of his irresistible will: all imperfection, all ugliness, all weakness and deformity, all frailty, infirmity, disease, deficiency and defect, every fault and failing, every blight and every blemish, every flaw effaced, purged, and purified. And when the last scar had been removed, the cleansing flames diminished and faded away. All this might have taken eons; it might have happened in the blink of an eye; I cannot say. But when the fire at last subsided, Tir Aflan had been consumed and its elements transmuted in a finer, more noble conception: recreated with a grandeur as far surpassing its former degradation as if an old garment had been stripped away and not merely restored, but replaced with raiment of unrivalled splendor. It was not a change, but a transformation; not a conversion, but a transfiguration.

The mudmen, whores, slaves and prisoners—all the Foul Land's wretched—were gone, and in their places stood men and women of stature and grace. The empty fields and forests were empty no longer; animals of every kind—deer and sheep, wild pigs, bears, foxes, otters, badgers, rabbits, squirrels, and mice, as well as kine, oxen, and horses—filled the meadows and glens and browsed the forest trails and ran among the hills and watermeads; trout and salmon, pike and perch, sported in the lakes and streams; the shining blue skies were full of birds and the treetops delighted in birdsong; the forlorn mountainsides, moors, and blasted heathlands wore a fresh glory all their own in the form of wildflowers of every shade and hue; the rivers ran clean and uncorrupted, the water crystalline and pure.

Tir Aflan was no more, Tir Gwyn stood in its place.

Tegid Tathal was the first to revive. He opened his eyes, stood up, and looked around. Scatha lay nearby, dressed now in a mantle of holly green with a belt of cornflower blue and a crimson cloak edged in green and gold. Gwion lay at Tegid's feet, and Bran beside him, and around Bran the Raven Flight as Tegid remembered them—but now the Ravens' cloaks were midnight blue and each wore a torc of thick-braided silver. Cynan lay a little distance away, his hand stretching towards Goewyn.

And all of them, Tegid himself included, reclothed in the finest apparel—of such material and craft, such color and quality as had never been known. Tegid, Scatha, the Ravens, every member of the Gwr Gwir and their prisoners—all arrayed in clothes of the most splendid color and craftsmanship.

The warriors' weapons had changed, too. The luminous luster of gold and bright-gleaming silver shone in the light of a dawn as clear and fresh as the first day of creation. The spears, both shaft and head, were gold, and golden too every swordblade and hilt. Shield rims, bosses and rings shone with silvery brightness.

Tegid turned his wondering eyes from the warriors and their weapons. He gazed skyward and saw the radiant heaven, alive with a living light. He saw the Foul Land made fair beyond words, and he began to understand what had happened.

Shaking, trembling in every part, he knelt beside Bran Bresal and touched him gently. The Raven Chief awoke and Tegid helped him to stand. He woke Scatha next, and then Cynan; Bran awakened the Ravens who, with Cynan and Tegid, began to wake the Gwr Gwir.

Scatha, her heart beating fast, ran to her daughter and knelt down beside her. Goewyn's hair was brushed bright and plaited with tiny white and yellow flowers. She wore a gown of hyacinth blue with a mantle of pearly white over it, and a henna-colored cloak sewn with plum purple figures. Cupping a hand to Goewyn's cheek, Scatha gently turned her daughter's head. Goewyn drew a deep breath and awoke.

"Llew?" she asked. Then memory rushed in upon her. "Llew!"

She jumped to her feet and ran to me. My body lay where Paladyr had left it. Arrayed like a king in siarc, belt and breecs of deep-hued scarlet, with scarlet buskins on my feet, I lay wrapped in a scarlet cloak; woven into the cloak in silver thread was the Môr Cylch, the Life Dance.

Goewyn lifted a cool hand to my forehead, then touched my face. Tears welled in her eyes as she felt my cold, lifeless flesh. Scatha came to stand beside her, and Cynan; Bran and the Raven Flight gathered around. As Tegid joined them, Goewyn raised tearful eyes. "Oh, Tegid, I thought..." She began to weep.

"He is dead, Goewyn," Tegid said softly, kneeling beside her. The bard placed his hand upon my still chest. "He will not come back."

"Look," said Bran, "his silver hand is gone."

They raised my right arm and saw that my silver hand was indeed gone, the metal replaced by a hand of flesh. Goewyn took the hand and clasped it to her. She pressed the unfeeling flesh to her warm lips and kissed it, then laid it over my heart.

"Where is Siawn Hy?" asked Cynan suddenly. "Where are Tángwen and Paladyr?"

Until that moment, no one had thought to look for them, nor, now that they did make a search, could they find them. The wicked ones had vanished, but not completely.

"Here!" shouted Cynan, closely scanning the place where Siawn was last seen. "I have found something."

The others joined him as he examined a curious spot on the ground. "What is it?" he asked, pointing at a small pile of powdery residue.

Tegid bent down and examined it. "All that remains of Siawn Hy," the bard announced at length.

It was the same with Paladyr and Weston, and all those who had willingly followed Siawn. The refining fire had burned away the dross and, when it had finished its purifying work, there was nothing left. Nothing, that is, save a handful of ashes soft and white as snowflakes.

Cynan wanted to gather the ash and throw it in the sea, but Tegid counselled otherwise. "Leave it," he advised. "Let the wind take it. There shall be no resting-place for these."

"What has happened?" asked Bran, trying to comprehend the changes that had been wrought in them and in the world around them. He spoke for many—especially the defectors who, in surrendering to me, had escaped the fate of their lord. Remade men, they simply stared in mute wonder at their transformed bodies and the world re-created around them, unable to comprehend it or their own good fortune.

Tegid lifted the rod of gold that now replaced his rowan staff. Raising his other hand over his head, he addressed the bewildered gathering: "The sound of the battleclash will be heard among the stars of heaven and the Great Year will proceed to its final consummation.

"Hear, O Sons of Albion: Blood is born of blood. Flesh is born of flesh. But the spirit is born of Spirit, and with Spirit evermore remains. Before Albion is One, the Hero Feat must be performed and Silver Hand must reign."

Lowering the rod, he stretched it over my body. "So it was spoken, so it is accomplished," Tegid said. "The Great Year is ended, the old world has passed away and a new creation is established." Indicating my crimson-clothed body, he said, "The Aird Righ of Albion is dead. The Hero Feat for which he was chosen has been performed. Behold! He has reclaimed Tir Aflan and brought it under his sovereign rule. Thus, all lands are united under one king: from this day, Albion is One. This is the Reign of Silver Hand. The prophecy is fulfilled."

Back through the mountains, now remade: glistening, silver-crowned giants bearing the wide, empty skybowl on their handsome shoulders. Pure white clouds graced the slopes like regal robes and raiments; sparkling streams sent rippled laughter ringing through the valleys, and mist-shrouded falls filled the heights with rainbows. The road was no longer; instead, a grassy path curved up through the high places and joined them with the lowlands beyond ...

Back through the moors, transformed into meadows of vast aspect, dotted with trees and brimming with sparkling spring-fed pools. Herds of deer and wild sheep grazed the grassy expanse; birds passed overhead in chattering flocks, or trilled their songs to a sky so fair and blue it made the heart ache to see it ...

Back through the hills and valleys, now made new: gently sculpted mounds rounding to grand crests and descending to shade-sheltered glens of solitude. The greens of the hills and glens were as verdant and various as the shifting hues of golden light that played on the cloud-dappled knolls ...

Back through the forest now remade: towering columns of magnificent trunks rising to a vaulted archway of a myriad spreading branches beneath a fine leafy canopy: nature's own sanctuary, illumined by a softly-diffused light. By day the grassy path was lit by an endless succession of falling shafts of sunlight; by night the moon and stars poured silver upon rounded boles and slender branches, favoring every leaf and limb with a delicate tracery ...

Back along the river, now a noble watercourse, handsome in its generous sweep and broad-bending curves, deep-voiced in the sonorous music of its stately passage. Swans and geese and other waterfowl nested in its reed-fringed banks; fish aplenty lazed in its cool shallows, and leaped in the sun-warmed currents of clean, clear water ...

Back through a world reborn: more fair than a loving heart's fondest dream of beauty, more elegant than delight, more graceful than hope. Back through Tir Gwyn they carried my body, back to the place where three swift sleek-hulled ships waited on the strand. And then back across a white-waved sea of startling color and clarity.

Back across this luminous, ever-changing firmament of liquid light they bore me to Albion. And though it took many days, my corpse showed not the slightest sign of decay or corruption. It was as if I slept; yet no breath stirred in my chest, and my heart was still and cold.

My corpse lay on a bier made from the silver shields of the Gwr Gwir bound to golden spearshafts. My scarlet cloak covered me and Goewyn rode, or walked, or stood ever by me. She would not leave my side for a moment. When the company stopped at night, she even slept beside the bier.

They reached Albion and in procession carried my body through a land familiar, yet transmuted into a higher vision of itself. Albion had been transformed into a wonder that swelled the soul with joy and made the breath catch in the throat, as if its former beauty had been but a reflection compared to the reality. For Albion now wore a splendor purer and finer than harpsong and more exquisite than music, and it made their hearts sing to see it.

The procession bore my body to Caledon, over the hills and across the plain, up Druim Vran to Dinas Dwr, where Lord Calbha and my people waited. Upon learning of my death, the people mourned with a deep, surpassing grief. The bones of Alun Tringad were interred in the dolmen atop the Hero Mound at the foot of Druim Vran. Professor Nettleton's head was buried there, too. My body, however, was placed in the king's hall to await burial, for Tegid had determined that I should be buried in a special tomb that he would build. Meanwhile, I lay on my golden catafalque in the king's hall, and Goewyn, inconsolable, stayed beside me day and night while they prepared the gorsedd.

One evening, Tegid came to the hall and knelt beside Goewyn. She was spending the night, like every other night, sitting in the antler chair beside my lifeless body. "It is time to release him, Goewyn," the bard told her.

"Release him? I never will," she replied, her voice softened by grief to a whisper.

"I do not mean you should forget him," Tegid soothed. "But it is time—and past time—for Llew to begin his journey hence. You hold him here with you."

"I hold him here?" Goewyn wondered. "Then," she said, reaching out to take my cold hand in hers, "I shall always hold him and he shall always remain here with me."

"No," Tegid told her gently. "Let him go. It is wrong to imprison him so."

Taking her by the shoulders, he held her at arm's length, staring into her eyes, willing her to look at him. "Goewyn, listen to me. All is as it should be. Llew was sent to us for a purpose, and that purpose has been accomplished. It is time to release him to continue his journey."

"I cannot," Goewyn wailed, grief overwhelming her afresh. "I shall be alone!"

"Unless you release him, your love will sicken in you: it will steal your life and the life of the child you carry," Tegid replied firmly.

Tears came to her eyes. She put her face in her hands and began to weep. "Oh, Tegid, it hurts," she cried, the tears streaming down her face. "I hurt so much!"

"I know," he said softly. "It is a hurt not soon healed."

"I do not know what to do," she cried, the tears falling freely.

"I will tell you what you must do," the wise bard answered, putting his arms around her. "You will give birth to the child that he has given you, and you will love the child and raise it in his memory." He took her hands in his. "Come with me, Goewyn."

She rose and, after a last loving look, went out with Tegid. Scatha and the Raven Flight were waiting at the hall's entrance. As soon as Goewyn and Tegid emerged, the Ravens entered the hall and came to the bier. They lifted the shield-and-spear litter to their shoulders and carried it outside; they then processed slowly through the crannog to a boat, and rowed the boat across the lake to where Cynan waited on the shore with horses and a wagon. Three horses—a red and a white, with a spirited black to lead them—drew the wagon; the horses' hooves and the wagon's wheels were wrapped in black cloth. Beside Cynan, holding a shield and spear likewise shrouded, stood Lord

Calbha, and behind them, unlit torches in their hands, thronged the people of Dinas Dwr.

The corpse was placed on the wagon, and the procession slowly made its way along the lakeside to the place where Tegid had erected the Hero Mound inside the sacred grove he had established for his Mabinogi. Mounting the long slope to the grove, the company passed by the mill, completed in my absence by Lord Calbha and Huel, the master-builder. As we passed, I blessed the mill to its good work.

The cortège entered the shadowed grove, dark under a sky of brilliant twilight blue. The gorsedd had been raised in the center of the grove—a hollow stone chamber, mounded with earth and covered over with turf, and surrounded by a ring of slender silver birches. Someone had left a shield beside the cairn, and upon entering the grove, I heard the croak of a raven. A swift shadow passed overhead and a great, black glossy-feathered bird swooped down and settled on the rim of the shield. Alun, I think, had sent a messenger to say farewell.

The golden bier was laid at the foot of the gravemound before the silent throng. The Chief Bard, standing over the corpse, placed a fold of his cloak over his head.

Raising his golden rod over me, he said, "Tonight we bury our king. Tonight we bid farewell to our brother and friend—a friend who did for us what we could not do for ourselves. He sojourned among us for a while but, like Meldryn Mawr, who held sovereignty before him, Llew served the Song of Albion. His life was the life of the Song, and the Song claimed the life it briefly granted.

"The king is dead, cut down in a most vile and hateful manner. He went willingly to his death to gain the life of his bride, and those of his friends whose release he sought and won. Let it never be said that he grasped after glory; let all men remember that he humbled himself, breaking his geas so that he might lead the raid on Tir Aflan.

"And because he did not cling to his high rank, great good has come to this worlds-realm. For in Llew's death, the Song of Albion has been restored. Hear, O Albion! The Great Year is ended, a new cycle is begun. No longer will the Song be hidden; no longer will it rest with the Phantarchs and kings to preserve it, for now the Song is carried in the heart and soul of every woman and every man, and all men and all women will be its protectors."

Tegid Tathal, Penderwydd of Albion, lowered his hand then, saying, "It is time now to release our brother and send him on his way."

He kindled a small fire and lit a torch. The fire was passed from brand to brand until all the torches glowed like stars in the night-dark grove. Then he directed the Ravens to lift the bier once more. Drustwn, Emyr, Niall and Garanaw, with Bran at my head, began, at Tegid's direction, to carry my body around the gorsedd mound slowly in a sunwise direction. The people, led by Tegid, with Goewyn walking directly behind him, Scatha on at her right hand and Cynan at the left, followed the body—and they all began to sing.

I was there with them in the grove. I saw the torchlight glowing on their faces and glinting in their tears; I heard their voices singing, softly at first, but more strongly as they released their grief and let it flow from them. They sang the *Queen's Lament* and it pierced my heart to hear it. Goewyn sang, too, head held high, eyes streaming with tears which threaded down her cheeks and throat.

I could feel the weight of sorrow bearing down her spirit, and I drew near to her. *Goewyn, best beloved, you will live for ever in my soul*, I whispered in her ear; *truest of hearts, your grief will ease*.

Tegid led the funeral procession once around the mound... and then a second circuit... and a third. At the completion of the third circuit, the people formed a long double line, holding their torches high. They formed the Aryant Ol, the Radiant Way by which a king's body is conducted to its rest. And, in the time-between-times, I was carried to my tomb.

The Ravens, tall and grim, shouldered the bier and, with slow, measured steps, began moving towards the gravemound along the Radiant Way. Tegid, with Goewyn and Cynan behind him, lofted his torch and the three followed the Ravens up the Aryant Ol and into the cairn. They placed the bier on a low stone pallet in the center of the chamber and, one by one, made their farewells, each kneeling by the body and touching the back of the hand to his forehead in a final salute.

Finally, only Cynan, Goewyn, and Tegid were left. Cynan, tears clinging to his eyelashes, raised his hands to his throat and removed his gold torc. He placed the ornament on my chest and said, "Farewell, my brother. May you find all that you seek—and nothing you do not seek—in the place where you are going." With that, his voice cracked and he turned away, rubbing his eyes with the heels of his hands.

Goewyn, eyes bright with tears in the flickering torchlight, stooped and kissed me on the forehead. "Farewell, best beloved," she said bravely, her voice quivery and low, "you go, and my heart goes with you."

Tegid handed his torch to Cynan and reached into the leather pouch at his belt. He withdrew a pinch of the Nawglan, the Sacred Nine, which he deposited in the palm of his left hand. Then, taking some of the Nawglan on the tip of his second finger, he drew a vertical line in the center of my forehead. Pressing his fingertip to the Nawglan again, he drew a second and then a third line, one on either side of the first—both inclining towards the center. He drew the gogyrven, the Three Rays of Truth, in the ash of the Sacred Nine on my cold forehead.

"Farewell, Llew Silver Hand. May it go well with you on your journey hence," the bard said. Then, quickly planting his torch at the head of the bier, he turned away to lead Goewyn and Cynan from the tomb.

The Ravens, waiting outside, began to close up the entrance with stones. I watched the cairn opening grow smaller, stone by stone, and I was on the inside, looking out. I saw the faces of those I had loved: Scatha, Pen-y-Cat, regal, brave and beautiful; Bran Bresal, Chief Raven, dauntless lord of battle; the Raven Flight: Drustwn, Emyr Laidaw, Garanaw Long Arm, and Niall, stalwart companions, men to be trusted through all things; Lord Calbha, generous ally; Cynan, steadfast swordbrother and friend of the heart; Goewyn, fairest of the fair, wife and lover, forever part of me; and Tegid, wise Penderwydd, Chief Bard of Albion, truest friend—whose love reached out beyond death to smooth my passage.

I saw the people, my people, passing the stones hand to hand up the Aryant Ol to seal my tomb. And then I heard Tegid's voice, clear and strong, lifted in a song which I recognized as a saining song. Cradling his harp, his fingers playing over the sweet-sounding strings, he sang:

> *In the steep path of our common calling,*
> *Be it easy or uneasy to our flesh,*
> *Be it bright or dark for us to follow,*
> *Be it stony or smooth beneath our feet,*
> *Bestow, O Goodly-Wise, your perfect guidance*
> *Upon our kingly friend,*
> *Lest he fall, or into error stray.*
>
> *In the shelter of this grove,*
> *Be to him his portion and his guide;*
> *Aird Righ, by authority of the Twelve:*
> *The Wind of gusts and gales,*
> *The Thunder of stormy billows,*
> *The Ray of bright sunlight,*
> *The Bear of seven battles,*
> *The Eagle of the high rock,*
> *The Boar of the forest,*
> *The Salmon of the pool,*
> *The Lake of the glen,*
> *The Flowering of the heathered hill,*
> *The Craft of the artisan,*
> *The Word of the poet,*
> *The Fire of thought in the wise.*
>
> *Who upholds the gorsedd, if not You?*
> *Who counts the ages of the world, if not You?*
> *Who commands the Wheel of Heaven, if not You?*
> *Who quickens life in the womb, if not You?*
> *Therefore, God of All Virtue and Power,*
> *Sain him and shield him with your Swift Sure Hand,*
> *Lead him in peace to his journey's end.*

The opening in the cairn was little more than a chink in the stone now. And then that small hole was filled and I was alone. Tegid's voice as he stood before the sealed gravemound was the last thing I heard. "To die in one world is to be born into another," he called to the people of Dinas Dwr. "Let all hear and remember."

The fire-flutter of the torch filled the tomb, but that faded gradually as the torch burned down. At last the flame died, leaving a red glow which lingered a little while before it went out. And darkness claimed me.

How long I stood in the rich, silent darkness, I do not know. But I heard a sound like the wind in bare branches, clicking, creaking, whispering. I turned and saw behind me, as if through a shadowed doorway, the dim outline of a white hillscape, violet in a blue-grey dawn. Instinctively, I moved towards it, thinking only to get a better look.

The moment I stepped forward, I heard a rushing sound and it seemed as if I were striding rapidly down a long, narrow passage. And I felt a surge of air, an immense upswelling billow like an ocean of air flowing over me. In the same instant, the pale violet hillside before me faded and then vanished altogether.

Trusting my feet to the dark path before me, I stepped forward. The churning air swelled over and around me with an empty ocean's roar. Emptiness on every side, and below me the abyss, I stretched my foot along the swordbridge and stepped out onto that narrowest of spans. In the windroar I heard the restless echo of unknown powers shifting and colliding in the dark, endless depths. All was darkness—deepest, most profound darkness—and searing silence.

And then arose the most horrendous gale of wind, shrieking out of nowhere, striking me full force, head on. It felt as if my skin were being slowly peeled away, and my flesh shredded and pared to the bone. My head began to throb with pain and I found that I could not breathe. My empty lungs ached and my head pounded with a phantom heartbeat.

Ignoring the pain, I lifted my foot and took another step. My foot struck the void and I fell. I threw my hands before me to break the blind fall; my palms struck a smooth, solid surface, and I landed on all fours in the snow outside the cairn in the thin grey dawn.

"Llew...?" It was Goewyn's voice.

39

The Endless Knot

I raised my head and looked around to find her. The effort released something inside me and cold air gushed into my lungs. The air was raw and sharp; it burned like fire, but I could not stop inhaling it. I gulped it down greedily, as if the next breath would be my last. My eyes watered and my arms and legs began to tremble. My heart pounded in my chest, and my head vibrated with the rhythm. I squeezed my eyes shut and willed my heart to slow.

"Lew..." came the voice again, concerned, caring. I felt a light touch on my shoulder, and she was beside me.

"Goewyn?" I lifted my eyes and glimpsed a trailing wisp of reddish hair—not Goewyn, but her sister, the Banfáith of Albion. "Gwenllian!"

"Lew... Lewis?"

My eyes focused slowly and her face came into view. "Gwenllian, I..."

"It's Susannah, Lewis. Are you all right?"

From somewhere in my mind a dim memory surfaced.

"Susannah?"

"Here, let me help you." She put her arms around me and helped me stand. "You're freezing," she said. "What happened to your clothes?"

I looked down to see myself naked, standing in about an inch of light, powdery snow. The wind sighed in the bare branches of trees, and I stood outside the narrow entrance to a hive-shaped cairn, reeling with confusion, despair breaking over me in waves, dragging me under, drowning me.

"Put this on," Susannah was saying, "or you'll catch your death." She draped her long coat across my shoulders. "I've got a car—it's on the road up the hill. We'll have to walk, I'm afraid. Nettles didn't tell me to bring any clothes, but I've got some blankets. Can you make it?"

I opened my mouth, but the words would not come. Very likely, there *were* no words for what I felt. So I simply nodded instead. Susannah, one arm around my shoulders, put my arm around her neck and began leading me away from the cairn. We walked through long grass up a snow-frosted hill to a gate, which was open. A small green automobile waited on the road, its windows steamed over.

Susannah led me to the passenger side of the car and opened the door. "Just stay there," she said. "Let me get a blanket." I stood staring at the world I had come to, trying to work out what had happened to me, grief powerful as pain aching in my hollow heart.

Spreading one blanket over the seat, she swathed another over me, taking back her coat as she did so. Then Susannah helped me into the car and shut the door. She slid into the driver's seat and started the car. The engine complained, but caught and started purring. Susannah put on the heater and defroster fan full blast. "It'll warm up in a minute," she said.

I nodded, and looked out through the foggy windshield. It took all the concentration I could muster, but I asked, "Where are we?" The words were clumsy and awkward in my mouth, my tongue a lump of wood.

"God knows," she replied above the whir of the fan. "In Scotland somewhere. Not far from Peebles."

The defroster soon cleared a patch of windshield which Susannah enlarged with the side of her hand. She shifted the car into gear and pulled out onto the road. "Don't worry," she said. "Just sit back and relax. If you're hungry, I've got sandwiches, and there's coffee in the flask. We're lucky it's a holiday and traffic will be light."

We drove through the day, stopping only a couple of times for fuel. I watched the countryside rush by the windows and said nothing. Susannah kept clearing her throat and glancing at me as if she was afraid I might suddenly disappear—but she held her tongue and did not press me. For that, I was profoundly grateful.

It was late when we reached Oxford, and I was exhausted from the drive. I sat in my blankets and stared numbly at the lights of the city from the ring road and felt utterly devastated. How could this have happened to me? What did it mean?

I did not know where I would go. But Susannah had it all worked out. She eased the car through virtually empty streets and stopped at last somewhere in the rabbit warren of Oxford city center. She helped me from the car and I saw that we stood outside a low door. A brass plaque next to the door read D. M. Campbell, Tutor. Susannah pulled a set of keys from her pocket, put a key in the lock and turned it.

The door swung open and she went before me, snapping on lights. I stepped into the room and recognized it. How many lifetimes had passed since I last stood in this room?

"Professor Nettleton told me to give these to you," Susannah said. She pressed the keys into my hands. "He isn't here—" she began, faltered, and added, "but I suppose you know that."

"Yes," I told her. Nettles, I suspected, would never return. But why had I come back? Why me? Why here?

"Anyway," she said, her keen dark eyes searching my face for the slightest flicker of interest, "there's food in the larder and milk in the fridge. I didn't know who or how many to stock up for, so there's a bit of everything. But if you need anything else, I've left my number by the phone, and—"

"Thanks," I said, cutting her off. "I'm sure it's ..." Words escaped me. "It's fine."

She gazed at me intently, the questions burning on her tongue. But she turned towards the door instead. "Sure. Umm ... well." She put her hand on the doorknob and pulled the door open. She hesitated, waiting for me to stop her. "I'll look in on you tomorrow."

"Please, you needn't bother," I said, my mouth resisting the familiar language.

"It's no bother," Susannah replied quickly. "Bye." She was out of the door and gone before I could discourage her further.

How long I stood, wrapped like a cigar-store Indian in my blanket, I could not say. I spent a long time just listening to the sounds of Oxford, a crashing din which the heavy wooden door and thick stone walls of the professor's house did little to shut out. I felt numb inside, empty, scooped hollow. I kept thinking: *I am dead and this is hell.*

At some point I must have collapsed in one of Nettles' overstuffed wing chairs, because I heard a scratch at the door and opened my eyes to see Susannah bustling into the room, her arms laden with parcels and bags. She was trying to be quiet, thinking me asleep in bed. But she saw me sitting in the chair as she turned to pile the packages on the table.

"Oh! Good morning," she said. Her smile was quick and cheerful. Her cheeks were red from the cold, and she rubbed her hands to warm them. "Tell me you *didn't* sleep in that chair all night."

"I guess I did," I replied slowly. It was difficult to think of the words, and my tongue still would not move properly.

"I've been up since dawn," she announced proudly. "I bought you some clothes."

"Susannah," I said, "you didn't have to do that. Really, I—"

"No trouble." She breezed past me on the way to the kitchen. "I'll get some breakfast started and then I'll show you what I bought. You can thank me later."

I sat in the chair without the strength of will to get up. Susannah reappeared a few moments later and began shifting parcels around the table. "Okay," she said, pulling a dark blue something out of a bag, "close your eyes."

I stared at her. Why was she doing this? Why didn't she just leave me alone? Couldn't she see I was in pain?

"What's the matter, Lewis?" she asked.

"I can't."

"Can't what?"

"I can't do this, Susannah!" I snapped. "Don't you understand?"

Of course she didn't understand. How could she? How could anyone ever understand even the smallest, most minute part of all I had experienced? I had been a king in Albion! I had fought battles and slain enemies, and had, in turn, been killed. Only, instead of going on to another world, I had been returned to the one I had left. Nothing had changed. It was as if nothing had happened at all. All I had done, all I had experienced meant nothing.

"I'm sorry," Susannah said, with genuine sympathy. "I was only trying to help." She bit her lip.

"It's not your fault," I told her. "It's nothing to do with you."

She came to me and knelt beside the chair. "I want to understand, Lewis. Honestly. I know it must be difficult."

When I did not answer, she said, "Nettles told me a lot about what was happening. I didn't believe him at first. I'm still not sure I believe it. But he told me to look for some things—Signs of the Times, he called them—and if I saw them, I was to go to that place—he even gave me a map—and wait there for someone to show up." She paused, thoughtfully. "I didn't know it would be you."

The silence grew between us. She was waiting for me to say something. "Listen," I said at last, "I appreciate what you've done. But I need..." I was almost sweating with the effort, "I just need some time to work things out."

She gave me a wounded look and stood up. "I can understand that. But I want to help." She paused, and looked away. When she looked back, it was with a somewhat forlorn smile. She was trying. "I'll leave you alone now. But call me later, okay? Promise?"

I nodded, sinking back into the all-enfolding chair, back into my grief and pain. She left.

But she was back early the next morning. Susannah took one look at me and one look at the room and, like a rocket blasting off, she lit up. "Get up, Lewis. You're coming with me."

I had no will of my own any more, and hers seemed powerful enough for any two people, so I obeyed. She rummaged through the untouched packages on the table. "Here," she said, thrusting a pair of boxer shorts into my hand. "Put these on, for starters."

I stood, the blanket still hanging from my shoulders like a cloak. "What are you doing?"

"You've got to get out of here," Susannah replied tartly. "It's Sunday. I'm taking you to church."

"I don't want to go."

She shrugged and shook out a new shirt, cocking her head to one side as she held it up to me. "Put this on," she ordered.

She dressed me with ruthless efficiency: trousers, socks, shoes, and belt—and then professed herself pleased with the result. "You could shave," she said, frowning. "But we'll let that go for now. Ready?"

"I'm not going with you, Susannah."

She smiled with sweet insincerity and took my arm in hers. Her hands were warm. "But you are! I'm not leaving you here to languish all day like a dying vulture. After church I'll let you take me out to lunch."

"I know what you're trying to do, Susannah. But I don't want to go."

The church was absolutely packed. In all the time I'd lived in Oxford, I'd never seen so many people at a church service. There were a thousand at least. People were crammed into pews, and lined up in the wide windowsills all around the sanctuary. Extra chairs were crowded into the back in every available space. The kneeling-benches had been pulled out and placed in the aisle to accommodate the overflow. When that did not suffice, they opened the doors so the people standing outside could hear.

"What's going on?" I asked, bewildered by the noise and hubbub. "What's all this?"

"Just church," Susannah said, puzzled by my question.

The service went by me in a fog. I could not concentrate for more than a second or two at a time. My mind—my heart, my soul, my life!—was in Albion, and I was dead to that world. I was cut off and could never go back.

Susannah nudged me. I looked around. Everyone was kneeling, and the minister—or priest, or whatever—was holding a loaf of bread and saying, "... This is my body, broken for you..."

I heard the words—I'd heard them before, many times; I'd grown up hearing them, and had never given them a thought beyond the church sanctuary.

This is my body, broken for you...

Ancient words, words from beyond the creation of the world. Words to explain all that had happened to me. Like a star exploding in the frigid void of space, understanding detonated in my brain. I knew, *knew*, what it meant!

I felt weak and dizzy; my head swam. I was seized and taken up by a rapture of joy so strong I feared I might faint. I looked at the faces of those around me: eager in genuine devotion. Yes! Yes! They were *not* the same; they had changed. Of course they had. How could they not change?

Albion had been transformed—and this world was no longer the same, either. Though not as obviously manifest, the great change had already taken place. And I would find it hidden in a million places: subtle as yeast, working away quietly, unseen and unknown, yet gently, powerfully, altering everything radically. I knew, as I knew the meaning of the Eucharistic words of Holy Kingship, that the rebirth of Albion and the renewal of this world were one. The Hero Feat had been performed.

The rest of the service passed in a blur. My mind raced ahead; I could not wait to get outside and bolted from the church as soon as the benediction was pronounced. Susannah caught me by the arm and spun me around. "You worm! You could at least have pretended to pay attention."

"Sorry, it's just that I—"

"I've never been so embarrassed in all my life. Really, Lewis, you—"

"Susannah!"

That stopped her. I took her by the shoulders and turned her to face me squarely. "Listen, Susannah. I have to talk to you. Now. It's important." Having begun, the words came rolling out of my mouth in a giddy rush. "I didn't understand before. But I do now. It's incredible! I know what happened. I know what it's all about. It's—"

"What *what* is all about?" she asked, clutching my arm and eyeing me carefully.

"I was a king in Albion!" I shouted. "Do you know what that means, Susannah? Do you have any idea?"

A few nearby heads swivelled in our direction. Susannah regarded me with faint alarm, biting her lower lip.

"Look," I said, trying a different approach, "would you mind if we didn't go out? We could go back to Nettles' place and talk. I have to tell somebody. Would you mind?"

Overcome with relief, she smiled and looped her arm through mine. "I'd love to. I'll fix lunch for us there, and you can tell me everything."

We talked all the way home, and all during lunch. I put food in my mouth, but I did not taste a single bite. I burned with the certainty of the truth I had glimpsed. I had swallowed the sun and now it was leaking out through every pore and follicle. I talked like a crazy man, filling hour after hour with words and words and more words, yet never coming near to describing the merest fragment of what I had experienced.

Susannah listened to it all, and after lunch even suggested that we walk by the river so that she could stay awake and hear some more. We walked until the sun began to sink into a crisp spring twilight. The sky glowed a bright burnished blue, red-gold clouds drifted over emerald hills and fields of glowing green. Couples and families ambled peacefully along the path, and swans plied the river like feathered galleons. Everywhere I looked, I saw tranquility made visible—a true Sabbath rest.

"You were right," she said when I at last ran out of breath. "It *is* incredible." There was more, much more to say, but my jaw ached and my throat was dry. "Simply incredible." She snuggled close and put her head on my shoulder as we turned our steps towards home.

"Yes, it is. But you're the only one who will ever know."

She stopped and turned to me. "But you've got to tell people, Lewis. It's important." I opened my mouth to object and she saw it coming. "I mean it, Lewis," she insisted. "You can't keep something like this to yourself. You must let people know—it's your duty."

Just thinking of the newspapers made me cringe. Reporters thrusting microphones and clicking cameras in my face, television, radio—an endless progression of sceptics, cranks, and hectoring unbelievers ... Never.

"Who would believe me?" I asked hopelessly. "If I told this to anyone else, it would be a one-way ticket to the loony bin for yours truly."

Maybe," she allowed, "but you wouldn't actually have to *tell* them."

"No?"

"You could write it down. You know your way around a keyboard," Susannah pointed out, warming to her own idea. "You could live in Nettles' flat and I could help. We could do it together." Her eyebrows arched in challenge and her lips curled with mischief. "C'mon, what do you say?"

Which is how I came to be sitting at Nettles' desk in front of a testy old typewriter with a ream of fresh white paper, with Susannah clattering around in the kitchen making tea and sandwiches. I slipped a sheet of paper under the bail, and stretched my fingers over the keys.

Nothing came. Where does one begin to tell such a tale?

Glancing across the desktop, my eye caught a corner of a scrap of paper with a bit of colored ink on it. I picked up the scrap. It was a Celtic knotwork pattern—the one Professor Nettleton had shown me. I stared at the dizzy, eye-bending design: two lines interwoven, all elements balanced, spinning for ever in perfect harmony. The Endless Knot.

Instantly, the words began to flow and I began to type:

It all began with the aurochs ...